# SPOKEN

# Spoken

## Mary Statham

TIKI PRESS

Spoken is a work of fiction. Any similarity to actual persons or events is purely coincidental.

**Tiki Press**, Westbank, BC, Canada
Web Address: www.tikipress.info,  Email: tikipress@hotmail.com

ISBN-10:  0-9865269-1-6
ISBN-13:  978-0-9865269-1-6

For Kelly and Matthew, whose words were always magic.

# Acknowledgements

There are so many people to whom I'm grateful that I could probably write another book just to list them. I'm tempted to in any case, just to make sure I don't hurt any feelings. The truth is that all my friends and family have had a hand in this novel, and in encouraging me when I faltered in its writing. I'm especially grateful to all my friends at Dragon Writers, for their ongoing support and gentle butt-kicking as required. I have to thank my sister June for allowing me to borrow not only her name but liberally from her character, and for all her knowledge of the Monashees. Kelly and Matthew never gave up on me, even when I did. Joy, my agent, who has always believed in me. Michelle, who encouraged my writing back in my misspent youth. Susan, who never lets me forget that I'm a writer. Thank you, Dara, Chris, and Ben, for helping to make me the person that wrote this book. And finally, I am deeply grateful to Mr. Tolkien, for teaching me early in life that any road can lead to any where. How delicious it is to find new roads and new places to go.

# Prologue

In the beginning, there was the Word, spoken by the unknowable Voice. From the Word came all things, both that which is understood and that which remains a mystery. The Word was neither good nor evil, only the strictest definition of all things. It categorized and delineated and designated each and every aspect of Creation, from its foundation to its annihilation.

The Universe, once set into motion, evolved in ways that defied the intrinsic definition set by the Word. It twisted under the weight of an impossible task until at last it buckled and broke. It is the greatest of miracles that the Universe did not end with the sundering of the one perfect Word. For instead, the Word broke into many smaller words, some greater than others. Each defines a piece of Creation, and all are linked by their nature. All words seek to return to the primeval Word. Thus it is that Being and Unbeing seek to join. Should these two greatest of the remaining words ever join completely, our existence would return to that defined by the first Word. All things would be as in the beginning; without form or movement.

The greater words must be protected from their own natures. The lesser words must be harbored and tended that they do not sow corruption among the purest natures of other words. You that tend the libraries of Creation, watch well your words, and do not fail. There is no death that cannot begin a new life, and no life that cannot result in the death of all.

# Chapter 1

Granny Rosie looked up from the worn old book in her hands, her eyes wide and solemn in the candlelight.

"Never forget, Rosanna. Everything is connected to both the beginning and the end. What we do tips the balance for everyone."

Rosanna sighed. Every year at solstice the family gathered together to tell the same stupid story and pretend that the world might end. Every morning after, the sun rose anyway. No one else, not even Rosanna's pagan friends, did any such thing.

"I won't forget, Granny. You've been telling me for as long as I can remember."

Granny nodded.

"But there's a difference between being told and remembering, isn't there?"

"Well, I'm here, so I can't have forgotten," Rosanna replied.

Rosanna had driven on black ice all the way up to Granny's little cabin in the Monashee mountains just to be with Granny on this one surviving family occasion. She had spent the last half hour of the trip listening to her snow tires scrabbling for purchase in the snow, and Granny's driveway was practically vertical. It was a long, difficult drive for eggnog and treats.

Granted the eggnog and fruitcake were nice, but if you were going to have a holiday tradition, why did it have to be the weirdest one possible?

"Rosanna, I think you have a doubt," Granny said. Everyone called her Granny, even people who had no relation to her. Granny Rosie was the kind of person that became the hub of any community she joined. She had faded blue eyes and hair the color of moonlight on snow, and a smile that opened hearts. Rosanna's heart had been open, too, and Granny Rosie had filled it all up. But that was a long time ago, now.

"I have lots of doubts," she said. "Starting with whether or not I'll make it home in one piece. Have you seen the snow on the highway?"

Granny brushed the comment aside.

"That's not what I mean, and you know it isn't. What about the story?"

Rosanna tucked her feet up under her and twined a long brown curl around her finger, trying to decide what to say, and how to make it as inoffensive as possible.

"Isn't it supposed to be Christmas time?" Rosanna asked evasively.

"You become a Christian this year?" Granny asked.

Rosanna shrugged. She'd sampled a half-dozen churches in the last couple years, but none of them had really stood out for her. She was, she supposed, a little too accustomed to making up her own mind. Religions seemed to want to do it for her.

"Well, no. But it's Christmas time anyway," she said. "That's what all the stores say. And Rudolph's been on TV, that must mean it's Christmas."

"But you're not a Christian?" Granny asked. Rosanna shook her head.

"It sounds a little crazy to celebrate the birthday of someone you don't know and don't believe in."

"And this is so very sane?" Rosanna asked. "I don't believe this, either."

Granny sighed and looked a little sad. She reached out and cupped Rosanna's chin in her fingers, smiling wistfully into Rosanna's deep brown eyes.

"You used to," she said. Rosanna shrugged in response. She remembered believing, remembered it with painful clarity. She'd waited for every word, wondering which one would be the magic one, and none of them were.

"I used to believe in the Easter Bunny, too. Sometime in my mid-twenties I figured out that the brown stuff bunnies make isn't chocolate."

"Now that's just cynical," Granny said. "Just because you stop believing in something doesn't mean it stops being true. The flat-earthers still fall down instead of up."

Rosanna had to laugh.

"You are so weird, Granny." They grinned at each other.

"Anyway, we digress. You have a doubt?"

"Granny, it's just a story. I've never heard it from anyone else, and it's silly. I'm happy to celebrate the longest night with you, but I don't buy this stuff."

Granny smiled, and patted Rosanna's cheek. When Granny smiled like that, the longest night didn't even exist, everything was sunrise and birdsong.

"Good. I'd hate to think I'd raised a girl who didn't think for herself." She looked at her hands for a moment.

Rosanna's parents had died in a mountaineering accident when she was two. She had fuzzy memories of smiles and kisses, and she treasured them. But Granny had been Rosanna's world for every minute after that. They'd lived all over the country, from east coast to west, and a dozen places in between. Every time they moved, Granny would turn acquaintances into friends, and friends into family, so Rosanna had never lacked for aunts and uncles and cousins. She'd been a little short on best friends and boyfriends, though. Granny was the focus of any picture, and Rosanna always felt like part of the underpainting, like that little something no one notices until it's pointed out.

"I tried so hard to be what you needed," Granny said. "People who won't define themselves too often get defined by someone else."

"That's hardly been the problem. I've got a definition and no one likes it."

Granny looked honestly shocked.

"You don't really believe that, do you?"

Rosanna shrugged again.

"Does it matter what I believe? Everyone else has their own opinion of me, and that's the one that seems to matter in the world."

"You know what they say about opinions?" Granny asked.

"No, what?"

"They're like assholes, everyone's got one." Granny chortled.

"I can't believe you said that," Rosanna said.

"So, and I said it anyway, right?"

"Yeah, and your point would be?"

"You don't believe in the Word, and I said it anyway. Doesn't it matter at all that I believe it?"

Rosanna really wished it did matter, but she was tired of fairy tales and nonsense. Granny Rosie could say the most absurd things, and people would believe it. Rosanna herself had believed every word for the longest time. But little girls grow up, and it wasn't fun any more.

"It makes me wonder what's in the eggnog, that's all it does." Rosanna looked into her cup.

"There's only a little rum, child. But the truth's in my story," said Granny solemnly.

"I don't believe it." Rosanna said. "I don't know what the point is to it. It's like telling the same joke over and over, until it doesn't mean anything."

Granny frowned.

"Doesn't it make you want to ask questions? Doesn't it make you imagine everything as one vast Word?"

"Granny, I'm not seven years old any more. I'm sorry; I would be if I could, if that would make you happier. But here I am, and you get what you get."

"I'm not getting anything, Rosanna," Granny said. "You're all closed off. All I get is the surface you, the picture and not the word."

"Granny, that's just…look, I don't go anywhere for anyone else. Isn't this enough? That I'm here? That I'm listening?"

Granny reached out to tap Rosanna's cheek.

"Are you listening, Rosanna? Are you hearing?"

And that was just one condescension too many.

"Granny, what the hell does this have to do with me? Why are you telling me this crap? What do words have to do with anything? Can't we just talk like normal people? God, you're driving me nuts!"

Granny leaned back in her chair and smiled a perfectly contented smile. If she'd been a cat, someone would be missing a pint of cream.

"Finally!" she said. "My girl, I was beginning to think you'd never ask."

Rosanna nearly walked away then, never mind four hours on the snowy highway at night.

"So, then why? Why can't we have a normal holiday?"

"Not that," said Granny. "The other question."

Rosanna tried to remember what she'd said. She remembered saying Granny was driving her nuts, and that wasn't changing any time fast. What had she asked? It was like a lesson Granny was waiting for her to repeat, and Rosanna knew too well how long Granny could wait.

"You mean," Rosanna asked, "why do you tell this story?"

Granny Rosie beamed again.

"Very good, that's exactly the one."

"I'd really rather you told me why we can't talk like normal people," Rosanna said, but Granny ignored her.

"Here," she said, "more eggnog for a toast."

Rosanna accepted it with a sigh. There was no rushing Granny in a mood like this. Sometimes it was like she had a detailed script for how a conversation was to go, and she'd just ignore any spare line that didn't fit her ideal.

"To knowledge," Granny said, raising her glass. Rosanna lifted hers in turn, and repeated the toast.

"To truth," Granny said, raising her glass again, and Rosanna followed suit.

"To tradition," Granny said with finality, draining her glass. Rosanna did the same, feeling the warm alcoholic glow of a bellyful of rum. She wanted to raise a toast to rum, but the eggnog was gone.

"I tell this story," Granny said solemnly, "Because it's true."

Rosanna rolled her eyes. All this build up for what? "I don't believe it," Rosanna said.

"I can't change what you believe, but I can't change what's true, either. You never asked me before why I tell this story, but now that you have, I can tell you."

"I did too," Rosanna protested. "I know I did."

"Maybe," Granny admitted. "Maybe once. But some answers only come it time."

Granny stared into the fire, and a dark flicker of emotion crossed her features. Rosanna hadn't seen it often, and she was never quite sure what it was. Granny was like an open book with a chapter written in invisible ink.

"Look, I was sure you believed it, or at least were pretending to. It just seemed...I don't know, like an old superstition, so I let it be."

"Have you known me to be superstitious, Rosanna?"

"Not about anything but this," she said. "Honestly, the idea of you with religion scares the heck out of me."

Granny laughed, but Rosanna was serious. Granny had never seemed defensive about it, just serenely certain of her position. It was the closest Granny had ever come to expressing an interest in faith. Granny Rosie was a force to be reckoned with all on her own. The thought of her with New Age fire in her eyes was downright terrifying.

"So I'm not superstitious, nor religious, and I believe this. What does that lead you to conclude?"

"It makes me wonder what kind of mushrooms you grow around here," Rosanna said.

Granny chuckled again.

"I won't vouch for the other folk around here, but I don't much bother with mushrooms. It's not an entirely illogical question, but assuming I'm not on drugs, what conclusion does that lead you to?"

Rosanna sighed resolutely. She couldn't see a way out of this conversation.

"Okay. Assuming you're not crazy or stoned, I guess a reasonable conclusion would be that you have reason to believe it."

Granny leaned back and grinned, and Rosanna felt the warmth of parental approval even over the lingering heat of the rum in her eggnog. More than twenty years couldn't dull the hunger for that smile, for that particular expression that said Rosanna was all any daughter could be.

"Well, Rosanna, you know you're named after me, right?" Rosanna nodded.

"And I was named after my grandmother, back down generations. I got all the old lists somewhere in one of my books, but that's not so important. You just have to understand that we're an old family."

Rosanna nodded. As a child she'd browsed through books of old photographs of long-dead relations. She'd envied the little girls their lacy dresses and perfectly curled hair. Rosanna had always been more of a jeans and t-shirt girl, and her unruly nest of curls had never looked so sleek and lovely.

"We came to this continent long ago, but we weren't the first here, you know that, right?"

"Well, yeah. The native Americans were here first, and before that probably the Neanderthals and long before that the occasional dinosaur."

"There's no need to get snippy with me, Rosanna," Granny said. The temperature in the cabin seemed to drop a little.

"Sorry," Rosanna said.

"No, you're not, but there's still no need to take that tone with me. You asked, I'm answering." Rosanna wanted to bury her head in her hands.

"I'm just kind of having trouble seeing the point to all this."

"That's because I'm still getting there. Be patient."

"I'm not good at patient," Rosanna muttered.

"Don't I know it," Granny said. "Once you have a goal in mind, you can't get there fast enough. You were a horror when you started walking."

Rosanna didn't remember walking, but she remembered reading under her covers at night just so she could find out the end of the story. She never jumped to the end, though. She always wanted to know the why's and how's of every conclusion.

"Put another log on the fire, would you?" Granny asked.

Rosanna did, and then poked at the embers until the wood caught properly. Snow tapped and whispered against the windows of Granny's little cabin. Firelight flickered nimbly across the warm golden beams and floor. Of all the places Granny had ever lived, this one seemed most her own.

"Where was I?" Granny asked when Rosanna sat down again.

"Fossil record," said Rosanna.

"All right then. When our people came here, we were friends with the folks already on the land, and they told our people about the people that came before."

"I was kidding about the Neanderthals," Rosanna said.

"Hush," said Granny, and something in her tone called Rosanna's sarcasm to heel as if it were a troublesome puppy. She was a little girl again, waiting for Granny to tell the really good part of the story. If she closed her eyes, she could almost imagine herself curled up in Granny's lap again.

"The people that came before, they were Librarians. They kept the First Words."

Firelight flickered across Granny's cheek, spawning little shadows that danced around her mouth. Granny watched Rosanna intently, clearly expecting a response. There was a long and awkward silence.

"I'm still waiting for the joke," Rosanna said finally. "Do we have a mystical connection with the Dewey Decimal System, too?"

"No joke," Granny said. "They were magic because they could use the greater words. Language defines reality, and they knew the right words."

"Language describes reality. It's not the same thing." Rosanna said.

"And you the linguist? You think that's entirely true?"

"Of course it is!"

"You tell me that language doesn't divide like the cells of a living thing, doesn't grow and change with the world around it."

"Sure, but that's because the world changes, so words have be made to describe the new things!"

"Says who? Who told you that was the order of things?"

"No one had to, it's just common sense."

"There's no such thing as common sense. Sense is almost impossibly uncommon."

"Granny, you sound awfully, awfully senile just now."

"Don't sass me. This is serious."

"It can't be. Look, this is the new millennium. People don't...words aren't magic. God, the whole idea of magic is archaic and stupid and, and fluffy! Magic words? I mean come *on*!"

"Do you remember Becky Martin?"

"Vaguely." Rosanna remembered her with painful clarity. Becky had been her best friend in ninth grade, until she'd become markedly more attractive and popular than Rosanna. Somehow, (not any how in particular) rumors had surfaced that she wasn't as virtuous as she might be, and her popularity had been replaced with notoriety.

"She was a nice girl, wasn't she?"

"Yes. She didn't deserve what happened to her."

"Do you remember what turned the tide?"

Rosanna had the uncomfortable feeling that Granny knew exactly what she'd done to Becky, and exactly what it had cost both of them. The two girls had never been friends again, but Rosanna had watched Becky's fall from grace with shame and sorrow.

"Yes. Someone called her a slut, and she believed it."

Granny nodded.

"Someone defined her with a word, and she became it, right?"

That was more responsibility than Rosanna was prepared to accept.

"No, everyone else believed it so strongly that all she could do was act the way they expected her to. Small towns can be mean."

"No one believed it before the word was spoken, not even Becky. She was a good girl in every way. But once she was named, the world changed, even her, to accommodate the word."

"No. I don't buy that, either."

Rosanna's voice was firm, but her conviction wobbled a little. It had been eerie how quickly opinions had turned against Becky, and how virulent the responses to her had become. It hadn't been like the surfacing of a rumor at all, but more like everyone had woken up knowing that Becky Martin was not and never had been a Good Girl.

"Granny, I can't..."her voice stumbled off into silence. She remembered saying the word, remembered the strange twisting inside her as the sound left her. She had put every scrap of her adolescent angst and jealousy into that syllable, and flung it at Becky's back.

"I know you spoke the word, Rosanna. I felt that power when you did it." Granny's eyes were solemn. "It was the only time you ever truly disappointed me."

Rosanna gulped back tears. She knew it wasn't the only time, but she expected it was probably the worst.

"I didn't mean for it all to go like that. I tried to take it back, to defend her, but no one would listen."

And it hadn't mattered anyway. Rosanna had still been insignificant and unremarkable. It had been better after that, though, because Rosanna knew what she was capable of, had understood that she was intrinsically untrustworthy. Once she'd realized that, it had been easier to accept her isolation.

"A word spoken can sometimes be retracted, but never unsaid. You learned that, didn't you?"

Rosanna nodded silently. Becky had fought the definition for a while, and then it was like she was lost underneath it. The sweet, pretty girl that had been Rosanna's friend turned into a Madonna-wannabe, almost overnight.

"Do you know what happened to her?" Rosanna asked.

"I do. Are you quite sure you want to know?"

Rosanna nodded again, despite the conviction that she really didn't want to know at all. Becky deserved this, at least, that Rosanna know the consequences of what she'd done.

"She was killed by one of her tricks down in Toronto. Killed for twenty dollars and some drugs. The guy turned himself in. Said he didn't know why he'd done it, just that he had to." Granny said it in a monotone, as if these were words she'd long heard in her head, but never spoken.

The words felt like a slap. Tears rushed up behind Rosanna's eyes, but the shame and regret were hotter still.

"I'm sorry," she whispered.

"I know you are, my girl, and I'd never have said anything about it, except that you need to know this. Words have power."

"Okay, power maybe, but magic?"

"What else do you call it when two thousand perfectly sane people forget something they've known all their lives? And they forget it all at once? And instead remember something completely opposite, but they believe it anyway? You think that happens because of something in the water?"

"People always respond to rumors," Rosanna said. "Like all that stupid crap about the movie stars. All that has to happen is for some idiot to make it up, and half the continent believes it."

"Don't you think that argues my case rather than yours?" Granny replied with a smile. "And how often do those rumors become true after the fact, hm? What about Brad and Angelina, then?"

"Oh God, please don't talk about them." Rosanna rolled her eyes. "What's so frigging fascinating I've never understood."

"Me neither. It's boring stuff, but because someone says it's scandalous and fascinating, people believe it is. Don't you think that's magic, in a small sordid kind of way?"

"No. It's human nature and the power of the media."

"Those sound like magic words all in themselves. I want you to really think. What makes it scandal? People break up, get together, and divorce; lots of people all the time. Why is it only scandalous when it's printed?"

Granny had a point.

"Okay," Rosanna said, rolling her eyes again. "I'll agree that words have power." She raised a hand to stop Granny's rebuttal. "But I'm not buying into magic."

Granny smiled with satisfaction.

"What's the difference?" she said.

"What?" Rosanna understood the question perfectly well, but she wanted a moment to consider her answer. Arguing with Granny Rosie was a lot like dancing blindfolded in a room full of bear-traps.

"I know you're stalling. Stop trying to convince me you're right, and just answer. What's the difference between power and magic?"

"Magic is just superior technology," Rosanna said.

"Don't plagiarize Arthur C, Clarke to me, my girl. I want to know what *you* think the difference is."

Rosanna paused. She hadn't really thought about it much before, not since she'd researched religion.

"Okay. Magic is doing the impossible by unreasonable means," she said at last. "And power is doing the highly unlikely by improbable means."

"That's a pretty fine line, Rosanna. Who draws it?"

"I don't know," Rosanna shrugged. "The universe, I guess."

"Why don't you bring that bullshit back in spring and fertilize my garden for me, will you?"

"Granny!" Rosanna said, shocked. Granny Rosie swearing was still a new phenomenon.

"Rosanna!" Granny said, raising her eyebrows into an imitation of Rosanna's expression. She looked longingly at the bottom of her glass.

"Do you have any more?" Rosanna asked, seeing the motion. Rum sounded good now. Maybe even tequila. She was feeling far too sober for this conversation.

"I'm all out. There's still rum, but I don't care for that straight," Granny said. Rosanna grimaced at the thought. Silence trickled in between them, and Rosanna had the faintest flick of hope that this very strange talk might be over.

"Look," Granny said at last. "You're balking at the word. You see the concept of magic played out all around you, but you're stopped by a word. Doesn't that speak to the word's power?"

"Power, but not magic," Rosanna said.

"You are so ruddy stubborn! Where did you ever get that from?"

"It's the company I keep," Rosanna said, looking pointedly at Granny.

"You were born stubborn," Granny said. "I never thought you were born blind, though. Why can't you see it? You've had it in front of your eyes all your life, and you just can't...no you *won't* see it."

Rosanna threw up her hands.

"See what? Granny, you're talking like this is all real, like it all matters."

"Power and magic are the same, like good old Arthur's advanced technology. They both describe manipulating the world in ways that don't seem logically possible, or even likely. How could that not matter?"

"But gossip? Where's the magic in gossip? It's stupid," Rosanna said.

"The magic of a few gossipy words fed the Spanish Inquisition. Heretic. Witch. Devil-worshipper." She paused. "Haven't you ever wondered how such a relative few could hold all Europe in terror? It was words, Rosanna."

"Still, that proves power and not magic. I mean, if power is magic, that would mean the wind is magic, or...nuclear missiles are magic. It's nutty."

"So what would you call real magic, then?" Granny asked. Rosanna thought about it for a moment.

"I don't know, I don't read that kind of book," Rosanna said.

"You used to," Granny said. "Why did you stop?"

Rosanna remembered the fairy tales, and looking for pixies in the garden.

"Because it wasn't real. Because I never found a fairy. Because it made me feel stupid and ordinary and you did that just fine."

"Rosanna!" Granny's jaw had dropped. She was old suddenly, diminished by Rosanna's words.

"I'm sorry," Rosanna said. "I didn't mean that."

"I think you did," Granny said. "I really think you did."

"It's all right though, Granny. It's okay. I *am* ordinary, and that's okay."

Granny shook her head.

"And what would it mean if you weren't? What would it mean if you had power all your own, something you inherited like your brown eyes?"

"Then it wouldn't be me being extraordinary anyway, would it? It'd just be a leftover from someone else. An accident."

"Do you honestly think so little of yourself?"

The sorrow in Granny's eyes was a little too close to pity.

"I do fine. I know who I am and where I stand. No one can take that. All this crap about magic, it's just a way to pretend something ordinary isn't. That's a good path to a broken heart."

Granny shook her head.

"Rosanna, you've asked the right question, you've earned the answers, but you don't want them?"

Rosanna shook her head.

"It's not a matter of not wanting. I don't believe them. Where's the proof?"

Granny set her mouth in a firm line.

"You aren't supposed to ask that question yet," she said. "You aren't ready for the answer."

"I think you can fertilize your own garden, Granny. This is all bullshit. I don't know why you want to do this to me."

"I don't want to," Granny said. "That's the worst part. If I could keep this from you, I would, but you've asked, now. Those words have power."

"Just stop it," Rosanna said. "I want to go to bed." She stood up.

"Wait," Granny said. "Please, just wait a moment." She looked up at Rosanna with sorrow and dismay mingled in her eyes. That was new. Rosanna hadn't seen Granny sad very often at all. She settled back into her chair.

Granny nodded.

"Thank you," she said with genuine gratitude. "I know this isn't easy, my girl, I know I haven't made it so. But there are rules."

"Granny, I'm still sitting here because I love you. But I'm awfully close to fed right up. What is it, exactly, that you're trying to tell me."

Granny closed her eyes briefly, and murmured something low and melodic. It might have been a song or a prayer, or only a string of sounds. A spark from the fire floated out under the mantel, then drifted lazily across the room to hang, perfectly still, a bare centimeter from Rosanna's nose.

She backed away hurriedly, but the spark stayed exactly where it was, pulsing a little as if to a heartbeat. She reached out a hand to touch it, and heard a crisp little chuckle, like the sound of a pinecone popping. The spark danced away from her touch. Suspended in the glow was a tiny figure, unmistakably the pixie she had never found in the garden.

For a moment, wonder filled her up, stole away every pretense of adulthood. Then another emotion came, something darker and wilder, a thick stew of every fear and disappointment she'd ever experienced.

"Stop it, Granny," she said.

"You asked for proof," Granny said. "Isn't this proof?"

"I don't know what this is, but it isn't proof."

"What? What do you mean it's not?"

Rosanna clenched her fists furiously, refusing to look at the little creature, the little daydream that glowed in front of her.

"I don't know what it is, and I don't care. I don't believe in magic. I believe in tricks and lies and power, but I *don't* believe in magic. I won't."

:"But look at it, Rosanna, look!"

"No," Rosanna said. "Make it go away." She closed her eyes tight, ignoring the cinnamon smell of the warm little spark. "I don't care what it is, I've had enough."

"You stubborn ass!" Granny said, with rising fury. "You ask questions, and I answer them. When you don't like the answers you close your ears and eyes? I thought I raised you better than that, I really did."

"Good night, Granny," said Rosanna. Ignoring the spark, ignoring the pain and anger in Granny's voice, and ignoring the voice of common sense, Rosanna stomped outside to her car. It was cold, but it would warm up.

She listened to the sound of the growling engine and ignored the smell of cinnamon that had pursued her even into the car. Nothing else did.

# Chapter 2

Rosanna spent an uncomfortable night in her car. She ran the engine until she was warm enough to sleep, and then woke up again when the temperature dropped too low. Granny's cabin looked snug and welcoming, just a few steps away, but Rosanna wasn't interested. She'd rather be cold in the real world than toasty warm in a delusion. Admittedly, the delusion became more attractive as the hours passed and the chill deepened, but Rosanna wasn't giving in.

Finally, at around seven, she woke up and decided that this was enough. The sun had not yet even kissed the mountaintops good morning, and probably wouldn't for a good couple hours. Still, it was late enough that she could expect coffee and breakfast at the nearest truck stop or town, and coffee sounded awfully damn good just now.

There were no lights on in the cabin, but that didn't mean much. Granny could quite happily have breakfast by firelight, and smoke still trickled out of the chimney. Rosanna considered saying good-bye, but what would she say after that? Worse, what would Granny say? Rosanna edged past the memory of the firelight pixie, and remembered the strange conversation, instead. Granny needed to be right, Rosanna knew. It wasn't always a flaw, it made Granny Rosie tough and independent. But sometimes it made her condescending and sometimes it just made her weird. It had been a crazy talk, and Rosanna was relieved to find she didn't want to think about it. Not wanting to think about it gave her permission not to, so she focused on getting her car safely down Granny's impossible driveway.

Snow had been falling all night, but it was the cold sandy snow of low temperatures and high altitude. It crunched under her tires like pieces of Styrofoam. The driveway still felt slick and unsafe, but once Rosanna got to the highway she drove with more confidence. The roads up here wouldn't forgive excessive speed, but Rosanna knew her way well enough to make decent time.

It was eight when she reached the first of the tiny towns that nestled among the mountains here. Some of them were barely more than two houses and a gas station, but they clung to the highway like snow-dusted barnacles. Logging trucks had to come through, and there were tourists in the summer.

Rosanna pulled into a little gas station and filled the car. A restaurant opened off the cash desk, but the lights were off, and Rosanna resigned herself to junk food for breakfast. The cashier was a little wren of a woman with long brown hair and friendly eyes.

"You're out early," she said.

Rosanna nodded and yawned. The woman chuckled in commiseration.

"I'm just opening up," she said. "Coffee's on, and I can do breakfast for you right quick, if you want."

"Coffee, definitely coffee," Rosanna said. "Probably breakfast too, once I'm awake."

The woman smiled again, and unlocked the door to the café and turned on the lights. Rosanna had steeled herself, expecting harsh fluorescents, but the light that filled the room was mellow and welcoming. They paused at the cash register so Rosanna could pay for her gas, and then walked together into the restaurant.

The tables were covered in stereotypical red and white checked tablecloths. Each one had a centerpiece of pine cones glued together and sprinkled liberally with glitter, in preparation for Christmas, most likely.

The waitress waved a hand.

"Take your pick," she said. "Not much of a line this early. Give it an hour, though, and you'd be waiting right enough."

"Really?" Rosanna asked. The waitress laughed at her surprise.

"You'd be amazed," she said. "There's more folks hidden up here than there are pot plants, and that's saying somewhat." Rosanna smiled.

She picked a table near the window. The air off the glass was chilly, but sunlight was creeping across the sky like a slow blush, and she wanted to watch. Her waitress came back with a pot of coffee and some silverware. The cup was almost too hot to hold, but Rosanna warmed her hands on it anyway.

The waitress brought a menu over, and Rosanna ordered bacon and eggs.

"Perfect," said the waitress. "I'll make enough for two." Rosanna grinned. She'd never been much of a morning person, but this woman clearly was. She was as brilliantly cheerful as the day promised to be.

Rosanna gazed into her coffee, hearing the clatter and bustle and sizzle of work being done in the kitchen. The steam twined lazily up and out of her cup; dancing to some sinuous music that she couldn't hear. '*Magic,*' she thought. That dancing little mote of fiery life had been so real, so tangible. She could still smell its spicy scent all around her. But magic was for children, or for people who didn't know better. Rosanna lived in a world where words described the universe, not where they defined it. It was absurd. If words could change things like that, all Rosanna would have to do is rename herself, and she could be someone else.

She paused in her thoughts. People did that all the time, didn't they? Changed their names and changed themselves? Murderers became someone else's neighbor, that nice man down the street.

She sighed. It was too much for so early in the day. But Granny had been so convincing. Or so convinced, rather, and that was even more alarming. If Granny wasn't crazy (and Rosanna couldn't quite believe she was) then she was telling the truth. Not just *a* truth, even, but also *the* truth, and Rosanna's entire world would have to change. And didn't that support Granny's case as well? That a world could change because of the words of one person?

The waitress set a plate generously heaped with food, bacon and eggs and hash browns and toast. It looked like enough for a small family, but it smelled glorious.

"Anything else?" the waitress asked. "Shot of whiskey in the coffee, maybe?"

Rosanna arched an eyebrow.

"Whiskey? Before noon? Before sunrise, even?"

"Sometimes it's called for," the waitress said. "You look like maybe this is one of those times."

"Maybe. Crazy relatives can do that to a person." She hadn't meant to say the word 'crazy', hadn't even meant it in the privacy of her own thoughts but the waitress just nodded in commiseration.

"My family would drive anyone to drink," she said. "Even before the sun is up. Hell, especially before the sun is up, 'cause then you know you've got a whole day with the buggers."

Rosanna laughed.

"Anyway," the waitress said, "sun'll be up soon, and after that, whiskey's fair game. Let me know if you want some."

"I dunno, do you suppose we could mellow out the relatives instead? Might take less whiskey, that way. More economical."

"I suppose that depends on whether you make it yourself or not. Moonshine's cheaper, but harder to sneak into someone's coffee."

Rosanna chuckled.

"You think I'm kidding?" the waitress asked. "Isn't only home-grown out here, it's home brewed, too. You should see our farmer's markets."

The waitress took her own breakfast to another table and began to eat.

Rosanna's breakfast was perfect, salty and fatty and full of cholesterol. She could feel her arteries hardening as she ate. She'd just put marmalade on her last piece of toast when a bell jingled at the door, announcing another arrival.

A man walked in, accompanied by a wash of cold air. He was so extravagantly bundled up that she could only tell his gender by his walk. No woman had ever acquired quite that swagger, at least not that Rosanna had ever known.

He was covered head to foot in thick winter clothing, most of it in shades of brown and green. His scarf was bright red, and covered in frost from his breath. His eyes were blue, and when he smiled at Rosanna, charming crinkles surrounded them. She smiled back, and he began to shed layers of clothing, turning his wardrobe back in time from deep winter to perhaps late autumn. First the scarf came off, revealing a close-cropped thatch of salt and pepper hair. Next he took off the heavy gloves. He shucked his snow pants without a sign of self-consciousness, and hung them on a peg beside the door. Under the coat, he wore a sweater and jeans: comfortable and serviceable clothing that was well worn but not threadbare. His smile was warm and mischievous as he looked over at Rosanna again.

"It's a little early for tourists,"he said from the doorway. "The beach isn't even open yet. Give it a month."

The waitress finished her last bite of breakfast, looked up and smiled at the newcomer.

"Thompson!" she said. "Don't you have any place better to go?"

"June, my love," he said, "anywhere you are is the best place in the world."

"You've just been spending too much time at high altitudes." June said, laughing. "Scrambled whatever passes for brains in a man."

"Possibly," he said. "But who needs brains when you have beauty?"

"Let me know when you find some," June said wryly.

Thompson took her hand in his, and kissed it.

"No greater beauty than yours, my dear," he said. June pulled it away, the smile on her face fading a little.

"Ah, give it a rest. You want to be fed or not? I'm not inclined to flirting this morning, so you'll just have to find some other way to amuse yourself."

"I am mortally injured," he said.

"Call search and rescue," June replied. "Meantime, coffee's in the usual place. How many eggs?"

"Make it three and bacon," he said. "I've been busy, and it's a wee bit chilly out there today. Little chilly in here, now that I mention it."

"Funny how the word 'no' can drop the temperature," June said, and bustled off to the kitchen.

Thompson watched her go, an appreciative gleam in his eye. Then he sighed and shrugged, and turned to Rosanna.

"You wouldn't tell a poor man 'no' before the sun was even up, would you?"

"I might," she said. "It would depend what he asked."

"What if he asked to share your table, in a completely non-threatening manner?" He waggled his eyebrows suggestively.

Rosanna laughed. The contrast between his tone and his expression was ridiculous.

"You do mean to sit at it, and not on it," she said, "right?"

It was his turn to chuckle.

"Well, if that's what you're offering, I'll take it," he said. "Just a tick." He walked to the coffee pot and poured himself a cup. He sat down and took a sip.

"I may live," he said. "Caffeine and company, what else could I want?"

"Breakfast, I expect," Rosanna said.

"Oh, eventually," he replied. "June's quick in the kitchen, if nowhere else."

"That's more than I needed to know," Rosanna said.

"Course it is," he replied. "That's why it's fun to say it."

"Mm-hmm," Rosanna replied. She would have liked to take offense, but couldn't quite manage it. Between the friendly grin and easy charm, it was hard to find him anything but endearing.

"So what brings a fair city flower out to this weed patch?" he asked. "It's a little early for swimming, unless you like frostbite."

Rosanna shivered at the thought of the lake. Its waters were chilly even in the middle of the warmest summer, and the only reason it didn't freeze over was that it was so deep.

"Visiting," she said. "My Granny lives out this way."

"My Granny did too," he said. "Born and died in the same house. Not many folks can say that any more."

"Well if they've died, I shouldn't think they'd say much of anything," Rosanna said.

"Depends who you ask," Thompson said. "My old auntie swears she chats with Granny every day down at the end of her garden."

Rosanna shook her head.

"Too much homegrown?" she asked.

"Ah, you've met her, then," he replied with a grin. He stuck out his hand.

"I'm Thompson," he said. "Thompson Trapper." Rosanna shook the offered hand.

"Rosanna Buchon," she said. His hand was warm, and large enough to engulf hers. His fingers were callused, but his nails were clean and neatly trimmed.

"Now that's a proper handshake," he said. "Nothing at all like wringing a dead fish."

"My Granny always said no woman should be ashamed of a firm grasp on reality or on a handshake," Rosanna said. Her thoughts shifted back to the fire lit conversation. Rosanna had always depended on Granny's grasp on reality, hadn't she?

"Penny for your thoughts," Thompson said.

"Hmm?" Rosanna replied absently.

"Your face just clouded right over there, for a second. Sun's out again now, though, and isn't it pretty."

She blushed. She hated the rush of heat to her face and ears, it made her feel like she was twelve again, talking to the first boy she ever liked.

"I think you might still be snow-blind," she said. "Or possibly June's right about the high altitude."

"Come on, now," he replied. "Pretty little thing like you must hear about it all the time."

"Not usually before breakfast," she said.

"Well, then, I'll tell you again once I've eaten," he said.

"And then will you hit on the waitress some more?" Rosanna asked.

"I'm an equal opportunity flirt," he said. "Any woman's a beauty, and all of 'em ought to be told. I make it my mission to do so."

June brought Thompson's breakfast and set it down in front of him.

"I heard that," she said. "You are a danger to yourself and others, Thompson, and you ought to have a warning label."

"I have one," he said with a grin. "Wanna look for it?"

June snorted. She turned to Rosanna. "I got a shovel out back you can beat him with if he bothers you," she said. "I've had to use it a time or two myself."

"I'll keep that in mind," Rosanna said.

"You hear that?" June said to Thompson. "You behave yourself, or else."

"I always behave myself," he said, as June walked away. "Bad behavior is still behavior, after all."

Thompson ate with a neat economy of motion that saw the food disappear quickly. Rosanna sipped her coffee in the companionable silence and watched a forget-me-not sky bloom behind the shining tops of snowy mountains. Every surface beyond the glass shimmered and sparkled. Even the road looked like a moonstone path that shone among the shadows cast by snow-laden trees. Snow never looked so fresh or perfect in the city. It was always an inconvenience, there, something to be tamed and corralled and cursed.

Thompson finished his toast and pushed his plate away with a contented sigh.

"Lord it's nice to have someone else do the cooking," he said.

"And the dishes, I expect," Rosanna said. Thompson nodded his agreement.

"I don't mind it so much," he said, "it's just that there's always more."

"It's one of the inconvenient things about being alive," Rosanna said. "There's always something more that needs doing, or wants doing, or can't possibly be avoided."

Thompson nodded again.

"Mind, up here, there's more than a few ways to avoid life," he said. "Some do it with 'herbal supplements', if you catch my meaning. Me, I think life's already magic enough without extra pretty colors to distract from it."

"Magic?" Rosanna asked, lifting an eyebrow. "You seem a little pragmatic for that particular word."

Thompson nodded to the snowy landscape outside the window.

"I can be as pragmatic as I please, and that still looks like magic to me. Always does, that first morning after a snow."

"I dunno," Rosanna said. "I always thought magic was unicorns and fairy tales, bad fiction, maybe."

"There's been some fine writing about magic," Thompson said. "The Bible, for instance. That one's full of magic."

"I'm shocked," Rosanna said.

"No you aren't," he said. "You just think that's the polite thing to say."

She chuckled.

"All right, you got me. I've always found it kind of amusing when Christian groups decide to boycott fantasy novels. Seems like their own special book has a lot in common with them."

Thompson peered around, as if looking for zealots in the corners of the room.

"Careful now, you never know who's listening." They shared a smile.

"Anyhow," he said, "magic hasn't ever been about only the good stuff. Haven't you read Grimm's fairy tales? All kinds of dark magic. People been watering it down for years, trying to take the spookiness out of shadows."

"Doesn't it seem just a little gullible to you? I mean believing in either? I like what I can touch, what I can measure."

"Can you measure your thoughts?" he asked.

"No, but someone somewhere can. They can measure the brainwaves, the electrical activities."

"But they can't tell you why you do it, how you do it. They can't tell you what you think, or how much a thought weighs."

"Who cares?" Rosanna said. "They can measure it in lots of other ways, and I know I have them."

"It matters to you, though, right? What you think?"

"Of course," she said.

"Even though you, personally, can't weigh or measure it? You quantify it with your experience, right?"

"Yeah," she said.

"Well then, that makes you a wizard, doesn't it. Or sorceress, or whatever title strikes you as befitting your noble abilities."

Rosanna laughed.

"Just call me the magical librarian," she said. "She sings, she dances, she files."

"The what?" Thompson said.

"I work at the college library," she said. "I'm just finishing up my degree, and I've got to pay the bills somehow."

"That's a kind of magic all its own then, isn't it? You create order out of chaos using a system that drives most people to drink."

"It's not *that* complicated," she protested.

"Sure looks like it from the outside," he said. "Most things, even simple things, do."

"That sounds like my Granny," Rosanna said. "That woman seems to surprise me just for fun."

"I thought that was a Granny's job," Thompson said. "My own Granny could be downright astonishing. She could put back more whiskey than all us boys put together, and be sober enough to wrestle a bear afterwards."

"Brown or Grizzly?" Rosanna asked sweetly. Thompson roared.

"Both," he said. "Consecutively or at once."

"So I'm sure you were no problem at all," Rosanna said. Thompson winked.

"Nah, she didn't start wrestling bears till after I left home. She said they kept her in practice for me."

"Uh-huh," Rosanna said. "No wonder she needed the whiskey, then."

"Lordy, girl, you're a sharp one!" Thompson said. "I think I might be in love."

"Again?" Rosanna asked. "I thought June was the light of your life."

"Sky's got more than one star, doesn't it? Got lots of room in my life for lights."

"Ah, but you don't see the stars when the sun is out. Isn't one really big light enough?"

"Sometimes," he said with a grin, "enough is never enough."

"Hence the heaping great pile of fibs," Rosanna said. "Do you actually expect people to buy this stuff?"

"Not really," he said. "But it passes the time." He grinned. "You're still here, after all, aren't ya?"

"Ah, and now the ulterior motive appears," Rosanna said. "Here I am, poor little fly, tangled in your web of words."

"Ah, the magic of a word," he said, and grinned.

Rosanna froze.

"What?" she asked.

"Hmm? What did I say?" Thompson asked. "You've gone white."

"What was that about magic?" she asked.

"Just a joke, city-Rose," he said. "I'd bespell you if I could, but all I've got in my bag of tricks is a pack of words and a decent line or two." He looked at her appraisingly. "'Course, if you think that'll work, my cabin's just a bit of a ways up yonder."

Rosanna barely heard him. The light of the little fire-pixie shone in her eyes, its scent filled her mouth. Granny Rosie had spoken a word; some *word* and that little thing had come out of the fire. Not a hallucination, not a trick, but the most important thing she'd ever seen, and Rosanna had *walked away*. Without a word in reply.

"Rosanna?" Thompson asked, from some great distance. "Rosanna, are you all right?"

"I...yes, I'm okay," she said. "I just think...I think I may have made a mistake."

"A big one or a little one?" he asked.

"I don't know," she said. "Could be huge though. Could be enough to cost me the person I love best in the world."

"Your Granny?" he asked. She looked up at him startled.

"How did you know?" she asked.

"Wasn't much of a guess," he replied. "She's the only person you've even mentioned. So I'm assuming that if there's a jealous boyfriend I need to watch out for, you don't much care for him."

"No jealous boyfriend, no," she said. "No boyfriend at all. Just books, and Granny."

"Need 'em both, hey?"

"God, yes," she said. "One wouldn't be near enough without the other."

"So, what's the mistake?" he asked.

"She told me..." Rosanna looked into his frank blue eyes, measuring him. He was charming and funny, but still a stranger, and she owed Granny more respect than to be giving family confidences away over coffee and toast. "She told me something important to her. I didn't know how to take it, and I left."

"That's a mite vague," he said. "Big secret or little one?"

"Huge one," she said. "Bigger than your biggest fib ever."

"Oh now," he said, "I can't imagine any secret that enormous even fitting under the same sky as my whoppers."

She smiled.

"You'd be surprised."

"Probably," he said. "So what makes it so big? Why did you leave?"

"Because it changes everything, it changes my whole world and everything in it. Even me. Especially me."

"Well, that's a big secret, then" he conceded. "But even secrets don't get to change what already is. A secret can't unmake you, or anything about you. Might need to shift definitions a bit, but you're still who you were before she told you."

"I'm not sure I believe that," Rosanna said. "That's why I left."

"Look now," he said, pointing outside. "Those woods are full of secrets that you might never know."

"Like fairies?" Rosanna said, "or bigfoot?"

"Never seen any sign of either, that doesn't mean they aren't there. What I think is squirrel prints could just as easy be sign of some tricksy magic critter having a good time."

"So?"

"What do you mean 'so'? What I see or don't see doesn't change what's there. What your Granny knows or doesn't can't change you. Not unless you allow it."

"What are you saying?"

"Ah, I'm not saying much of anything. Just hate to see you so riled up, that's all. We were having such a nice little conversation." He smiled ruefully. "I spend too much time on the mountain to get as many of those as I'd like."

"What do you do up there?" she asked.

"I run a trap line, do a little prospecting. Some gold still washes down the river, I keep looking for the source."

"Sounds…peaceful," she said.

"Not hardly, though it probably sounds like it to someone as hasn't done it. Winter's hard up here."

"So why do you stay?" she asked. "Why not do something else?"

"Because somewhere up there is riches, and I know it," he said. "All those little scraps have made me hungry for the big score, and I'm too stubborn to give up on it." His blue eyes gleamed. "Much like following June, I suppose."

"Did I hear my name in vain?" June said. She brought the coffee pot over, and Thompson accepted another cup.

"Not for me, thanks" Rosanna said. "Too much more of that and I'll be vibrating."

"Now that sounds fun," Thompson said with a leer.

"I still got that shovel," June said.

"I'll hold him down, you pummel him with it," Rosanna said.

"Now that *really* sounds fun," Thompson said. Both June and Rosanna flushed, and he roared with laughter. June walked away, the backs of her ears still pink.

"Now that was a good one," he said.

"You are a terrible man," Rosanna said severely.

"That's no secret," he said. "I do my best to advertise most thoroughly."

"All right then," she said. "What would you do if someone told you the one thing that made it look like you were a truly good guy at heart, not a lecherous flirt with a roving eye? What would you say to that?"

"I'd say screw it," he said. "Nobody defines me but me. My life, my soul my hands, I decide it all."

"What if you thought they were telling the truth?"

"What's truth? Everybody's got some kind of truth, doesn't mean I need to buy it."

"And if you respected their opinion?"

"Everyone's got an opinion," he said.

"Like assholes," she murmured.

"Exactly. Maybe I'd listen, but I'd make up my own mind. And if I didn't like what it all meant, why I'd change myself until I was exactly what I wanted to be."

"But you'd listen?"

"Hell, why not? Everybody listens to my stories, whether they buy 'em or no. It's at least good for passing the time."

Rosanna nodded. She had a choice, and walking away from Granny was not the one she wanted to make. But choosing to listen didn't mean choosing to believe, it didn't have to mean anything more than what it was.

"Thanks," she said. "I think I needed that perspective."

Thompson looked puzzled.

"Well, if I was helpful, I'm glad, but I don't know that I said anything particularly earthshaking." He tapped the back of her hand with his fingers. "Mind you, if you've an interest in earthshaking, I'm the one to provide it."

Rosanna laughed.

"Thank you, perhaps another time. I think I better get back to Granny before she decides never to speak to me again."

"Well, at least let me buy you breakfast," he said. "That way you'll owe me one next time you come by this way, and I'll have an excuse to sit with you again." Appreciation glimmered in his eyes, and his smile warmed the air between them.

June walked to the table and set down the bill. Thompson took it before Rosanna could even look at it.

"Call it country hospitality," he said.

"Call it hopeful," June muttered to Rosanna, and they shared a sly smile.

"Come back any time," June said. "There's almost always coffee, and don't forget the whiskey's on at sunrise.

Rosanna thanked her, and thanked Thompson, then walked out to her car. She started the engine, and began the cautious drive back to Granny's place. As she drove out of the parking lot, she caught sight of Thompson in her rear-view mirror watching her pull away. She smiled at the memory of his voice and charm, and then applied her attention to the winding road.

# Chapter 3

The return trip to Granny Rosie's house was not comfortable. Rosanna considered turning back, and even stopped by the side of the road to argue with herself over it. The truth was complicated. Rosanna and Granny almost never fought, Rosanna having long ago learned the virtue of graceful retreat. She kept her opinions to herself and Granny seemed to accept this as the natural order of things. But Rosanna possessed strong opinions, and not expressing them had slowly built a wall between her and Granny, one that she wasn't sure Granny even knew existed.

So Rosanna's first inclination was to avoid the conflict altogether, to go back to her simple, dusty little life and forget anything had ever happened. It would have been almost a relief to remove herself from Granny's world, to set aside the expectations she'd always felt but that Granny had never expressed.

Her second inclination was to go in raging, to snarl and roar with righteous indignation. Granny had kept things from her, important things that might have changed everything, might have changed Rosanna and saved her from that sad, dusty little life to start with. She wanted to blame Granny, to savage her.

Her third inclination was to be good, to go learn at Granny's knee. It might be nice to be the child again, to let Granny hold the answers and not be required to find answers of her own.

On the whole, she despised all her inclinations equally. None of them seemed true to the wonder she felt when she thought of the fire pixie, or to the complicated mix of fear and longing that filled her relationship with Granny Rosie. It wasn't as simple as any of those inclinations suggested. Leaving her would be horrible, hurting her would be worse. And Rosanna would never be a child again, no matter how she sometimes ached to be.

So she fought each inclination to a surly impasse, and decided, finally, only to go to the door, and see what happened next. It seemed the course of action least likely to drive her crazy.

The driveway was almost worse by daylight, when she could clearly see the glassy slope. Snow tires hardly seemed sufficient, she found herself wishing for chains, or perhaps climbing pitons.

The cabin nestled snug and silent among glittering drifts of snow. Smoke still lofted up the chimney to be whisked away by the breeze. Rosanna parked her car and walked to the door. On any other occasion, she might simply have walked in and announced herself. Today, she knocked.

She heard faint sounds of movement inside, and then the door opened. Granny stared out at her silently. Rosanna rocked from foot to foot, but Granny opened the door no wider than it took for them to see each other. Rosanna was the first to break the awful, storm-charged hush.

"I'm back," she said. Granny said great volumes of nothing. Her face might have been carved out of ice.

"Can I come in?" Rosanna asked. "I think...I think we may need to talk."

"Oh, so *now* you want to talk," she said. "How nice for you. Why don't you send a card, instead?"

"Granny, don't be impossible," Rosanna said. "It's freezing out here."

"Don't expect it to be much warmer in," Granny said, but stepped back from the door. She turned her back before Rosanna was even past the threshold. Rosanna saw age in the slope of Granny's shoulders.

"Coffee's on the stove," Granny said, then walked to her chair and sat down. She had a mug on the table beside her, and a photograph album lay open on the floor.

Rosanna slipped off her shoes, then helped herself to coffee and doctored it liberally with sugar. Granny made camp coffee, the kind that could dissolve fillings. The clink of the spoon on the side of the cup hurt her ears. Granny's silence roared.

Rosanna took a deep breath, then sat in the chair opposite Granny. She sipped the coffee, more as a delaying tactic than out of real interest in it.

"So," Granny said at last. "You're back. I suppose I ought to be grateful."

"Grateful? What do you mean grateful?"

"Well, how often does a poor crazy old woman like me get such an exalted visitor?"

"I never said you were crazy," Rosanna said.

"You might as well have, the way you stomped out of here."

"Well what did you expect? I mean, God, Granny, you spring this on me after all these years? You don't think it's reasonable I might be a little overwhelmed?"

"Don't be such a child, I've been preparing you for this your whole life."

"A child? You have *got* to be kidding me."

"I said it and I meant it," Granny replied. "Only a *child* could be so unspeakably rude."

"This is not how this is going to go, Granny," Rosanna said. "You don't get to accuse me of anything when you're the one who's been keeping secrets."

"I don't have to accuse," Granny said. "You're the one that left me wondering all night if you were ever coming back, if you were even *alive* out there."

"Cut the drama," Rosanna said. "I didn't even leave your yard, and if you could have spared just a second from that self-righteous wrath, you were perfectly capable of checking."

She thought for a second.

"Besides, I drove off this morning, and if you didn't hear that, then you're a heavier sleeper than you used to be."

"Doesn't matter," Granny said. "I'm not going to beg anyone to come back to my own damn house."

"Beg? Holy crap, Granny, do you actually believe this stuff you're saying?"

"You walked out on ME Rosanna, after I told you the most important thing I know. You threw it back in my face, everything I gave you, you threw it away like it was garbage."

"I just couldn't take it in, so I left for a while. You want to read insult into that, that's your responsibility, not mine."

"No, of course not, you're not a responsible sort, are you?"

"And what is *that* supposed to mean?"

"Every time something gets difficult, a relationship a job, whatever, you walk away."

"So now this is going to be about how I fail you? Great, let's get it over with," Rosanna said. "I'm pretty tired of you not saying it, and meaning it all the same."

"You don't fail me, you fail yourself. Over and over you do it," Granny said. "For heaven's sake, you file books for a living. Didn't you ever want more?" Rosanna tasted fury in her mouth, acrid and burning.

"Of course I wanted more, don't be stupid. But I didn't know there *was* more, did I? I didn't know all these lovely little secrets you kept from me. Are there more? How many lies did you have to tell me over the years?"

"I didn't lie," Granny said, looking down at her hands. "I just never told you everything."

"A lie of omission is still a lie. And a half-truth is more false than an outright lie. *You* taught me that, remember?" Rosanna set her cup down. She didn't know if she was going to spill it or throw it.

"There are rules, Rosanna. I couldn't just tell you everything, it had to happen in a certain way."

"Is it in the rules that you have to lie?" Rosanna asked.

"Maybe. What do you care? It's got nothing to do with you, does it? You get to walk away whenever you please."

"That's interesting. As soon as I call you on something, we're back to how disappointing I am."

"So stop disappointing me, and I'll be able to stop talking about it."

"And should I apologize for that? For not being able to meet impossible standards? For being human? God, how can you breathe up on that high horse?"

"You haven't apologized," Granny said. "Not once, you haven't said you're sorry."

"I'm tired of being sorry. I'm tired of apologizing for my life, for my self. I'm tired of never being what you want, and always having to be sorry for it."

"You owed me more than that, girl. You owe me everything you are."

"Even the disappointing parts?"

"Don't you talk to me like that, you haven't the right."

"Make up your mind. You're mad because I left, you're mad because I came back. There's not going to be any winning this, is there?" Rosanna felt her fingernails biting into the palms of her hands. She didn't remember clenching them, but forced herself to relax the fists she'd made.

"Who says it's about winning?" Granny asked.

"It's always about winning with you. All those years, Granny! All the times I failed you and you wouldn't tell me how! You made me feel like nothing, never good enough, never anything enough."

"That wasn't what I wanted you to feel."

"But you're not sorry for that, right? I'm supposed to be falling over myself to apologize for walking out ONCE when you've been turning your back on me all my LIFE!"

"Don't you yell at me!" Granny shouted. "You don't have the right! Don't you *dare* yell at me in my own house!"

"What *do* I have the right to, then? I don't have the right to your honesty, your respect, your love. Was it just obligation, then? All that time?"

"Of course not, I've always loved you."

"Bullshit. People who love each other don't tell lies."

"You can moderate your language *and* your tone, young lady," Granny said.

"Oh, no, you don't get it both ways, Granny. You don't get to be the good mama and a liar in the same conversation. Pick one."

"Damn it, every parent has to tell some lies, to protect their children."

"I haven't been a child for a long time now. But you held onto your pretty little fib."

"I'm telling you, there are rules. I couldn't tell you until you asked the question, it would have put you in danger, and until you showed interest, it was possible you couldn't even use the words. What would be the point?"

"It might have been nice to know exactly *how* I was such a disappointment," Rosanna said, looking down. "It might have been nice to know that it wasn't really something I did, just something I was. Or wasn't."

"I'm not…I haven't been disappointed in what you are," Granny said.

"That's not what you said earlier."

"I want more for you than the life you have, that's all."

"And why do you get to pick?" Rosanna asked. "Why does my life have to be good enough for you?"

"Because I've been holding your birthright for you, all these years, and never knowing whether you'd ask me for it. Because I need you to be strong enough for what I've given you."

"How would you know? Who made you the judge?"

"I have to be the judge, you're my responsibility."

"I am more than old enough to be my own responsibility," Rosanna said. "Whether you like what I do with it or not." She paused.

"What is this really about, Granny? If this was my birthright, why now?"

"Because you asked the right question," Granny replied.

"Last night, I was sure I'd asked the question before. I know I did." She remembered asking, now, she remembered wondering why her family didn't talk about Baby Jesus, why they talked about the Word, instead.

"You were too young, Rosanna, much too young." Granny said. "I had to protect you. It's not an easy burden, what I do...what your mother did."

"So you tell me now, and you're surprised I freak out? That I get overwhelmed? What did you expect, for God's sake?"

"I expected you to be..."Granny's voice dropped. "I expected you to be like your mother when I told her. I expected you to already know it was true, somewhere inside you."

"I never even knew her," Rosanna said. "All I ever knew was you, and I never thought you kept secrets from me."

"Every person has places in them that no one else ever goes."

"But this wasn't your secret to keep from me. You said it yourself, this is my birthright. So why didn't you tell me?"

"I knew you weren't ready for it. I didn't think you'd ever be ready for it. And you proved it."

"You gave me no room to prove anything else. You gave me no choice but to walk away. And even then, I came back. You didn't pursue me, I came back to you. What does that say about ready?"

Granny shook her head.

"I protected you." She said. "I did what was best."

"It's not turning out so great, is it?" Rosanna said. "I trusted you all my life, and here is where that lands us."

"You trusted me until last night" Granny said bitterly. "Until I told you the most significant thing I know."

"Don't you get it? It wasn't just magic, Granny, it was about *us*, about you and me."

"That's not true," Granny said. "It doesn't mean anything about you and me, or what we've been to each other. After Lillian died, you were my world."

"I don't want to be a replacement for my own mother," Rosanna replied. "If that's all I am to you, get a dog. They're easier to train."

"How can you say that to me, Rosanna?"

"I can say that because I am stronger and smarter and braver than you believe. I am ready to walk away rather than let you fold me into some new pocket of your life. My life isn't much but it's MINE and you don't get to define me."

Granny let her breath out in a huge bellow of laughter.

"Oh, finally, Rosanna, oh finally!"

Rosanna deflated in puzzlement.

"Do you need to be so cryptic? Could we just argue like normal people?"

Granny chuckled, and all the age seemed to slip off her shoulders again.

"We aren't normal people, my girl, and that's the truth."

"I don't feel like I'm done arguing," Rosanna said.

"You probably aren't, and we can talk more later, but it's time to sort out where we've come to."

"What?"

"You're goggling like a goldfish, girl, close your mouth."

"But I'm still mad."

"Me too, but like I said, there's time to sort that out later. Right now, right this minute, you've passed the next test, and there's not a moment to lose."

"TEST?"

"Oh hush, now. We were really fighting, about real things, but in there, you said the last of the key words. I don't define you."

"Oh crap, tell me this isn't going to go on forever? Do I have to learn a special handshake, too?"

"Only if you want to. Otherwise, I'm just going to tell you the rest of my secrets. Interested?"

"Just tell me if I really disappoint you," Rosanna said. Granny shook her head wearily.

"I'll admit it, though I don't like to. You're right. I was disappointed and I treated you badly, waiting for you to take up the work. I love you, Rosanna, and I was wrong. I'm sorry."

"You're what?"

"Come on, you don't really expect to hear it twice in the same day, do you?"

Rosanna chuckled.

"No, I suppose not. I'm sorry I walked out."

"I figured there was a good chance you would. Didn't know if you'd come back, didn't even know what to hope for."

"Ouch."

"Don't take it that way, that's not how I mean it."

"So what do you mean then?"

"This work is what killed your mother, Rosanna, it's what took my daughter from me."

"Why didn't you tell me when I asked? It might have made this easier. Didn't you think I could do it?"

. "It's not that, not at all. You were too young when you first asked, and I was too afraid."

"Afraid?" Fear was something Granny put into other people.

"I couldn't stand to lose you, not after Lillian," Granny said. "Losing one daughter to the Word is one too many. Two might break me.

"So my mother knew magic," Rosanna said. "Real magic."

Granny nodded.

"More than knew, she was a prodigy, someone with a powerful innate understanding of the words."

"You mean she was…what, a wizard?" It was absurd.

"Not precisely," Granny said. "Not in the way of Harry Potter and his lot."

"Okay, so not a wizard. A what, then?"

"A Librarian," Granny said. Rosanna laughed, she just couldn't help it.

"A librarian? A mighty magical librarian? What did she do, hunt down people with late fees?"

Granny smiled. It wasn't a real smile, but it was a valiant attempt. Rosanna stopped laughing. Something in Granny's face spoke to old, old wounds. Rosanna had enough respect for Granny's strength that the idea of Granny hurt was sobering.

"Not just any librarian, Rosanna. A true Librarian, one who tends to the great Words, and gathers the lesser. She was brilliant."

"And I guess I'm nothing like that."

"Nothing? Oh child, every time I look in your face, I see more of her than you'll ever guess. Every day of your life I saw something in you that reminded me of my lost Lily."

"I never felt that way, Granny." Rosanna said. "I always thought…well, that you'd rather have her."

"I'd rather have had you both," Granny said. "I'd rather she had a chance to raise her daughter. But she didn't." There was a long silent moment in the cabin as each of them examined the shape of her losses.

"Why didn't she, Granny? Why didn't she stay with me? Was it really an accident? Or something else?"

Granny sighed.

"It was something else, of course," she said. "She was building a Library, one meant to house the greater Words. She made a mistake, and she wasn't strong enough. Words can bite their speaker, if she doesn't have control. Lillian didn't, no matter what she thought."

"A word…a word killed my mother?"

"That was the instrument, yes. Truth is, I killed her. I failed her. I was her teacher, and I didn't teach her well enough. She died because of me."

"I don't believe that, Granny. If that was so, every driving instructor in the world would be a murderer."

"You're kind, but you don't know," Granny said. "She was brilliant, I told you that, and I was so proud of her. She asked the questions young, started training early. Building a Library is most often the masterwork of a Librarian, one they take on late in life." Granny paused, and memories flickered in her eyes.

"Get me that album will you? The one on the far left." Granny pointed to her bookshelves. A book in tattered blue bindings stood next to the other photograph albums. No other of them looked as worn.

Rosanna took a sip off coffee. It was lukewarm, and she wished she had some of June's whiskey for it. She brought the album to Granny, and moved her chair in close beside her.

Granny opened it, and the first picture was one Rosanna remembered. It had been framed, and had hung in every house they ever inhabited. Rosanna's mother smiled warmly and waved at the camera.

"Oh, she was such a ham for the camera, that one. Never could have a nice dignified portrait, not even on the most important of days."

"What day was it?"

"It was the day she died, my dear. The day she meant to seal the Library and finish the work of it. I think she expected to build a half dozen of them before she died." Granny shook her head. "Didn't quite manage the one."

"Are you disappointed in her?"

"No, just myself."

"But why not? She's the one who messed up, not you."

"I'm the one that didn't train her, and I was right there, Rosanna, right there when she died. If I'd seen the flaw, I could have stopped her in time. And she died in front of me. Just dropped, all broken inside."

"God, Granny, I'm sorry."

"That's not why I'm telling you this. I'm telling you this so you know the danger, so you believe it. Lillian never really did, it all came too easily for her, and no smaller mistake ever bit her hard enough to teach the lesson."

"So, what is it you're saying then? Don't do this? Are you trying to talk me out of it all?"

"I can't do that, Rosanna. It's your choice now, to take up the work or no, but you have to know what it could mean, you have to really understand that you could die because of it."

Rosanna paused for a long moment, staring at her mother's picture. This was a woman she didn't remember, someone she only knew from Granny's stories. But this near-stranger was dead because of Granny's secret, gone and lost forever. What reward could be worth that risk?

"Why do you do it, Granny?"

"Because it needs to be done. When the words get loose, if they get loose on their own, sometimes they only join the rest of language. Didn't you ever wonder where new words came from?"

Rosanna shrugged. "I guess, " she said. "I just assumed they sort of grew out of other words."

"Sometimes, yes, out of a new need. But sometimes, they're just part of the greater Words gone astray. When that happens, the power in them becomes dilute, spread out over all the people that speak it. That means one tiny piece of magic is unmade."

"So? That doesn't seem like such a big deal."

"No, probably not in itself. But if it ever comes to a point where magic is entirely gone from us, when the process of spontaneous creation is removed, chaos and Unbeing will have free reign. Everything we know will cease to exist."

"That sounds a little far-fetched. How do you know?"

"I don't, not entirely and for sure, but I believe it. As magic fails and chaos deepens, I see human souls hungering for chaos and destruction."

"Haven't we always?"

"To some extent, but the process of diluting words took much longer. It's all gathering momentum."

"I don't think I can buy that. I mean, responsibility for the whole of being seems a lot for a few librarians to handle."

"So don't buy it, I don't need you to. What's true is that preserving the Words preserves the magic. We are as much guardians of magic as of words. That's what got me in at the start."

"So, magic like what? Like that fire fairy?"

"Just like. Imagine if her word got spread out over the Internet. She'd thin out until she ceased to exist."

"But I thought you just made her from the word you spoke."

"No, I called her by her true name, a single syllable of the greater Word of which she's part. There is a world of magic that you know nothing about. Wouldn't you like to?"

"Is it worth it? Worth the risk I mean?"

"I think so. But the risk isn't just from the Words themselves. Only sometimes does a Word get lost, sometimes a person collects them and twists them and sets them on the world. Magic can be malign, too, if the will that calls it is."

"That sounds dangerous."

"More than dangerous, deadly. These people will kill for more of what they've got."

"But why? Why would they do that?"

"I don't know, really. You know that saying about absolute power, right?"

"Who doesn't. But cliché aside, why do you *think* they do it?"

"I think they do it for fun. I think they like to be secretive and powerful and know more than other people."

"Yuck."

"It's not so different from me, really. Just the way that power is directed."

"Ummm so you only use your power for good then?"

"Nothing so super-hero. I think of myself as a keeper of rare creatures. Magic will die without me and other Librarians."

"So that's what you're asking then. Whether I'm willing to put my life on the line for an endangered species?"

"Near enough."

It wasn't fair for Granny to have talked about secrets and power and knowledge. They were all things Rosanna craved. She found herself hungry for magic, too, for another taste of the mystery and wonder of that little fire creature.

"Well then, call me ecologically conscious, I guess. I'm in."

Granny sat back with a satisfied smile.

"Thank God, girl, I thought you'd never get there."

# Chapter 4

It was cold out, but Granny had extra scarves and mittens, and Rosanna always brought heavy winter boots in her car in case of emergencies. The sky was open and clear above mountains that looked sharp enough for a camera commercial. Sun was a brilliant dazzle on the new snow, but a keen little breeze stole its warmth away.

"It's another ten minutes for me," Granny said over her shoulder. "Probably closer to a day and a half for you. Lord, girl, you're slow."

"I'm not exactly accustomed to wading through nine feet of snow, you know," Rosanna replied. "I live in a city, remember? With snow plows and sanding trucks?"

Granny snorted.

"Why you'd want that much distance between you and the real world, I'll never understand."

"The city's part of the real world, too, Granny. God, you'd think I lived on Mars."

"Sometimes I wonder. Pick it *up* Rosanna. The faster we're done, the faster you'll be in by the fire."

Rosanna growled under her breath, but there wasn't any point in arguing. Granny was already forging ahead at a ridiculous pace, and the sight of her bony old backside was all the goad Rosanna really needed. Granny was too old to outpace her granddaughter, for heaven's sake. It just wasn't polite.

They pushed through the snow until they reached the edge of the pine forest. There was little snow under the protective branches, though now and again the wind would knock some loose, and it fell to the forest floor with a sound like a solid smack with a feather pillow. The smell of pine was strong and rich as they walked through drifts of old needles, and it felt warmer with trees to cut the wind. Rosanna's nose was still numb, but her fingers seemed to be recovering feeling. Granny still walked indecently quickly, but Rosanna managed to catch up.

Granny looked her up and down critically.

"You don't get out much, do you? I thought you city folk believed in gyms and such."

"Some of them do," Rosanna said. "I believe that winter was made for hot chocolate and good books."

"It shows. You're out of shape."

"I am not!"

"Well, I suppose round is still a shape," Granny said, and grinned.

Rosanna reached up and batted at a snow-laden branch over Granny's head, and managed to cover them both equally with snow. Granny laughed.

"You want to play that way, my lass, you might consider getting yourself out of the way first."

Rosanna chuckled.

"I'm out of practice, I guess. Is it much farther? I don't mean to whine, but it's ruddy cold out."

"We're almost there," Granny replied. "I'm trying to decide which to show you first."

"Which what?"

"The grave or the thing that made it necessary."

"Oh."

There was a deep and heavy silence, broken only by the creak and rustle of pine trees above them.

"I think the grave first. I never want you to forget what can happen. Knowing makes the best part of caution."

Rosanna nodded. When she was a child, she'd imagined finding her mother's grave, and played that it was all a mistake, that her mother wasn't really gone, just waiting to be rescued. This was not as she'd pictured it. Knowing that there was a place where her mother's remains lay made it permanent, final. Somehow, it was like losing her for the first time.

They walked in stillness for a while, each immersed in her own thoughts. Granny's face was tired with sorrow, lined and hollowed by it.

"It wasn't your fault," Rosanna said, not knowing if it were true, but certain that it had to be said.

"You weren't there."

"It doesn't matter. Her mistake isn't your fault. Are my mistakes your fault?"

"Maybe."

"Don't evade me. Sometimes people make mistakes even with the best education, the best parents. You must know that."

"I suppose. But Lillian was mine, Rosanna. It's different."

"I bet every parent thinks that. But it's not, and you're still beating yourself up for it. Wouldn't you like to stop?"

"I don't dare," Granny said. "Not when you're taking up the work now, too. I don't dare forget for a moment that my failures cost the people I love best. I don't dare."

Rosanna couldn't think of anything that would answer the pain and resolve in Granny Rosie's voice. She closed the space between them, and put her gloved hand in Granny's. Granny looked up with surprise, but held to Rosanna's hand in return, tears rising up in her eyes until the blue seemed almost silver with the shimmer of them.

Abruptly, they broke through the dense tree cover, and stepped out into a little clearing. The air here was warm, and green grass covered the forest floor. Rosanna looked down, and found that the green ended abruptly, as if a wall separated spring from winter. A large stone sat in the middle of the space, a simple piece of granite whose center had been hollowed out to form a little basin full of clear water. A channel cut in the rock allowed a trickle of water to seep down its mossy side and into the earth at its foot. There, a thick stand of white lilies bloomed, and their scent filled the clearing like a psalm of grace. Rosanna released Granny's hand in surprise.

"This is…this is impossible," Rosanna said, but found herself pulling off her gloves and loosening her scarf.

"Not impossible, not even terribly difficult," Granny said. "The spring was here, warm but not really hot, so I gave it a place, and made it so the warmth would linger. It took a year or so before everything grew in, but it's been like this since." She paused.

"It was the last syllables of your mother's being that provided the power," she said.

Rosanna walked to the pool, and dipped her hand in it. Water bubbled up from the bottom of the basin, and flecks of sand moved lazily in the current. It was just warm, not quite hot enough for a bath, and it smelled a little of the minerals it had leached from the earth on its journey to the surface.

"This is her grave?" she asked.

Granny nodded.

"But she's not buried here. We don't do things that way." She brushed the surface of the spring with her fingers, just a caress.

"When she died, I pulled apart the words that held her body together, and linked them to this place." Her face closed tight over that memory, and her eyes became opaque, like black ice. After a breath or two, she shook her head, and put the sorrow away.

"She's part of everything now. I think she'd have like that. She was always a fanciful child."

This was far beyond Rosanna's most romantic imaginings. This was a little chapel devoted solely to the memory of her mother. She bent to smell the lilies, and tears burned behind her eyes. Her chest was tight with the effort of holding them in.

"I was starting to think no one else would ever come here," Granny said. "I'd want to release the word before I died, else it might be lost. It's a small one, a simple one, but sometimes small and simple mean more than great and complicated."

Rosanna nodded. Granny rested a hand on her granddaughter's shoulder.

"I was starting to think no one would ever weep here but me," she said quietly, and that set loose the tears, like a wind in a rain-heavy tree.

"I don't remember her, Granny," she said, and turned into the waiting arms. She buried her head and sobbed into Granny's shoulder. "I want to remember her! It's not fair, I want to remember!" Granny stroked her hair, and said nothing, let the words spill as they would.

"I thought that seeing her grave would make me remember, but I just don't. I just...when I smell those lilies, it smells like her, that's all."

"That was her perfume, love. She always wore that scent."

"Then I do remember?"

"A little," Granny said. "You used to tell me little things, like how momma made tea for breakfast, or that her favorite blanket was blue. But things fade when you're so small. It's not your fault, Rosanna."

That set her off again, and Granny patiently waited out the storm as Rosanna began to release a lifetime of unshed tears, unspoken sorrow.

After a while, the storm eased, and Rosanna pulled away, wiping her eyes with hands that trembled. Granny offered her a tissue.

"I've got more," she said with a gentle smile. "I always bring them when I come here."

"I can see why," Rosanna said. "It's beautiful, but it's so sad."

"Mostly in winter it's sad. In summer, in spring, the birds fill the place, and there's other flowers in the grass. Everything grows less in the winter, but in summer, that grass comes up to my hips, and this place is all color and sound. She'd have liked that, too."

"I can't see how anyone wouldn't," Rosanna said, "It's amazing." She paused.

She paused. "Granny, there's something I've always wondered, but never asked. I guess I thought they died together, but...where's my father?"

"Your who?"

"My father. Did he die with her? There aren't any pictures, and you never talk about him."

"I...Rosanna, when you say that, I just can't think. All the words and the thoughts just pour out of my head."

"You can't have forgotten a whole person, can you?"

"I shouldn't think so, but...whenever I think that word, everything scatters."

"Repression, maybe? From a trauma?"

"Oh, I don't think so. Something's wrong."

"Well, clearly, but what?"

"I don't know, but my best guess is that I've been spelled."

Rosanna wanted to scoff with a lifetime's accumulation of healthy skepticism, but it was not possible, not in this place. Magic was here, was real, she could see and touch and smell it.

"So why? And by who?"

"Whom" Granny corrected absently. "What were we talking about?"

"My father," Rosanna said.

"Your what?"

"Granny, this is getting old. I keep trying to talk about my other parent, my mother's husband, the sperm donor, and you keep going senile on me."

"Say that again," Granny said urgently, "just the last bit."

"Sperm donor? I wouldn't have thought you'd like that one, Granny."

"I don't, but I can focus on it sideways. The other words just slip away. We've got to get to the Library, Rosanna. If I've been affected by a Word, it must be one of the greater ones, and that worries me."

"Does this mean you don't remember my…"

Granny hushed Rosanna before she finished the sentence.

"Don't," she said. "Not unless you want to have to do the whole thing again. The other words probably trigger the spell."

Rosanna put her gloves back on, and wrapped her scarf around her. She looked around the dell. It seemed wrong to leave in a hurry. Granny saw her hesitation.

"I am sorry, Rosanna, truly I am. I hate to rush you like this." She paused. "You can come back whenever you wish, stay however long you like. But this other thing frets me deeply. I want to deal with it while I can even remember that it's a problem."

"I could remind you," Rosanna said. "I don't mind."

"Shouldn't like you to think I've *really* gone senile. It's best not to wait."

Rosanna nodded, sighed, and steeled herself to step back into winter. Even so, the cold immediately regained possession of her fingertips and the end of her nose. She shivered, and followed Granny further up the mountain. Granny Rosie set an even quicker pace, despite the grade. Rosanna was grateful to have someone break a path through the snow, but she panted with the effort of keeping up. She really wasn't in the best of shape. She was sweating under her heavy coat, but her fingers remained stubbornly cold.

"Granny!" she shouted. "Can you slow down a little? I'm dying, here!"

Granny turned back, and peered down the steep slope.

"Girl, if you can't keep up with an old granny, it's no wonder you haven't kept a man. They're twice the trouble!"

"Not hardly!" It wasn't the best repartee, but it was all Rosanna could manage between gulps of air.

"Follow my track, Rosanna. I'll meet you up there. I want to see if anyone's been mucking about. It's not too far now."

"That's what you said when we left the house," Rosanna muttered, but Granny was already forging ahead. Rosanna sighed, readjusted her scarf, and followed suit.

Granny climbed rapidly, then stopped to wave. Rosanna couldn't spare the effort to wave back, but she was heartened when Granny then disappeared from view entirely. That meant that the hill must end, although she supposed it might easily just lead on to another. She didn't have enough energy for both walking and pessimism at the same time, so she focused on Granny's trail through the snow, and on forcing her burning muscles to propel her upward.

She was so focused, in fact, that she nearly stumbled when she did finally reach the end of her ascent, as if she'd climbed a stair that didn't exist. She sighed, puffing and steaming in the cold air. She turned to look behind herself, and was embarrassed to see how small a distance she'd actually come.

She spotted Granny a little ahead. A tumble of loose stone had sheared off the mountainside sometime long ago. They lay strewn about like a careless child's toys, some covered in snow, some swept bare by the wind. The breeze was stronger up here, crueler, too. It sliced through her mittens and  coat, chilling the sweat on Rosanna's body and stealing the heat of her exertion.

Granny sat on a rough boulder in the middle of the debris, watching Rosanna's progress with amusement.

"Maybe it's time for more gym and less hot  chocolate, hm?" she said.

"If you were not my venerable old Granny," Rosanna said, "I think I'd give you the finger."

"Obscenity is the last refuge of the ignorant, "Granny said. "Surely you can think of better?"

"Maybe, but I can't breathe well enough to be creative."

Granny chuckled. "You'll get used to it," she said. "And it's not so bad the rest of the year."

"That's not very comforting, considering that winter lasts nine months up here."

"Does not."

"It most certainly does. You had snow in May this year, I remember it."

"Just a bit. And it melted."

"Still."

"Stop whining. I'm too old to keep correcting you, and you're too old to need it."

Rosanna stuck out her tongue.

"Very mature. In any case, welcome to the Library."

"Where?"

Granny indicated the stones with her hand. "All around you."

"You're kidding me, right?"

"Not about this. Here, come sit with me."

Rosanna did, and felt a deep warmth surge through her from the boulder. All at once she was perfectly comfortable, from her toes to the tip of her nose.

"Did you do that?"

"No. That's residual power from the Library, something your mother set up to keep herself comfortable, I suspect." She peered at Rosanna. "She probably couldn't stand the cold, either. Thin city blood, maybe."

"I notice you're not in a hurry to move," Rosanna said.

"Don't be impertinent. I'm old enough to be your grandmother." She grinned, and Rosanna smiled in answer.

"Any roads," Granny continued, "this is it. This is what she died trying to make."

"It doesn't look like much." Rosanna had pictured something grander than a scramble of broken rock.

"It's not supposed to," Granny said. "Being ordinary makes for good camouflage. And it isn't finished, not quite." She sighed, and gestured at the other stones again. "All this is supposed to be a single stone, a sealed Library. As it is, each piece holds some Word, or portion of one. Lillian nearly had it all, and then some flaw broke it all apart again. She was nearly buried under it all." She shook her head. "I can still remember it all so clearly. Sometimes I wish I could forget."

They sat in silence except for the thin whistle of the wind.

"Any sign of someone else around here?"

Granny shook her head.

"No, but the wind could erase tracks, and any roads, it wouldn't have to be a recent visit to have stolen the Word." She shrugged, and brooded silently.

"So how does this all work?" Rosanna asked at last.

"That's simple enough," Granny said. "Because of the flaw, the words escape. It's slow, but they do."

"But why? I don't get it. Why would they do that? I mean, power or not, they're just words, aren't they? Don't they have to be spoken?"

Granny sighed. "It's so ruddy hard to explain," She said. "You'd think it'd be simple, like you say, and in some ways it is. Maybe that's *why* it's hard to explain." She paused again.

"Okay, think of it like this. You know how if you drop, say, a car in water, the water will rush to fill it up?"

"Yeah, the pressure equalizes."

Granny nodded.

"Like that, only it's existence and non-existence, chaos and order that are trying to balance out."

"Um… you say that like it might make sense."

"God you can be dense."

"Look, you're the one explaining. If the explanation sucks, it's not my fault I can't follow it."

"All right, all right. Let me try to make it really, really preschool for you."

"Feel free."

"Everything either exists or doesn't."

"Okay so far."

"Good. So existing and not existing balance out."

"What?"

"Every force has its equal and opposite, right?"

"Okay, I guess I can buy that. So...not-existing is the opposite of existing?"

"Right. Not just destruction, but annihilation. Ceasing to be at all."

"Okay, so which are the Words?"

"They're a force for Being. They are drawn to balance out Unbeing, like water into the car.'

"It's a stretch, but I think I can get there. But if that's so, why wouldn't you want the Words to just cancel out the Unbeing? Wouldn't that be a good thing?"

"If that's what would happen, maybe. But like I told you, the Words get into language instead, they become diluted, and they don't have any power in themselves any more."

"Which would mean...what?"

"That Unbeing would be bigger than Being, and  'poof', there goes everything."

"Everything?"

"Everything."

Rosanna shivered, even though her body was quite warm.

"But you can't know that, can you?"

"Only in degrees. I've seen words slip into common usage, and the Beings they described disappear. Fairy folk used to be common when I was a girl, though they were always reclusive. People learned their names, and the fairies disappeared."

"But it's still just a theory, right?"

"So's Mr. Darwin's theory on Evolution. Can't prove it exhaustively, but you can see it in action."

"I...it's too big."

Granny nodded sagely. "I know. That's why I bring it down to caring for the magic. For me, that's the part I can understand. I can't imagine caring for the whole of everything, so I take care of what's small and here. What I know and can touch."

Rosanna chuckled shakily. "Think globally, act locally?"

"That's it exactly. It's important to know there's a big picture, but it's more important to do everything you can than worry about what you can't."

"Are there more Librarians out there?"

"Oh yes. Lots of us keep in touch. I'll introduce you."

Rosanna couldn't muster much enthusiasm for that idea. Everything was so new, so overwhelming, and everyone else would only know more than she.

"Couldn't one of them do this?"

"No," Granny said. "It has to be you or me, and I'm not strong enough any more. Not that I'm dying or anything, but it takes control I just don't have after all these years. Plus I think my memory may be about full." She smiled wryly.

"Why us? Why does it have to be us?"

"Part of who Lillian was is embedded in this Library, broken down as it is. It couldn't be remade from scratch without destroying that. We've got a connection to her, we can mend it without…without losing that last little piece of her." Granny looked down at her hands, her shoulders rigid with unspoken emotion.

"But how can I do that? I didn't know her, and I have no idea what I'm supposed to be doing. I mean…what if I break it by accident?"

"God damn, Rosanna, do you think I like asking this of you? I know you're untrained, because I haven't trained you. I've spent all these years raising you, trying to bring you into your own abilities. When I finally moved back here, there wasn't enough of me left to do the job!"

"I…are you blaming me for that?" Rosanna's eyes closed against the answer. The wind seemed cold again, despite the heat of the Library. Granny was silent.

"Because I don't see how that's fair," Rosanna said. "You never told me, you never asked me, you never even hinted. And when I wasn't satisfactory, I'm sure you could have left me with someone else while you did your important work." She paused to wipe angrily at her eyes. Tears wouldn't do her any good. They never had.

" It probably would have been nice not to have the inept, untalented, bad excuse for a replacement hanging about to remind you of Lillian."

"Rosanna…" Granny didn't seem to be gearing up for a fight. There was no anger in her tone, but no apology either.

"Don't, okay? I know we stopped fighting back at the house, but those things…they still stick in what you say, and how you say it."

"I know. I know they are, and I don't know how to stop."

"So what am I supposed to do? Just take it?"

Granny shrugged uncomfortably.

"I'm old, Rosanna. It's hard to change."

"Bullshit. Old has nothing to do with it. It's just hard to change. And you want proof, right? That I can do this?"

"Some part of me does, yes. You haven't exactly filled me up with confidence in you."

"You haven't exactly filled me up with confidence in myself, either. Look, you're the expert on words. Why don't you look at yours? Ask what they mean to you, ask why. You've got a choice in what you say and think."

"I don't much care for advice from someone your age."

"I don't much give a damn what you care for. If we're doing this, we've got to do it as a team. You can't be boss, and I can't be slave. Teaching doesn't work that way."

Granny snorted. "It did when I was young. I had a terror of rulers for years."

"Well, it doesn't work that way any more, and it sure as hell won't work that way with me."

Granny Rosie sighed heavily, and a little of the tension eased from her shoulders.

"Your mother never talked to me that way," she said, but it was an observation, not an accusation. "She never asked why, she just wanted to know how."

"Is that okay?" Rosanna's throat closed a little. "Would it be okay if I was different from her?"

Granny nodded, wiping furtively at her own eyes. "I guess it would. It might be hard though. It might mean…letting go of her."

Granny turned and cupped Rosanna's cheek in her hand.

"I'm afraid to let her go, Rosanna. And I'm afraid you'll fail, and I'll have to let you go, and when that happens…there just won't be anything left for me to hold at all."

Rosanna's fingers covered Granny's gently. Her other hand brushed away a tear that trembled down Granny's weathered cheek.

"Then let's be a team. We can do this together. God, Granny, with you as backup, anyone could do anything at all."

Granny smiled and patted Rosanna's cheek. "Flattery will get you most places," she said, and the weight of the moment lifted from them both.

"So what is it, exactly, that I have to do?"

"Well, I know the flaw is here, but I don't know quite where. The stones all contain Words, but sometimes they slip out. Mostly they've been smaller ones, or parts of greater ones, but they're all important. Once you contain these, it'll be your job to seek out the lost ones, if you can."

"So this isn't a once-only gig?"

"'Fraid not, my dear. Clear your calendar."

"Great. Maybe we should get started, then."

"All right. So you feel the power in the stone under our collective butts, yes?"

"Yeah."

"I want you to listen to it."

"With my butt?"

"No need to get cheeky." Granny grinned, and Rosanna groaned. "Just...listen. Like it's a radio station you can't quite hear. It might help to close your eyes."

Rosanna shut her eyes, feeling the steady thrum of energy beneath her. The wind hummed around her. She heard Granny's breathing, then pulled in to hear her own, and her heartbeat, pulsing to the power of the stone. For a long moment there was nothing but those sounds, and she found herself drifting in the darkness behind her eyelids. Then the throb deepened, rushing up and through her into a sound. It was a nonsense syllable, nothing she recognized from any language she'd ever studied. But she knew it, now, and knew what it meant. It was a Word, like a beat of the world's enormous heart. She opened her eyes.

"I heard it!" she said. "I heard it! It was like...it was like..."

"Never mind," Granny said with a smile. "I know what it was like. Makes it seem a little more worthwhile, doesn't it."

"I...yes, I guess it does. I didn't imagine. Is it always like that?"

"You get used to it, a little. The wonder never goes away, though. It's pretty heady stuff, to hold the powers of creation in your mind."

Rosanna frowned.

:"But you said there were people that don't use it that way. I don't understand. How could you do anything else with it?"

"The powers of destruction can be just as addictive, I imagine."

Rosanna shook her head. She couldn't imagine not being touched by that experience, not being awed. Yes, it was exciting, but it was spiritual, very nearly religious. She listened to the Word, felt the stirring of its syllables in the heat of her blood.

"So can I use it, now?" she asked.

"You can," Granny said. "That one's embedded in the keystone, so its syllables can be spoken, and not lost." She waved around at the debris field again. "Unfortunately, only some of these here are actually embedded."

"I could feel that Word sort of....bound to the stone, like it was part of it. Is that what you mean by embedded?"

Granny nodded. "That's it exactly. " She stood up and walked to one of the smaller stones and rested her hand on it. Rosanna followed suit. It was easier to the hear the Word this time, but it didn't have the same sense of permanence as the keystone.

Granny watched her face intently, and nodded to Rosanna's questioning glance.

"That's the difference. See, a Library is most like a geode. The inside is very structured, and when the whole thing is together, each part lends integrity to the other."

Rosanna pictured this in her mind, a cavernous crystal library. She laughed.

"It's the original crystal ball, isn't it?" she said. "Let me tell your future…"

Granny chuckled. "I never thought of it quite like that, but, I suppose it could be. Anyhow, the keystone is intact, and the structure of it is intact, but the rest has fallen away, like this bit here." She tapped the stone under their hands. "It's got Words in it, right enough, but without the structure, they slip away, trying to…" she paused for a second "equalize the pressure, like you said."

"But why did it break? Did she do something wrong?"

Granny shook her head. "I've never been able to figure it out. Near as I can tell, something was flawed in the physical shape, that the pieces didn't come together as they ought."

"What could do that?"

"Like I said," Granny replied, an old irritation rumbling in her voice. "I don't know. And you *know* I don't much like having to say that."

"Okay, but, theoretically? Something in the rock? Something distracting Lillian? I mean, I don't want to put it back just the way it was, do I?"

Granny shook her head slowly. "No, I suppose not. But… all these years I've only been thinking about finding the flaw and fixing it. Not about why it's there to start with. Doesn't that seem strange?"

"More than strange, Granny. I mean, you've been obsessed by this forever, and all you've gotten to is blaming yourself for not training her right. Let's imagine you trained her just fine. What would make this happen?"

"Well, I've checked the stones themselves, and there's no inherent flaw. She picked 'em well, took her time, found their connections to each other." Pride glimmered in Granny's eyes. "And the keystone is perfect."

"What about the weather? Lightning, maybe?"

"No, she chose a good clear morning, and there wasn't any kind of rockslide."

"An animal? Could something have attacked her?"

Granny froze, and Rosanna feared she'd hit a sore spot. She wasn't really up for more quarreling. But Granny said nothing, though her face paled

"Granny?" Rosanna said, with growing alarm, "are you okay?"

Granny nodded mutely, then moved stiffly to the keystone and seated herself on it again. She stroked the stone absently, as another might pet a cat for comfort.

"Granny, please!" Rosanna knelt down, and looked up into familiar blue eyes. Those eyes were silver with tears again, and Granny's hands shook when Rosanna took them in her own.

"What is it?" Rosanna begged. "Are you sick?" She looked around with growing panic. She had no idea how she'd get Granny back to the house from here, let alone whether there was ambulance service so far up in the mountains. But Granny finally shook her head, and met Rosanna's gaze.

"It wouldn't have been an animal, Rosanna." She said. her voice was as pallid as her skin. "Lillian had a way with the wild things, and she would have set wards to protect them as much as her." She shook her head. "Why didn't I ask?" She said to herself. "It's such a simple question. Why didn't I think of it?"

"Think of WHAT, Granny? You're dithering, and I didn't think you knew how!"

Granny drew Rosanna back into focus.

"Sorry, m'dear. It's just...it's just too enormous a thought."

"Great. Okay. So you're back with me. Would you please tell me what you're talking about?"

"An animal couldn't have done this, Rosanna. A human could. Someone could have attacked Lillian, or the Library."

"You mean...oh God, you mean she was *murdered*?"

"It would..." Granny gulped back tears," It would make sense, wouldn't it? Nothing else I've looked at could explain what happened." She turned her pale, frightened eyes to her grand-daughter. "But why didn't I think of it? Why didn't I ask?"

Rosanna sat in stillness, considering the question. She could practically hear Granny reassembling her self-recrimination to fit this new question. But that wasn't any kind of answer to this.

"Why didn't you ask it, Granny? What made you not ask?" Rosanna said urgently.

"I don't...I don't know, Rosanna. I just never did, it just never...until you started asking me, the words never occurred to me before."

"Okay...so is it like what happened when I asked about my..."she paused, hating the levity of it "my sperm donor?"

Granny's eyes snapped back into focus, and Rosanna saw a comforting spark of rage ignite there.

"Yes," she said, muscles jumping in her jaw. "Just like that, actually. What a thorough little murderer he must have been, killing my memories as well."

"Can you remember anything at all about...that murderer?" she asked. "Can you get to the memories like that, or do I need to keep saying the other?"

"No," Granny said, with a fierce little grin. "I seem quite able to hold onto that word." She paused. "It's like searching a deserted part of the house," she said at last. "The doors are stuck, and I can't quite get in. But at least now I know they exist." She looked around her. "The Word that did this might have been taken from this very place, by the one who killed her."

Rosanna shuddered. "Can we fix that? I mean if it's a Word doing it, can we undo it?"

Granny shook her head. "It's not so simple, I'm afraid. That kind of thing would have to be renewed, the Word spoken over and over. By now, it's probably as much part of me as the sound of my heart."

Rosanna was appalled. It was like a rape that couldn't be stopped.

"We can't leave it like that," Rosanna said. "There's got to be something I can do."

"There's no point, child."

"No point?"

"Don't raise your voice, Rosanna, I have the most awful headache." Granny scooped up some snow and held it to the back of her neck. "It's probably from sneaking under the spell."

"But how can there be no point? Some bastard is…is inside your head! How can there be no point in stopping that?"

"Look, the easiest way to remove this would be to have the speaker dead. That's the best state of affairs. Everything else requires careful study." She shook her head. "Rosanna, we are creatures of Being, you, me, everyone. Words are inherent in us. If we were to pull apart the wrong one…"

"You'd die?"

"Worse. I wouldn't be me. Imagine we took away the part of me that knows you. Or knows the Words."

"But this…isn't it the same? Isn't this just as bad?"

"We can't take the risk, not until you know enough to stand on your own."

"Oh great, so everything has to hinge on me again."

"It always has, dear one."

"That's not terribly comforting."

Granny shrugged. "Should I get you a warm blankie and some hot milk, then?"

"Ha, ha."

"You said it yourself, Rosanna. Can't be both ways. You're an adult. There's no room here for coddling."

"What about supporting then? Aren't we supposed to support each other if we're a team?"

"Support doesn't mean letting you sag, darling girl, and I'm not just talking about lingerie. You have to believe you can do what's necessary."

"Do you?"

"Not sure, but I'm hopeful." She stood up again, and peered into the sky. The sun was sliding towards mountain peaks. Rosanna hadn't thought they'd spent so long, but days were short this time of year, and this far north.

"We should be getting back," Granny said, and Rosanna groaned. Granny laughed. "Come on, there's a fire and enough warm blankies for both of us."

Rosanna lifted her warm (and reluctant) butt off the keystone, feeling strangely bereft without the rhythm of the Word beneath her, but it shone in her memory, its syllables clear and lovely. She and Granny walked carefully down the snowy slope. In its way, the descent was as difficult as the ascent had been. It required careful concentration to keep footing on the slippery surface, and underneath the drifts pockets of shale shifted under their weight.

They had nearly reached the bottom when a strange sound lifted on the wind. Rosanna lifted her head, trying to identify it, or its source. Granny's head came up with a snap.

"Do you hear that?" she whispered, and Rosanna nodded. "What is it?"

"Keep walking," Granny said, "and keep your voice down. Someone is speaking things better left unsaid."

"What? What's going on?" Rosanna hissed. Granny shook her head impatiently. "No time, girl. Keep moving. Lillian's grave might be protection enough."

They stumbled and slid down the last of the rocky incline, and the eaves of the forest were only a few meters away. The smell of pine was a welcome promise of safety. The sound on the wind rose to a growling roar, and something appeared between the women and the trees.

It was low to the ground, a twining sinewy creature, like smoke loosely contained by a body. There was no sense of malevolence about it, but the sound of it made Rosanna's skin crawl. Its head was as sleek as an otter's, though it did not seem to have eyes. It stood on four short, powerful legs, each tipped with blunt claws. The head followed the women's movement, tracking them either by sound or scent. When they froze, it slunk slowly towards them, making a quiet keening sound that seemed to vibrate right through Rosanna's bones.

Rosanna made to back away, but Granny seized her arm. "Don't. Move." she said, the words barely more than a breath. The creature's head snapped up at the sound, and it moved more certainly towards them, the drilling whine rising in pitch and volume.

Granny spoke a syllable, and Rosanna recognized it as a Word, though she didn't know it or its purpose. She and Granny both rose soundlessly off the snow. The animal homed in on the sound again, closing the distance between them until its sound was nearly unbearable. Granny began to back away from it very slowly and at an angle. She pointed the other way, and Rosanna moved slowly to flank it on the other side. Since they were off the snow, their feet made no sound. It was a strange sensation, but Rosanna had no leisure to enjoy it. She didn't know what the thing was, but her primal self was screaming for flight, and it was all Rosanna could do to keep herself from running full-speed to the shelter of the trees.

The thing stayed where it was, its blind head still pointed to the place where last they'd stood. As Rosanna passed, she saw large ears pressed tight to its skull. It had no discernable nose, but its lip lifted a little to display teeth like obsidian knives, translucent and perilous. The wind rustled and hushed through the tops of the trees, a protective screen of sound that masked her breathing.

Granny reached the edge of the woods first, and gestured for Rosanna to keep moving. Rosanna stepped under the shadow of the trees with relief. Granny pointed the way into the wood, and Rosanna walked as quickly as she could without brushing up against the trees. Then, shockingly loud, Granny shouted.

"Hey! Over here!"

The thing whipped around and skimmed across the snow towards Granny. Its cry was vicious, exultant.

Granny said nothing else, but fled into the woods, away from Rosanna. Rosanna looked around her wildly. She could see the tracks she and Granny had made previously, and the direction of the grave was clear. But that thing was so fast, and Granny had no right to be taking such chances. They'd gotten by it, hadn't they? She couldn't hear its cry at all, anymore, but it could still be anywhere. They shouldn't be separated.

She followed glimpses of Granny's movement into the woods, and caught up with her. There was no sign of their toothy predator.

"What are you thinking, girl? Get away!" Granny said.

"But it's gone!" Rosanna said. "It didn't follow you in."

"It couldn't hear me," Granny said. "But I bet that murderer knows lots of words! God dammit, I need you safe!"

"And I need *you* safe! Why did you yell?"

"I wanted to give it a place to focus. I didn't think it would be so ruddy fast. It might still be around!"

"What are we supposed to do?"

"We've got to find some kind of shelter," Granny said. "Let's get to the grave, there's some protections there, if we can make it."

Rosanna listened, but there was no longer any whisper of the strange word hanging on the chill breeze.

"It's gone, isn't it?"

"That one might be. Get moving!"

They hurried into the deepening shadows of the woods. Daylight was failing quickly, and the temperature dropping as well. Granny seemed to know her way well enough, but every sound was a threat to Rosanna, and she could hardly breathe under the weight of her fear. She cringed away from contact with the trees, from anything that might give away her position. They skimmed just above the surface, and Rosanna was grateful there were no obstacles.

Finally a last glimmer of light shone on green grass just a little ahead, and Rosanna was nearly giddy with relief. Granny seemed to relax a little as well, though she kept turning around, trying to see everywhere at once.

"I've got to release the Word, Rosanna," she said. "I can't maintain it and keep running like this, I'm getting tired."

"We're almost there," Rosanna replied, and Granny nodded. They dropped to the cushioned floor of the forest, and their feet rustled through the fallen needles.

No burring whine met the sound, but they still walked cautiously. Granny was still nearly silent on the soft floor of the forest, but Rosanna found her own footsteps terrifyingly loud. They stood panting in the glade for a moment, saying nothing.

"Let's go," Granny said in a low whisper. "Might be it's gone, might be not, but I'll feel a lot safer with walls between me and it."

"What was it?"

"Don't know, don't care. It didn't look like it wanted to curl up and be a nice doggy to me."

"Me neither." Rosanna shuddered. "Magic made that? I'm supposed to take care of that?"

"Equal and opposite, Rosanna." Granny said. "Not all things in creation are pretty, not all magic is pixie-dust."

"If it's safe here, couldn't we just stay? It's warm enough, we'd be okay."

"There's no telling if it's safe, or if the thing is just not following. Besides, there are other Words, and I wouldn't want to meet any of them on a dark night in the woods. You?"

Rosanna shook her head, and sniffed back a tear.

"We will get out of this, Rosanna."

Rosanna clung to the comfort, and tried to ignore her misgivings. No matter what Granny might promise, clearly there were things that even she couldn't handle.

Granny took Rosanna's hand and led her back into the woods. It was full dark now, but Granny knew her way regardless. Rosanna released the hand, and clutched to Granny's arm like a blind woman. They passed through the shadows without incident, and soon saw the glow of moonlight on snow.

"Last leg of it," Granny whispered, and Rosanna nodded. They stepped out, but with the first crunch of boots in snow, a familiar keening cry pierced the silence.

Once again, Rosanna's feet lifted a little off the surface, but Granny's mouth was set with the effort, and her arm trembled in Rosanna's grasp. They had crossed nearly half the distance to Granny's cabin without seeing the beast at all, but when Rosanna chanced a glance over her shoulder, she saw a shadow on the snow, like blight on a flower. It stood rigidly just a few paces from where the women had exited the forest, and its head turned eagerly, searching for the sound of them. And then the wind dropped off. The trees settled into deep silence. Rosanna's pounding heartbeat thundered in her ears, and her breathing was ragged and noisy.

The thing's cry rose again, louder, hungry. Its teeth glimmered in the moonlight, and it glided towards them with frightening speed.

Rosanna and Granny dropped to the ground.

"Too tired,' Granny gasped. "Run!"

Rosanna draped Granny's arm around her own shoulders, and heaved herself forward. The tracks of their previous passage were clear, and Rosanna could smell the smoke of Granny's fire. Surely they couldn't be far? She didn't dare look over her shoulder again, but she heard no sound of movement, and the things cry disappeared abruptly. Maybe Granny had some kind of protection here? Granny stumbled, and Rosanna gasped with the effort of keeping them both upright.

The light of Granny's cabin slid into view, and she nearly sobbed with relief. Then a shadow detached from the pools of darkness between snowdrifts. A vicious whine lifted on the night air, sharp enough to pierce right through Rosanna's skull. Granny tried to push away.

"Go!" she gasped. "Get out of here!"

"No chance," Rosanna said.

The thing insinuated itself across half the distance between them. Rosanna stood stock still, but she couldn't help her heartbeat, or breathing. It lifted its lip, and teeth glinted in the moonlight in a mockery of a smile. It danced a little to the left of them, with puppyish, playful steps. Rosanna chanced a step forward, trying to get around it, but it snapped those teeth with a clash, and slid back to the right of them. Despite the threat, it did not leap to the attack, but merely stood, keening and grinning horribly.

Rosanna took another step, trying to flank it again, but once more it blocked her passage. Each step she took brought her and Granny closer, but it did not attack. All at once, she had the impression that this was exactly the point. It knew her only safety was ahead, so it was forcing *her* to walk into its jaws. Fury rose up in her.

"Get out of here!" she shouted. "Get away!"

It bared its teeth again in that parody of a grin, but did not move. Its cry increased in volume until Rosanna could barely stand the pain of it. Then she remembered the Word, the single Word she knew, and its purity, and she was enraged even further. This *thing*, whatever it was, was a hideous misuse of an amazing power. She didn't know why, but she spoke a single syllable of that Word, and wind sprung up and snow rose around the beast in a dizzying whirlwind. Rosanna took advantage of the distraction, and ran with all her remaining strength, nearly carrying Granny. She held that syllable in her mind as they ran, ignoring the pain of her muscles, ignoring her terror. They had nearly reached the porch of Granny's house when she stumbled over an obstacle hidden in the snow. She fell hard, and her head slammed into the planks. Starbursts of light exploded behind her eyelids as she clung to consciousness. Granny groaned on the ground beside her. The Word slipped away, and the beast's cry rose to a scream.

Rosanna gave a little cry, and struggled to her feet. She pulled Granny up, and they stumbled together towards the house. Rosanna flung open the door but the monster reached them at the same moment. It leapt at Granny, and she fell forward as it ripped through the layers of her winter clothing with savage slashes of its teeth. Rosanna shrieked, looking for a weapon. Granny must have been knocked out by the fall, because she made no sound until the thing tore into her shoulder. She screamed then, high and horrible. Rosanna grabbed the shovel from beside the back door, and brought it around in a furious arc. It hit the thing's head resoundingly, and it released its grip on Granny's flesh. It shook its head, and tried to back away, but Rosanna pursued it with wild swings of the shovel. She made contact against its shoulder, then square across its muzzle again. Its cry dropped away to a whine, and it turned and ran back the way they'd come.

Rosanna flung the shovel away from her, and took hold of what remained of Granny's coat. She dragged her over the lintel and into the warmth and light of the kitchen. Granny did not move or make any sound, and Rosanna wept desperately as she slammed the door and barred it.

She ran to the living room and pulled a blanket off the sofa. She was shaking so that she could barely stand, and she dropped to Granny's side with a sob. Gently, she lifted Granny's head and put the blanket under it. Granny made no sign that she was aware, or even alive. Rosanna could not see if Granny was breathing from this angle, but she didn't dare turn her until she knew the extent of the injury. She pressed her fingers to Granny's throat, hunting for a pulse, terrified that there might not be one.

At first, she felt nothing but the trembling of her own hand, but then, a beat. And another. It was slow, but steady. Rosanna dropped her head into her hands and cried in relief and terror and fury. For the moment, that was all she had left.

# Chapter 5

Rosanna's sobs clawed the inside of her chest like wild animals, and she could not stop their escape. Between rasping, whooping gulps of air she struggled to regain control, but the image of that *thing* would not leave her mind's eye, and its cry seemed to have torn a hole in her thoughts. Panic poured through her, and would not recede.

Was the door locked? She looked up, and it was, but that wasn't enough. She wanted to feel that it was barred, that she was safe, so she tried to stand. The floor tilted beneath her, and her head throbbed. Warm blood ran down her face from her forehead. She remembered falling, and seeing stars, but everything else had been more important. She still needed to know for absolute certain that the door was barred, so she crawled over the kitchen floor. Every movement sent spikes of pain through her head, and she wanted nothing more than to lie down and sleep. She reached the door, and checked it. Her fingers were comforted by the solid wood. She pressed an ear to the door, but there was no sound of the beast. She had no desire whatever to open up and take a look. The thing had been solid enough when she hit it, but she had no way of knowing whether something like that could be hurt, let alone killed. The terror receded a little, and she found herself able to take a real breath. She was so tired, though, more tired than she thought possible. Her head drooped, and blood began to drip off the end of her nose.

She knew this wasn't a good sign, and she knew that people with concussions must be kept awake. But how did you know it was a concussion when you were having it? She held her hand out and said "How many fingers am I holding up?" But it wasn't particularly funny, it was possible that nothing would ever be funny. How could laughter live in the same world as that creature?

Granny. Granny was hurt. She scrabbled away from the door, frantic again. How could she have left Granny there? Her thoughts were strangers, things glimpsed from a distance and through fog. All the same, Granny needed her. Granny never needed anyone, and now she needed Rosanna.

Rosanna lifted the remains of Granny's jacket away from the bite there. Rosanna's attack with the shovel had kept the thing from tearing out a chunk of flesh, but there was a circle of puncture wounds from the top of Granny's shoulder to half-way down her rib-cage. There was blood, but not as much as Rosanna had feared. One of the punctures was no more than a finger-width from Granny's throat. Rosanna's world shivered and faded towards gray when she saw that. This was how close she'd come to losing Granny forever, how close she'd come to watching Granny's life pour out on the kitchen floor.

Rosanna didn't know what to do. Her head pounded, and blood continued to flow freely down her face. One fat drop splashed onto Granny's back, livid against the pale skin. She ought to do something about that, she knew, but she could hardly think. She so desperately wanted to sleep. A strange high hum filled her ears and she felt herself sliding toward the floor. She shook her head, and forced her eyes open. There was no time for this, no time for weakness.

She needed to clean both their wounds, but she couldn't think how to do it. Water, that was what she needed. Water and cloths. The kitchen looked miles long, with the sink at the other end, but she had to get there. She tried to stand again, but the floor pitched wildly and tilted her back on her knees. That wasn't going to be much good. Crawling it was, then. The kitchen was small and there was scarce room for her to move around Granny. Dizziness made Rosanna clumsy, and she jostled Granny more than she wanted to as she made her awkward way across the room.

Granny made no sound, and Rosanna stopped twice just to check her pulse. It was slow, but strong. Granny was still in there, somewhere.

Rosanna levered herself upright by clinging to the cabinets. There was a basin in the sink, and a dishcloth hung over the faucet. She poured warm water into the basin, watching it fill until the reflected lights started to dance her to sleep. She lifted her head again, and braced herself against the  counter. She wasn't made for this, she knew. She was made for the city, for dangers she knew. She couldn't exactly call the police and ask them to arrest a fanged terror. The police…that thought wandered hazily through her muddled thoughts for a moment. Granny had a phone. She looked at the basin of water. What should she do first?

"I'm not *made* for this!" The husky shout startled her, and Granny twitched. Rosanna turned, and slid back down the cabinets, holding tight to the basin of water. The room wanted to pitch her sideways, she knew, but she was stubborn, and only spilled a little water.

She wet the cloth and pressed it to her forehead. The pain went from a sullen heat to a firestorm at the touch. She whimpered, and more tears slid down her cheeks. She was ashamed of them, of what they said about her. What did she know about pain? Granny might be dying. She knew that she had to slow her own bleeding before she could help, but it hurt so much, and she had never wanted sleep more desperately. She was hungry for it, starving for it, and she felt the world slowly closing towards darkness. Her hand fell away from her scalp, and the wound shrieked a protest. She shook her head slowly, trying to clear the shadows from the corners of her vision.

She rinsed the cloth, wrung it, and pressed it to the cut again. She knew you were supposed to apply pressure to a wound, but she couldn't remember why, or how she knew. The knowledge was simply there, with no attachment to memory or understanding. After a while, the bleeding slowed, though it did not completely stop. The water in the basin was clouded with her blood, so she made the slow journey back up to the sink to dump it. She watched it curl around the drain and away with detached interest. Then she rinsed the cloth in fresh water, and filled the basin again. She crawled back to Granny, dragging the basin with her.

Granny moaned at Rosanna's touch, and she chose to believe that was a good sign. She bathed the bite mark as carefully as she could, but tatters of Granny's jacket were stuck to the blood, and she winced every time she had to tug to clean them away.

"Sorry, Granny, sorry," she said, over and over. Granny did nothing more than twitch in response, but Rosanna found the sound of her own voice comforting. It was a real sound, a familiar one, and it did not demand anything of her.

Even when she'd cleaned away the blood, the bite was ugly. Each puncture was puffy and hot to the touch, like a bee-sting. Granny started to shiver, so Rosanna took off her jacket and used it to cover the Granny's back. What now? What should she do now? She was so tired that the room rocked her like a cradle, her own heartbeat was a lulling murmur. She could nap a little, couldn't she? Just a little? Granny wasn't bleeding any more.

Then Granny coughed, a wheezing, hoarse gasp for air. Rosanna jumped at the sound, awake again, if only for the moment.

"Granny?" she said. "Are you okay?"

"Stupid question," Granny said faintly, her voice muffled and weak. "Can't breathe." She flailed a little, trying to turn herself over, but all she managed was a kind of clumsy shrug.

"You're bitten on your back," Rosanna said. "I don't think…should you lie on that?"

"Can't breathe!" Granny said again, more urgently. "Help me!"

Rosanna wanted to weep again. What was she to do? Granny was the one that knew things, she was the one that got things done. She didn't want Granny's bite to start bleeding again, but Granny's breathing became increasingly labored.

"Wait!" she said. "Let me help."

"Can't breathe!" Granny repeated, panic louder than her voice.

Rosanna pulled Granny's uninjured shoulder towards her, trying to roll the older woman and use her knees as a support. Granny gasped and a trickle of blood seeped from one of the punctures, but her breathing eased. Rosanna bundled up her jacket and put it under Granny's head.

"Better?" she said. She wanted to sound business-like, cheery. She was the nurse here, the comforter.

Granny rolled her eyes up to Rosanna's face, and focused with a visible effort.

"You look like hell," she said. Rosanna tried to laugh, but a sob escaped her instead. She swallowed it back.

"So do you," she said.

"How bad is it?" Granny asked.

"Me or you?"

"Either," Granny said.

"I hit my head, but I'm okay. You've got a big bite on your shoulder, but it didn't bleed too much."

"You don't look okay," Granny said. "I don't feel okay."

"We *are* okay. We're alive, and I think that thing's gone. Everything will be fine."

"Don't jolly me, Rosanna. I still can't hardly breathe, and I feel like my back's on fire."

"But I washed it," Rosanna said. Her head drooped with weariness. What else could she do? What else was there to do?

"I can call the ambulance," Rosanna said. Wasn't that right? That's what you do in a city, that's the sensible thing.

"Can try," Granny said. Her voice was slowly winding down, slipping away towards a whisper. "Don't feel so good."

Rosanna checked Granny's pulse again and saw a thin thread of black pulsing under the skin at Granny's throat. It throbbed with Granny's heartbeat.

"Granny?" she said "What does it mean when there's black in your vein?"

"Means poison, mostly," Granny said. "Means dying."

"You can't be poisoned. I don't know what to do for poison. Maybe you're allergic."

"Allergic to poison," Granny said with a faint smile. "Like most folks."

"You can't do any dying, Granny. I can't fix dying." First aid hadn't covered dying, only injured. For dying you called the hospital, and the doctors fixed it. Not Rosanna, she of the broken head and maimed thoughts.

"You don't make sense," Granny said. "You okay?"

Rosanna laughed, but only a little. More would have been hysterics, and she was not going to be hysterical. Her head pounded in time to stifled laughter.

"Don't worry about me. What do I do? I'll call…" the thought spun out, reaching for a conclusion. "I'll call 911!" She said triumphantly. That's the thing you're supposed to do. She knew she'd remember eventually.

"No time," Granny whispered. "I'm burning. Oh God, oh help me, Rosanna, help!"

Pain glazed over Granny's eyes, and turned her voice from a whisper to a moan. What was Rosanna to do? All she wanted was sleep and she was forgetting everything else, moment by moment.

"How?" she said. "I don't know what to do!"

Granny started to shiver more violently, then to shake. The line of black had crept up to her chin, and Rosanna saw it had spread across her chest, as well.

"Use the Word," Granny said. "Now."

"What Word? I don't know how!"

"Do it. Do it or I die."

Rosanna wanted to shriek, to retreat into the comfort of sleep. But if she ever woke from that, she'd wake to Granny dead. There was no room for walking away, no room for failure. She was a finger's width from losing Granny again, right now.

All things are made of Words. She knew this, all things that exist are part of Being. That meant Granny, too. She laid her hand on Granny's forehead, closed her eyes, and listened. There was nothing at first but the slow vertiginous swing of the darkness behind her eyelids. And then she heard the Words, the very sounds of Granny's soul. Around that pure, bright chorus of perfect sound was another. It was the sound of the beast's cry, a violent cacophony that was tearing Granny's Being to pieces.

She opened her eyes again. She knew that, she knew that there was poison. How did this help? How could anything help? Granny was the mender, the doer, the leader.

Granny's eyes had closed, and her breath came only in shallow, hungry gasps. A net of black now covered her hands, and was creeping up her face. No time. Rosanna had no time to be stupid. She remembered the Word she'd heard at the keystone, its warmth and integrity. It was whole. It knew how to be whole. Maybe Granny needed to know that? Maybe it would help?

Rosanna and Granny were both out of time. Granny's eyes rolled back in her head, and her body arched in a terrible convulsion. Rosanna spoke the Word.

Granny's eyes snapped open and she screamed. She convulsed so violently that she threw Rosanna back. Granny's body rippled like a flag in a gale, and she screamed again.

"No!" Rosanna shouted. "No, I didn't mean it!" She knew she'd failed, knew she'd watch her failure kill the only person she knew how to love. That would be all, the end, and she would sleep and never wake up. She let herself slide to the floor, waited for sleep to catch her and carry her away.

And then Granny spoke.

"Damn, girl," she said. "That hurt."

Rosanna opened her eyes, and saw Granny looking back at her. The black lines were gone, and her breathing was easy and regular.

"Granny?"

"Yes, love. You did good."

"I did?"

Granny nodded with a weary little smile.

"Got to sleep now."

"Oh, me too," Rosanna said, but Granny shook her head.

"You bumped your head real bad. You got to stay awake." Granny sighed. "Sorry, I got no choice." Her eyes slid closed, and she started to gently snore.

Stay awake? How was she supposed to stay awake? She looked at Granny's closed eyes with relief and envy, and she couldn't say which she felt more. She'd never been more exhausted. Using the Word had wearied her as well, and she needed sleep like a junkie needs a fix.

Maybe coffee would help. She looked around the kitchen. She was sure all the makings were here somewhere, but equally certain that caffeine alone wouldn't keep her eyes open. Time for help.

She pulled herself upright, as if her body were a puppet that she could manipulate, but not necessarily inhabit. The floor still slanted treacherously, and she felt poised to fall off it at every step. She tottered into the living room and collapsed into Granny's easy chair. She picked up the phone, but she didn't even know who to call. Was this still an emergency? The nearest hospital was in Nelson. By the time anyone got here from there, she might already be taking the nap you don't wake up from. The phone beeped angrily, and she put it back in the cradle. Okay. Can't get help to come here. Maybe she could go to help? But who?

The thought of coffee wandered through her thoughts again, and she remembered the little café, June's little café. It wasn't that far, maybe twenty minutes. Could she stay awake that long?

She found herself nodding off as she considered the idea. It wasn't as dark outside now; the moon must have risen. Was it late? Time had ceased to flow in the usual way the moment the monster had begun its pursuit. Moments had leaped and skipped, too fast or impossibly slow, and only now did they seem to be returning to an orderly procession. She looked at her watch, but her eyes wouldn't focus properly. It was only when she closed the left eye altogether that she could make out the time. It was half past seven. That was impossible, she knew. She'd spent a lifetime running down the mountain, and another one watching Granny die on the kitchen floor.

The café might be open, then. What if that thing was still outside? She couldn't fight again, she knew. All she wanted was to drop into the lovely warm arms of sleep. Granny was safe, wasn't she? Wasn't Rosanna due a little nap, just as a reward? She sighed. Granny wasn't there to kick her ass, so Rosanna figured it might be her own job to do it, this time.

She walked unsteadily to the window. There was so sign of the beast, and no sound of it. She listened, with that particular intensity she was learning to use, and heard nothing but the murmur of a small magic keeping the cabin warm, and keeping it safe. She felt sure that nothing would pass these walls without invitation. Outside the window there could be anything at all, but Granny was safe inside. Safer than Rosanna, just at the moment. She wondered if she could heal herself, and nearly laughed. She could barely manage her physical being at the moment.

Her coat was still in the kitchen with Granny, but Granny always kept sweaters by the door for visitors. Rosanna shrugged into one, noticing vaguely that her shoulders hurt, maybe from the effort of getting the beast off Granny's back. Her head hurt too much to even bother tallying up other damage.

She opened the door as quietly as she could, listening for any sound of attack. There was none, so she stepped out, and staggered to her car. The cold air woke her a little, and it felt good on her head. She stooped for a handful of snow, and pressed it against her hurt. It stung, but the cold was a beautiful relief. Her keys were in her purse, in the car. There wasn't much chance of car-jacking hereabouts, and Rosanna had a talent for losing keys. The car started with a whine of protest, but it started. It wasn't near as cold as it could be this time of year, but Rosanna's breath still frosted up the inside of her windshield. The heater soon took care of that, but as the car warmed, Rosanna felt herself drifting towards sleep, the world becoming a mix of dream and reality. She rested her head against the steering wheel, and considered again just fading out. The car's motor dropped from a whine to its usual mellow purr, and the change was enough to wake her again.

She put the car into gear, surprised at the stab of hot pain that shot up her arm. She'd forgotten about that, but it had been waiting quite patiently to remind her. She snarled at it, but at least the jolt woke her up a little further.

She backed down Granny's drive as slowly as she could. She knew that if the car got out of control there would be no chance of her regaining it.

She sighed with relief when she felt her back tires inch out onto pavement, and made a slow and awkward sweep onto the highway. There were no lights out here, none of the comfort of city surroundings, but the moon was bright and clear, and the stars danced in a perfect black-velvet sky.

The drive was painfully slow, and she stopped twice to scoop up some snow. She put one handful on her forehead, and the other on the back of her neck. It was enough to keep her conscious through all the bumps and weaves of the little road. No other vehicles passed her, and she wasn't surprised. The darkness and stillness ought to be menacing, she supposed, but where her fear had lived was now a memory of action. She remembered the solid sound of the shovel hitting the creature. She remembered saving Granny. Surely if she could do these strange and miraculous things, then she must be able to drive a little ways down a mountain road.

Her head was drooping again by the time she saw the lights ahead. The gas station was lit, but there didn't seem to be lights on in the café. Rosanna didn't know whether to scream or cry. Where else could she go? Nelson was too far. She had spent all her willpower getting to this spot, and there was nothing left for her to move on. She pulled into the gas station anyway. What else could she do? She could go back to the cabin, but she didn't know if she could make it. The still night weighed down her eyelids until she could scarcely keep them open. She felt herself slumping against the steering wheel, and sat up with a jerk. She thought she ought to put the car in park at least, so she did. Her wrist yowled a protest, but she was too tired to listen. Should she turn the motor off? She wanted to be warm, but that would make her sleepy, but falling asleep in the cold could kill her, too. She watched her thoughts ramble in a bemused little tangle of unfinished processes. It was almost entertaining, like watching clowns take prat-falls.

A sharp rap on her window pulled her out of the muddled circling of her thoughts. She looked out, and saw June peering in. June's eyes widened when she saw Rosanna's face, and she tried to open the door. The safety locks were on. Rosanna fumbled for the switch, and managed to roll the window down.

"Holy     shit!"     June     said.     "What     happened     to     you?"

"I fell," Rosanna said. What else could she possibly say?

"What, onto a pit bull?" She shook her head impatiently. "Never mind that, let's get you someplace warm."

"Warm sounds nice," Rosanna said vaguely. June reached in and turned the keys. The car rattled once, and then the engine stopped.

June was shorter than Rosanna by nearly a foot, but she slid her shoulder under Rosanna's arm, and half carried her into the café. It seemed a much longer walk than it had been before. When was that? Rosanna couldn't remember. June didn't struggle under Rosanna's weight, though Rosanna was clumsy with fatigue and dizziness. She bumped her bad wrist on the way through the door, and cried out. June hissed in sympathy, but kept up the momentum. Soon Rosanna sat at one of the tables. June looked at her critically, then hurried to the kitchen. She turned on some lights there, and came back with a bag of frozen peas.

Rosanna looked at her blearily.

"Peas? Thanks, but I'm not really hungry."

"Idiot. It's the best thing next to an ice pack. You can put in whatever shape is best for you. But you better get that on your forehead. Looks like hell."

Rosanna obeyed, and the cold quieted the throbbing enough that she dared close her eyes, just for a moment.

"None of that, now," June said. "You been thumped pretty good, girl. Who did this?"

"Nobody," Rosanna said, fighting her eyes open again. "My Granny and I were chased by an animal. I fell."

"Wouldn't be a two-legged animal would it? I got no patience for men that hit women. Not much patience for the women that puts up with it, neither." She scowled.

"No, honest, it was just an animal."

"What kind, then? Bear? Wolf?"

"I don't know. It was dark." Which was true, in its way. The beast had been dark as rage, dark as revenge.

"I got no patience for lies, neither. What was it?"

"You wouldn't believe me."

"I don't believe you now, so how's that a loss?"

"It was something I've never seen before. It was black, and low like a dog, but it howled like a buzz saw. It appeared and disappeared, and I hit it with a shovel."

"That sounds like the truth, I guess, though I doubt that's all of it. Besides, you're a city girl, ain't ya? Coulda been anything."

"I suppose."

June looked at her critically, and Rosanna met her eyes as frankly as she could. June's face swam in and out of focus, but Rosanna could see the sharp suspicion soften into concern.

"Don't matter much, anyhow," she said at last. "You got hurt, and that's enough to know. Just don't you lie to me."

"I won't," Rosanna said, and under June's gaze, the assurance took on the weight of a promise. "I won't," she repeated.

"Good enough, then," June said. "Let's look at the damage, hey?"

June left Rosanna holding the blessedly cold peas to her head, and returned with a bowl of steaming water in one hand and a stack of towels in the other.

"All right then, first the head," June said. "You see okay? Anything double?"

"Things are fuzzy, but not double."

"Good enough. You been throwing up?"

"No, just really dizzy. And really tired."

"All right then, well, I'm going to clean this mess up, and we'll see whether I think you ought to get flown to the hospital."

"No, really, that's not…"

"Did I ask your opinion?" June said, with relative good nature. "You come here for help, you get it by my rules. All right?"

Rosanna nodded.

"Good. Now, plain old concussion, we'll just wake you up every hour, make sure you ain't planning on staying asleep. You got a skull fracture, girl, you gonna be airborne before you can count your feathers."

"How will you know?"

"Like I said, we'll clean this up and have a look. Don't look like you got any place sunk in, and your eyes look to be reacting together. Now shut up and let me fix you up some."

Her smile took away any sting that might have been in the words, and she carefully bathed Rosanna's forehead. It hurt, but she took pauses for Rosanna to reapply her makeshift ice pack. A few fresh dribbles of blood trickled down into Rosanna's eyebrows, but June cleaned them up, too.

"Well," she said at last, "you still look like hell, but at least you don't look like something from a slasher flick." She examined the injury critically. "You could probably stand for a couple stitches there, and I could do it, but foreheads are hard to stitch. They move too much. I got some butterfly bandages, they'll do you just as well."

"You're the boss, boss," said Rosanna.

"Damn straight," June said with her first real grin of the evening. She bandaged Rosanna's forehead. "Now then," she said. "What else you done to yourself?"

Rosanna tried to remember, but between the warmth of the café and the comfort of June's presence, her thoughts were drowsy, nebulous things.

"Never mind," June said. "I can see you don't care much. Let's get you lying down, you can have a bit of rest. I'll be waking you up though, so don't get too comfy, got me?"

Rosanna nodded. June led her back to the kitchen, and then through it to a small room. It contained a sofa, a ragged recliner, and a desk covered in books.

"I do my books here some nights," June said. "Sometimes I get snowed in, and sometimes I'm just too damn lazy to drive home. The sofa folds out."

She settled Rosanna in the recliner, and set up the bed. It was the most beautiful thing Rosanna had ever seen, and she said so.

"Got to have a concussion," June muttered. "Quit the crazy talk and go to sleep."

June helped Rosanna out of her coat and shoes, and then tucked her under the covers.

"You need anything, you yell, all right?"

Rosanna nodded.

"You're awfully nice," she mumbled. June chuckled in reply, and turned off the light.

"Less talking more sleeping," she said, then closed the door behind her.

Rosanna tumbled gracelessly into sleep, plunged into it like an inept diver. It seemed a very long way down into the darkness, and she was grateful for it. She thought she heard voices, somewhere up above the surface, but she didn't care. All that mattered was the bliss of closed eyes and drifting mind.

Far too soon, she heard June's voice. Rosanna groaned and tried to ignore it, but June shook her awake.

"C'mon, sleeping beauty. Time for wakey."

"I take it back. You're not nice. You're evil."

"Thanks for noticing. C'mon, don't give me a rough time. You know you got to wake all the way up. You do that, have a little to drink, then I'll let you sleep some more."

"I'm not thirsty."

"Do I sound like I give a shit? Nobody's gonna die in my bed, girlie, so get your ass up and out of it."

Rosanna groaned again, and dragged herself out from the cozy nest of covers.

"Besides," June said. "You got a visitor."

"A what?"

June shrugged. "You want to find out more, you're gonna have to come see." Her eyes were shadowed, but she said nothing more. She waited until Rosanna was standing, and then slid under her arm as a support.

"Not much of a crutch," June said, "but I'm the best you'll get just now."

"What kind of hotel is this anyway?" Rosanna said. "Abusive staff, faulty crutches…"

"It's hillbilly hotel, that's what it is. You be a very good girl, and maybe you'll get moonshine in your coffee in the morning."

"Not now?" Rosanna's head ached with every step and bump, though June made the walk as easy as possible.

"Not now, no. Gotta wait to make sure you aren't going to try for the really big sleep."

They walked out through the kitchen, and into the café. The lights were on low, and Rosanna was grateful for it, through the dazzle of her headache. June led her to a table and helped her ease herself into a chair. Her wrist snarled at her when she put too much weight on it, and June noticed the wince.

"Lord, was there any place you *didn't* get hurt?"

"Doesn't feel like it. It's just my wrist though, not as bad as my head."

"Come off it, I saw that look. It hurts pretty fine all on it's own, don't it."

"Yeah, okay, it hurts." Rosanna looked around as June examined the wrist. "I thought you said I had a visitor?"

"You do, he's just answering a call of nature."

Rosanna's sleeve was tight around the wrist, and June sighed at the sight of it.

"I hope it's not broken," she said. "It looks like crap, but if your head's anything to go by, it's probably hard as rock."

"Why are you being so nice to me?" Rosanna said. "I'm practically a stranger, I show up here and bleed on your floor, but you're still being nice to me!"

"Would you like me to stop?" June asked, with a smirk and a raised eyebrow.

"Not especially, but really, why? I could be a serial killer, for all you know."

June chuckled. "Not hardly. Anyhow, you needed it. What was I gonna do, tell you to go away? Tell you I was busy?"

"But that doesn't answer the question."

"So maybe it doesn't. Look, that's how it is here. We're the backside of nowhere, and if we don't help each other out, we're all screwed."

"But…"

"Don't you ever, ever stop talking? You're worse than a blue jay."

"Ouch!" Rosanna yelped as June tried to undo the cuff of her sleeve.

"I'm gonna get some scissors," June said. "Don't go anywhere, now." Rosanna stuck her tongue out. It was so good to taste laughter in her mouth, it washed away the last remnants of fear that lingered there.

Rosanna was busy examining her scraped hand when her visitor returned from the washroom.

"Evening," he said casually. "Come here often?" It was Thompson Trapper, his short hair spiky from having been under a hat.

"Often enough," Rosanna said. "I think it's starting to become a habit." She looked outside, at the pale ribbons of moonlight wound through the branches of the trees. "Isn't it a little late for dinner?"

Trapper sat down opposite her with a casual grin.

"Yes actually, but I thought maybe June would be interested in dessert." He winked.

"Sorry to ruin your plans, then," she said. "I could go bleed somewhere else, if you'd rather not be disturbed."

He waved a hand airily.

"Nah, nah, don't bother yourself on my account. Though it looks as if you've had some bother already."

"I fell," she said. "It hurt."

"I'm sure." He paused, and she let silence flood in and fill the space. Seconds ticked by. Finally he said, "So you're not going to tell me what happened, then?"

"No, I don't think I am," she said. "Ask me tomorrow, maybe." He nodded.

"Well, truth is," he said, "I saw you drive by, and you looked like a drunk driver. You came right past my place, weaving all over the road." He shrugged. "I don't have a phone, so I figured if you weren't here, I could call the cops." He leaned forward and smiled at her. "I didn't know it was you, though, else I'd have flung my body on the road to slow you down."

The smile was right, and the words were light and flirtatious, but something flickered behind his eyes, like a hint of deeper emotion. He put out a hand and tilted up her chin, as if to get a better look at her wound, but the touch was nearly a caress.

"Trapper, can't I leave you alone for a minute? God, leave the poor girl alone! She's got headaches enough without adding you to them."

"I'm hurt," he said, and he took his hand away, but his fingertips trailed just a little along the line of her jaw. Rosanna flushed and ducked her head.

"Got the scissors," June said, and shooed Trapper over to another chair. She cut away the blouse. The wrist underneath was swollen, but June didn't think it was broken. Rosanna could move all her fingers, it just wasn't any fun.

"Thompson," June said, "go be useful and bring this girl in some snow. There's a towel by the sink, you can fill that up."

'Yes ma'am, thank you ma'am, pleased to be of service, ma'am," Trapper said with a servile little bow. She waved a dismissive hand at him.

"Rosanna," she said, "let's see if your eyes are still working together."

As soon as Trapper left, though, June showed no more interest in the state of Rosanna's pupils.

"Did he have anything to do with all this?" she asked.

"Thompson? I…well, no, it was some kind of animal."

"What kind of animal?"

"I told you…"

"I know what you told me, tell me the rest."

"Look, I don't know how…"

"We don't have time, he'll be back any second. Do you think he had anything to do with it?"

"Not that I know. I thought…I thought he was your friend."

"Trapper's everyone's friend. Thing is, not much of anyone is his."

"What?"

The bell on the door jingled as Trapper returned. Rosanna pressed the snow against her wrist, and it eased the pain a great deal. June caught her eye and shook her head.

"Thompson was just telling me he saw me drive by," she said, and June frowned at her. "I guess he was worried."

Trapper smiled.

"We take care of each other, we back-country folk. I wouldn't have wanted anyone to end up stuck in a ditch, or off a cliff."

"So where is your place, Trapper?" June said. "I thought you kept yourself up the mountain, away from the road?"

"I do, but I've got a base camp closer to the road. Easier to get supplies in by stages, you know?"

"Lucky you were around then, I guess," Rosanna said.

"Trust a man to show up after the trouble's over," June said.

"Of course, dear lady, how else can we nurse poor, helpless women back to health?"

"No helpless women here," June said. "Whatever it was attacked Rosanna, she beat it away with a shovel. Not bad for a city girl." She turned and grinned at Rosanna, and Rosanna felt a rush of pride.

"Not bad, indeed," Trapper said. "What was it that attacked you?"

"I don't know," Rosanna said. "It was…well it was almost dark, and I just know it was kind of dog-shaped, and it howled." All the things she couldn't say bubbled in her mind.

"Wolf maybe?" Trapper offered.

"I don't know," Rosanna repeated. "I don't really know enough about animals. And anyway, I hit my head so hard I'm probably not remembering right." She shook her head, and her eyelids started to droop again.

"I'm really tired," she said. June nodded.

"I'll go get you a glass of water and some ibuprofen," she said. "That should help with the swelling in that wrist. I'm betting you still have a hell of a headache, too."

"Yeah," Rosanna said. "I don't feel quite as dizzy, though, just tired."

"I still don't want to just let you sleep," June said, "but you can lie down again, and I'll wake you up in an hour or two."

"Make it two? Pretty please?"

"All right, two then." June turned to Trapper. "And what about you, Prince Charming? Since the lady fair doesn't need rescuing after all? You headed home?"

Trapper nodded. "I better," he said. "But I'll come back in the morning to check on our city blossom." He smiled warmly at Rosanna, and she blushed again.

June shook her head.

"Utterly shameless," she said.

"Utterly," he agreed. "Who could resist a woman who's too concussed to argue?"

"Yuck," said Rosanna. "I'm going to bed." Trapper had just opened his mouth when both women said in chorus

"ALONE."

# Chapter 6

It was a long night, as much for June as for Rosanna. It was twelve hours before June finally felt safe enough to just leave Rosanna sleep. Rosanna woke in the dim fastness of the back room, not sure of the time or even the day. Her body ached all over, but the dizziness was gone, as well as any trace of vertigo. Her clothes lay in a heap beside the bed. Sometime in the night she must have taken them off, but she didn't remember doing so. It was very peculiar to wake up naked in a strange bed. She hadn't done that in a very long time, but she smiled at the memory. It had been lovely, that time, however brief.

A thin line of light shone under the door, and by it Rosanna found a switch for the lamp beside her bed. The light, though small and mellow, still blinded her for a second, and the pain in her head snarled.

Next to the lamp was a phone, and Rosanna's next thought was for Granny. She couldn't believe she'd left Granny alone, with whatever was out there. She dialed the number with a shaking hand. It rang twice, three times, and then Granny's voice lit the line like an epiphany.

"Rosanna?" she said, before Rosanna could even say a word.

"It's me," Rosanna said. "Are you…are you okay?"

"Oh my girl, oh my brave girl, I'm fine." There were tears in her voice. "I knew you'd gone, even asleep, but when you didn't come back…"

"Granny, god I'm so sorry. I just woke up now."

"Where did you go? Are you in hospital?"

"No, I went to the little café. I couldn't…I didn't know what else to do."

"June's place? You couldn't have done better!"

"I know. She kept me up through the night, bandaged me up."

"Bandaged? Bandaged what? Are you okay?"

"I hit my head pretty good when I fell, and I think I sprained my wrist."

"But otherwise? You're not bitten?"

"No, it only got you. How are *you* doing?"

"Better. You did a good job, lady mine. No finesse, of course, but who expects finesse? You're a natural, sure enough. I don't know how I didn't see it before."

"I don't know, Granny, but if you want to fight about it, you're going to have to wait until I'm a little stronger."

Granny laughed. "Didn't I say you were out of shape? Lord, when you were younger a bump on the head just made you more stubborn to keep going."

"Age gets us all, I guess."

"It does indeed." Granny paused, and sighed. "I'm sorry Rosanna. It's my fault, all of it."

"How can it be your fault?"

"I should have guessed there might be trouble. I should have made my house protections better. I could have kept us at Lillian's grave. I'm getting old, girl. Old and stupid."

"Look, anyone who can run down a mountain like you is NOT old."

"'T'isn't all about running." Rosanna could almost hear Granny shaking her head, putting the thought aside. "This isn't the time for that. You coming home soon?"

"Do you mind if I have breakfast first?"

"'Course not. I think I'll have a bite myself. Another bite, I guess." Rosanna groaned in response.

"I think I liked you unconscious," she said. There was a pause on the line.

"You did good, girl. I'm proud."

"I…yeah, I did. And I'm proud, too."

"Good," Granny said. "I'll see you in a while."

"I love you Granny," Rosanna said, surprised as the words sprung to her lips. It had been a long time since she said them with such depth of sincerity.

"I love you too," Granny said. "Anything else is incidental."

Rosanna brushed away a tear.

"See you soon," she said.

"See you soon," Granny said. Rosanna hung up the phone and sat for a long moment in the stillness of the little room. Somewhere outside, she heard the muffled sound of movement, but it was comforting to sit in this little cocoon, and let the world go on without her, for at least small space of time.

Her stomach interrupted her thoughts with a loud growl, and she chuckled. That was all the time she could apparently spare for cocoons or contemplation.

She eyed her clothes with distaste. There was blood all over them, and the sleeve of her shirt was in tatters. She put them on all the same. She stripped the sheets off the bed. They were bloody as well, but only a little, and she was relieved to see it hadn't soaked through to the mattress. She folded the sheets (even though she knew they'd need to be washed) because it seemed the polite thing to do, and then stowed the bed away. She turned off the lamp, and walked to the door, led by the light at its bottom. She opened the door, and the bright lights of the kitchen pierced right through her eyes and into her aching head. She squinted, sighed, and stepped into the kitchen anyway.

June wasn't in sight, but there was bacon on the griddle, and the gurgle and glorp of coffee brewing. Rosanna looked around with interest, and a growing appetite. She thought it might have been the scent of bacon that had woken her. Everything seemed so mundane and comfortable. It was hard to believe that the malice she'd fought could exist in the same world as bacon and coffee and toast.

Rosanna took a side trip to the washroom, careful to avoid the mirror. Everything hurt, but she really didn't want any visual reminder of that. When she came back, she could hear June's voice, but still not see her.

Just as Rosanna was about to seek her out, June came through the swinging doors with a bump. Her brown hair was neatly braided into two pigtails that came just past her shoulders. In this light, her eyes were a dark forest green, but Rosanna remembered them being brown the night before. June smiled, and gave a little wave.

"Well look who walks again!"

"Thanks to you," Rosanna said. "And I really can't thank you enough."

"Jeez, first conversation of the day and I already have to tell you to shut up."

Rosanna shrugged, and grinned. "I have that effect on a lot of people," she said.

"No doubt. Want some breakfast? There's whiskey for the coffee."

"Is it still before noon?"

"Only barely. I won't tell if you don't."

June paused to turn the bacon and crack a couple eggs onto the griddle.

"Bacon or sausage?" she said.

"Bacon," Rosanna said. "I like cholesterol."

June nodded again. "Just let me get this order out, and I'll fix us up something. It's only Seth Gordon, and then we'll have a minute."

"I can't stay too long," Rosanna said. "I'd like to get back to Granny as soon as I can."

"Are you telling me you left someone else there?" June's eyes lost their warmth.

"She's okay. I called her first thing when I woke up." The accusation on June's face lost its edge, but did not entirely disappear. "She was all right when I left. She told me to come."

"There's more you aren't telling me, isn't there." It was a statement, not a question, and Rosanna would not dissemble. June had earned honesty, and beyond that, Rosanna enjoyed the easy friendship that was growing between them.

"Yes, there is. Lots more. And I don't have the right to tell you until I talk to my Granny. Is that okay?" June nodded slowly, her eyes never leaving Rosanna's. Rosanna saw then that they were hazel, brown and green flecked with gold.

"I guess that's fair," June said. She turned back to the cooking food. "Damn," she said. "I was supposed to scramble those. You like easy-over?"

"I like food," Rosanna said with a laugh.

June cracked another couple eggs, and put some more bacon down. "You might as well have this," she said. "Seth never tips anyway, so he can just damn well wait."

Rosanna laughed, and tried (without success) to feel guilty for pre-empting Seth's breakfast. June slid the bacon and eggs onto a plate, dropped a couple pieces of toast on it, and said, "Eat up. Might as well sit in the dining room. It'll piss Seth off, but he'll survive. Help yourself to coffee, there."

Rosanna took her plate through the swinging doors and into the dining room. Out side the windows, snow sparkled and gleamed in the clean sunlight. This too, seemed to deny the dark beast she'd defeated. Defeated was a nice word, and she rolled it around in her mouth, sampling it. Yes, that had a good taste to it. She smiled to herself, and sat down with her breakfast.

Seth was a sullen older man with thinning black hair and a paunch. He looked at her disagreeably, and she smiled anyway. He snorted and turned his eyes to the kitchen door.

Rosanna chuckled to herself, and tucked in. Coffee could wait, she decided. It would still be warm, and she wanted her breakfast while it was hot. She savored every bite, the rich smoky taste of the bacon, and the satisfying crunch of buttered toast. When she finished, she leaned back in her chair, enjoying the view. Frost had left a little forest of ferns and fanciful towers etched onto the glass. She reached out a finger to trace them, and to her surprise, heard the quiet murmur of a Word. It was a small one, like the faintest whisper of wind over water. She listened to it, marveling, considering that even frost was made of a power that she, *she* Rosanna might learn to understand and use. She listened, and stored the syllable in her mind. There was a space there, she found, something like an empty bookshelf. She'd never known it was there, but somehow, she must have known that it was empty, for the Words there filled it perfectly, and some gnawing hunger inside her was sated by their acquisition.

June came out with Seth's breakfast, and he grunted at her, just as disagreeable as he'd been with Rosanna.

"God you're an ass," June said, and Rosanna stifled a laugh. "Haven't you even got any manners?"

"Not when my food's late. Probably cold, too."

"It's not cold, and you know it. Get over it." She turned away without another word, and walked to the coffee pot. Seth snuffled a little, like an unsatisfied badger, and started to eat.

June came back to Rosanna's table with two cups of coffee in one hand, and a bottle of whiskey in the other.

"How do you do that without spilling?" Rosanna asked, as June deftly set the cups on the table.

"Practice," June said. "Lots and lots of practice. You still want that whiskey?"

"I shouldn't…"

"Aw, c'mon. We earned it, I think."

"You talked me into it," Rosanna said with a smile. "I guess we did."

June poured a dollop of whiskey into each mug, and sat down across from Rosanna. She raised her cup.

"Here's to a fierce woman!" she said, and they clinked cups. They sat in companionable silence for a while, each absorbed in her own thoughts.

"I don't think I can ever repay you," Rosanna said at last. "I think you saved my life. Thanks."

"Don't be stupid. You can repay me. You buy breakfast, you replace my first aid supplies, and we're square."

"That's not what I mean."

"I know it's not, but you can't repay anything else. It's just...it's just being a good neighbor, a good human. I don't do it for you particularly. Anybody showed up at my door in that shape, I'd do the same."

"Thanks anyway. Gratitude is the same thing you know, being a good human." June ducked her head and shuffled her feet a little.

"Yeah well, you're welcome, so quit talking about it."

Seth cleared his throat noisily. "You too busy to bring a paying customer some damn coffee?"

"It's over there, Seth. You got legs, get it yourself. Everyone else does."

"Well, maybe I'm not everyone else, then."

"True 'nuff. You're the most ornery cuss around."

Seth's lumpy face split with a wide grin, displaying a mouthful of yellowed teeth.

"You always could talk your way to a feller's heart," he said, and got up to fetch his own coffee.

Rosanna smiled and clinked her cup with June's again. June looked up at her, surprised.

"To a fierce woman!" she said, and June laughed and met the toast. The whiskey was good, a cheering heat that eased some of the aches in Rosanna's muscles. June nodded in satisfaction.

"Looks like you needed that," she said. "Taken a little of the starch out of your shirt."

"I didn't know I was still so wound up," Rosanna said. "I'm not used to this kind of stuff, I guess."

"Don't get used to danger, girl, that's how you end up dead." She wore a silver chain, with a pendant that disappeared below the collar of her shirt. June pulled it out. The pendant was a large tooth. It had a hole drilled through it, and a loop of metal that attached it to the chain. Rosanna looked up at June questioningly.

"Big cat," June said. "Cougar."

"Where'd you get it?"

"From the cougar, stupid."

"Well, yeah, I assumed that. I mean *how* did you get it. There's got to be a story."

June leaned back with a satisfied grin, and dropped the chain down her shirt again.

"Course there's a story," I just haven't had anybody new to tell in such a long time, that I'm kinda enjoying myself."

"I can tell." Rosanna resisted the urge to stick out her tongue, but only just. June's continuing silence was a tease, and Rosanna knew it, and didn't ask again. June let the silence stretch out a little further, then chuckled again. "You're a stubborn one, too, ain't ya."

"Anyone who spends ANY time with my Granny ends up either stubborn, or railroaded. And railroaded gets dull, believe me."

"Well, then, here's the story. I got hunted by a cougar. I was hitching a ride. Don't look at me like that, I was young, and the world was safer. Anyhow, the bugger was creeping up on me when I finally caught a ride with some drunk asshole in a truck. Wasn't sure which was worse."

"Yeek! Are you serious?"

"About which?"

"Smartass, about the cougar. I can believe drunken assholes, especially in a truck."

"Straight up. Scared the crap out of me, so I got me a big knife, almost a machete. Made me feel braver 'bout assholes and cougars both." Rosanna nodded. June's eyes turned a deep brown as she remembered, and Rosanna could well picture June with a giant knife strapped to her thigh, like some wild vestige of a less civilized age.

"Anyhow, don't know if it was the same one, or another, but we met on a trail. Me, now, I'm just the right size to be cougar-prey. Not too big, not too quick. He musta thought he found an easy meal." She grinned, and her teeth glinted in the new sunlight. "So I saw he was gonna jump, and I figured if he was gonna get me, he was damn well gonna work for it. Braced that knife. He batted at it, cut his paw, got mad, and jumped anyway."

"Oh my god! Are you serious?"

"You keep asking. Don't I look serious?" June shook her head. "Never mind, I get your meaning. Yeah, it's true. He jumped, I stumbled, and he ended up on my knife. I got out of the way of them claws fast as I could, but I didn't know he was dead right away. I was just waiting to die." She shrugged. "Part luck and part nerve, I guess, but he's dead and I'm not. I wear that tooth so I remember all the time I got is time I stole from that furry bastard. It's all time I won for my own self."

"Holy shit. And he didn't leave a mark on you?"

"I didn't say that," June said. "I got a good scar on my one side where he tried to tear in, but he mostly missed. Guess he was too busy dying."

Rosanna shook her head.

"I don't think I'm in the same fierce league as you, June. You're kind of in the major league and I'm just a junior almost wannabe."

June laughed.

"Don't sell yourself short. Fierce is fierce." Her eyes focused sharply on Rosanna's. "So let's talk about what happened yesterday."

Rosanna looked over at Seth and hesitated. June looked over her shoulder, then at the clock.

"Seth, you're late. If you don't get home, Marion is gonna know you went for breakfast without her."

Seth looked up at the clock with a guilty start, and set his cup down. He put a crumpled bill and some coins on the table, then hurried out of the café.

"If that boy thinks for a minute that his wife don't know where he goes, he's dumber than he looks, and that's saying somewhat." Her smile glinted again. "Marion's just grateful to get an hour alone of a morning." The smile lingered, but her eyes were intense.

"So? What happened?"

"I...like I said, there's things I just don't have the right to tell you."

"So don't. I don't need everything, just tell me what you can."

Rosanna did her best to sketch the story without filling in too many details. June didn't interrupt, and it was a relief to tell it all, to spill out the fear and fury and desperation. To her embarrassment, she felt tears rise in her eyes, but she let them fall. It seemed as if the telling eased the ache in her thoughts as the whiskey had eased her body. When she was done, the two women sat quietly for a long moment, listening to the companionable ticking of the clock.

"Seems to me," June said at last, "seems to me that our stories ain't so different, really."

"No, I guess not. But it's so much easier to think of you as brave, than me."

"You're one of them kind of girl, hey?"

"One of what kind?"

"The kind that only thinks nice things 'bout other people."

"I guess," Rosanna said. "I haven't had much call to think nice stuff about myself."

"You just ain't had practice. Time to start." June put a hand on Rosanna's shoulder and closed the distance between their faces until their noses nearly touched. "Repeat after me," she said, humor and intensity mingled in her voice. "I am a fierce woman."

"You are a fierce woman," Rosanna said with a grin, but June just shook her shoulder, and frowned. "All right, all right," Rosanna said. "I am a fierce woman."

"Damn straight. And a fierce woman got no reason to be afraid in any place she calls home, right?"

"I guess."

"Good. You wait here."

June picked up Seth's dirty dishes and took them into the kitchen, then Rosanna heard the office door swing open. Within a few moments, June returned with a black nylon something that turned out to be a sheath. In the sheath was a very long, very solid blade. It was smooth and sharp, with a slight curve to it. Rosanna held it gingerly, but its weight denied half-measures. She wrapped her hand around the hilt.

"This is the knife that killed a cougar," June said. "You take it now."

"I can't do that," Rosanna protested. "I don't even know I killed anything!"

"You meant to, and that's enough," June said. "I won't argue, and you will take it, so save your breath, and just say 'thanks'."

Rosanna took a deep breath, readying arguments, and found she didn't care to use them.

"Thanks, then," she said.

"You're welcome. You get some other thing come after you, you just brace yourself and let it take a swipe at that blade. Most critters is wise enough to back off, once they get to bleeding a bit."

"But not all of them," Rosanna said. "Not that cougar, anyway."

"Not all, no," June said. "But knowing you got fangs too takes the scare out of things, gives you more room for fierce." She grinned, showing even, white teeth, and her hazel eyes flashed.

Rosanna thought of the monster again, of fleeing down the mountain in darkness and terror, of the bite on Granny's shoulder. If there was room in her life for that malignancy, there was certainly room in it for fierceness, and for a sharp knife. The sheath had a clip on it, and she hung it from a belt loop. It knocked awkwardly against her thigh, and June shook her head.

"Ain't gonna do you much good there, girl. You gotta be able to draw it. It's got a belt, you can strap it to your thigh."

"I'll look ridiculous." It was one thing to imagine the wild and wary June decked out for an adventure movie, but Rosanna?

"You think a cougar's gonna care? You're not in fashion central, here."

Rosanna fumbled with the straps, and despite the way the efforts hurt her wrist, she welcomed them, welcomed the chance to saddle up and prepare. Ever since Granny had spoken, Rosanna had simply floated on the surface of events, neither directing nor assisting her progress. Perhaps it was time to do both. With the weight of that knife, she could almost believe she'd the right to choose a destination, as well.

June sat back and looked at Rosanna with satisfaction.

"Suits you," she said.

"But what about you?" Rosanna said. "I don't want you to end up some *other* cougar's lunch, just because I've got your knife."

"You think that's my only knife? I bought me a new one after that, kinda saved this one for luck. And maybe for you."

"I never would have believed I'd need one, you know," Rosanna said. "I just haven't had that kind of life."

"Life is what it is, Rosanna. It changes, and if you don't change too, it'll run you down. I think you got it in you, though."

"Thanks. That's good to hear."

June nodded. They sat and sipped their coffee, and Rosanna got up to fill their cups after a long and comfortable silence.

"So listen," June said. "Since I made it clear you're a fierce woman, I don't want to be telling you your business."

"But?"

"But what do you know about Thompson Trapper? He a friend of your Granny, or something?"

"Well, no, not that I know of. I just met him here, the other day."

June frowned.

"He's awful friendly with you, then, isn't he?"

"I guess I just assumed he was that way with everyone. I mean, he was with you, the other day."

June bobbed her head side to side in an indecisive sort of way.

"Yes and no. He can be flirty that way, sometimes, and mostly he seems harmless."

"I hear a 'but' coming on."

"Yeah. There's something about him that bugs me. You get any bad feelings about him?"

"Well, no, not really. I thought he was kinda cute, in an older-man kind of way."

"Oh, no denying cute. Sometimes dangerously cute. But he doesn't quite…fit. I don't know how else to say it."

"Doesn't fit? Like a bad suit? What?"

"Kinda like a bad suit, yeah. Like this place here, doesn't fit him, and he don't fit it. Like he's a kitten on the outside, but the cougar ain't far away."

"No, I didn't feel anything like that. What are we talking about here, fierce woman's intuition?"

June looked troubled.

"Do I sound crazy? I mean, more so than usual?"

"I don't know. What kind of things don't fit?"

June shrugged.

"It's some little things. He talks too smart for one, educated. There's folks here got good educations, but we rub off on each other after a while. Roughen each other up, some."

"Kinky," Rosanna said, and grinned.

"Not like that! Well, not *only* like that, anyhow. I don't feel much like speculating. But he's different. It's like he talks country 'cos he can, not 'cos it comes natural."

"I don't think I'm enough of an expert to say," Rosanna said, frowning. "But he seemed genuine to me."

"Like I said, he's a likeable fellow. He's everyone's friend. But no one knows much about him. He doesn't drink down at the Legion, he don't hunt with buddies. All we know is a name and a smile."

"But how long has he been here?"

"I can't remember," June said. "It's like he's always been here, and I want to just like him, but there's some kind of edge to him, something that backs me off."

"Aren't there other people like him, trappers and stuff?"

"Girl, this isn't the eighteen hundreds no more. Fur coats come from farmed minks. Ain't even legal to trap beaver no more. Nobody's ever seen him selling or even wearing fur. He's always got money, but no one round here buys from him."

"He said he found some gold up there," Rosanna said. "Maybe it's just more than he says?"

"I don't know. Most places good enough have already been prospected, and if it's good, why doesn't he have a claim and a mine? Just don't make no sense to me."

Rosanna remembered the weathered smile, still brilliant and charming, and the easy flow of his banter. She did like him, and she couldn't find anything sinister about it.

"One other thing," June said after a moment's thought. "How did he know you were here last night?"

"He said he saw my headlights," Rosanna replied. "It's not that surprising, is it?"

"He's never come down for anyone else," June said, "and the Ranier boys got drunk enough to run down the mailboxes and go half-way up the mountain trying to get away from the cops. That's right along the same stretch, and he didn't even know about it till he came in the week after."

"Does that have to mean anything?" Rosanna said. "Maybe the timing was bad, or he was out in the woods." She wasn't sure why she was defending him, only that it seemed silly to worry about one man, however peculiar, when there was a whole world of new dangers out there. She put her hand on her knife, and traced the grain of the sheath with her fingertips.

"I don't know if it means anything, and that's the truth," June said. "I just thought maybe you ought to be told. Since he seemed to take such a shine to you and all."

"You think so?"

June snorted. "Practically had to kick him out the door when you crashed, last night. He was watching your door like a love-sick pup."

Rosanna blushed, and June chuckled.

"For all that, he's a fine looking man," she said, and Rosanna's flush deepened. "But I guess you noticed," June added. "Unless that's sunburn?"

"You're a wicked woman," Rosanna said.

"Why thank you for noticing," June replied, and they laughed together.

"Anyhow," Rosanna said, "I should probably head back to Granny's."

"Your wrist be okay for that?" June asked. "You don't seem dizzy at all today, but you're still favoring that wrist. And, o' course, you still look like hell."

"And thank *you* for noticing. But yeah, I think I'll be okay, it's not that far and I can stop if I need to."

The bell on the café door jingled, and both women looked up to see Thompson come through the door, so bundled up that only his red scarf gave away his identity.

"Speak of the devil," June murmured, but Rosanna only shrugged. He'd said he'd come back, so it wasn't so very surprising.

"Good morning, Thompson," Rosanna said. "You here for coffee or company?"

He shucked his cap and outer layer of clothes before he answered.

"Any chance of both?" he asked. "And please call me Trapper. hardly anybody calls me Thompson unless I'm in trouble."

"You must hear it a lot, then," Rosanna said. June snorted.

"Most of what he hears ain't near so polite," she said. "You want breakfast, Trapper?"

"Just coffee, oh jewel of the mountains. Had a bite earlier."

"Well, then, it's in the usual place, and I'm quite comfortable where I am, thanks."

Trapper poured himself a cup, then turned back to the women.

"Anyone else need a warm-up?"

"We are talking about coffee, right?" Rosanna asked.

"For the moment," he replied. "But I'm sure we could find other things to talk about, should we apply ourselves to it."

"And thirty seconds into the conversation, he's already hitting on the girl. You're consistent, I'll grant you that," June said. Rosanna blushed again, and Trapper grinned and shrugged. He brought the coffee pot over and topped up their cups.

"Can't seem to help myself," he said. "When there's such a wealth of beauty in the world, why wouldn't I try to collect some?"

"From what I've seen," Rosanna said, "you're trying to collect it all."

He shrugged again. "At least that way I'm bound to end up with *some*," he said.

"God I love a desperate man, don't you?" June asked. Rosanna thought it wisest not to answer, and lifted her cup to her lips instead.

"Take that as a yes," June said, and she and Trapper grinned at Rosanna's discomfort.

"So anyhow," June said to Trapper, "You feel like being useful this morning?" Trapper waggled his eyebrows lecherously.

"What'd you have in mind, lady fair?"

June snorted. "Lordy you're hopeful. I thought maybe you'd take Rosanna home, if it's not too far out the way for you. Seein' as you said you saw her go by last night?"

"I said I can drive myself," Rosanna said. "Honestly, it's not that bad, and it's not that far."

Trapper watched the careful movement of her injured wrist. His eyes seemed to tally the damage, and Rosanna was very glad she hadn't looked in the mirror.

"Well," he said, "far be it from me to contradict a lady, but you aren't exactly convincing, since you look you got the worst of ten rounds with a bear. Besides, you wouldn't rob a poor mountain man of an opportunity for chivalry, would you?"

Rosanna opened her mouth to say that she would, indeed, do that very thing, but caught June's glance and subsided.

"I'd take you myself," June said, "but I've got my morning rush coming on, and folks round here get right nasty without their coffee."

"You've done enough for me, honestly," Rosanna said. She was humbled by June's generosity, the simple and forthright manner in which she'd given aid. Somehow it meant even more to know that June would have done the same for anyone, to know that she, Rosanna, was no less or more important than any other injured body in the world.

"If you thank me again, I swear I'm gonna smack you," June said, and Rosanna stifled the words before she could speak them. June nodded in satisfaction. "So, she said," you up for it, Trapper?"

"Absolutely. Can I finish my coffee first?"

"Be my guest," June said. The bell on the door jingled again, and an androgynous bundle of winter clothes clomped and stomped through the door.

"Diane!" June cried happily." Girl, I haven't seen you in ages!"

Rosanna and Trapper sipped their coffee, watching June bustle about. Before they'd finished, three more people had arrived, and molted their winter coats. Rosanna finished her coffee, and looked up in time to see the bottom of his mug as he tipped the last mouthful back.

"You set?" he asked, and Rosanna nodded.

"Just let me say good-bye to June," she said. She stood, feeling every bump and bruise and ache, and walked stiffly to the kitchen.

"We're on our way," she said, and June looked up from her cooking.

"You take care, girl, and stop in again. Can I call you to see how you're doing?"

"Sure!" Rosanna said. "I'm staying with my Granny now, and I probably will for a while yet. There are some things…some things I need to sort out."

June looked at her for a long moment.

"You gonna tell me whole story, sometime?" she asked, and Rosanna nodded.

"I think you've earned it," she said. "And I trust you." She patted the knife on her thigh. Its weight was becoming familiar already, familiar and comfortable.

June hugged her, gently enough to accommodate injuries, but warmly enough to convey affection.

"You write the number beside the phone out front," she said. "I'm sorry to leave you with that rascal, but I don't know what else to do."

"I'm sure it'll be fine," Rosanna said. "I'm a fierce woman, right?"

"All the same, you take care. I don't know for sure that there's anything off, but you had enough adventure yesterday."

"That's saying a mouthful," Rosanna said. June turned to flip eggs and sausages.

"You get going," she said. "And give me a call when you get home, all right? I don't like to worry."

"Talk to you soon," Rosanna agreed, and stepped back out into the restaurant. Trapper was already bundled up again, except for his hat and scarf.

"Can I start the car for you?" he asked. "You don't look dressed for the weather."

Rosanna handed him the keys, and in a moment heard the engine snarl and mutter, then start with a surly whine. She wrote Granny's number on the pad beside the phone, and took one of the home-printed cards that sat by the cash register. Her own sweater hung on a peg beside the door, and she put it on with some disgust. The front of it was stiff with blood as well, and it crumbled and crunched as she pulled it on. She very desperately wanted a shower. She thought hopefully of Granny's big old tub, and decided a bath would be fine, too.

She *wasn't* dressed for the weather, she knew, so she waited for the car to warm up. She passed the time reading the assorted notices and messages posted on the wall beside the coat-pegs.

The door opened, ushering in a wash of cold air, and Trapper stomped his feet just inside it.

"You ready?" he asked. "The car's warm enough, I think, even for a frail and wilting city blossom."

"I'm not *that* frail," Rosanna said, and tapped her knife. Trapper's eyes lit on it, and smiled.

"We'll make a bear-fighter out of you yet," he said, and walked back out to the car. Rosanna zipped her jacket and stepped out into the chill.

The air was cold and sharp, and she had to take shallow breaths, or it made her cough. The sky was clear again, though a bank of clouds hovered nearly out of sight to the north. The sidewalk was a little slick, though June had put salt down to help break up the ice. Rosanna walked gingerly to the car, feeling thirty years older than she was. She opened the front passenger door and folded herself down onto the seat. It took some doing, and it hurt, but she managed. Thompson watched her with concern, but said nothing. Rosanna was glad of it. Sympathy might have allowed the little tears of pain to become a larger flow, and she was pretty sure that fierce women didn't cry.

Thompson drove well, and she nearly drifted off to sleep. She wasn't accustomed to having anyone else do the driving for her, and it was pleasant to be able to just enjoy the scenery.

"Where along here is your place?" she asked. "Will you be okay to get back to it?"

"I get most everywhere by shanks' mare," he said. "It's not too far from where we are now. We getting close to your Granny's place?"

"Next turn," Rosanna said, "about a klick on and then a right."

"Ah," he said. "Down by the Johnson's place."

"I don't really know," Rosanna said. "Granny doesn't talk about her neighbors, really."

"That's unusual," Trapper said. "Most folks around here need gossip like they need air."

"Granny's not exactly a usual kind of person," Rosanna said, and Thompson smiled. He turned, and whistled at the sight of the driveway.

"You got good tires on this thing?" he asked.

"Yup," Rosanna said. "I've made it up twice now, though I wouldn't want to try if it snowed too much more."

"Somebody ought to sand this," he said, and started up the steep grade.

"Granny doesn't get too many visitors, I guess. And she's got a four-by-four. She doesn't drive much, but when she does, she means it."

Trapper chuckled, and they made the last little rise up to the cabin. It looked snug and peaceful, not at all like the site of a duel to the death. Snow padded the roof and eaves, and heaped up around the steps.

"So?" Trapper said. "Where to next?"

"The cabin's good," Rosanna said.

"Yes, but where's the cabin?"

"It's right there," Rosanna said. "I thought I was the one with the bumped head." She looked at Trapper, wondering what the joke was. He looked right at the cabin, but his glance seemed to pass over it or through it. He truly couldn't see it.

And then Rosanna remembered Granny's protections. She didn't know how they worked, or what they were, but could they do this?

She reached out a hand and touched his that lay bare on the steering wheel. With that new intensity, she *listened* and heard the sounds of his Being, the Words that made him up. Over and through that song, winding like a poisonous snake, was the sound of last night's beast. He met her eyes, opened his mouth to speak, and she threw open the car door and fled, heedless of what he might do. She sprinted across the remaining distance as best she could, and pounded on the door. She looked around wildly, but he wasn't pursuing her, simply sitting in the car with his head on the wheel.

Granny opened the door, and Rosanna flung herself through it. She stumbled on the lintel, and fell past Granny and into the living room.

"Shut it!" she gasped. "He's out there!"

Granny shut the door. Rosanna picked herself up, and braced her back against the door, waiting for the next monster to arrive.

# Chapter 7

Rosanna knew that this was in no way the correct response of a fierce woman. She was certain that June would have snarled, drawn her knife, and confronted the varlet, and then no doubt skinned him and made gloves from his hide. All the same, she was quite content to huddle against the door like a frightened child. It had been too much, she decided, simply more than she was equipped to handle. She was not designed for such stresses, for as flexible a world-view as her life now required.

"How good are your protections?" she asked. Granny looked at her, bewilderment and annoyance tangled in her expression.

"Against what?"

"Against a bad guy," Rosanna said.

Granny sighed.

"I wish you'd quit panicking and just tell me what's going on."

"The guy...the one who sent that thing, he's right outside."

"Be reasonable, Rosanna, he couldn't possibly find this place. My protections are that good, at very least."

"Oh, he could find it if someone directed him, don't you think?"

"Yes, theoretically, but who…" The question trailed off. "You didn't. Rosanna, you DIDN'T!"

"I didn't know!" She couldn't believe she'd been that gullible. Just a nice guy, right? And June had even said to be careful. She should have known from the start. Men just didn't take to her. She was too smart and not pretty enough. But he had been…he had been kind.

"Rosanna, calm down and tell me what's going on. Good god, I have a little nap and you blow the world to bits!"

"A nap? You could have died!"

"We've no time for quibbles, Rosanna, no time! What happened?!"

"I met him at the café, he drove me home, when he got here he couldn't see the place, and heard that *monster* inside him." She shuddered, hearing again the inimical wrapped around the glory of a soul.

"Does he have a vehicle?"

"No, but he's in my car!"

"Dammit, where's your sense? Didn't I always tell you never to get into a car with strangers?" Granny drew the curtain back from her front window.

"There's no one in it, Rosanna."

"Oh god, where'd he go?"

"I don't know! But there's no bumps against the protections, I'd feel that. Your car is still running, but there's nobody in it."

Rosanna straightened up, and felt the weight of her knife again. She flushed with shame. This was not how a cougar-hunter dealt with danger. She stood beside Granny.

"Let me see," she whispered. Granny looked at her with sour amusement.

"It's a little late for caution, dear. Might as well speak out loud." She made room for Rosanna all the same. Granny was right, there was no one in the car. Both doors were open, and the engine was still purring contentedly.

"Where'd he go?" she asked, looking around. Even if he were walking, there ought to have been some sign of him, but the only prints visible were Rosanna's. The snow beside the driver's door was undisturbed.

"Creepy," she said.

"Exceedingly," Granny said. "On the other hand, that gives us a moment to catch up."

"Should I go turn the car off?" Rosanna asked.

"Give me a second," Granny said, and murmured a Word. Her eyes went a little vague for a half-minute or so, then snapped back to their usual keen focus.

"I can't feel him out there at all, and that's not good, neither. Either he's gone or he's hidden himself, and no matter which it is, that's more power than I'm strictly comfortable with." She paused, thinking and tapping a finger against her teeth.

"You might as well go and do that," she said. "I'll keep an eye out here, but you be quick about it. I don't like this much at all."

Rosanna stepped out into the sharp, cold air, hurried to the car and turned it off. The seat was still warm from the weight of Trapper's body, and she shivered. He could have done anything, and she never would have had a chance. She took the keys out of the ignition and closed both doors, one hand on the hilt of her knife. She wasn't sure she was capable of using it, even should the need arise, but it was good to know she had the option.

Granny stood at the door, and closed it tight behind Rosanna.

"So," she said. "you've been busy, my lass. Make any new friends?"

Rosanna made a face.

"You didn't exactly give me much choice, you know."

"What, I sent out invitations for Mr. Nasty? All I did was go to sleep."

"Great job, Gran, have a snooze while I deal with a concussion all by my lonesome."

"You're resourceful, I figured you'd cope. You did cope, didn't you? You still look like hell." Granny waved a finger warningly. "But that's still no excuse for fraternizing with the enemy."

"Granny, I don't mean to sound ungrateful, but you're taking this awfully lightly. You feeling okay?"

Granny Rosie laughed, and pulled Rosanna into a warm hug.

"Oh my girl, I'm just so glad we're both alive. I haven't the heart to be cranky with you, not when you've done so well." She pulled back, and brushed Rosanna's hair back from her forehead. "You know you've done well, don't you?"

Rosanna felt hot tears rising up in her eyes.

"Oh Gran, god! I thought you were going to die! I thought I was going to die, but it was worse thinking that you...that I..."

Granny Rosie nodded, and drew Rosanna back into her arms. They stood for a moment, each nursing her private terror, and drawing strength from the other's heartbeat. After a moment, Granny broke the embrace, wiping her face with the back of her hand.

"Well, now, that's quite enough of that, I think. Tell me what happened."

Rosanna started talking about June and the café, but Granny stopped her.

"But the hound, girl, what happened to it? I remember being bitten, and that's something I wish to hell I could forget. But after that?"

"I, um, hit it with the shovel." She shrugged, embarrassed now to say it. It sounded such a mundane way to deal with a magical creature. Granny nodded in satisfaction, though.

"Best thing, girl. Go with your instincts, you can trust 'em. And it worked, didn't it? Us not being ghosts and all?" Rosanna nodded, feeling again the slow, encouraging kindling of pride. She hadn't even needed a knife. Maybe June was right, after all. Maybe they *were* in the same league.

"Anyway," Rosanna said, "then you were poisoned, and I used the Word from the keystone. I thought I did it wrong, Granny, I was so scared I'd killed you!"

"Phew," Granny said. "No wonder it stung." She paused, immersed in her own thoughts for a moment. "I didn't expect you to cure me, you know, just to give me space to fix it myself. But you did it all the same, all untrained." There was wonder and pride in her voice, and when she met Rosanna's glance, it shone in Granny's eyes like an epiphany. "Just like your mother, Rosanna. Lord what a marvel the world can be."

"So then I went down to the café, like I said, and June helped me out. Granny nodded.

"I've always liked her," she said. "Such a sensible girl."

"Well, she was great, but then Trapper came to the café, and offered to drive me home. June said there was something not right about him, but he seemed nice enough."

"Was he cute?" Granny asked sharply, and Rosanna's ears burned.

"Sort of, in an older-man kind of way," she said, just as she'd said to June. Granny's gaze didn't relent, and finally Rosanna threw up her hands. "Yes, okay, attractive and nice. Twice my age probably, but even so..." Rosanna didn't want to give up the memory of the sparkle in his eye, or the honey and silk tone of his teasing. But that sound, that one other sound, it was enough to tear those memories to ribbons. She felt like a friend had died. Granny put a comforting hand on her shoulder.

"I'm sorry, Rose-girl, truly. 'Tisn't ever easy to be betrayed. So what then? How did you place him?"

"Like I said, he drove me home, and when he couldn't see the place...somehow I knew, or guessed. I touched his hand, and I heard that same sound, the poison-sound that was in you." She shuddered. "It was horrible. It was like...like walking in a rose-garden and smelling a corpse."

Granny Rosie nodded, and leaned back, thinking.

"Well," she said at last, "I don't know what to make of it all just yet, but there's no point huddling behind the door. Let's have some coffee and think on it some. You had breakfast?"

"Breakfast yes, but the ibuprofen's starting to wear off. Have you got any?"

"In the bathroom, under the sink. Bring me a couple while you're at it, would you? That shoulder's still some tender. Maybe you can look at it once I've had something to eat."

"Sure," Rosanna said. "And I'd like to have a bath, if we can spare the time."

"We better spare the time," Granny said. "you look like something out of a horror movie."

Rosanna turned on the light in Granny's little bathroom, and regretted it. The woman in the mirror was not a pretty sight. The cut on her forehead was covered fairly well, but a bruise extended above both brows, and she had a shiner on the left side. She was lucky, she knew. If she'd been just a little closer to the porch when she fell, she could easily have lost an eye. There were scratches across her cheekbones and neck that she didn't remember acquiring. Probably they were from the run through the forest. She looked at her wrist critically. It was bruised and swollen, but she could move all her fingers, and, (if she gritted her teeth) she could rotate the wrist itself.

She stripped off her clothes, wincing and muttering at all the different aches. She had some deep, ugly bruises on her ribs that she didn't remember acquiring, along with myriad others on her shoulders and shins. She felt old, and stiffer than a life sentence.

She filled the tub half-way. She longed to fill it to the top and soak those aches away, but there really wasn't time, so she settled for a quick scrub and a wishful sigh. She wanted to wash her hair, too, but if she had to go out in the cold again, wet hair would be a bad idea.

Granny knocked on the door when Rosanna had almost finished.

"Got some clean clothes for you," she called, and opened the door to tuck them inside. Rosanna dried her self off , rooted around under the sink, and came up with Granny's first aid kit. There was peroxide in it as well as ibuprofen. Rosanna clenched her jaw and swabbed some of the disinfectant onto her cuts . It bubbled and stung, and Rosanna hoped it would keep the wounds from getting infected and scarring too much. She dressed in the jeans and sweater Granny had brought. On top of the pile of clothes there had been a pair of Granny's wooly socks, and Rosanna pulled them on happily. All the fabrics felt stiff and uncomfortable against her bruises except for the socks. Rosanna found room to be grateful for small luxuries.

She brought the kit out into the kitchen with her. Granny had started a pot of coffee, and was busy burning toast by the time Rosanna arrived.

"Lord girl, you look worse every time I see you. Could you do something about that? You'll put me off my food."

Now that Rosanna had leisure to notice, Granny was not looking her best self, either. There was a grayish tinge to her skin, and deep hollows under her eyes. Her movements were as quick and bird-like as ever, but there was a hesitation to them, a barest suggestion of weakness or uncertainty.

"I beg pardon your majesty. I don't want to offend your delicate sensibilities." Granny stifled a laugh and looked at Rosanna severely.

"I should think not!" She looked at the kit in Rosanna's hand. "You found it okay?"

"Yeah, not a problem. I'll just get a drink of water. You want some too?"

"Yes, please."

Rosanna poured a couple glasses of water, and took several ibuprofens. Granny took as many, and Rosanna glanced at her sideways. Granny met her eyes.

"Something to say?" she asked. It was a tone calculated to terrify, and it had worked on Rosanna, both child and adult, for years out of mind. Rosanna squared her shoulders, and tried to remember that she was fierce.

"Granny, you don't look too well, either. Did I do something wrong?"

"I'm just old, Rosanna, thanks for reminding me."

"Give me a break," Rosanna said. "You've been old for a long time and never looked it."

"Smartass," Granny said.

"Better a smart ass than a dumb one, I always say," Rosanna replied. "So? Are you going to tell me, or what?"

Granny Rosie sighed. "Look, it really just is my age. You did great, like water into wine, but I'm old, and my body doesn't bounce back the way it used to."

"I don't really want to imagine your body bouncing, back *or* forward."

"I'll have you know that there was quite a lot of interest in how my body bounced, once upon a time." Granny leered.

"Now there's a visual that will haunt me," Rosanna said. "I think I'm scarred for life."

Granny looked up at Rosanna's forehead.

"Could be, but they're scars honorably earned, I think."

"Could I heal it? I mean so it doesn't scar?"

Granny shrugged. "Might be. But like I said, it's honorably earned. Why not wear it proudly?"

"It might detract from my perfect profile, is all," Rosanna said, and grinned. The smile pulled at the cuts and scratches. "No really, wouldn't it be better to be all fixed up?"

"Yes and no," Granny said. Rosanna sighed.

"That's annoying, you know. Couldn't you go right to the definite answer?"

"Not really. I would if I could, but this...well, this is one of the primary conflicts among Librarians and their counterparts."

"Counterparts?"

"Don't interrupt while I'm waxing didactic, will you? It's distracting."

"Ooo, nice vocabulary, Gran. By all means, wax away."

"It's like this," Granny Rosie said. "I collect Words with the intent of storing them in a Library. I believe that keeps them safe, keeps them from being degraded or diluted by use or time."

"But don't you use them?"

"Yes, but only sparingly. Once they're in the Library, their original state is preserved, but they can still be change over time, with use."

"But if they're in the Library, what does it matter?"

"In the Library or no, it's still the same Word. The Library gives that pure state some protection, allows for a certain level of safe usage. But if we overdo, we could damage the Word ourselves, we who are supposed to guard them."

"So how much is overdoing?"

"I don't know," Granny said.

"Oh my god, it's those three little words I never expected you to say! Is that twice now in an entire lifetime?"

Granny scowled at Rosanna.

"You know, you can be a real cow," she said.

"Moo."

"Lovely. You have just the right face for it."

"Came by it honestly," Rosanna said. "It's genetic."

"ANYway," Granny said, dragging them back to the topic, "everyone has a different idea of what 'too much' is."

"And your idea?"

"I think that anything past the very bare necessity is wasteful, and very nearly sacrilegious."

"You're kidding me, right?"

Granny shrugged.

"Okay," she said. "maybe it's all about thrift. Maybe I'm a miser. But Words are sacred to me, and I just can't see using them for the every-day. It's like wearing your best evening dress all the time, just because it's pretty."

"But it's not like that, not really. It's just using what you've got."

"In a sense, I suppose, yes."

"Anyway, we're not talking about frivolity, really. We're being tracked, and I'm not at my best, and neither are you. Isn't that need enough?" Rosanna asked.

"It's for that same reason that I'm reluctant to use the Words on healing. Our bodies are doing that, and who knows what greater need we'll have?"

"You use a Word to keep the house warm, don't you?"

"Yes and no. I use the Word to speak to the creature that keeps my house warm. In return for her help in holding warmth, I provide her with the wood she needs as fuel, and with a safe place to exist."

"But couldn't you just use another Word to chop the wood for her, instead?" It seemed a waste to have access to such power, not be able to use it. What was the point of magic if you had to lock it away in a Library and leave it there?

"Maybe, but I wouldn't."

"But why not? Isn't it just part of the same process?"

"Because it makes the holy mundane," Granny said. "Because I'm already made up of Word, and if those ones can suit the need, it's wasteful to use another."

"I'm not sure I buy the mysticism, Granny. I mean, I even heard a Word in frost on a window. If it's so fragile, how could they still be there?"

"Did you hear any Words when you sat in your car?"

"Well, no, but I wasn't really listening, you know, not that way."

"You won't hear one, except in an old car, or an especially loved one. We've used those Words so often, that they've lost their power, and cars are just things, rather than expressions of Being."

"That doesn't make sense. A thing is or isn't, right? Would that mean that everything that exists is made of Words?"

"Everything was, but when a Word is spoken too often, it loses the power to create, and becomes a definition instead of a definer. Then the thing defined becomes an expression of Unbeing, or chaos."

"Come on, you're saying my *car* is on the dark side of the Force?"

"No, it just isn't on the light side. It's a void. If the void outweighs the Being, then we will no longer live in a world of Being, but of chaos. Or possibly no world at all. Many of us believe that when Chaos and Being are exactly equal, everything will cancel out."

"Many? Not all?"

"No, not all. But I do."

"And I'm just supposed to take your word for it?"

"You could do worse. But no, you aren't. You're supposed to make up your own ruddy mind about it. But for the moment, would you just trust me? We haven't got strength to spend on healing, not if there might be worse on the way."

Rosanna shrugged. She remembered how much it had tired her to heal Granny. And besides, it hadn't exactly looked comfortable. She figured if Granny could tough it out, there was no way she, Rosanna, was going to start the whining.

She poured a cup of Granny's caffeinated sludge, and added enough sugar and milk to make it drinkable. The toaster popped, and Granny took a pot of marmalade down from the cupboard. It was hidden up on the topmost shelf, and Rosanna looked away with a smile. She'd been notorious for finding the jam and eating it right out of the jar. Granny had kept finding new hiding places, and Rosanna had kept finding new ways to get into them. Even now, when they hadn't lived together for years, it was still up and out of sight.

Granny turned from her toast in time to catch Rosanna's smile, and smiled back at her, a grin of shared affection for that contrary, clever child.

They walked back into the living room, and Granny settled into her favorite chair with a wince.

"Don't you tell me that's just old age," Rosanna said.

"All right, I won't. Just don't ask."

"You're sure I did okay?"

"Rosanna, honest to god, you're such and old auntie! Let me have some breakfast, then you can have a proper gasp and cluck over it all."

Rosanna decided that even fierce women might pick their battles, and concentrated on her coffee. It wasn't anywhere near as good as June's, but it did *smell* rather like coffee, which was always at least half the point in having coffee at all.

Granny finished her toast and licked marmalade from her fingers.

"I suppose you had a much nicer breakfast, then," Granny said.

"Rather, yes. But if you don't ask me about it, I won't have to tell you."

"Lord, how did I ever raise such a mouthy child?"

"The question is probably more how you'd ever manage *not* to raise a mouthy child." Rosanna paused. "Was my mother, too?"

Granny rolled her eyes.

"She was a mistress of mouthy, my Lily. She could have taught graduate courses in the subject by the time she was nine." Granny set her plate and cup beside her chair. "And I'm supposing you still want a look at this shoulder, yes?"

"You're supposing right. Tell me honestly, how much does it hurt?"

"More than a stubbed toe and less than an aneurysm. I think. Never had an aneurysm, but it probably hurts more than a stubbed toe."

"And you say I'm mouthy."

"You are."

"Quit stalling and take your shirt off."

"Lord, I haven't heard that line in a score of years."

"God, Granny, are you *trying* to blind my mental eye?"

Granny unbuttoned her shirt. Even from the front, Rosanna could see a line of deep, purple-black bruises. Granny struggled a little with the shirt, until Rosanna couldn't watch any more, and moved to help. Granny didn't protest, and soon sat topless. She didn't seem terribly self-conscious, but she crossed her arms over her breasts. Granny had never been especially well-padded, but her collar bones stood out sharply, and the skin stretched too tightly over her ribs.

Rosanna set the shirt down, and turned to examine Granny's shoulder. The punctures were no longer hot, but ugly bruises stood out around every one, and spread up the back of Granny's neck beside. Rosanna touched one as lightly as possible, but Granny hissed with the pain of it.

"How can you stand to have your shirt on this?" she asked.

"Well, I didn't want to hang around naked, and I didn't much care for the state of my last shirt" Granny replied. "Besides, I had a bath when I woke up. You do with what you've got, right?"

"I guess, but Gran…these look awful."

"Any blood?"

Rosanna looked closely, and saw that the holes had scabbed over quite firmly, and showed no signs of seeping.

"No, none that I can see." She left her hand on Granny's skin, and *listened.* There was no overt sound of the poison, but there was a subtle discord in the music of Granny's body and spirit. It wasn't so much a sound as a lag, a stumble, where there shouldn't be one.

"Stop it, girl, I can hear myself quite clearly, thank you all the same," Granny said, and pulled away from Rosanna's fingers. "All we need now is some peroxide, I think, just to be sure."

"But..."

"I don't want to hear 'but', all right? I'm a woman grown, and I don't need anybody fussing over me as if I weren't."

"Ow," Rosanna said. There was a thick silence in the room for nearly a minute.

"I'm sorry, my dear, truly. Can we chalk it up to not my best day?"

Rosanna nodded. "I guess we can."

"Are you sure I can't do something else about this? I just...I hate seeing it."

Granny smiled, a pallid and weary excuse for her typical grin.

"You're a soft-hearted wench for someone with such a hard head," she said.

"Now there's the pot and the kettle," Rosanna replied.

"Ah, but which is which, I'm wondering?" Granny smiled again, and this one was closer to the usual standards.

"Does it matter? Anyway, can I? Help, I mean?"

"Just peroxide, girl. Anything else will have to heal itself."

"But why? And it's not just being frugal, because there is something still wrong with you."

"I know there's something wrong, but I don't know what, and I don't know how to find out what."

"Can't I just listen?" Rosanna asked. "That worked with the poison."

"Right enough, but that was clear and obvious. This is…something else."

Rosanna dripped peroxide onto the wounds, and Granny sat still for it, though her face paled, and a muscle jumped in her cheek. The scabs bubbled up, and Granny growled in her throat.

"Lord I hate that stuff," she said, and Rosanna nodded in sympathy.

"Do you think I should put dressings on these? They're closed, but I don't know what'll happen if you get to moving around." Granny sighed in response.

"I suppose you ought to," she said. "I'd hate to start bleeding at an inopportune moment."

Rosanna was as gentle as she could be, and spread a large dressing over the bite. It didn't quite cover the entire thing, but Rosanna didn't think Granny could take much more of her ministrations. She taped it down, and helped Granny back into her shirt.

"So now what?" Rosanna asked.

"That's the question, isn't it," Granny said. "I don't know. Any ideas?"

"Not really, but a few questions."

"Like?"

"Like why would someone attack us to start with, and why would it be Trapper?"

Granny shook her head slowly.

"The only reason I can think of is that someone knows of the Library. But that doesn't make sense, only Lillian and I knew of it."

"And my…" Rosanna hesitated, "sperm donor?"

"Lord Rosanna, I'd completely forgotten about that again." She frowned. "You know, it's an awful lot like my own protections. If I look at it directly, I can't see it at all, and I can only catch a glimpse out of the corner of my eye."

"Maybe we need to unravel that spell, Granny. Maybe it would help us figure out what's going on."

Granny nodded, and dropped her chin into her hand.

"The problem is, girl, I'm plain worn out. I don't know how to unravel it, and I don't think I could anyhow."

"So what do we do? Can you teach me a Word that would do it?"

"It's not likely to be my own Words as set the spell, except..."

"Except what?"

"Except that if they're from Lillian's Library, they'd be accessible to anyone who knows how to get them. I know some of those Words, but not all of them. They've been leaking out of the stones as the Library erodes."

"So you mean someone else could learn them?"

"Learn them, or catch them in a Library of their own, or trap them in their own memory."

"Trap?"

"You know, catch and hold it there. Words caught like that will degrade and lose power, which makes it a very selfish and destructive way of keeping them."

"But trap...as in Trapper? Could he have set the spell?"

"Possibly, but how would he know how to find the Library? Why would he set such a spell on me in any case?"

"Maybe he was a friend of my parents," Rosanna said. There was another thought, a quiet flicker of a thought, that she repressed as soon as she thought it. She waited for Granny to speak the same thought, the same unsettling idea, but she didn't.

"It's possible. Too bad I didn't see him, that might of broken the spell for us altogether."

"Okay, but if a Word from my mother's Library set the spell, could another release it?"

Granny shook her head. "You quit thinking that right this instant, my girl. You are not going out there alone, and I am in no shape to accompany you."

"But if the spell makes you forget, what else does it do? Maybe it's making you stay sick, or maybe it'll make you forget something else important. How can we risk that?"

"Rosanna, please!" Tears welled up in Granny's eyes. "Please don't ask me this, don't ask me to let you risk yourself for me."

"It isn't just for you, Granny. If there's something wrong with you, that makes us a weaker team, and we can't afford that."

"That's a sneaky way to get around me," Granny said with a glare, "playing on *my* weakness. You aren't even trained!"

"You told me I could trust my instincts, didn't you? And my instincts tell me this is important."

Rosanna was surprised at the depth of her own conviction. It didn't come from belief in her own power, or fear of attack, but only from a deep certainty that this thing must be resolved, or there would be terrible consequences. Granny must have seen some of that on her face, for she nodded.

"All right then, all right. But let me teach you just a little before you go," she said.

Rosanna nodded, solemn and eager at once.

"Do you remember the little whirlwind you made the other night?"

"Yes, but I don't know how I did it."

"Think of the Word you took from the keystone, hear it in your thoughts."

Granny's voice receded as Rosanna fell into the syllables of that Word. She could hear, in some fashion, the different elements of it, how it tied together earth and air, fire and water.

"Good," Granny said, watching Rosanna's face. "You hear the elements, yes?"

"Yes," Rosanna said. It was difficult to concentrate on outside sounds and hold the Word in her mind at the same time.

"You can call those elements, use their power, but you must direct them with your will."

"But I didn't, not last night."

"You did it out of instinct, but you can do it consciously, if you choose."

Rosanna thought of the little whirlwind, and the biting ice-crystals within it. She knew the necessary syllables and was about to speak them.

"Not in the house!" Granny said sharply, and Rosanna drew out of her tight concentration with surprise.

"Was I really going to make it happen?"

"Yes, and all over my living room, to boot. Lillian was a disaster on legs when she started Speaking." Granny shook her head at the memory. "So don't! One living room tornado per life is my limit."

"What about the frost Word I found?"

"Don't use it," Granny said, "or only use it in direst need. You need to protect the Words you find until they can be placed within a Library."

"So can I go now? Is that enough?"

"No amount would be enough for this, but yes, go if you have to."

"I do have to. I'm not sure why, but I do."

Granny shook her head.

"I don't like being old, my girl, I don't like it at all. I should be doing and leading…"

"You should be in charge, you mean," Rosanna said, but without rancor. "You've always been good at being in charge."

"I had to be, you know," Granny said. "After Lillian died, there just wasn't anyone else to do the job."

"But you did it a little too well, Granny, " Rosanna said. "I never knew I could even *be* in charge, let alone that I might be good at it."

"But I tried to give you your head, to let you go out on your own, and you ended up filing books."

"And what's so different about this new job?" Rosanna asked. "I'm filing Words, instead. Seems a step down the ladder, promotion-wise." She grinned, and Granny Rosie laughed.

"As you will, then. I hereby demote you to Librarian. Welcome to the select few. You must now acquire quirks, tics, and neuroses to befit your station."

"Can't I just borrow yours?"

They laughed together, and hugged, and danger was outside the circle of their arms, entirely apart from them. There was no perfection in that circle, only a wondrous meeting of imperfections that somehow resulted in comfort, safety, and peace. Rosanna couldn't remember feeling any closer than this to anyone at all, not even Granny herself through all the years of Rosanna's childhood.

And then the moment passed, as all such perfect moments must, and Rosanna pulled away to arms' length. Granny took Rosanna's hands in her own and kissed first one, then the other.

"Go with my blessing, girl, and with all the courage you possess," she said, and Rosanna nodded.

"I don't know the way," she said. "Can you tell me?"

Granny shook her head.

"I've always been lousy at giving directions. Follow our tracks if you can, then use the Word. You'll find a way, I'm sure."

It seemed an enormous task with the single Word she knew, but Rosanna was fierce now, not any ordinary woman at all, and she *would* find a way. She kissed Granny's cheek, got dressed, and stepped out into the snow.

# Chapter 8

It was all very well to assume she'd find a way, Rosanna thought, but a little different to consider exactly *how* she'd find it. She walked to the back of Granny's house, and stood for a moment, reading the signs of her struggle the night before. That part was easy, since she already knew what the scuffs meant, but how would she do in the woods? Sometimes being a city girl had disadvantages.

The tracks leading away from the house were clear enough, but Rosanna hesitated. How could she know they hadn't been tampered with? There were so many what-if's that she couldn't even count them. She shrugged under the weight of her doubts, and stepped out into the snow.

She walked in her own tracks when she could; they stood out as blue hollows, like bruises on the fair white skin of the snow. She found it easier to walk in her own tracks than in Granny's. Not only were

Rosanna's feet bigger, but the length of Granny's stride was awkward for her. It was comforting, though, to see Granny's footprints, as if Granny were walking there with her. She looked over her shoulder at the cabin, missing its warmth already. The cutting breeze out here had an uncanny knack for finding every little chink in her winter clothing.

She thought she made good time, but it was difficult to say. The forest remained an indistinct shadow ahead, and it took all her concentration just to keep walking. Sunlight was a sharp dazzle on the snow, and soon it seemed to bore right through her eyes and into her skull. The pain of it latched onto the headache she already had, and doubled it. Her legs were sore and stiff from all the exercise the day before, and every little ache made itself known in exquisite detail.

She'd been walking with her head down for some time  when the snow suddenly thinned, and was replaced with a carpet of pine needles. She turned and looked behind her, but she could no longer see the cabin, nor even the little line of smoke that marked its chimney. She was relieved to step out of the glare, and the cool shadows of the forest soothed her headache some. Her legs were only a little sore now; her exertions had warmed the muscles and loosened out some of the kinks.

There were tracks in the pine needles, but they were not as clear as in the snow, and Rosanna knew she'd come to the end of her woodcraft, such as it was. She could see where the needles had been disturbed, but the patterns made no sense to her. They could as well have been made by Bigfoot as by she and Granny. Or by Trapper. It was a disquieting thought. On the whole, she decided, she'd rather meet up with Bigfoot than Trapper.

She thought she had a fairly good sense of the direction she needed to take, but under the eaves of the forest, one direction would look just like any other. What to do? What she needed was a nice little path, like Dorothy's Yellow Brick Road.

"Follow, follow, follow," she sang, just under her breath. Why wasn't it ever so easy in real life? She knew she could call a wind, but that would just further confuse the trail, and she knew she could Speak cold, but she was already quite chilled enough, thanks all the same. What did that leave? She thought longingly of the gentle warmth of Lillian's grave, that little oasis of gentler seasons in a desert of snow. Hadn't Granny said that was kept by a Word? Rosanna *listened* and caught, faint among the many sounds of the forest, a whisper of the Word, something that sounded like Granny's voice. It was too far away, though, and too faint, for her to follow with any certainty.

So now what? She needed a path! Or...a guide, perhaps? She didn't know how to summon a beast, or even one of the magic creatures Granny had spoken of, so it would have to be something else. She needed a compass that already knew the way, and that gave her an idea.

As a child, she'd been fascinated with the art of dowsing, had even tried it with considerable success. What if she could dowse for warmth?

Sticks were strewn all over the forest floor, but she wanted her hands free. So what did that leave her? She knew you could dowse with a pendulum, but that wouldn't be much better. Besides, the wind could easily confuse her results. All she really had was her knife. She was becoming accustomed to its weight against her thigh, and she could hear the Word that made it up. There was something of June in it, a sense of practical strength and straight-forward action. That was comfort in itself, as if June, too, stood beside her. She pulled the knife from its sheath, and admired its keen beauty. It was a thing made to conquer danger, and she drew strength from its nature.

This would be her first true act of magic, and her need was too great for failure. Granny counted on her, and wasn't *that* a kick to the head. Everything was turned around and widdershins. Granny needed someone, and Rosanna was exactly the person she needed. That had never happened before, though Rosanna had sometimes daydreamed about it.

She took a deep breath and Spoke the syllables for air and fire, fixing in her mind the need to find warmth. Air would determine the action and fire, the goal. She *heard* the new sounds join with the knife, in a way she hadn't expected. It wasn't simply that she'd laid a spell on something, those Words changed the nature of the knife, made it into a compass. She didn't think she'd be able to take that quality away, not without destroying the thing entirely. She understood a little better why Granny would be reluctant to mess with a spell laid on her very self. If that spell had become a part of Granny's self the way this one had become part of the knife, the act of removing it could destroy Granny. Rosanna didn't know what good she could do, but she did know she had to get to the Library.

Her knife now seemed to have more of a presence, almost a self, and it was impatient. It warmed against her thigh, and tugged. It wasn't much, simply a light pull against the strap that held the sheath to her thigh. Just to be sure, Rosanna turned back towards the warmth of Granny's house surely towards that source of heat. The knife didn't respond until she focused on finding Granny's house, then the knife started to pull in that direction instead. It was good to know that she could find her way back, and equally good to know that her compass wasn't going pick just any old random warm spot. She turned back towards the woods, and concentrated on Lillian's grave. There was a pause while the knife attuned to the new goal, and she felt a spark of irritation from the blade, and it heated up against her leg. It wasn't uncomfortable, but it was disturbingly sentient. What had she made, exactly? The idea that with two spoken sounds she might have created a life was disquieting.

She followed the steady pull of her compass, and walked as quietly as she could through the dense heaps of needles and twigs. It was probably pointless, but if Trapper was looking for her, she didn't feel inclined to make it any easier for him. It was hard to feel oppressed for long, though. The sun glimmered between the pine boughs, and left little scatters of light on the forest floor. She heard no bird-song, but a squirrel chattered somewhere in the distance. The trees creaked and whispered in quiet conversation with the wind that stirred their boughs. Her footfalls were muffled by the needles more than by her own efforts, and the rich perfume of pine rose up around her with every step.

Time slipped away from her, and she didn't mind its departure. She was making the best time she could, and it was pointless to spend effort on worry. She was hungry for the stillness, she found, and it surprised her. She'd always loved her city, its noise and movement, and had never much enjoyed her time in nature. Now though, she found a peace within her that mirrored that of the world around her. Maybe that was the difference, she thought. She'd never really felt peace within, so the city was the perfect reflection of her inner self.

Rosanna shook her head with a half-smile. Soon she'd be out here growing pot with the hippies, and talking about the brotherhood of man.

After some while walking, she saw the glade as a green shimmer against the browns and rusty golds of the forest. The light seemed softer there, and she loosened her jacket in anticipation of warmth. Her knife, too, seemed to anticipate their arrival, and jumped in excited little bumps against her leg. She patted it fondly, then stopped, surprised at the impulse. It truly was a little like a live thing. Not like a person, but like a dog, perhaps, an intelligent one.

Rosanna stepped into the warm circle of grass and dropped her coat with a happy sigh. And then she saw Trapper, kneeling by the stone pool, eyes closed as he breathed in the scent of the lilies. She froze, hoping he hadn't heard her, but he opened his eyes, and smiled at her with frank affection. She was pinned by that smile, just for a heartbeat. There was nothing of malice or danger about him, and he did not rise, but stayed kneeling and vulnerable. She turned to run out of the glade.

"Rosanna," he said, "please wait."

He still made no move to stand, but his eyes pleaded, and he stretched out a hand to her.

"What do you want?" Rosanna asked, after a long moment.

"Just to talk," he said. "Besides," he added, "if you leave without your coat, you'll freeze to death."

"You didn't care so much about me when you called that monster down on me," she said. She'd been a fool to discard the coat, to believe in any kind of safety. She bent to pick it up, not breaking eye contact, but he still didn't move, just sat there with pleading eyes, and an outstretched hand.

"I didn't call it," he said. "I was trying to get rid of it, and it poisoned me."

"You are so full of shit," she said, but his eyes did not shift from hers.

"If I meant you harm, don't you think I'd have done it proper?" he asked, and a crooked little smile quirked his lips.

"I thought you were just country folks, not a Librarian at all," she said.

"Never that," he said. "Never in a million years. They're good folks, but they got it all wrong."

"Got what wrong?" Rosanna shook her head. "Look, never mind. I don't have time to sit and chat. Go away or I'll kill you." She was surprised to find she meant it, and she dropped a hand to her knife.

"Be reasonable, city-Rose. I didn't come to hurt you, nor even to scare you. I came to talk. Won't you just talk? You can make up your own mind then, do what seems best to you, but what would it hurt to talk first?"

His tone was reasonable, and he stayed on the ground. She was out of his reach, even with his arm extended as it was. In her mind she thought of ice and wind. She hated the thought of disturbing this place, but if she needed to, she would.

"I can see you thinking up things to do to me," he said. "Can't say as I blame you, with what you've probably been thinking, let alone what you been told. Can we call truce?" He looked around him, and dropped his hand. "This place has always been precious, can't we keep the peace just for a little?"

She hesitated. It had to be a trick, but he seemed so…earnest. Besides, if he had poisoned Granny to begin with, maybe he would know how to cure her.

"You stay where you are," she said, "and I'll stay where I am. That's the only way I'll talk to you."

"Fair enough," he said, and settled down cross-legged on the grass. "So tell me what's on your mind?"

"You're the one who wants to talk," she said. "so do it."

"But I need to know what you're thinking of me," he said. "That's not so extravagant a request, is it?"

"Look, I heard that sound in you, the sound of the thing that attacked me and Granny. You can quit pretending to cordiality, okay? I know it's not real."

"Me oh, I can see why you'd think about doing me damage," he said. "I'm not pretending to anything."

"Liar," she said. "I don't know why I trusted you at all, but I did."

His blue eyes held hers steadily.

"Not lying," he said. "I was trying to draw the beastie off and it gave me a bit of a bite. I've managed to clear the poison out, now, but I was still working on it then."

"I don't believe you," she said. "If that's so, why didn't you see Granny's house?"

"I don't know who all she's got those walls up against, Rosanna, but could be anyone with a chance of Speaking couldn't see it."

"Granny didn't say anything like that," Rosanna replied, but she hesitated again. The number of things she didn't know so far outnumbered the ones she did that it should have been laughable. Except that it wasn't, except that everything Rosanna loved hung in the balance.

"She didn't say anything different, did she?"

"No, but still…when she was looking for you, she said she couldn't find you."

"Look, if you came up against an electric fence, didn't know how high the voltage was, or if the farmer had a gun…wouldn't you skedaddle?"

"But why wouldn't you wait to explain?"

"*Me* wait?" He laughed. "You hared out of that car so fast I'd have been explaining to the wind." He paused. "Besides, it looked to me like you'd made up your mind about things anyhow. Figgered I might as well give you some time to cool off."

"I still don't believe you. That sound…it wasn't just in you, it was *part* of you."

"'Course it was," he replied. "That's how I broke it down. Took it in, swallowed it up. Not that it weren't a bitter pill." He made a face. "But we've all got different ways to Speak our piece."

"So, very, VERY theoretically," Rosanna said, "what would you be doing out saving us?"

"I stay around here because of the Words," he said. "There's a broken Library up there, and its leaking. Words without a Speaker can be dangerous, so I catch them."

"I can believe that, as far as it goes," she said. "the question is what you do with them after you've found them."

"I didn't make that thing, if that's what you're saying. I'd been hunting it. Used to just be a wolf, poor thing, caught the wrong end of a Word. Turned into…well, you saw well enough, I'm thinking."

"Why didn't you just tell me? And why doesn't Granny know?"

"Your Granny…" he paused for a long moment, closed his eyes, then continued. "She never did much care for me."

"So she knows you?"

"Did, once upon a time. A long, long time, if you want to know the truth." He opened his eyes and looked at her. There was a kind of hunger in his expression, an ache of loneliness that awakened Rosanna's sympathy. "That was back before you were even born, of course, before you were even thought of."

"And how would you know?" Rosanna felt a flicker of premonition, and found that she was trembling.

"Ask me why I'm here," he said, not answering the question. "You're practically dying to ask me, I know."

"I hate games," she said. "and I'm still prepared to kill you." But the words didn't ring true anymore, and they both knew it. This trembling moment couldn't be halted by anything so simple as a death, not even if she wanted to.

"I come here a lot," he said. "It's my wife's grave."

"Liar," Rosanna said. "This is my mother's grave."

"Yes," he said, and his eyes held hers. "It is."

"You can't expect me to believe that," Rosanna said. The very logical part of her was screaming for proof, the slightly less logical was screaming for blood. Under it all, though, under it all, was a thread of doubt.

Thompson shrugged comfortably.

"'Course I don't," he said. "Great gods, what kind of fool would you have to be?"

"So?" she said. "Where does that leave us?"

"Same spot, city-Rose, right here and now. There isn't ever any where or any when else, 'cept in our imaginations."

"Come off it," Rosanna said. "This is where you tell me to search my feelings, right? God save me from cliché."

Thompson chuckled, and Rosanna found herself warming to the sound despite herself. It was not the maniacal laugh of your average villain. It was accessible, friendly, disarming. She didn't want to relax, and scowled at him.

"This isn't funny," she said.

"Sure it is," Thompson said. "It's always wisest to laugh at sorrow, don't you think? Anything else makes it important."

"What the hell do you want from me?" Rosanna said. "Why are you saying this? Are you just saving your skin?"

"Girl, my skin's safe from you no matter what you try," he said. "You're a natural, like Lillian, but you haven't been trained." He paused. "All the better, really. I've got a chance with you before those Librarians close your mind up tight."

"Wait, okay? Just wait!" Rosanna put a hand to her forehead. It ached, and her body ached, and adrenaline was eating up the very last of her energy. "Can you prove this?"

"Well," he drawled, "I don't imagine you've time for a paternity test, though that'd do the trick."

"Will you stop making fun of me?"

"Can't do it," he said. "Wish I could. This...this is how I deal with difficult things, Rosanna. I make them small and entertaining so they can't tear me to bits."

"Then what? How can you prove it?"

"Let me tell you about Lillian," he said.

"I never knew her. You could say anything."

Trapper nodded. "That's true," he said. "though you did know her, a little"

"I still don't remember," she said.

"So what would serve as proof?"

"I don't *know*!" she shouted. "I don't understand why you're even doing this" There was no room in her for this much hurt, no space. She'd dreamed of finding her parents alive and well, and each of those dreams rose up and mocked her.

"Do you think I'd cause either of us this much pain, just for fun?" he asked. His face was gray under the tan, and the lines around his eyes looked more like age than like character. Rosanna paused.

"All right," she said, after a breath or two. "So I'll grant you that. When *did* you decide that I'm your long-lost daughter?"

"Don't sneer," he said. "You don't know how it hurt me to lose you."

"Yeah, well, that's just pretty words until you can provide some kind of proof," she said. It was hard not to *want* to believe him. Not believing came quite easily, but the *want* sat beneath her breastbone and ached.

"You could ask your Granny," he said, and she stepped forward, hand on her knife.

"You bastard," she said. "you know she doesn't remember my father. You know she *can't* remember."

"I'll come with you," he said. "That'll break the spell I set."

"The one that's killing her?" Rosanna shouted. "That spell? I won't take you anywhere *near* her, and I'll kill you if you try,"

He shook his head.

"Honest to god, girl, you're worse than a bear with a toothache. The spell I set was only meant to take me out of her memory, it wouldn't cause any harm. We never much liked each other, but I got a lot of respect for her."

"Something is still wrong," Rosanna said. "Granny is still not well."

"Well, if she got tagged by the same beast I did, I'm not surprised. Nasty work, that one." He reached for his left sleeve, and Rosanna pulled her knife free.

"Simmer down," he said. "I just want to give you some proof, here." He rolled the sleeve up, and there were four dark, ugly bruises set around puncture marks, just like Granny's wound.

"You could have done it to yourself…" she said, but it was a half-hearted response. The marks were distinctive, and had only just closed over.

Trapper grinned and bared his teeth. "Don't have the overbite for it," he said, and chuckled. He looked up at her from under a weathered brow, and his eyes softened.

"Would it be so bad," he said, "to have an ally? Maybe to have a family?"

"But why…if it's true, why wouldn't you keep me?" The *want* inside her turned, and she felt it like a live thing, a small fluttering creature that would not keep still, that would not be silenced by cynicism. She watched Trapper's face as he folded in on his memories. There was an old pain there, and an old shame. But somewhere under it all, she thought, there were still secrets.

"When Lillian died, I wasn't fit for anything. I was injured when the Library blew out, and Lillian's death near killed me. I couldn't have been any kind of father." Tears filled his eyes with silver. "Lillian would never have forgiven me. A bad parent's worse than none."

"I don't know how to believe this," Rosanna said. "I just don't."

"Well, it'd be unfair to expect you to," he said. "At least all at once. But I wanted to tell you."

"Why? And why now?" There had been all those years she'd longed for a family. She'd filled her life with books, made those words her dearest companions. It could have been so different.

"When I got bitten, I nearly died. I wanted you to know, I guess, that you aren't alone. That you got more kin, somewhere in the world."

"Granny's my kin," Rosanna said. "She's been all my family to me all my life. If this is all true…why did you take her memory away?"

Thompson ran a hand through his short hair, then looked up at her again.

"If you're a little more inclined to chat," he said, "do you suppose you could sit down? My neck is starting to ache something fierce."

Rosanna didn't know what to think, or even what questions to ask. The possibility of a parent, a *father* had not crossed her mind in years. She'd put those fantasies away a long time ago, and now, here was this man, asking her to open them up again, asking her to believe what was once her fondest wish. The *want* within her fluttered again, painful and bright and undeniable. She folded down gracelessly onto the grass, each of her aches reasserting itself as she moved.

"Thanks," he said, then paused. "It was a selfish thing I did," he said at last. "I'm ashamed to admit it. But I took her memory of me so she wouldn't come find me."

"But why?"

"Well, first because she blamed me for Lillian's death, and second because I blamed her. I wasn't sure what it would come to if we ever had it out, and I couldn't deprive you of all your family at once." This still seemed an incomplete answer, somehow. The spell was so very thorough. It didn't seem like the actions of a grief-struck man trying to contain his anger. Another secret, Rosanna assumed, and quite sternly told her hope to contain itself.

"But why didn't you keep me? If you blame Granny, why send me to her?" She couldn't help the plaintive note in her voice. Granny was an amazing woman, but Rosanna had stood for so long in her shadow. Balance would have been nice.

"I told you, because I wasn't going to be any kind of parent to a baby girl, and no matter what her faults, Granny was still a good mother." He said it with a shrug, but it seemed to hurt him to admit her suitability as a parent.

"What do you mean, her faults?" Rosanna knew many of Granny's faults intimately, but she didn't care to have anyone else remark upon them. Especially not someone who was practically a stranger.

"Ah, she's a good enough woman, but she's a Librarian, and that twists a soul every which way."

Rosanna frowned at him. "I don't think Granny's soul is twisted, " she said "except by that spell you laid. It's messed her up somehow."

"If that's true, I'll come with you, and we'll break it. But that's not what I meant, really." He looked at her. "I won't be speaking ill of your Granny, so you can settle your feathers. But Librarians think they've got all the answers, all the responsibilities, and it knots them up inside, like it did Lillian."

"I don't know what you mean," Rosanna said. "I don't think Granny's knotted up at all." She couldn't help think of Granny's sternness, though, her unforgiving commitment to Doing The Right Thing. There had never been much room in their life together for compromise.

"No?" he asked, and raised an eyebrow. "Has she told you the whole spiel, about saving the universe by saving the Words?"

"Well, yeah, though I'm not sure I believe all that.".

"Good," he said. "So we're not too late in meeting. It doesn't make sense does it? If everything's made of Words, then it shouldn't matter if a Word is spoken or not, there will always be more."

"But Granny thinks there's a finite number, I guess, or that it takes something out of the world when a Word changes."

"I know she thinks that, it's what lets her believe Words are only the property of Librarians, that anyone else who uses them is a dangerous rogue." He smiled without humor. "And though I may be a rogue, and may be dangerous, I'm disinclined to let any secret society tell me so."

"And what do you believe about the Words?" Rosanna asked. She wanted to sneer, and she wanted to dismiss it all as lies and manipulations. But Granny was no less manipulative, however benignly so. And hadn't Granny said that Rosanna was to make up her own mind? Well, here was a chance.

"I believe they exist to be used, that it is their nature to change. What else makes sense? We have air to breathe, water to drink, and they exist without our saying so. I think the same is true of the Words." He lifted a hand and touched her forehead gently. Even that light brush of fingertips hurt her, and she drew back.

She didn't like this, the feeling that they might share the same disbelief. It felt too much like conspiring against Granny. On the other hand, it was so very good to be able to talk about it with someone else, anyone else. Even someone who might be…she shut the thought down before it finished

"Why wouldn't I mend you if I could?" he asked. "Words give me power to change the world, to make it better." He Spoke, and all the pains in her body melted away, disappeared like a whisper on the wind. She nearly sobbed with the relief of it. She hadn't known she hurt so much until it stopped.

"Granny said it was wasteful," Rosanna said. "She said it was selfish to use the Words up."

"It's selfish to breathe, isn't it?" he said. "Selfish to drink? Whatever you take could be taken by someone or something else. But you still need to do it, don't you?"

"I guess. But she thinks…" Rosanna paused.

"I've heard it all, believe me," Trapper said. "Every syllable, over and over again. And I don't buy it. Every time a baby is born, that child is made up of Words. Think about how many are born! How could there cease to be Words unless there ceases to be life?"

"What if using Words up does mean the end of life?" Rosanna asked.

"I can no more imagine the end of all life than the beginning of it," he replied. "And I seriously doubt that either is in my hands." He shook his head. "In any case, the changing of the Words keeps humans evolving. Vocabulary follows invention, and as long as we're inventing, we're creating words, too. Power is a tool, Rosanna. You can choose to use it, or choose to let it disappear. When they lock those Words in a Library, they close them away from life, from the natural process of change. They hoard a power they decline to use. It's ridiculous."

"I guess that makes sense," Rosanna said, and it did. It skipped mysticism and went right on to logic, where she was always most comfortable. But the fact remained that Granny held her beliefs for very good reasons, whether Rosanna understood them all or not.

"I can see why you and Granny wouldn't get along, then," she said. "But what about...what about my mother? Didn't she fight you on it, too?"

Trapper looked down at the grass, and for a long moment, there was only the quiet murmur of water in the basin.

"We fought about it, yes," he said. "But she was determined, and building that Library meant everything to her. I couldn't change her mind, and she couldn't change mine, so we let it be at that." He shrugged, but there was pain in the set of his features, something like a half-healed scar. "And when she died...well, it was all the proof I needed. If I thought it would help I'd melt the damned thing to glass."

"But it wouldn't?"

"I don't know, and that's the truth. Maybe the Words would go free all at once, and I'd get melted down myself. Maybe the Words would go back to wherever it is they come from. As it is, I do what I can. I try to catch 'em before they do harm, but I don't always manage. Words belong in the minds of people, not loose to wreak havoc." He looked up from the grass to meet her eyes. "It's another reason I have argument with the Librarians. If it's so great to trap the Words in stone, why do they make such damage when they escape?" He shook his head again. "Stupid. Stupid and pointless." He looked down at his hands. "And Lillian died for them, died for those ideas." He reached out a hand and tapped Rosanna's knee. "I want better for you, city-Rose, and you've great potential for it. We could change the world, you and I. Who knows what wonders are locked away in all the Libraries? We could set them free, give magic back to the world."

"Now that's almost as far along the garden path as what Granny thinks," Rosanna said, but the idea was exciting. Maybe magic wasn't failing in spite of the Librarians, but because of them.

"In any case, I suppose I've something to prove to you," he said. "I guess I better give Granny Rosie back her memories, though I guarantee you she's not going to thank me for them."

"You mean it?" she said. "You'll break the spell?"

"On my word as your father, Rosanna," he said. "I'll break the spell."

"Well, if it comes to it," Rosanna said, "I'm still not entirely sure I buy that, either. And if I do, that flirting in June's place was downright icky."

Trapper laughed, and the sound was a perfect accompaniment for the murmur of the fountain.

"Sorry, didn't know it was you," he said. "I ought to have guessed, but I'd forgotten Granny's maiden name. Wasn't till I thought of it after that I remembered. Coulda kicked myself six ways from Sunday over that one, believe me."

"So why did you really come to the café the other night?" she asked.

"I told you, I was tracing the beast. It bit me, and took off. Then I heard you Speak. Gods girl, you say the Words just as your mother did. Fair to stopped my heart, it did, hearing you, and knowing who you must be."

Rosanna nodded. It made sense. She wanted it to make sense, and that was terrifying. Could she trust herself to think when her heart was so ready to leap right in?

"You flirted with me then, too," she said, backing away from the hope. "Quite earnestly, I think."

"I didn't know what else to do," he said. "I didn't want June to know anything was up, and that girl's as quick as she is pretty, which says a mite. And I'd been bitten, and you looked like nine kinds of hell, and it was easiest just to keep up the act."

That made sense, too. This was perhaps the only time in her life that she wished things made less sense. Contradiction though it was, that would be less confusing.

"So what happens when you break the spell?" she asked at last. "I'm assuming you and Granny won't have gotten any fonder of each other."

"Nope, not likely," he said. "But I've learned a lot since those days, and I think I can hold up to her long enough to explain." He shrugged. "Otherwise I'm slag, I guess, and this conversation is pretty much moot." He paused. "If she does reduce me to bits, could you bury them here? I miss my Lillian, I miss her every day."

"We'll have to keep that from happening," Rosanna said. "At least until we can get that paternity test. After that I might let her have you."

Thompson chuckled. "You're so like your mother, girl. All sass all the time."

Rosanna looked around her. She didn't know if she still needed to go to the Library or not. Trapper's spell might be the problem, or it might not. And if it wasn't, maybe he could be an ally, someone to help her find the way.

Trapper got up first, and reached a hand out to her. She hesitated. The sound of the poison in him had stung her so deeply, that she could not even look at his skin without some trepidation. She expected to see the black threads running through his veins, but there was nothing there, just the roughened hands of a man accustomed to work. She took his hand, and *listened* but there was no sound but the Words that made him up, and she found she recognized some of them. She looked up and saw her understanding reflected in his eyes. He pulled her to her feet and into his arms, and hugged her hard. She fought her tears, but they came anyway, and she felt his tears hot on her neck. They stood, not speaking, simply being together. Rosanna remembered Granny's farewell hug, and stepped away, confused. Was this a betrayal? This was the man who had broken Granny's memories, and he was just a stranger.

Trapper seemed to understand, even to expect, her withdrawal.

"Give it time," he said. "Give *me* time, Rosanna. We'll do all right." He cupped her chin with his hand, and smiled at her.

She didn't know what else to say, and there didn't seem to be much point in talking about it any more than they already had.

"We've got time," she said. "I'm not sure Granny does, though, can we head back?"

"Do you know the way?" he asked. "I could track our way back, but it's going to be dark soon, and it'd be quicker if you can just lead."

"I have a compass," she said, and concentrated on finding Granny's cabin. The knife warmed, and gave a little pull back into the woods.

Trapper looked at the knife, and then his eyes got a little vague as he listened.

"Nice work, that," he said. "Granny?"

"Nope, me," she said. She glowed a little with the praise. She bundled herself back up in her coat and mittens and scarf, and stepped out of the glade.

The sun was dropping rapidly behind the mountains, and it set the high cirrus clouds alight with golden and rose fire. Rosanna stopped for a moment, looking up through the trees to admire the sky. Everything was happening so quickly, after so many years of nothing. It was hard to keep up, and she felt a little like she was drowning in it all. But the high, pale, sky was untroubled by her storms, and the peace of it buoyed her. Some things were too big to change, and she decided not to try. It would all be as it would be, whether or not she fought it. She turned and followed her compass back into the woods.

# Chapter 9

As the sun dropped, so did the temperature, and Rosanna was glad for Trapper's healing. She didn't want to linger out here any longer than she had to. Trapper kept pace beside her, and though she was soon puffing with the exertion, he showed no signs of fatigue. She stopped for a breather and looked at him with exasperation.

"Aren't you even a little tired?" she asked. He shrugged.

"I'm just country folks, remember? I spend my days in healthy exercise and my nights…in meditative contemplation."

"Uh-huh," Rosanna said. "I'm sure that's what you'd call it."

He shrugged. "Meditation is where you find it, you know. I've always found walking meditative."

"I thought meditation was about stillness," Rosanna said.

"For a learned person, you don't know much about the practical, do you," he said. It was Rosanna's turn to shrug.

"I've never really seen how meditation is practical," she said. "So I haven't much studied it."

"And how would you know, if you've never studied it?" he asked.

"So you're suggesting it is?"

"I've found it so," he said. "It clears the mind, helps me to focus on what I really want, and ignore all the other stuff."

"And what *do* you want?" Rosanna asked.

"Chiefly," he said, "I want to get in out of the cold sometime before the next ice age. So stop whining and learn, all right?" His tone was teasing, but there was real intent under it all. Thompson could be just as imperious in his own way as Granny could in hers. Rosanna sighed in the privacy of her thoughts. Why did everyone who entered her life seem to think they knew best what to do with it?

"I'm listening," she said.

"No, you're puffing and blowing like an asthmatic badger, but it'll do." Rosanna made a face at him. "That's very attractive," he said, "now you *look* like a badger as well." He paused. "Only this one needs more fiber in his diet."

"Did you want to actually say something, or are you just going to poke fun at me?"

"Can't I do both?"

"Clearly so," she said, and they smiled at each other.

"All right, then, oh impatient one," he said. "Lots of people think of meditation as a sort of break from the events of life, but it works best when it's part of life, instead." He gestured around him.

"All of this, mountains, sky and everything in between, is sacred, so everything we do here has the potential to be sacred, too."

"Whoa, are we skipping into metaphysical-land here?" Rosanna asked. "Because I don't think I brought any incense."

"Darlin', physical and metaphysical both contain the physical, right?"

"The words do, yes."

"Well then, the physical has a connection with the meta, right?"

"I guess so, though the etymology…"

"Stop being a scientist, and listen to the metaphor," he said. "Yeesh, I'm trying to keep it simple, and you insist on making it *not.*"

"Okay, okay," she said. "So physical is connected to the more than physical, got it."

"Right," he said. "So it's possible to be meditative in all you do, if you get the knack."

"But what's the point? If it's just my body, why would it matter if my meta-whatever is involved or not?"

He raised a finger and tapped the end of her nose.

"It makes the difference between doing and struggling," he said. "When I walk mindfully, I'm not fighting the world around me, and not arguing with my body. My truest destination is always right here, so I don't have to struggle to get to anywhere else."

"Sounds absurd," Rosanna said.

"I suppose it does," he said. "But you just try it. Don't focus so much on where you're getting to, just on each step as you take it. That way, you spend all your energy and concentration on here and now, where you need it."

"I suppose it's worth a try," Rosanna said. It still sounded pretty hippy-dippy to her, but he didn't look the least tired or out of breath, and he'd had a near-mortal wound less than twenty-four hours previous. A thought struck her.

"You're not cheating, are you?" she said. "Do you have some kind of magic going?"

He chuckled. "I never fight fair if I can avoid it," he said, "but I don't spend energy on something like that. My body can do it if my will directs it

Granny had said something similar, though the two of them seemed to come to the same conclusion from completely different directions. Perhaps that spoke for the conclusion's validity.

"So how do I do it?" she asked.

"It's no more complicated than I said," Trapper replied. "It's all a matter of focus. Pay attention to here and now. Don't fight thoughts of the future, just let them drift, and bring your attention back to what you're doing."

They started moving again, and Rosanna tried to follow his instructions, but she kept thinking of Granny, and then of Trapper, and then of a million other things. After a little while she stopped in her tracks with a growl of frustration.

"I can't do it," she said.

"I bet you're trying really hard," Trapper said. "I bet you're doing your utter best."

"Of course, I always do."

"Well, stop it. This isn't about striving, it's about acknowledging what already is. Some part of you already walks in meditation, because you walk without thinking about walking. So just think about walking for a while. Stop trying so bloody hard, you get in your own way."

They started out again, and Rosanna focused on her footing, feeling the shape of the ground underneath the pine needles. When the pull of her compass drew her attention, she focused on the movement of her muscles under the sheath. When her fingers got cold, she paid attention to the swing of her hands as she walked. It was restful to let the future be the future, and to hang in the moment of a single step.

By the time they reached the edge of the forest, Rosanna felt relaxed and alert. Thompson turned to her and smiled.

"Well done," he said. "We'll make a proper woods woman of you yet."

"You know," she said, surprised at the words even as she said them, "I think I'd like that. I never understood the whole fresh air and exercise bit, but this…I could get to like this a lot."

"Makes a world of difference, doesn't it, and it's all in how you look at a thing."

She nodded, looked at him, and turned the word 'father' over in her thoughts. How much would it change if she looked at him in that way? Not just an interesting and helpful companion, but a connection, and perhaps an obligation.

"I'm not sure how much farther it is," she said. "I'm not good at distances."

Trapper shrugged. "To tell the truth, I'm not all that anxious to get there," he said. He raised a hand before Rosanna could protest. "I know, I've got to see her, but Granny Rosie…well, she's a woman of immoderate temper." He smiled, and Rosanna realized how dark it had become. The moon was peeking up behind the mountain peaks, turning the sky a velvet silver, and the starlight shimmered on the snow; diamonds reflected in a perfectly still pool.

Her knife pulled impatiently against her thigh. It never seemed content while she stood still. She was surprised to find that she, too, was reluctant for Granny and Thompson to meet. That might mean choosing, and how do you choose? What would she be choosing? The past over the future? All the same, her body cooled quickly in the still night air, and beautiful as the moon and stars were, they granted no warmth.

She sighed and turned towards Granny's house, walking in her own footsteps again. It seemed impossible that these could still be the same footprints, softened though they'd been by the winds. Too much had happened for these to still have been made by her own feet, and her quiet little life seemed farther away than the moon.

Trapper walked beside her, but not in Granny's tracks. He was taller than her, and had to moderate his stride a little, but she thought they were still making good time. It was easier to slip into her meditation on motion, this time, mostly because she really didn't care to think over much about their destination, and what it might mean. She felt the snow crunch under her feet, and even had some sense of the ground underneath it. Her breath was regular and even, and though she was getting tired, it was a pleasant fatigue, a slow and warm reminder that her body was working as it ought.

She lost track of time once more, but soon she saw the twinkle of the lights in Granny's window. She paused for a moment.

"Can you see it?" she asked.

Thompson shook his head. "What should I be seeing?"

"I can just see the lights," she said, "but I don't think we're far. And it's mostly downhill from here."

"I don't know whether to be grateful or not," he said. "It's getting a wee bit nippy out, to be sure, but I doubt my reception is going to be any warmer."

Rosanna didn't know what to say to that, since it was true. Thompson patted her shoulder.

"Don't you worry, Rose my lass," he said. "Things will work out as they must, and you've no part in what happens between she and I."

"No part? How can you possibly figure that?"

"This story has been on hold for a whole lot of years," he said, "waiting for the last paragraph. It was written when you were only a baby, and though it affects you, it doesn't need to include you."

"Well, I'm kind of right here in the middle of it," Rosanna said. How could he imagine it didn't include her?

"Not a comfortable place, I imagine," he said, and Rosanna nearly laughed at the understatement. It was like saying Everest was high. All the same, it couldn't be put off forever, so she started to move again. She couldn't recapture her walking trance this time, and the snow seemed to pull at her feet, to drag her down and back.

"Ow!" Trapper said, and stopped abruptly.

Rosanna had started at his exclamation, and turned to look at him. A faint glow surrounded him, flickering like a miniature Borealis.

"What's that?" she asked.

"Granny's protections, I expect," he said. "I'm thinking she's upgraded the electric fence a little, I didn't get near this sting when I drove you home."

"I don't feel anything," she said.

"That'd be because her wards recognize you," he replied. "They're not especially fond of me, though. Not much of a welcome mat."

"So what do we do? I can go bring Granny out, I guess."

"How? She'll forget me the instant you mention me. No, best thing's probably if you share your recognition."

"What do you mean?"

"Well, if you declare me your companion, the wards will recognize me as yours, like your clothes, or your knife."

"What, I need to sign an affidavit?"

"Nothing so complicated," he said, and she could hear the smile in his voice. "You've just got to be touching me, and not be scared of me."

"Alrighty, then" she said. He took off his glove, and she looked at him curiously.

"Skin contact's best," he explained. She took off her own glove, and he clasped her hand. His hand was warm and calloused, and engulfed hers.

She stepped across the imaginary electric fence, and brought Trapper with her. She felt a tingle, just a hint of what he'd experienced, and a feeling of scrutiny, as if she were being carefully measured. She took another step forward, still holding Trapper's hand, and the tingle disappeared, as if the watcher were satisfied with what it had seen.

"Phew," Trapper said. "It almost wasn't enough. That wasn't just electric, it was barbed and possibly poisoned to boot."

"I guess that monster thing spooked her near as much as it did me. And if she's feeling weaker, it makes sense to protect her home. Better to avoid a fight than lose one."

"Well, she's nothing to worry about from me," he said, but Rosanna wasn't completely sure of that. The protections had been very...interested in Trapper, and he was a man capable of secrets, however open he wanted to appear.

The last stretch to the house seemed longer than the entire walk before. Rosanna knew it was just apprehension that weighed her down, but it felt like she was carrying a ton of it. It was one thing to tell Trapper he could come home with her, and another to have brought him through the fence, and right up to Granny's door. This wasn't a betrayal, was it? She looked sidelong at Thompson, but his head was down, and a frown creased his forehead. He looked old and tired, and those weren't words she'd expect to have to apply to him. She stopped a few steps from the door, and he paused, too.

"Maybe I should go first," she said. "Kind of...warn her, I guess."

"Of what? That someone she doesn't remember knowing is right outside? Sounds like a new game show, come to think of it."

Rosanna chuckled. "Come on down, you're the next contestant on Meet Your Life!"

"Meet your in-laws, more like," Thompson said, and sighed. "I don't know that anything you do is going to soften this one, city-Rose, but if you think it's worth a try, by all means, go ahead."

"I don't know that it'll accomplish anything either," Rosanna admitted. "I just can't quite imagine walking up to the door with you." She paused. "Is that okay?"

"Hell, girl, I'm half ready to hare it out of here. I'd be more than happy for a few breaths of respite."

Rosanna knew that feeling well. Granny didn't often get truly furious, but when she did, whole mountain ranges would collapse just to get out of her way. No matter what Thompson said, Rosanna knew that somehow, she'd end up in the middle, and Granny wasn't one to allow neutrality. You were with her, or against her, no middle ground.

She walked up onto the porch, took a deep breath, and knocked. Then she opened the door, and stepped gratefully into the light and warmth of Granny's kitchen. She closed the door again with a sigh of relief. Just for this second she could pretend nothing was different, nothing was wrong. She was simply Rosanna coming home to Granny's. It sounded like a fairy tale, and she desperately hoped that Trapper wasn't the big bad wolf.

"Hello?" she said. It was unusual for Granny not to have come to the door. She walked through the kitchen, not pausing to take her boots off. Granny could give her hell later, but she wanted to be able to get outside without any kind of delay. She took off her gloves and put them in a pocket, then unzipped her coat. She left the coat on, remembering how vulnerable she'd been in the glade when she took it off. Winter was as implacable a foe as any monster called by magic, and it wouldn't do her much good to survive the monster, and be killed by the cold.

She walked into the living room, tracking snow across the linoleum, and then onto the wooden floors. She winced a little, looking at her trail, thought about getting a cloth, and dismissed the thought as absurd. There would either be time for it later, or it wouldn't matter at all.

Granny was asleep in her chair, a blanket tucked up around her chin. She looked old, too, and Rosanna hated to see it. Granny's skin was drawn tight against her cheekbones, and her eyes were deep in shadow. Granny's hand, where it clutched the blanket, looked desiccated, like that of a mummy. Rosanna paused, terrified for a second, and then saw Granny's breath raise the blanket. Rosanna laid her hand on Granny's cheek, and Granny opened her eyes.

"Heavens girl, you back already?" she said. "Must have dozed off there for a bit."

"Probably did you some good," Rosanna said, but Granny caught her tone.

"Not looking so hot, am I?"

"Ah, give it up, Granny. You're the hottest octogenarian I know."

"That'll be septo, thank you all the same."

"You're cranky enough for octo," Rosanna said.

"Practice, that's all it is. And raising a teenager. That'd age anyone."

"Ha, ha," Rosanna said. "Like you didn't age me at all."

Granny sat up, and let the blanket slide down to her lap.

"So," she said, "what did you find?"

Rosanna didn't know how to answer that one.

"Well," she said at last, "I didn't make it all the way to the Library, but I'm hoping what I've found will set you to rights."

Granny sighed, and Rosanna was appalled to see tears in her eyes.

"Girl, I know you've good intentions, but there isn't anything short of magic that'll save me. What happened? I know it's a long way, I know it's too much to ask, but I'd hoped…"

"It's not like that, Gran," Rosanna said. "I found someone in the woods that might be able to help."

"The only one who has even a chance is the one who set the damned spell, and I doubt you found that one lounging about under a tree." She shook her head. "This isn't a fairy-tale, Rosanna, and the cure doesn't magically come to you. It's got to be *sought.*"

Rosanna felt anger creep up her neck and vibrate in the back of her head.

"You are so good at knowing everything, aren't you," she said. "It's your turn to listen for a change, all right? I wouldn't have come back for no reason, and I didn't just give up."

Granny's face settled into lines of impatience and disappointment.

"But you're here, aren't you. And you haven't even been to the Library. What help is that supposed to be to me?"

"I told you, I brought the man who set the spell."

"And who's that, pray tell? Some random stranger you met in the woods can cure what ails me?"

"God, I just want to shake you!" Rosanna shouted. "Would you just listen? For once in your whole damn life, would you *listen?*"

Granny shut her mouth with a snap, and her eyes glittered as she looked up at Rosanna. For what felt like the first time ever, Rosanna had Granny's complete attention, and it wasn't pleasant. She could hear the whispers of unspoken Words, just under the surface of the silence, and she paused to take a deep breath. And to take hold of her temper.

"All right," she said. "I found my...sperm donor." She hated the words, especially now that she could connect them to a face. "Or rather, he found me. He's agreed to remove the spell, in fact he says that seeing him should break it."

Granny looked skeptical, but the diamond-sharp fury in her eyes blunted a little.

"He found you? And you believe him?"

"He's been here all along, Granny. He's the one who brought me home."

"The one you said was the enemy?" Granny's anger whetted its edge again. "You mean you trust him now?"

"I…well, yes, mostly," Rosanna said. She wanted to be able to be certain, but she couldn't. There were still too many secrets, and too many unanswered questions.

"Mostly," Granny said, and her voice would have flayed the skin off any lesser mortal. But Rosanna knew, at least for this moment, that she truly was fierce, and she stood up to the verbal blow.

"Yes, mostly. Like I trust you," she said. Granny's mouth opened, but no sound came out. "I know he's got his own agenda and beliefs, and I know you do, too. I know he has a purpose he wants to use me for, and so do you. So isn't that enough of a starting place? At least you two already have those things in common."

"Do you think so little of me?" Granny asked.

"No," Rosanna said. "I think the world of you. I just don't trust you to run my life for me, okay? It's got to be my own job."

"And where does that leave us, exactly?"

"It leaves us here and now," Rosanna said. "If this has a chance of helping, we've got to try. If it works out, great, if it doesn't, I'll go to the Library."

Granny was silent for a long moment, and Rosanna heard only the tick and crackle of the fire. Then Granny heaved a sigh and nodded.

"I guess…I guess I owe you that, girl. I said you've got good instincts, and it's true." She paused, then gathered herself up, and put the steel back in her voice. "But you are not ever to speak to me in that tone again."

"Granny, I love you, but you're such a bitch!" Rosanna said. "I'm going to talk to you in whatever tone it takes to make you listen!"

Granny's jaw dropped, and then she laughed.

"We're a right pair of bitches then, aren't we?" she said. Rosanna laughed too, as much out of surprise as anything. Nothing was really okay, but their shared laughter let her believe that it all *could* be okay.

"So," she said. "Do you want to bundle up and come outside, or shall I bring the visitor in?"

Granny frowned. "Probably best I come out," she said, "though I'm not too keen on freezing my wrinkled old butt off. I've got protections inside the house, should we need them." She stopped and raised an eyebrow. "Which begs the question, how did your...friend get past my outer defenses?"

"I um helped him" Rosanna said, and steeled herself against the tirade to come. To her surprise, Granny only shrugged.

"In for a penny, and all that," she said. "It's a little late to worry about it now.

Rosanna waited while Granny bundled herself into suitable clothing, sweating in the warmth of the cabin. She didn't want to bother undressing just to dress again, but it was uncomfortable. She hoped Trapper was still there, but she didn't want to look for him. It was silly, but she felt as if as long as she didn't look, he might still be there.

When Granny was finally ready, Rosanna took a deep breath. Now came the tricky part.

"Gran," she said. "you ought to know that you and...this person, didn't part on the best of terms."

Granny Rosie snorted. "I rather guessed that from the spell, girl. Friends don't do that kind of thing to each other."

Rosanna nodded. "I just...I want you to remember that, okay? And it's been a long time, so maybe you want to...I dunno, hold back on your first impulse."

"That bad, eh?"

"Yeah, probably," Rosanna said.

"You're sure I ought to meet this person, then? Even with all that considered?"

"I think it's the only way to take that spell off, Gran, and maybe...well maybe then you'll heal properly."

"It's only a maybe, girl," Granny said softly. "No guarantees. Like I said, I'm old, and sometimes...well, sometimes it's just time to stop."

"Don't you even talk about that, I wouldn't be anything without you."

Granny shook her head. "T'isn't true, my girl, and I think you know it. You've a will and a power all your own. Not that I mean to die, mind, but if I do, you'll go on. I trust you to."

Rosanna closed her mouth on all the other words that wanted to come out. This wasn't the time, for one, not with Trapper just on the other side of the door. For another, they were pretty much out of useful things to say on the subject. It was true that Rosanna would go on regardless, and true that she finally felt her own worth, and beyond that, everything else was details.

"Ready then?" she said.

"No," Granny said, "but what the hell, let's live dangerous." Rosanna grinned at her, then turned and opened the door.

For a moment, she couldn't see Trapper at all as her eyes adjusted to the lower level of light, and she was afraid he really had bolted. But then she saw him, a dark shadow against the snow, just outside the reach of the windows' glow.

"Trapper?" she said. "Why are you way out there?"

"Safety," he replied, "just in case someone gets in an incinerating sort of mood."

Granny stepped out onto the porch.

"Who're you talking to, girl? Your friend? You know it's not polite to whisper."

"I'm not whispering," Rosanna said. "Can't you hear him?"

"She can't," Trapper said, "I was very thorough. Maybe too much, but your Granny can be right frightening when she wants."

"Come on," Rosanna said. "He's right over here." She stepped down onto the snow, still scuffed from her fight with the beast. Time had all gone strange, she no longer knew how long ago that had been. It might have been last night, or a century ago, it had all blurred into a montage of fear and running and confusion.

Granny followed Rosanna, but her footfalls were tentative, and she nearly stumbled.

"Watch your step," Rosanna said, and reached out a hand to Granny's shoulder.

"Watch your own," Granny said. "I think I'm old enough to stand on my own." Rosanna drew her hand back, but watched Granny sway a little where she stood.

"Well," Granny Rosie said, "whoever you are, come make yourself known. I've come as far as I'm likely to without sureties of safety."

Trapper walked slowly towards the light, and when the first glimmer of it lit his face, Granny drew in her breath sharply.

Rosanna first *heard* the spell unwind from around Granny's soul, and then the shouted syllable that sent a ball of seething blue fire at Trapper's head.

He dropped and rolled, and the spell passed over him to land in the snow a good distance behind him. There was a hiss, and a cloud of steam, and then a brief flare of light as the fire lit the grass underneath.

"Gran, stop it!" Rosanna shouted, but Granny Rosie had spoken another Word already, and that one hit its mark. It wrapped Trapper in a tight cocoon of lightning. He opened his mouth to speak, and the net tightened. He screamed hoarsely, and the net loosened again.

"Stop it?" Granny said. "Stop it? Do you know who this bastard it? I haven't even started yet!"

"I know he's my father!" Rosanna said. "I know that!"

"That's not all, Rosanna. He's a murderer." With a whisper, Granny tightened the net again, and Trapper screamed. His eyes were wide with pain, but the set of his mouth was determined and fierce.

"I don't care," Rosanna said. "You can't just torture him like that!"

"I can and I will!" Granny said. "And you should be the first to help me. He killed Lily! He killed your mother!"

Rosanna felt like all the air around her had been whisked away, and she struggled for breath in the vacuum. She looked into Trapper's eyes, but saw nothing there but the pain.

"I don't believe that," Rosanna said.

"He was the only other one that knew where the Library was!" Granny said. "He didn't approve of Lily's work, so he introduced the flaw! And bespelled me so I wouldn't remember it!" She yanked the net tight again, and Thompson's scream was a hoarse croak.

"Granny, stop it!" Rosanna shouted. "How do you know? At least let him defend himself!"

"Defend himself? What kind of idiot are you? He's a murderous bastard!"

"And my father!" Rosanna saw Granny weakening. Holding Trapper was taking more energy than she could afford, and she was standing only by the strength of her will.

Rosanna ran to Trapper, and thrust her hand into the tracery of power. It slammed through her like lightning, and without thinking, she Spoke a syllable of earth. The force grounded into her body and out through her feet. A wide circle of snow around her melted away in an instant, and she fell against Trapper's chest. Granny collapsed with an incoherent shout of helpless rage.

"Thanks," Thompson murmured. "Don't think I coulda gotten out of that one on my own."

Rosanna pulled back.

"Don't thank me," she said. "You've got answers I need, that's all." She couldn't quite imagine him as the murderer Granny claimed, but Granny hadn't seemed to have a doubt. Rosanna had never seen Granny violent, not once in the whole of their lives together. Rosanna pushed away from Trapper gracelessly.

She wondered if there would ever come a time that she wouldn't feel this exhausted. She could only dimly recall what it had felt like to be rested. Adrenaline had its uses, she knew, but she was tired of running on it. Her hand still tingled from Granny's lightning web, and the soles of her feet felt scorched. She wanted to run to Granny's side, to explain or apologize, or something, but she didn't know what to say, and she didn't believe she was able to run just now.

Granny's spell-casting had melted the snow around her, too, and the brown grass beneath was damp and warm, though the cold had already started to turn the moisture to ice. Rosanna knelt beside her, thinking that this was becoming too frequent an event. Granny opened her eyes, and looked up into Rosanna's face.

"Why did you stop me?" she asked. "I could do it in the heat of the moment, but not now." She shook her head. "Not in the cold." Granny started to shake, and to weep, and Rosanna wrapped her arms around her, surprised to find that she was crying, too. There had been too many heated moments, and too many cold ones, in the last few days. She was beyond her ability to adapt any more.

After a long while, Granny quieted, and struggled to sit up.

"Well," she said. "What now?" She looked around, and saw Trapper still standing where Rosanna had left him. Her eyes narrowed, but she made no motion to attack him again. Rosanna could *hear* all the Words just below Granny's skin, the ones that she desperately wanted to Speak, but Granny did nothing more than want to Speak them.

"So what is it you want?" she said, struggling to her feet. Rosanna helped support her, and took the opportunity to *listen* to Granny's state of being. The spell was gone, but there was still something slightly out of kilter, and Granny was still not entirely healed. Granny turned to scowl at her.

"Stop that," she said, "it's rude."

"I just wanted to know…"

"What, whether this monster was responsible for killing another of your relatives?"

"No, whether you were any better."

Trapper laughed, low but cheerful.

"Better? That old bird can only get worse. Tougher and meaner." He shook his head.

"This isn't helping," Rosanna said, but he just kept chuckling to himself. Rosanna could hear the Words Granny didn't say, could hear them like a shout.

"You need to step away now," he said. "Granny Rosie and I have a few things to sort out."

"I don't think that's going to happen," Rosanna said. "I think you should go away now. Maybe we'll have something to talk about when everyone has cooled down a bit."

"Oh, city Rose, I'm cooler than glaciers, cooler than the coolest cat that ever strolled the woods." The sound of poison lifted up in malevolent chorus from somewhere within his being.

"But I have you both now, and I know you both now, and I think we should all take a walk up the hill there."

Rosanna shook her head. That sound was like a rape of the very air around her.

"Oh, I don't think we'll be going anywhere," she said.

"Don't be foolish," he replied, "really, just don't. Without Granny, you have no protection at all. You led me through the strongest of her wards yourself. And you kindly rescued me from the best of her offense as well. Be a good girl, now, come here."

There was command behind the word, but Granny spoke another syllable and he staggered a little as his will rebounded off of hers. His smile slipped, and Rosanna was glad to see it go. It was the most terrible lie of all, she thought, that expression of open geniality.

"Aren't you tired of being alive?" he asked Granny. "I know you weary me something fierce."

He Spoke, and a dart of ice whipped out, driven by his will. Rosanna pushed Granny aside, and felt the cold sear past her cheek.

She cried out and Granny grabbed her arm and pulled her up onto the porch. Trapper sent another blade, but this one bounced off the invisible wall of Granny's shield.

She caught sight of his face again as Granny fumbled with the door. He was smiling, and the virulent song of poison twined around him like a welcome pet.

# Chapter 10

The two women stumbled through the door, and Rosanna heard Granny strengthening the wards on the door. From a great distance she noted all the elements in that spell, and she filed the information in her memory. There was a space between her and everything else; best of all between her and Trapper. Her father, the murderer. She might have laughed, were there any laughter left in her. So much for childhood dreams, then. That one had never entered her mind. It was pleasant to stand in the blurry embrace of shock, where nothing was sharp enough to hurt her, and the flow of blood down her cheek was little more than an interesting heat.

Granny grabbed a towel and pressed it to Rosanna's cheek, then pulled her into a fierce hug.

"Oh girl, oh my girl, I'm so sorry," she said. "I need time to tell you, and there isn't any." She shook her head. "He's capable of anything, I think."

Rosanna nodded. "What do we do?" She wanted to care, but couldn't. It was only Granny's urgency that led her to respond at all.

"He's inside my best protections, but I can shield the house, I think, at least for a while. I'm so tired, my dear, so very tired."

"I'm sorry, you know," Rosanna said. "I brought him here, and I'm sorry."

"Don't be stupid, girl, how were you to know? You did your best, that's what matters."

"I bet my mother did her best," Rosanna said. "And she's dead. Me too, I guess. It must be a family thing."

"Stop it," Granny said. "We're not going to die here. Lillian didn't believe him capable of murder, but we know better. That gives us an edge."

Rosanna laughed, but the sound was too bitter, too close to emotion. She cut it off and tried to retreat back into numbness.

"It does," Granny said. "So let's use it." She pulled the towel away from Rosanna's cheek. "Not deep,' she said, "but messy. It'll need stitches when we have a moment."

Rosanna put a hand up to her forehead.

"He healed this,' she said. "I guess it's a fair trade."

"Nothing fair about it, my dear, but we're not going to give him another chance." She looked out the window, and shook her head. "He's still just sitting there," she said. "Maybe he'll forget to get up."

"I can't kill him, you know," Rosanna said, and Granny turned with a glint in her eye.

"Don't you worry about that," she said. "I can do what's necessary."

"Then why don't you just go out there and do it?" Rosanna asked. "Haven't you got a gun?"

Granny shook her head. "Never needed one. And I wouldn't count on him sitting still to be shot. He may well be crazy, but he's the cunningest bastard I ever knew." She shook her head again. "Fooled us all for a while, and Lillian never could believe the worst of him." Granny sighed. "But that's long gone and ago now, and you are not going the way of your mother."

"No," Rosanna said, "I guess not. I guess I can't let that happen." In her mind she built a little space for her confusion and pain, and put them there. She knew she'd have to reckon with them eventually, but not now.

The world came into sharp focus, and Rosanna saw how gray Granny's face was, and how badly her hands shook.

"Granny?" she said. "Are you okay?"

"I'd like to lie, but that's not going to do you any favours," Granny said. She smiled, but it was a weak and lopsided version of her usual grin. "I'm tired. It wasn't the amnesia spell," she said. "I'm just old, girl, worn-out like a mother-in-law's welcome."

"I wouldn't know," Rosanna said. "I've never had a mother-in-law."

"Well, I've been one, and that son-in-law has worn my welcome out, sure enough."

Rosanna turned to the window, and saw Trapper standing now instead of kneeling. He was a terrible shadow, somehow, a darkness greater than the night could create alone.

"Rosanna!" he shouted, and both women started. The sound wasn't just outside; it was all around them, as if the words had been bellowed by the walls and floor of the cabin. "This can stop now," he said. "Come out to me, and we can leave your grandmother in peace. You're all I want."

Rosanna shook her head. Never. She spoke no Words, but let her negation chase the echoes of his voice out of Granny's home. Silence returned, heavy and deep as fog.

"Can I open the door? Without messing up protections, I mean?" Granny nodded, and Rosanna opened the door. She felt the shielding in front of her, as if she stood in front of a screen door.

"Go away," she said. "Go away and never come back. That's all *I* want."

He shook his head.

"Can't do it, city-Rose, can't risk it." He paused. "It's a shame, though. You showed such promise."

For a moment she regretted speaking about the Library, regretted any intimation that she might act against his will. Perhaps she could have lulled him into carelessness, and avoided this. But something in her rebelled against the deception, and she knew she couldn't have done it, any more than she could kill him. He had to be the only villain in this scene. Anything else would blur the lines between them, and she couldn't bear that.

"Please," she said. "If you ever loved my mother, please don't do this to me. Don't make me fight you. We only just met."

"All it takes is your promise, Rosanna. Promise me the Words, and promise me your loyalty, and we can leave here without a tussle." His voice darkened. "You don't want to cross me, and I don't want to kill you."

"Did you want to kill my mother?" she asked, and regretted that, too.

"No, but I did. And I can kill you, kill that cowering Rosie behind you. You can save her, Rosanna. Come with me."

Granny shouldered Rosanna aside.

"Get away from my door, you animal, or I'll put you down where you stand."

"You want an animal?" he asked, and laughed. Rosanna shivered. The sound of that laugh scraped across her skin and left her raw.

He lifted his head and howled to the sky, and she recognized the cry. It was the vile scream of the poisoned wolf. Rosanna *heard* him speak the Word, and knew for certain that this Word hadn't mutated on its own. He had taken a Word, something pure and lovely, and warped it to suit his desires. She thought of her own captured Word, that frail and perfect description of frost, and felt sick. How could he do it?

There was no time for philosophical considerations. The thing took shape as she watched, each thread of its being called to this place by Trapper's will.

"You don't have to do this," she said. "You could just stop. You're powerful, aren't you? Isn't that enough?" She heard the pleading in her tone, and hated it. She wanted to be wild and fierce. She dropped her hand to her knife hilt, but there was no comfort in it. She didn't know enough about fierce to hold it in her heart.

Thompson's howl stopped, and the creature arrived, whole and desperately malign.

'

"Yes," he said. "I'm strong." He gestured to the animal. "I can do amazing things. But it isn't enough. I want those Words, and they want me. I can't stop, you see? I've been wanting them so long it's like an itch in my brain." He smiled, a bitter twist of a smile that had nothing to do with humor.

"Besides," he said, "your Granny wouldn't let me live another day anyway."

Rosanna knew it for true, and found another thing to regret. No one of them could afford to walk away. She stifled a sob.

The creature's head turned, and its eyes lit on her. It took a step.

"Last chance, city-Rose," Trapper said. "I could let you go, back to your city, back to your books. Wouldn't that be easier? What do you care about a Library anyway?"

"You should go," Granny murmured. "Leave this to me. I never knew I'd bring this trouble to you."

"Don't be ridiculous. It's our trouble now, whatever he says. You can't honestly think he'd let me go? He just thinks it'll be easier to pick us off one at a time."

Granny nodded wearily.

"I hate it when you're right," she said. "That's my job, not yours."

Rosanna wanted to laugh, tried to, even, but the monster Trapper had called was stepping towards them again.

"I'll stay, thanks. I like it here." It was the bravest thing she could think to say, and it wasn't even decent repartee.

Trapper said nothing more, but turned his will on Granny's protections. Rosanna felt the clash of the Words, and understood that this was a contest of resolve as much as of magic. She felt the wards around them shudder, but they held. Granny's face paled, and she clutched at Rosanna's shoulder as if she might faint. Rosanna held up under the pressure, willing her strength into Granny. She felt Granny's hand grow cold, and whispered a Word of warmth. Granny looked at her in surprise, as if she'd forgotten that Rosanna was really there. Rosanna met her eyes.

"Let me help," she said. "Tell me what you need."

"I'll hold," Granny said, with gasping little hitches in her voice. "You attack. Distract him."

Rosanna thought of her meager stash of Words. She knew that complicated things could be done with simple building blocks, but she had no time to consider. She thought of her little frost Word, and discarded the idea. She would not sully it by use, not as Trapper had done. Instead, she thought of ice and wind, and flung the Words at him. A tornado of ice crystals leapt up around him, and his voice stumbled for a moment. The ruined wolf paused, and turned to look at him, and Rosanna understood that it was as much a danger to Trapper as to her and Granny. Perhaps he'd gotten bitten learning the same lesson.

Thompson pulled up a curtain of fire, and it swept Rosanna's snow spell away. She felt the power rebound with a snap and a sting of cold. She shuddered with it, and Granny squeezed her shoulder.

"Not too hard, girl, not too heavy. If he breaks a big one, it could kill you just as easy as he himself."

'What if he breaks your wards?"

"I can ground some of it out," she said, but there was doubt in her voice, and Rosanna recognized a half-truth. She had to find a way to stop him before he broke Granny's protections.

His voice strengthened, and Granny staggered under the force of his renewed attack. Rosanna watched the wolf turn again and step towards them. It seemed to her that it was reluctant, and she wondered how much of its true nature remained. Wolves don't hunt humans, not if they can avoid it. She listened, straining out all the outside sounds she could, and caught the sound of it once again. It was true that the Word had been broken to this new use, but underneath that was still the sound of the wolf, and also the power that rode it.

Granny groaned, and Rosanna felt the shields around them flutter. The whole house shivered, and the windows rattled.

"Granny," she said, and Granny Rosie looked at her with eyes nearly blinded by pain and effort. "Granny, trust me," she said. Granny responded to the intensity as much as to the words. "Always," she said.

Rosanna stepped through the door and outside of Granny's wards. Granny cried out in protest and Rosanna shouted over her shoulder.

"Trust me!"

She didn't see Granny's response, but she felt the wards strengthen. Thompson paused in his attack.

"Well now," he said. "Come to your senses? I guessed you for a smart girl."

"Not exactly," she said, and he shrugged. "Been wrong before, I reckon," he said. "I'll plant roses on your grave, then."

The wolf-thing lunged at her, its mad eyes glowing. Granny screamed behind her, but Rosanna had no time for that. She opened her arms as if to welcome its attack, then spoke a Word of ice and wind, this one designed to hold it still.

"Interesting trick," Trapper said. "Let's see how long you can hold it." He continued his assault on the house.

Rosanna felt the poison of the creature seeping into her, simply by way of the Words that held it. It was if the thing weren't really venomous, but contagious instead. She struggled to hear again the pure sounds underneath the corruption, but it was much harder with those razor teeth so close to her flesh.

She sank further and further into the sounds that made the creature up, until she wasn't sure she'd ever find her way back to health and reason. The poor animal was insane with pain and rage and terror. She hadn't expected to pity it, but she did, and that pity served as a catalyst, it seemed, for some primal part of the animal recognized it, welcomed it, and she heard the true Words of it, felt them shining through.

She seized onto that sound, and Spoke it. All around that true core were wound strands of fire and earth, binding and warping it, so she Spoke water and earth, clean sounds of balance and peace. The dark compulsions began to strip away, first slowly, then more rapidly, until she could no longer follow the progression.

She released the wolf, still Speaking its truest nature, and the shadows around it dissipated and the mad fury flowed out of its eyes like water released from winter's grip. She fell to her knees, still holding it, and not knowing how to let go. She heard Trapper cry out, and then everything was still except for the murmur of Granny's wards. She opened her eyes, and the wolf stood frozen in mid-leap in front of her. She released it, and it shook itself. It stared up at her with cool gray eyes, and she readied herself for an attack. Even if it weren't bespelled, there was nothing safe about a wolf an arms-length away.

It shook itself again, lifted its muzzle and howled. To her delight, Rosanna heard the true sounds of the wolf's being reflected in the howl. It was all the gratitude she needed. The wolf barked sharply, then headed away across the snow. It glanced at Trapper and lifted its head to scent the breeze. It gave another little bark, then hurried on and away.

Granny stumbled through the snow and nearly tackled Rosanna to the ground.

"Oh my girl!" she said, over and over. "Oh my brave girl."

"We don't have time for this," Rosanna said, hugging her back. "We've got to go." Granny pulled back.

"There's no need," Granny said. "I felt that backlash, and he's down. That would have killed anyone."

Rosanna shook her head. "Don't you watch horror movies?" she said. Granny looked at her blankly. "The bad guy's never dead," Rosanna said.

"This isn't a movie," Granny said. Rosanna looked over at Trapper. He lay very still, and a thin stream of smoke or steam lifted off his clothing. Perhaps she'd killed him after all. She put her head on one side and listened. The Words that made him up were so loud that they nearly deafened her. How could anyone be so powerful? The fire and fury of him should have split his skin with its intensity.

"Granny, get moving," Rosanna said. "Head to my car."

"But my wards…"

"Will kill you when he breaks them," Rosanna interrupted. 'There is no time for this, get going."

"But my house!" Granny Rosie cried. "My pictures! They're all I've got left of Lillian!"

"Head for the car, I'll meet you there," Rosanna said. There was no way she could save the house, but she couldn't bear to lose what little scraps she had of her mother.

Granny wasn't moving swiftly enough, so Rosanna got under her shoulder and half-carried her to the porch. Granny shook her off, and headed to the car around the corner. Rosanna ran through the door and into the living room. She hated to let it go. Every nook was packed with Granny's life and memories. She took as many photo albums as she could carry in one arm. She looked around wildly, wanting to save it all, and heard the murmur of a Word. The fire-pixie floated by the hearth, radiating concern and worry. Rosanna didn't know what to do.

"We've got to leave," she said. "You should run." The tiny creature hesitated and then floated to just a centimeter from her nose. It was achingly beautiful, and she resented her urgency. "You should run," she said again.

Suddenly the walls around her shook violently, and the pixie floated even closer, and laid a tiny hand against Rosanna's forehead. Warmth flowed out from that touch, filling her whole body with a cinnamon-sweet heat. Around her the cabin began to shake itself to pieces. Glass exploded out of the window-panes, and a thousand shimmering knives flung themselves at her. There was no time to think or even to breathe. She threw herself at the floor, knowing it was ridiculous and futile, but still trying to live through it. After a second, she opened her eyes. A glittering spear of glass spun like an arrow, not more than two centimeters from her left eye. As she watched, it melted, evaporated into nothing. The walls and ceiling still shook and groaned, but the glass, all of it, was gone. The fire sprite took its hand from her skin, though she still felt the warmth of its touch. It darted in close, and she closed her eyes involuntarily. She felt it brush each of her eyelids, and thought it had kissed her there.

She opened her eyes again, and it nodded solemnly, and then pointed to the window. The frame twisted and shuddered under the stresses put on it, but it was still a clear route out, and it wouldn't require passing in front of Thompson. She heard his voice in the destruction around her, and wanted to weep. There might be a chance for that later, but she knew her time in this house was measured in seconds. She wrapped her arms tightly around the photo albums, and plunged through the window-frame. Something sharp snagged her shoulder as she passed it, but she was through and gasping on the snow before she could register pain. Granny sat in the passenger seat of the car, her face drawn and her eyes wide. Rosanna pulled herself to her feet, and into the car.

"What are you still doing here?" she said, and flung the albums into the back seat.

"No keys and no you," Granny said. "Can't leave without both."

"The keys are in the ignition!" Rosanna shouted, and started the car. "Damn it, Granny, I just lost my father. I can't lose you, too!" Tears welled up, hot and furious, but there was still no time for them. She let them run over her face, let them sting in the cut on her cheek, and jerked the car into reverse. It groaned and bucked, unhappy at such abrupt treatment, and for a breathless second, she thought she stalled it out. When they started to move back, she forced her foot to press slowly on the gas. They'd only gone a few meters when a concussion rocked the car.

In front of them, Granny's cabin buckled in on itself, then flew apart. A piece of wood slammed into Rosanna's windshield, and left a spider web of cracks in front of Granny.

"No!" Granny cried. Rosanna hit the gas harder, and heard the tires scrabble on the ice. They caught, and the car roared down Granny's driveway. Rosanna was glad for the slope, for the mercy it granted. She couldn't see the ruin of Granny's home, and she couldn't hear Trapper's voice.

She skidded out onto the highway, turned sharply and sped away. She had no destination but 'away', and for the moment, that was enough.

# Chapter 11

Rosanna pulled her gloves off with her teeth, one at a time. She was ready, and perfectly willing, to head back to her city. She and Granny Rosie could get lost in that other world, and even Thompson, trapper that he was, might never find them. Her cheek hurt, and as the adrenaline wore off, her hands trembled. Granny looked at her with worry.

"Maybe you'd best pull over for a breather,' she said. "Not that the ditch doesn't look comfy, and all, but there's likely rocks under that snow."

Rosanna shook her head.

"We've got to get away," she said.

"That's all very well in the short term, but I believe you're bleeding all over your nice clean car, and if I don't stop to pee there's going to be a mess on this seat, too."

"For God's sake, you're worse than a child," Rosanna said. She smiled, and the expression felt strange on her face, as if she'd forgotten how to do it.

"You'd know," Granny said, and reached out to pat her hand. "We're far enough for the moment."

Rosanna ignored 'for the moment', and settled on the words 'far enough'. She slowed the car, and pulled over. She put the car in park, but left the motor running. The gas tank was a little over half-full still, and that would be enough to get them out of the mountains, if not all the way home.

Granny reached for Rosanna's hand again, and then pulled her into a fierce hug. Rosanna rested her aching cheek on Granny's shoulder, and waited for the tears, but they didn't come. Perhaps she'd built too solid a wall against them. When she closed her eyes, all she wanted to do was sleep. The night had gone on forever now, and she hadn't had a rest since June's place.

After a little while, her shoulder hurt too much to hold the embrace. Rosanna knew it was only a moment's respite, but she was glad of it. There was too much to think about, and too little of her left for it.

"Rosanna," Granny said. "You are bleeding like a stuck pig. Could you stop it, please? It's most unladylike."

Rosanna chuckled.

"Sorry, Gran. Didn't mean to offend."

Granny smiled in response, and the expression looked foreign on her face, too.

"We should get a look at that," she said, but Rosanna shook her head.

"I don't have any way to deal with it, even if we look now. Besides, we're not all that far, and he…"she gulped for air, just at the thought of him "might have a magic carpet or something."

"So what, then?" Granny asked. "You shouldn't go on much further like that, and we're certainly not going to make it to Nelson."

Rosanna knew that the 'we' was charitable. Granny might well make it on her own, but Rosanna was going to pass out, from fatigue if not from blood loss.

"For now," she said, "we should put pressure on it. She pulled her scarf from around her neck, and found that her winter clothes were becoming uncomfortably warm. She undid her zipper, but left the coat on. The cold was as fierce an enemy as Thompson, and she didn't want to be vulnerable to either. She wondered if she'd ever feel safe again. She'd never had a real enemy before, not even counting antagonistic professors.

Granny tied the scarf around Rosanna's upper arm. Rosanna gritted her teeth and told her to tie it tighter. It hurt now, searing and seething like a burn. She put her hands on the steering wheel and looked out the windshield. Granny's side of the glass was a haze of cracks, and she was surprised it hadn't broken entirely. She was grateful for this single bubble of warmth and safety, but she wished she knew just how safe it was. Where was Trapper? Was he following? Had they slowed him down at all?

At the thought of him, her hand dropped to the knife strapped to her thigh. It bumped against her, a little throb of comfort, like the touch of a beloved pet. Could she use it if she had too? She'd said she couldn't kill him, but what if that were her only choice?

"I think we should head to my place," she said. "It'll be safe for a while, at least."

"How safe, and for how long?" Granny replied, and shook her head. "We can't leave him with the Library."

"Screw the Library, Gran. I just want to go *home*." The word hurt her mouth, and she remembered again the destruction of Granny's house.

"It won't work that way, Rosanna. You can access Lillian's Library. If he could do it, he would have, long ago. He needs you."

"All the more reason to run, then," Rosanna said.

"And you'll run forever? Every place you hide, he'll destroy."

"I'm younger, he'll die before me."

"There's no guarantee of that, and you are being pig-headed."

"I learned that one from the best," Rosanna said.

Granny reached out and took Rosanna's hand. It trembled and fluttered in Granny's grasp like a frightened bird.

"Please, Granny," she said. "*Please.* I can't do any more. I'm done."

Granny pressed Rosanna's hand to her weathered cheek.

"This won't go away, my lass, my love," she said. "I'd take from you if I could. I'd give every other power up, just for the power to take this away."

Rosanna nodded, and retrieved her hand. She rested her forehead on the steering wheel. The big picture was too much, so she narrowed her view.

Granny stepped out of the car and did what she needed to, down in the ditch and just out of sight. Rosanna could barely stand to see her disappear, and held her breath until Granny was visible again.

Granny opened the door and settled into her seat again.

"Well then," she said. "That's a load off of my mind." It was an old line, and Rosanna was glad that she wouldn't be expected to laugh at it. That would have been too much to ask.

"So?" Granny said. "Any bright ideas?" Rosanna sat quietly, and listened to the comfortable purr of her car's engine.

"We need a safe place to check this shoulder out," she said. "June's got first aid stuff, I know." The smile this time came a little easier, though it still fit strangely on her lips. "We can talk about everything else after that, okay?"

Granny nodded, and Rosanna put the car in gear and started down the highway again. It wasn't a solution, but it was a plan, and that would do for now.

# Chapter 12

The drive to June's café stretched out interminably, and Rosanna's eyelids grew heavier by the minute. She opened her window, and let the cold air slap her awake, but it was a temporary solution. She no longer knew how far she had to drive, nor how far she'd come, only that her world had narrowed to headlights on the yellow line. She wondered if the scope of her life would ever widen again, or if it would always be this string of crises. Lord, how she missed boredom, and the mundane.

Granny had offered to drive, but she looked even worse than Rosanna felt. Her skin was pale except for dark hollows under her eyes and cheekbones. She looked withered and ancient, and her voice quavered when she spoke. Rosanna had turned her down, and Granny had accepted it without complaint.

Rosanna could spare little attention from the effort of driving, but she spent that little worrying about Granny.

When at last she saw the lights of the restaurant, she nearly sobbed with relief. Granny woke from her restless doze, and her head snapped up.

"We there?" she said. It would be hard for her to make out their surroundings through the ruined windshield.

"Yeah," Rosanna said. "I hope she's still there."

"And if she's not?"

"We'll think of something,' Rosanna said. "I've got to rest, at least. Maybe get a little sleep." She was prepared to break in, were it necessary. June would forgive her, she thought. Her choices were as narrow as her focus, these days.

She pulled in to the gas station, and then circled around the building to park behind it. It wasn't much in the way of concealment, but she needed to make the attempt.

She and Granny shambled to the door, each supporting the other as best she could. The gas station was open, but the restaurant lights were out. Rosanna didn't know if June employed anyone else, but she hoped not. She rang the bell, and when there was no response, rang it again louder.

"Keep your shirt on," June shouted, from somewhere back behind the desk. "I heard you the first time, and now you're just pissing me off."

"Sorry," Rosanna shouted. "Just wanted a cup of coffee."

June came into view wearing a cheerful grin that slid off her face as soon as she saw the two women.

"Shit, girl," she said. "You didn't have to dress up for me again." Rosanna was glad for the business-like surprise in June's voice. Compassion might have broken her, might have thrown her to her knees at least. But this, she could handle just fine.

"I missed you," she said, and June laughed. "I probably wouldn't have recognized you without some bruises." She marked Rosanna's condition with sharp eyes, and though her grin faded a little, she did not let it slip again.

"Come this way," she said, and lifted the bar at the counter. She turned the 'open' sign around, and switched off the outside lights as Rosanna and Granny limped through the door behind her.

The door led back into June's little office, and Rosanna led Granny to the hide-a-bed. They both collapsed gracelessly onto its cushions. Rosanna closed her eyes as the room spun lazily around her, and she hated to open them again. The feeling of 'safety' was better than a shot of brandy, and all the muscles in her neck and shoulders released. She felt poisoned by her own adrenaline, and was glad to feel its buzz fade.

June closed the door behind her and pulled a curtain across it. Rosanna looked at the door out to the kitchen with sudden longing. She couldn't remember what she'd last eaten, nor when. June saw the look and shook her head sternly.

"You are not getting a bite to eat until you stop bleeding on my furniture," she said, and Granny Rosie chuckled.

"I always did like you,' she said, and June smiled.

"Don't know me very well, do you? I am not a likeable kinda girl, trust me."

"Careful," Rosanna said. "She's fierce."

"Wicked fierce,' June agreed. "Now shut up and try to stop bleeding. Again."

She left, and Rosanna heard her clattering around in the kitchen a little, but the sound faded out and she dropped into an uncomfortable doze. She woke with a start as June and Granny began to peel off her coat. Adrenaline tried to kick in again, but Rosanna was too tired for it. When they untied the scarf around her upper arm she felt an unpleasant rush of heat as her shoulder began to bleed again.

"You know," June said, "I don't think half-explanations are going to do it this time." She looked appraisingly at Rosanna's shirtsleeve, then took out a pair of scissors and cut it off before Rosanna could protest. It was soaked in more blood than she wanted to see anyhow, so she was just as glad when June dropped it in a trash bucket and out of sight.

"I don't know what to tell you," Rosanna said, and June shook her head.

"You don't have to tell me much until you're not bleeding, and maybe you get some sleep. Just tell me if you're in trouble."

Rosanna nodded, and Granny gave a half-hearted chuckle.

"Big trouble, then," June said, and Rosanna nodded again. "Is it the kinda trouble likely to follow you here?" she asked, and Rosanna looked at Granny.

"It's the kind of trouble like enough to follow us to the end of the world," Granny said. "But I'm hoping it won't catch us up for a little while."

"But it could come here," June said, and it wasn't a question.

"We'll go, June," Rosanna said. "I didn't think and I didn't know what else to do." She looked around for her coat, and saw it draped over the office chair. When would she learn not to let it out of her reach? She tried to get up, but couldn't.

"Oh yeah," June said. "I can see you'll be jogging out of here any minute." Rosanna looked up into those warm hazel eyes, and was amazed to see the smile in them. How could June smile?

"You don't understand," Rosanna said.

"Nope," June said, "I don't. Don't care, neither. Whatever it is can wait until you're patched up a little. I'll want to know it all."

Rosanna remembered the devastation at Granny's cabin, and closed her eyes against the memory.

"He destroyed Granny's house," she said. "He can do anything."

"That's good to know," June said. "But you're still bleeding. Sit still and be quiet. In that order." She turned to Granny. "Lord she's a talker, must be yours." That surprised a laugh out of both Granny and Rosanna, and June nodded in satisfaction.

"Better," she said. "Ain't no trouble that can't be laughed at." She looked at Rosanna's cheek, then at her forehead. "Hm, she said, "rotating injuries. I thought that only worked with crops." Rosanna opened her mouth, but shut it again when June glared at her. June nodded again. "That's right, I get to comment, you get to take it. You need stitches on that one." Granny nodded.

"I told her she would," she said. June turned that stare on her, and Rosanna was amazed to see Granny Rosie, the Great and the Terrible, wilt.

"I don't want to hear from you neither," June said. "You look like shit, and I'm not taking any lip from either of you."

June got a bowl of warm water and some cloths, and started cleaning Rosanna's cheek.

"You are gonna owe me a mess of new linen," she said, and Rosanna shrugged. Her eyes watered as June washed away the dried blood. She felt the uncomfortable warm drip of blood down her cheek again, and June put another towel on her shoulder to catch it. She pulled out a length of black thread and a needle.

"This won't be much fun," she said. "You want a shot of something first?"

"Like what?" Rosanna hated the hope in her voice, but June only smiled.

"Still got whiskey," she said, "plus some special brownies in the freezer. I wouldn't suggest anything stronger, though."

Rosanna's experiences with pot were limited, so she opted for the whiskey. She didn't want to muddle her mind more than it already was.

June poured each of them a generous shot, and even Granny downed hers in a gulp. Rosanna hadn't seen Granny drink much more than the occasional beer, but if ever there were an occasion for hard liquor, today would qualify.

Rosanna focused on the heat in her throat and belly as June put a half-dozen stitches in her cheek. The tugging made her queasy, but the flow of blood down her cheek stopped. June stood back to examine her work.

"Well," she said, "you ain't the bride of Frankenstein, but you'll do. Now the shoulder."

June looked at the ruin of Rosanna's shirt and shook her head.

"You're supposed to keep the blood in, you know," she said, and Rosanna smiled. The heat of the whiskey had settled to a comfortable glow, something that loosened her muscles enough that a smile very nearly came naturally, at least until it pulled on the stitches.

"I needed an excuse to see you," she said.

"What, my coffee wasn't good enough?" Rosanna shrugged, and June said, "and what about that Trapper, he's a bit of a draw, ain't he?" Rosanna stiffened, and Granny drew in a breath. June took a step back and looked at both women.

"Hm," she said, and that was all, but her eyes darkened, and her mouth drew into a sharp line. The shoulder was a nasty gash, and Rosanna was surprised it hadn't hurt more. It hadn't seemed like more than a tug when it happened, but the muscle was exposed. Rosanna only looked once. Even with the whiskey, the sight made her a stomach shift. June stitched that one as well.

"You ought to see a doctor," she said. "But I don't suppose that's in your plans today."

Rosanna shook her head, and looked at Granny Rosie. Granny's eyes were closed, her chin resting on her chest. Her skin was nearly translucent, as if Granny were fading away to a shimmer of her old self, and Rosanna ached to see it.

"I don't know what's in my plans,' Rosanna said softly. "I don't have plans. Just…situations."

"Sometimes, girl, that's all you get. Ain't always got a choice in the matter, neither." June got another chair from the dining room and sat down.

"So," she said. "What first, sleep or explaining?"

"What would you prefer?" Rosanna asked, and June shrugged.

"I'd rather see you sleepin' than hear you talkin', but if it's as bad as you think, maybe I ought to know."

Rosanna nodded. "Then you'll know whether you should kick us out sooner or later," she said.

"Stop it," June said. "You're being stupid and it don't suit you." She leaned forward and put her hand on Rosanna's uninjured shoulder. "I don't back down from fights, remember? And I don't back out on friends." She gave the shoulder a little shake. "No matter how annoying." Rosanna wanted to try another smile, but found herself crying instead. She didn't know how to explain anything, and she didn't know how to thank June, and all in all, it didn't seem like she knew very much of anything.

June let her cry, then offered her one of the clean cloths.

"I'll put it on the tab," June said, and Rosanna snorted a laugh and wiped her nose.

"So," June said. "Tell me a story."

"Well," Rosanna said, after a lingering pause, "do you believe in magic?"

"Dunno," June said. "Never seen any. Mind you, I've never seen Spain, either, and I'm pretty sure it's there all the same."

The whiskey bottle still stood on the desk, and Rosanna picked it up. June lifted an eyebrow.

"For this, I need whiskey?"

Rosanna shook her head.

"But you might for this," she said, and Spoke the little frost-Word she'd found here, not so long ago. A delicate lace of ice crystals spiraled out from her fingertips, swept up the neck of the bottle and stopped with a delicate 'ping' at the bottle's mouth.

June looked at it appreciatively.

"Say," she said, "that'd be nice at beach parties." She took the bottle from Rosanna and examined it. The tracery smudged and blurred with the heat of her fingers. She tipped the bottle up and took a healthy swig.

"Right," she said. "Can you prove Spain?"

Rosanna laughed, and Granny started awake with a snort.

"Hmm?" she said. "What's the joke?"

"Me, I think," Rosanna said. "Are you the punch line?"

"Don't tempt me, my girl," Granny said, and Rosanna delighted to hear some of the old spark in Granny's voice. "What are you two giggling about?"

"Rosanna showed me a magic trick," June said. "So now what?"

"Well," Rosanna said, "suppose there's someone who wants magic only I can unlock for him…"

"And suppose," June said, "you don't want to, yeah?"

Rosanna nodded.

"So let me think," June said, "who around here could possibly not be what he says he is?" Rosanna nodded.

"It's worse than that," Rosanna said. "He says he's my father."

"He *is* your father," Granny said, and the colour faded out of her cheeks again.

"Family reunions are such a bitch," June said. "But they only sometimes end up with someone's house blown up." Her tone was dry, but she reached out and put the bottle back in Rosanna's hand. She rested her arm on Rosanna's shoulders for just a moment, and Rosanna could have wept again for the comfort in that touch.

"So," June said. "Why don't you just get the hell out of here?"

"He'll hunt me," Rosanna said, and her head drooped under the weight of that understanding. "Wherever I go, he'll hunt me." Her head came up again, and she put her hand on her knife. "And I think I'd rather see him coming."

"Best way," June said. "A wolf you can back away from, a wolf is mostly sane." Rosanna remembered Trapper's wolf, remembered its eyes and nodded. June pulled her pendant from under her shirt, and clenched a fist around it. "A cougar is crazy, and you're crazy if you turn your back on it." She smiled at Rosanna. "Anyway, we're fierce, right?"

"June, this isn't your fight," Rosanna said.

"You are so frickin' dense," June said. "We're friends, ain't we? The fierce women's club?"

"But you hardly know me!"

"I know you're a good person, and I know you need me. I know the land around here 'bout as well as anyone will. I been runnin' around these mountains so long, I'm practically a wild thing myself." She grinned again, and showed a lot of even, white, teeth. Her eyes were green and gold now, like sunlight through leaves.

"You got the brains and I got the beauty," she said, and laughed. "At least 'till your face heals up."

"I don't know that I've got much for brains, just now. They feel pretty thoroughly scrambled." Rosanna looked around. "I don't even know what time it is."

"What time does it feel like?" June asked.

"Bedtime," Granny said, and Rosanna nodded her agreement.

"All right then," June said. "It's bedtime."

"I don't know if we can afford the time to rest," Granny said. "He can be a stubborn little cuss, clear enough."

"Takes one to know one," Rosanna said, and Granny took a half-hearted swing at her.

"Abuse!" Rosanna said. "Did you see that?"

"I seem to spend an awful lot of time telling you to stop talkin'," June said. "Do you suppose you could spare me the effort this once?"

Rosanna smiled. The expression rested easier on her face now, like a frightened animal returning to its home.

June got new sheets and remade the bed, and Granny and Rosanna curled in, side by side. It was a small bed, but Rosanna was grateful for the heat of Granny's body next to hers, and for the soft hush and hum of her breathing. June had turned the lights out, but a thin line glimmered under the door, and Rosanna was comforted by that, too, and by the casual noises of June at work in the kitchen.

She wanted to sleep, she was desperate and dizzy for it, but her busy mind wouldn't rest. She didn't know what to do next, or even what her options were. She still didn't think she could kill him, but she didn't want to die at his hands either. The sound of Granny's breath was precious, and she treasured it, tucked in close beside her worries, and let it lull her to sleep.

She woke to a gentle shake of her shoulder. Light from the kitchen backlit June so that it took Rosanna a drowsy moment to identify her as a friend. Granny snored beside her, so Rosanna moved the bed as little as possible when she got up. If Granny could wring a little more sleep out of this break, all the better.

June stood nearby, and Rosanna had reason to be grateful. She ached.

"Was there ever a day I wasn't in pain?" she said mournfully, and June chuckled.

"I dunno," she said. "But think how you'll enjoy it when you get one."

They walked together to one of the dining room tables. All the shades were drawn, and the kitchen light was the only one on. June had lit a candle for this table, and the little globe of golden light was gentle on Rosanna's eyes.

Rosanna looked at her watch, but somewhere in the course of things, she'd smashed the crystal.

"My watch says about half past whenever," Rosanna said. "What time is it?"

"Little after seven," June said. "Sunday crowd won't be wanting breakfast for a few hours yet, lazy bastards."

"How long did we sleep?"

June shrugged. "A while," she said. "Not near long enough, by the looks of you."

"I don't think a week would be long enough," Rosanna said, and tried to stretch some of the aches out of her shoulders. It didn't help, and the pull against her stitched arm hurt. She sighed. She looked up, and saw June's frown.

"What?" she said.

"I don't mean to be unkind," June said, "but you just ain't cut out for this size trouble."

"Is anyone?"

"I dunno," June said. 'but why don't you just magic yourself better?"

"It takes energy," Rosanna said. "And if I do it wrong…" she paused. "Would you let someone do surgery on you if they'd never held a knife?"

"That'd depend how desperate I was," June said.

"So let's say I'm not quite that desperate. Yet." She wondered what it had cost Trapper to heal her. She hoped it had cost him more to hurt her, but she wouldn't have taken bets on it.

"What about your Granny?"

"She could probably do it, but she's tired."

"She's more than tired," June said, dropping her voice. "Besides, that's not what I meant. I mean, can you heal her?"

"I wouldn't want to do surgery on her, either," Rosanna said.

"I think you might be runnin' out of choices there," June said. "She don't look any better now than she did before you lay down."

"I know," Rosanna said, and didn't know where to go from there.

"Would a hospital help?"

"Might," Rosanna said, "but I don't know. Granny just says she's old."

"She'd know," June said. They sat in stillness for a while, each pursuing a solution in the privacy of her thoughts.

"Got room for another hen, there?" Granny said, and they both startled at the sound of her voice. June pulled out a chair.

"Sure 'nuff." she said. "You two want breakfast? We should keep it simple so it don't look like I'm home." Granny and Rosanna nodded.

June stepped into the kitchen, and Rosanna looked at Granny. Even in the candlelight she looked wan, and her eyes were huge and pale in a face made of shadows and angles. Granny reached out and put a hand gently against Rosanna's injured cheek. Her eyes were full of sorrow.

"Oh girl," she said, "oh my girl." She dropped her head into her hands and began to weep, a slow drawing cry that seemed to pull her apart. Rosanna dropped to her knees beside Granny's chair, and wrapped her arms around Granny's shoulders. She couldn't bring herself to say it was okay, and she didn't know how to comfort when she herself felt so divorced from comfort and safety. All she could do was hold Granny, and wait for the sorrow to ebb a little.

"I don't know what to do," Granny said at last, her words muffled by her hands. "I'm ashamed to say it, but I don't have any idea."

"Granny, should we get you to a hospital?"

Granny shook her head. "There's no point," she said. "It isn't my body that's ailing, it's my spirit. I'm worn out, and I can feel myself unwinding, second by second." She lifted her face from her hands, and met Rosanna's eyes. "'m dying, my girl. That's what's true. Might be age, might be the bite, but I'm dying, and I don't want to." She shuddered, but did not drop her face again.

Rosanna wanted to turn from Granny's gaze, to see anything but the truth of her words, but she would not meet Granny's courage with cowardice.

"Trapper had a bite from that thing," she said. "He seemed okay. Maybe you'll get better."

"Firstly, he's younger than me. And second, maybe he's dying, too, and just doesn't know it yet."

"One can hope," Rosanna said.

June came back to the table with a tray laden with bowls and cups. The bowls were full of hot oatmeal, and the cups were full of steaming coffee.

"Could I have a drink of water?" Rosanna asked. The coffee smelled delicious, but she craved nothing so much as plain water. June nodded, and returned with a pitcher and some glasses.

Rosanna covered her oatmeal with cream and brown sugar, and started to eat. She found raisins and sunflower seeds and chunks of apple in her cereal, and though she'd never been much of an oatmeal fan, she asked for seconds. Granny cocked an eyebrow at that.

"I do remember a certain amount of screaming and whinging about oatmeal, sometime in your past," she said, and Rosanna shrugged.

"Yours never tasted like this,' she said. "And just because I'm a librarian, it doesn't mean I'm interested in eating paste."

The coffee was wonderful, and Rosanna sat back with a sigh. She wanted to relax, sternly told her muscles to take the rest while they could, but it was impossible. Trapper was out there, and Granny was dying. The word was foul in her mind, polluting any sense of respite she might have enjoyed.

June gathered up the dishes and took them back to the kitchen. Rosanna offered to help with the dishes, but June just laughed.

"Dishes?" she said, "who's doing dishes? I can put 'em in the dishwasher and run 'em later." She returned with the coffee pot, and sat down with an easy grace that Rosanna envied. She envied, too, the simple assurance that there would be a 'later'.

"So," June said. "We got a plan yet?"

Rosanna meant to laugh, but the sound came out as more of a strangled moan.

"Sounds like a no," June said. "Granny?"

Granny sat very still for a moment, until Rosanna thought she wasn't going to answer. Every second of silence pulsed more panic through her veins. Granny had to have a plan, didn't she?

"I think we have to hunt him," she said at last, and Rosanna was astonished at the sorrow in Granny's voice. Granny met Rosanna's surprise with a level stare.

"I could kill him in the heat of a moment," she said, "but it's a different thing to plan a man's death. He wasn't always…" she paused, and swallowed hard. "He wasn't always a bad man. He just learned too much, and didn't understand enough."

"And he's a bad man now?" June said.

"I don't know," Rosanna said, and that was the crux of it. He hadn't seemed a bad man, not until he'd threatened, not until he'd ruined Granny's house.

"He's a dangerous man," Granny said.

"They all are," June said. "How dangerous?"

"I think…" Rosanna paused. "I think he's more than a little crazy."

"Ah," June said. "That's always the worst. You can guess what a complete headcase might do. The other ones are tricky."

"Rosanna," Granny said, her words heavy with regret, "he's got to die."

"Stop it," Rosanna said. "I know what you're really saying. You're saying he has to be murdered. You're probably saying I have to do it."

Granny shook her head. "I'd never ask that," she said. "This monster is at least partly my making. I'm supposed to be the guardian of this Library, and I've failed it. Failed you, too."

Rosanna opened her mouth to protest, but Granny shook her head.

"If I hadn't been so scared to lose you, I would have started training you long ago. You'd be ready for this. I let you down. I screwed up."

After all the years that Rosanna had longed for Granny to admit to a mistake, any mistake, this was not the moral victory she'd always imagined. Granny had turned out to be merely human, after all, and Rosanna missed her invincibility. It had been impossible to meet unstated standards of perfection, and that had always hurt. This was worse, and Rosanna had no way to soothe this hurt for either of them.

"We just didn't have enough time," she said at last, and Granny smiled faintly.

'There's always lots of time until there isn't any," she said. "You'd think an old lady would remember that."

"Well then" June said, "if we're done planning funerals maybe we could figure what we're going to do first."

Rosanna was grateful again for June's solidity. There was no denial in her voice, but neither was there despair. Rosanna squared her shoulders, and met June's eyes. June nodded with satisfaction. "And there you are again," she said, "a fierce woman, right enough."

June began to gather the dishes, but stopped, her head cocked to one side.

"Thought I heard something," she said. The wind outside was rising, flinging snow against the windows and muttering at the door.

"Rosanna," the wind said, and the voice was Trapper's, everywhere at once. June dropped the dishes, and stood perfectly still.

"Thompson Trapper," she shouted. "This here's my place and these folks are my guests. You just get your ass off my property."

"June," the voice said, "oh pretty little June. I've always liked you. Haven't I been a good customer? A good friend?"

"Don't matter," June said. "I won't have people hunted in my home. Now git!"

June sounded so like a mother chasing children off her porch that Rosanna laughed. And Granny turned to her with an amazed smile.

"We don't want any more of this," Rosanna said. "Can't you let it go?"

The wind rattled the restaurant, and two of the windows cracked with the pressure.

"I want what I'm due," Trapper said. "I spent my life for that Library, lost my wife for it."

"Killed her, you mean," Rosanna said. "Was it worth it?"

"No," he said, "but it will be, as soon as you unlock the Library for me. That's the only thing that could make it all mean something."

"And if I won't?"

"This is an old conversation," Trapper said, the words seeping through the floor and walls. "If you die, if your grandmother dies, maybe the Library will release. You're the end of the line. That's enough of a chance for me. You can live or die, it's up to you." Rosanna stood and put her hand on her knife.

"You're crazy, and I won't give it to you." She did not shout, but the words hung in the air like a promise.

"Good enough," bellowed the wind, and all the windows exploded in. Granny spoke a Word, and the shards of glass dropped in a circle around the women. She sagged, and Rosanna moved to support her.

Granny clung to Rosanna's arm, and she and June helped pull her to her feet. Rosanna felt the Words of Granny's being, and the tight web had loosened till it was more like a net, and Granny's life was slipping through the holes. She Spoke one of the Words she heard there, saying it like a prayer, and felt a trickle of her own strength seep into Granny. Granny looked up at her with angry eyes.

"I told you I'm dying," she snapped. "Save that for yourself."

"I can't just…" Rosanna said, but June shook her head.

"We ain't got time for a chat, now haul ass!"

The wind continued to rise, and Rosanna realized she could hear the Words that made it up, too. She stored them in her mind, syllables of air and ice. They were different from those in the Library, but she felt that they belonged with her. His use of them was a violation of their purity, something like a rape.

She Spoke one of them, and felt his will upon it. She applied her own will, and the strain was immense, like a tug-of-war with a river. She let the Word go, and Spoke another, a small Word of stability, and another of ice. They made eddies in the wind, little breaks in the current that drained the strength out of it, no matter how much energy he poured into them. The tempest around the restaurant finally dropped altogether.

"You're a natural, all right," he shouted through a shattered window pane. His voice, unaugmented, was distressingly human. It made him a person again, rather than just a force. She could hear pride in it as well as a measure of condescension.

"But you don't know enough yet," he said. "Granny Rosie ought to have taught you your limitations, at least."

"I don't believe you have any," Granny said, her voice for Rosanna alone.

"Still," he said, "you've only proven yourself at making things. Can you unmake them too?"

He spoke a Word, something that tugged horribly at Rosanna's being. It was the antithesis of any other Word she'd heard. She listened to it, but did not add it to her own lexicon. It was something primal, like the void before the light, and she did not know how he could bear to know it, let alone to Speak it.

Granny screamed, a hoarse and horrible sound that nevertheless cut through Trapper's voice. And then Rosanna felt Granny's response. She Spoke the Words of her own being, spun them out of herself and into a cocoon around the three of them.

Rosanna tried to scream, tried to stop her, but once begun, the process had a momentum of its own. Around them, Trapper tore the building to pieces, and then the pieces into smaller fragments, until they were surrounded with a cloud of shimmering dust. There were no Words in that, no sense of being, but only the malice of Trapper's will.

The cloud collapsed upon them, all the weight of the restaurant, and also of Trapper's madness. Granny shouted, and Rosanna felt the last syllable spin out of her to complete a bubble around them. It held, and made a tracery of light against the crushing darkness. Rosanna heard one more Word, something of ice, and the ruins froze solid.

"Good-bye," Trapper said. "It's a shame, June. I always meant to bed you."

Granny tumbled in a heap, and Rosanna fell with her, trying to hold her up, and hearing only silence where Granny's soul ought to be. She listened and listened, catching the echoes of Granny in the protection she'd woven, but that was all there could ever be now. Only echoes.

# Chapter 13

Rosanna rocked Granny's body in her arms. She wanted to weep; the tears were hot and fierce behind her eyes, but she couldn't. She didn't know why. Was there something wrong with her? Granny was dead. She'd bought Rosanna's life with her own. Someone touched her arm, and she brushed it away. Yes, Granny had bought Rosanna's life. Bad bargain, at best. Someone touched her arm again, and she pushed the hand away more violently. Trapper would have to die, of course. Rosanna thought about killing him, about spinning him away, syllable by syllable. That would make sense. The hand touched her again, and she flailed out at it.

June grabbed her by the wrists.

"Rosanna!" she said, but Rosanna was beyond hearing anything but the last echoes of Granny. "Rosanna!" June shouted. "Your Granny would be ashamed of you!"

Rosanna froze, trapped by the thought. There was always lots of time until there wasn't any. She threw her head back and screamed. The debris around them shivered with the force of the sound, and June cried out and covered her ears with her hands. Rosanna opened her mouth to scream again, and June slapped her smartly across her uninjured cheek.

"We got no time for that," June said. "I don't know how much we have, but that's wasting it." Her voice was even and intense, and the last sounds of Granny's spirit echoed in it. "I don't know nothing about this shit, and if you go crazy on me, I'm all alone and hip-deep in it. Don't do that to me, Rosanna."

There was no note of pleading in June's words, only a straight-forward statement and demand. Rosanna nodded, and swallowed her scream. There might be time for it later, or not, but it was still true that she had no time for it now.

She opened her eyes. She hadn't realized she'd shut them. Granny's web held an open space in the debris, like an air-bubble in a lava flow. Rosanna tested the web as best she could, but she simply didn't know enough to guess how long it would hold, or even why it still existed after Granny's death. She traced the murmur of syllables, and found that one of the Words was linked to Rosanna. The spell had been set by Granny's death, but it was maintained by Rosanna's life. So long as she held, so would their protection.

"So?" June said. "What the fuck is going on?"

"Granny made this," Rosanna said. "But she connected it to me. Looks like it'll last as long as I do."

"Well," June said, "that's kinda good news and bad news for me, ain't it."

"I'm sorry," Rosanna said. "I screwed everything up. We should have run for it."

"What you sorry for?" June said. "Wrecking my place? Killing your Granny?"

Rosanna's head snapped up at the bluntness of the questions.

"Yes," she said.

"Then you're a fuckin' idiot, because you didn't do none of that," June said. "That bastard out there, that *man*, he's got those things to be sorry for, and you don't. If you say that again I will slap you into next week."

"But…"

"Shut it," she said. "You got one enemy more than you need already, don't you go adding yourself to the list."

"Thank you," Rosanna said. The guilt didn't ease, but June's words gave her permission to let it go for now, like the scream. Maybe later. June put a hand on Rosanna's shoulder, and they sat together for a moment, with Granny still lying across Rosanna's lap. There was too little room to move around her, and Rosanna knew what needed doing. She hated the thought, it was all too soon, too fast, and she still wanted to wait for Granny to awaken. She brushed silver hair from Granny's cheek, and a few of her tears escaped the confines of 'later' and dripped off her nose. She looked into June's eyes.

"We can't function with her here, can we," Rosanna said.

"No," June said, and that was all.

On a deep level, Granny's body was still made up of Words, not the ones that had been her spirit, but the smaller, stronger, and stranger ones that defined her physical being. They were whispering into silence, but Rosanna craved the sound of them, the last vestiges of Granny's being.

Not knowing exactly how, she called those Words into herself. They were foreign and peculiar, but they fit into the space where she stored the syllables she learned. As they came, Granny's body thinned into a mist, and then disappeared. Matter became energy, and Rosanna accepted *it* into herself. Some of her exhaustion eased, and she felt herself strengthened.

Rosanna lifted her eyes to meet June's. They sat in a silence punctuated only by the groans and squeals of their frozen prison.

"So," June said. "What now?"

"You're asking me?"

"Ain't no one else to ask, I'm sorry to say."

Rosanna nodded, and swallowed back more tears. Those too, would have to wait. Assuming she survived, Rosanna would be very busy for a while.

"Well," she said, "I'm not even sure which way is up, let alone out, and that stuff is frozen solid." She could hear the magic holding their prison around them, and there was nothing subtle about it. She didn't know how to pull it from Trapper's will.

"It's like being caught in an avalanche," June said. "Only I don't expect Trapper called search and rescue for us."

"What about your customers? Might they get to us?"

"Maybe," June said, "but one problem is the same here as under an avalanche. We don't got too much air in a pocket like this."

Rosanna hadn't thought of it, and didn't want to now.

"Plus," June said, "I'd assume we was dead, if I was anyone else. Wouldn't you?"

Rosanna didn't bother to answer that. The restaurant had been pulverized.

"Can't you just melt it?" June asked. "You know?"

Rosanna sighed. "What I don't know is a whole lot more than what I do. I can feel what he's done out there, but he's stronger than me, and I doubt that would work." She shrugged. "But it's worth a try."

She called up one of the syllables from her Library, one of warmth and grounding. Cautiously, she Spoke it, not putting too much of her energy behind it, but testing Trapper's spell. The cold around them seized onto Rosanna's little thread of warmth and seemed to pull it out of her, pulling Rosanna's strength with it. It was a horrible feeling, like watching herself bleed to death. She broke the Word off, but she could feel Trapper's will coursing around their little shelter, watching and waiting. Any Word she spoke would require extending herself beyond Granny's protections and into that snare.

"Well," June said. 'That didn't look good."

"What?"

"You got real pale there, and looked like you was going to fall over."

"Yeah, that's how it felt. That's not going to work."

"Fine," June said. "So we can't burn through it, can we sneak around it?"

"I don't know how," Rosanna said. "I'm so lost without Granny, I don't know where to go or how to get there."

"Well girl," June said, "we'll just have to buy you a compass, hey?"

Rosanna's knife throbbed against her thigh, and she gasped.

"What now?" June said. "You okay?"

"I...yeah, but I think I have something Trapper's forgotten."

"And that is? A rat-trap for magicians?"

"No," she said. "A magic compass."

"You're shitting me," June said. "Really?"

"Really," she said, and explained about the knife. She took it out of the sheath, and the two women examined it.

"Looks different," June said. "Never had that red edge before." She tested the blade, and drew her finger back with a hiss. "Sharper, too."

Rosanna nodded. The thing seemed happy to be in her hand, and thrummed gently with pulses of warmth. "The question is, how do I use it?"

June shrugged. "Hell, I can't make sense of a normal compass. I got one in my head that works better."

"Well then, which way should we go?" Rosanna asked.

"It don't work like that," June said. "I know the mountains and I get a sense of where I am. Sitting still like this, in the dark...we could be in outer space for all I can tell."

"How do you escape an avalanche if you get caught in one?"

June shrugged.

'Well, actually, we got an advantage in knowing which way is down," she said. "In the snow you can't always tell. So, assuming you got a little air, and assuming you don't freak out, you got to move in little bits, work yourself free without upsetting the snow more."

"That sounds pretty similar, all right," Rosanna said. "If I try to just break out, the spell will get very, very unhappy. So maybe if we move just a little, it won't." She looked around her at their tiny bubble.

"But I don't know if this will hold once I break through it. And if it collapses..."

"Then we're screwed," June said. "But no more than if we sit still. Gotta take a risk to get a return, right?"

"I guess," Rosanna said, "but it's a hell of a risk."

"Damn fine return though," June said, and managed a smile. It was miles from her usual grin, but the courage of it warmed Rosanna. She nodded, and reached out to stroke the web of light around them.

Granny was still there, as long as Rosanna's blood moved in her veins. She didn't know what would happen to the web if she broke through, but, like June said, they couldn't very well just sit here. She supposed Granny would always be in her veins, one way or another.

"Well, compass," she said, "I want to go home." The knife leaped in her hand like a fish. "But gently!" she said, and it quieted to an excited vibration. It pulled her hand a little to the right, chose a spot between the strands of Granny's web, and stayed there, thrumming.

"I guess this is where we start," Rosanna said. She took a deep breath, and let her weight follow the knife. She sank through the debris to her wrist, feeling the weight of Trapper's spell all around her. The knife found a way around and through the spell. As Rosanna shifted, Granny's web moved to accommodate the movement, and she felt a whisper of hope.

"June," she said, "I think the web might be meant to move. Can you come right up close to me?"

"Closer than this? Girl, you owe me a dinner," June said, and put an arm around Rosanna's shoulder. Rosanna smiled.

Rosanna braced her right hand with her left, and followed the knife into the ice and debris. It was strange to move through what looked so solid, but the knife burrowed through as if it were little more than loose soil. Rosanna stopped when her face reached the edge of their bubble. She didn't want her face in that, any more than she'd want it in polluted water. Besides, if the web didn't move, what would happen? It still looked solid, and it still exuded malice. June's arm tightened around her shoulders.

"Go on," she said quietly. "We got no choice. You can do this"

"But…"

"Don't matter. Just do it."

Rosanna shuffled her body as close to the edge of their bubble as she could. She took a deep breath, then edged into the debris field on her knees.

She opened her eyes, not having intended to close them, and found that the web had clung to her, and so had their little air pocket. She let a breath out that she hadn't realized she was holding

"That wasn't so bad," June said, and Rosanna smiled.

It hadn't actually been. Rosanna's face hadn't really touched the ice; the web had gone first, bringing the air with it.

They moved painfully slowly, but Rosanna's compass never wavered. Her shoulder ached from holding it, and her knees were bruised and raw from the uneven surface below them. Rosanna suspected that would have been much worse without the web. The light brightened bit by bit, and Rosanna began to dare to hope they might get out, that there might be an after.

But then what? What if he was out there? He wouldn't expect her to escape, but how arrogant was he? How sure? Her knife hit clean air, and Rosanna sat back.

"I'm through," she said, and June heaved a sigh of relief. Her arm tightened in a hug.

"Well?" she said. "Now what?"

"I don't know if he's out there," Rosanna said. "If he is, I don't know what I can do about it."

"We can't stay here," June said. "It don't matter if he's out there or not"

"I don't…I don't want to let go of the web," Rosanna said. She hung her head and a few tears trailed down her cheeks. "It's all that's left of her."

"Don't be an idiot," June said, but gently and with a hug. "You're what's left of her."

Rosanna nodded.

"What do we do if he's there?" It felt like hours had passed, but time was impossible to guess.

"Running sounds like our best plan" June said. "If we can get to my truck, I got some cold-weather gear. Maybe we can get help."

"Yeah right, I can just hear it. 'Come hunt the crazy magician that blew up my Granny's house', We'd get lots of help, especially of the pharmaceutical variety."

"That wouldn't be the craziest story we've heard up here," June said. "But what? You want to do this alone?"

"He's my responsibility, June."

"And he's my enemy, now." June's voice was low and growling. Rosanna shivered.

"I wouldn't want to be your enemy, I think."

"No, you wouldn't. And you wouldn't be stupid enough to manage it. He's underestimated both of us. We got the advantage, there."

"Some advantage." Rosanna felt June shrug.

"You take 'em where you find 'em," she said.

"Anyway, I'm not sure what direction we're facing, except that I asked to go home."

"You got a magic compass," June said. "Why don't you ask it?"

Rosanna laughed. For all that she was the magic-user, she still wasn't used to the idea.

'Compass,' she thought. 'Which way to June's truck?'

The knife pulsed and pulled a little to the left and ahead.

"It's pointing mostly right in front of us," Rosanna said.

"Good," June replied. "No matter where we are in this mess, it shouldn't be too far."

"And if he's there?"

"We'll do our best to kill him," June said, and that was all there really was to say about it. And really, what more was there?

Rosanna had a thought.

"What about my car?" she said, but June shook her head.

"It might be closer, but we don't even know if it's still there. Might be packed around us."

Rosanna groaned.

"And me without crazy bastard insurance. Do you suppose this comes under an act of God?"

"I hope so. Don't have crazy bastard insurance myself and this place..."her voice shook a little. "This is all I got."

Rosanna rested her head on June's shoulder for a moment, the closest she could get to a hug. She was ashamed that she hadn't thought of June's loss in the immediacy of her own. June took the comfort wordlessly, and tightened her arm around Rosanna in thanks, then released her grip.

"That's enough of that," she said. "Best get on with it, don't you think?"

Rosanna pushed the last little way through the debris and out into open air. They both tumbled out into the snow. It was cold, but Rosanna reveled in the cleanness of it, in the lack of hate. She looked around, but there was no obvious sign of Trapper. June lay in the snow for a moment, too, taking in great breaths of cold, clean air. She took Rosanna's hand, and tugged. She stayed bent low, and Rosanna took the hint. After that long stint of crawling she badly wanted to stand and stretch, but not so badly that she wanted to risk their skins for it.

Skins...maybe this had been a snare, just intended to hold them till they were too weak to struggle. If that were so, he ought to be watching. June pulled at her hand again, and Rosanna realized she'd stop to think. This was no time for it. The two women moved as quietly and quickly as they could through the snow. They were both soon shuddering with the cold, but the truck wasn't far, up under the shelter of some trees.

June took one look over her shoulder, shook her head, and kept going. Rosanna spared a glance, and shuddered the harder. The gas pumps still stood, but the restaurant was nothing more than a pile of dust and ice. There was no sign of her car, but it could have been hidden behind the devastation.

They reached the truck without being smashed to pieces themselves. June edged them around behind the ancient blue monstrosity, and they peeked up over the box, looking for Trapper. There was no sign of him, though the spell over the debris-field held.

"He's got to maintain the spell," Rosanna whispered. "He doesn't know we're out."

"Can you find him?" June whispered back.

"Don't think so. pretty tired. Maybe in a little while?" She could hear the faint whisper of Trapper's voice, holding the ice and hatred together.

"Can you convince him we're still there?"

Now that was an idea worth considering. It must take a good bit of energy to hold onto this thing, and if he were distracted and tired when they found him, so much the better. June's teeth were chattering, and so were Rosanna's, but she didn't want to draw his attention, not until she'd set up her distraction. She Spoke a tiny syllable of warmth and air, told it what she needed. In the end, she held a little spark, something about the size of a mouse. It was a separate thing from her, not so much a spell as a little magical construct. She sent it back to Trapper's monster of a spell. It nibbled cautiously at the edges, not enough to invite a full-scale attack, but enough to suggest someone were struggling against the bonds. Rosanna grinned. She liked the idea of *him* ragged and weary, just for a change.

"Safe to go?" June stuttered.

"Safe as it will be."

There was a wooden storage locker in the box of the truck. June opened it up and took out a couple worn winter coats and some mittens. Rosanna sheathed her knife and shimmied into a jacket. The fabric was stiff with cold, but Rosanna didn't yet dare use magic to speed the warming. June pulled another jacket on, and pulled the hood up. She blew on her fingers for a moment, then shoved her hands in her jean pockets. Even cold as they were, the thick layers of wool and eiderdown were a comfort against the chill of the morning air. Rosanna was grateful there was no wind. June hunted for her keys, and didn't find them, but she had a spare hidden in the box. She grinned.

"Be prepared," she whispered.

"Girl scouts?"

"Drunk father," June whispered back, and grinned.

They eased open the passenger door, since it was farthest from the restaurant. Trapper might be miles away, or just hidden in the trees. The longer they could hold off alerting him to their escape, the better. As soon as they got into the cabin of the truck, Granny's web flared, and filled the space. It warmed almost immediately, and Rosanna could have cried with relief. It wasn't gone after all. She tested the strands with her mind, and found them all just as strong as when Granny had cast it. They pulsed slightly with her heartbeat. Whatever it was, it wasn't going away any time soon. She blinked away a tear, and June caught sight of it. She patted Rosanna's arm with hands made clumsy by cold and exhaustion. She took a long look at the remains of her home and livelihood, and her mouth thinned to a cold, hard line. Her eyes were nearly brown in the new light, with golden fires burning in their depths. No, Rosanna would not want June for an enemy, but she did not pity Trapper.

June fumbled with the keys, shuddering so with the cold that finally Rosanna dared the quietest Word of warmth that she could manage, whispering it into Granny's web in hopes that it would mask the sound. She sent a little trickle of that heat under the hood of the truck as well. June nodded her gratitude, then stopped, just on the verge of turning the key.

"Old truck," she whispered. "Loud."

"Should we push it out?"

June shrugged, fatigue in every line of her, and Rosanna shared it. But if they could sneak away, with Trapper none the wiser, they would have the advantage of time and surprise. The two looked at each other and sighed. June put the truck in neutral, then edged the driver's side door open. Rosanna took the long step down on the passenger side, and they braced themselves against the door frames. The snow was well packed, and the truck moved with relative ease, but they were both near the edge of their physical limits.

They got it out onto the road, turned looking down the long slope past the diner. Turning the truck right around was beyond their abilities, but they had a chance of sneaking by without turning the engine over at all. They gave the truck one last push, then both climbed in. The truck rolled quietly, and painfully slowly at first. Rosanna couldn't help but watch the café as they passed it. Her car was still there, mostly intact from the look of it, as were the gas pumps. She shuddered to think what Trapper might have done with all that fuel.

They picked up speed, finally passing the clearing around the diner. June stared straight ahead, her jaw clenched and her mittened hands tight on the wheel. She waited a little longer, then turned the key in the ignition. The engine started without complaint, though they winced at the loudness of it, even from this distance. June put it in gear, and the old truck picked up speed, leaving ice and ruin behind.

# Chapter 14

The shocks on the old truck squeaked and bucked over every little bump in the road, but the cabin heated up quickly. Rosanna turned around often, but there was no sign of pursuit, and finally she decided she was just too tired for vigilance. If Trapper was coming after them, a few seconds' notice wasn't going to make any difference. At this point, there was nothing she could do about it anyway. She was dead tired, and she ached all over. The wounds June had stitched pulsed protest with Rosanna's heartbeat. There was no other specific complaint that suggested deeper injury, but she felt almost exactly as if a building had collapsed on her. Granny's web had expanded to cover the inside of the truck, and she drew both comfort and sorrow from it. The feeling of Granny was so strong in it that Rosanna could almost hear her voice, but that only served to remind her that she'd never hear Granny's voice again. A tear overspilled her eye and got tangled in her stitches. She brushed at it carefully. June glanced over at her.

"You holdin' up?" she asked.

"I guess so," Rosanna replied. "You?"

"More or less," June said. "I'm tired and I'm hungry."

"Me too. Any ideas?"

"Yeah, actually. There's folks around here I could go to, but I don't want to bring that bastard down on 'em."

Rosanna nodded.

"I shouldn't have…"

"Shut it," June said. "I don't want to hear that crap from you ever, you got it? What he did ain't your fault."

"But your place…"

"Just shut it. You're too tired for guilt and I'm too tired to talk you out of it. Waste of energy either way."

It was true. Like grief, guilt would have to wait.

"So where are we going?"

June handled the beast of a truck deftly around curves and up icy slopes.

"We can go up to the hot springs," she said. "I got some supplies stashed there. Sometimes a girl's got to get away. There's sleeping bags and a tent in the box."

"Is it far?"

"A ways," June said. "Maybe far enough that Trapper won't think about it."

Rosanna wrapped her arms around herself. She wasn't used to being prey yet, it wasn't her first thought that he might or might not know a place. All she wanted was rest and food, and a moment or a day to settle back into her own head.

Rosanna looked at her watch, and the broken crystal looked back. She'd forgotten about that.

"I wonder what time it is," she said. It was strange and unsettling to not know the time, to not have an accounting of moments spent struggling or fleeing.

June shrugged. "Daytime, I guess." She peered up at the sky. "Maybe noon? Don't make much difference. It'll take us 'bout an hour to the turnoff, maybe twenty minutes after that, if we don't get stuck."

"Stuck?"

"Ain't much but a logging trail," June said, "at least where we're going. There's hotels and stuff further along, but I don't mean to be easy to find."

Rosanna nodded. A hotel sounded nice, but she didn't think she'd survive having another building dropped on her head. She shuddered, thinking of ice and hatred pressing down around her. They should have died there, she knew.

"Won't people be worried about you?" she asked.

"Probably," June replied. "Better they're worried than we're dead. You know what all he can do? Can he find us?"

"I don't know," Rosanna admitted wearily. "There's so much I don't know." She paused. "But I hope that if he thinks we're still trapped, he won't be looking."

June nodded. "By now someone is probably trying to dig us out," She said.

"He may have to let go of the spell for that," Rosanna said. "I don't know."

"Well, no point worryin' over what we can't know," June said. "We just gotta get someplace safe." She bared her teeth. "Then we hunt."

"I've never gone hunting," Rosanna said. She patted the knife at her thigh, and it gave a little pulse of warmth.

"Done some hunting," June replied, "but never hunted a walking magical asshole before."

Rosanna laughed, the sound bright and loud over the squeaks and groans of the truck. June smiled her approval.

"You wanna rest for a bit, that's fine," June said. "You still look like shit."

"Thanks, you're not exactly looking fabulous yourself," Rosanna said. It was true; June had an enormous bruise on her right cheek that blossomed purple up to her temple and into her hairline. Her brown hair was matted with mud, and her features were sharp with fatigue, as if the skin were drawn too tight across bone and muscle.

"I could drive," Rosanna said, then paused, as June shifted gear. "Maybe. I haven't driven a standard in forever."

June shook her head.

"I don't want to spend the time switching," she said. "Besides, I know where we're goin', you don't. Just sleep a little. I'll wake you if I need keepin' awake."

Rosanna nodded, and closed her eyes. She was too tired to argue with sense, or even nonsense. She dozed lightly, woken often by the lurch and squall of the truck. She felt dreams hemmed around her, and she was just as happy to avoid them. She couldn't afford those dreams yet, not until there was safety around her in some measure. She slipped easily between slightly dizzy wakefulness and incomplete sleep.

She woke fully when the truck turned off the highway and onto a road that was more pothole than road. The first stretch of it was asphalt, with only a light covering of snow, but soon there was only a snowy track leading up the side of a steep hill and towards the mountains. She yawned and stretched, and winced at the stiffening of her bruises.

"Better?" June asked.

"Some," Rosanna said. "Are we close?"

"Bout twenty minutes, long as we don't get stuck."

The sun was mostly hidden behind thick pine forest, but sunlight still splashed off of deep snow on the road. There were drifts among the trees, but only where the trees were far enough apart to permit it. There had been some traffic on the road, but not enough to clear it, and nothing since the last snow. June's truck grumbled and moaned, but it didn't seem to have much difficulty with the terrain. They reached the top of that long slope, and looked down into a valley, the grade so steep that Rosanna thought skis might be a better choice of transportation.

June looked at Rosanna's expression and chuckled.

"It's not so bad," she said. "This truck has done it a thousand times."

"Yeah but there's no tracks! Are you sure we're in the right place?"

"I'm usually the one that makes the tracks," June said. "Don't be chicken."

"I'm not...okay, well, yes, I am a little. But it looks like we could just slide down on our butts."

"You can go that way, if you want," June said. "Me? I like heat."

Rosanna stuck out her tongue, and June stuck out hers, and they laughed at each other.

"This ain't the first time I done this," June said. "Grab hold, sit tight. We're almost there. Hot water and whiskey. Oh, and food." She grinned, then growled a little as the expression pulled against tender muscles.

"Maybe even aspirin," she said.

"For that I'll brave a ski hill," Rosanna said, and took hold of the handle above the door. June moved the truck forward slowly, and it lurched into the deep snow. Chunks of ice and snow flew up on the windshield, and June turned on the wipers to clear them. Rosanna found she had to brace her feet, as well, to keep from being thrown around too painfully. It was like riding a boat in a storm, up and over the waves of snow.

June drove cautiously, but not too slow. Rosanna's worry calmed a little, simply by virtue of June's nonchalance. Maybe this was a big deal for city girls, but country girls clearly took it all in stride. The grade lessened, then evened out, and Rosanna saw steam a little further ahead. The truck grumped and squawked up over one last snow drift, and June pulled to a stop. Rosanna looked around in disappointment. Somehow she'd hoped for cabins or pools, maybe even the security of a house. Instead she saw a few cedar boxes up among the snowdrifts, and even getting to those promised to be cold work.

"Is this it?" she asked, trying not to wilt. Fierce women didn't wilt, she was sure.

"Yup," June said. "Told ya, it ain't much, but at least it's private."

"But where will we stay?"

June sighed.

"I told ya, I got a tent in the back." She turned the truck off, and looked at Rosanna.

"You're not gonna wimp out on me, are ya?" she asked. Her tone was light, but her eyes were dark brown with concern.

Rosanna shook her head.

"No, I'm sorry. I'm just...I'm just really tired." To her own mortification, she started to weep.

"I'm sorry," Rosanna said, and repeated it over and over. June scooted across the seat, and put her arms around her, rocking gently. The tears tangled in Rosanna's stitches, and stung and burned, but there was no injury worse than her fatigue at that moment. It pulled all the fire out of her, and left her sifting the ashes for some scrap of intention or ability.

Rosanna sniffled at last, and pulled herself upright.

"I'm not going to wimp out, I swear. It's just..." she could feel the tears prickling behind her eyes and scrubbed them impatiently. "I'm just a little out of my element, here." She said at last.

"First element is snow," June said. "I'm tired too, but we need a place to lie down, and we need food, and we need a good stiff drink while we soak."

Rosanna nodded. All this made sense, and it also made sense to stay away from civilized places, not just to evade Trapper themselves, but to keep other people safe from him. But she was a city girl, always had been. When she camped, it was only ever at someplace with room service.

"C'mon," June said. "Sooner we set up camp, sooner we can crawl into a hot spring and a bottle."

Rosanna climbed down from the truck. Granny's web clung to her has she moved, and sank through her clothes and disappeared. She could still feel it, though, and Hear its protections, like an echo of Granny's voice. Outside, the snow was up over her knees, but still fairly soft and easy to move through. June opened the box in the truck, and pulled out the tent and sleeping bag.

"Come on and get one of these," she said. "I don't want to get snow on 'em."

Rosanna shuffled through the snow around the front of the truck. It was chilly out, but not unpleasant in the shelter of the trees. Rosanna looked up, and saw patches of blue among the waving branches. A light wind shushed through the needles, and a bird called somewhere off in the distance. The truck still ticked as it cooled, an enormous blue beast settling down for a nap.

The sleeping bag June handed to Rosanna was surprisingly light, and June smiled at her surprise.

"There are some things you just don't go cheap on," she said. "Being warm is one of 'em." She passed the other bag to Rosanna as well. "If you can carry both, I'll get the axe. I got firewood in my stash, but I don't want to come back for it if I don't have to."

Rosanna nodded. The bags were lighter than some purses she'd carried. She followed June into the snow between the cedar boxes, and she finally got to see what they were. Black plastic pipes poked up from them, two to each box, and poured water into hot-tubs that looked large enough to hold a dozen people each. The water steamed invitingly, and she sighed, just looking at it.

"Come on," June said. "Camp first, soak second. I don't know 'bout you, but as soon as I soak I'm gonna want to sleep."

It made sense, but Rosanna followed only reluctantly. She didn't even mind the strong sulphur smell of the water, she just yearned for the clean heat of it.

"Anyway, there's a better spot further in, by my stash," June said. "Stone pools you don't even have to climb into. We'll camp there."

There was little sign of human intrusion. Some of the paths looked like they might have been flattened down earlier in the winter, but nothing very recent. When she looked in the pools, she saw a fair layer of pine needles suspended near the bottom of them, and bits of leaf danced around on their surfaces. It was comforting to feel this place wasn't tended, nor overly populated. She saw deer tracks in the snow, but hers and June's were the only human tracks. The stillness settled into her and eased a little of the terror from her muscles. There was a deep calm here, a peace that seemed almost holy.

Rosanna shuffled along in June's tracks, past the pools and into the shadows of the trees. The snow was less there, just a thin covering over the pine needles with an occasional drift. June's stash proved to be a sturdily built pine box with a padlock on it, hidden behind a screen of bushes.

"We can set up right here," she said, gesturing at the needle-strewn forest floor. "No need to sleep on the snow."

Rosanna thought that she could probably sleep standing upright, and not care about the snow, but perhaps this would be a more comfortable option. June unfolded the tent, which was surprisingly modern-looking. Rosanna looked questioningly at it, and June chuckled.

"What, us hillbillies ain't allowed nice toys?"

"It's not that," Rosanna protested. "It's just, your truck, you know…seems kind of…well-worn."

June laughed. "My truck is a heap of shit," she said, "except that it does what I need it to. I had an old army surplus tent for ages, but it blew away on me one night. This one ain't blown away yet. Guaranteed not to, even. Plus it's easy to set up, even in the dark."

Indeed, it seemed not to be set up so much as shook out, like a blanket that magically unfolded into a tent with a little vestibule. Rosanna helped stake it down, and the fly over it. June opened a valve on a rolled-up mat and threw it inside, and it began inflating itself, just as magically as the tent had erected. She took the sleeping bags out of their stuff-sacks and lay them over the mat.

"So?" she said. "What first? Food or soak?"

"I have to pick?" Rosanna said mournfully, and June laughed.

"Well, hot food will take a bit, but I've got some dried fruit here. That tide you over?"

"Sure."

"Fine then, we'll take it to the pool. Got extra towels and blankets. Almost like I spend time up here in twosomes," she said, and winked. She packed some bags and bottles into a little day-pack and shrugged into it.

"Almost," Rosanna said. "How uncanny that you were prepared like this."

"Oh yeah, uncanny, that's me."

"I wasn't going to mention it, but now that you have…"

"When I want your opinion, I'll give it to you," June said, and thrust a towel and blanket into Rosanna's hands. They were both stiff with the cold, but Rosanna was grateful for June's forethought, whatever wicked behavior had incited it.

"Just gimme a sec," June said, "I'll set up the heater before we go down, so it'll be warm in the tent when we get back."

"Oh luxury," Rosanna said, and June smiled. The heater was hardly recognizable as such, just a little plate with a propane bottle attached. June set it up in the vestibule as well, making sure it didn't touch the sleeping bags, then zipped the fly.

"It'll turn off if it tips," she said. "I tested that myself. Let's go."

Rosanna struggled to walk, and June put an arm around her waist. They leaned on each other gently, like two friends tipsy enough to need support, but sober enough not to want to be burdensome. It wasn't a long walk, but the slope down to the pools was slippery in places where the snow had drifted over stones. They went slowly, and Rosanna could see the steam rising ahead long before she saw or heard water.

They came first to a well-weathered outhouse, and both women stopped to use it. Rosanna would almost rather have peed in the snow, but then again, she wasn't sure she would have been steady enough to avoid soaking her boots. It wasn't a particularly offensive outhouse in any case, and the graffiti was entertaining. It was a little bit more of a walk to the change house, which was only big enough for the two of them. It was little more than a shed with rough plank walls, but the floor was satin-smooth, warn so by many feet, and it was warm. Rosanna looked at June questioningly, and she smiled.

"The spring comes up under us, and runs down to the pools. Whoever built this didn't want cold feet, I guess."

"Is it old?"

June shrugged. "I guess. It was here when I was a kid. Doesn't get used so much now that they put the pools in."

"I kind of like it," Rosanna said. Something about that age appealed to her, felt comfortable and comforting. She set her blanket and towel on the floor as she undressed. She wanted to be shy, but June stripped with such a relentless lack of self-consciousness that Rosanna had to follow suit. Her various stitches pulled and complained, but she ignored them as best she could. Granny's spell was a pale golden light that shimmered just beneath her skin, doing its best. she thought, to help mend her various hurts. Granny's hands could still give comfort. She shook her head, and let the thought go. She wasn't ready to stand here naked and weep. She already felt too exposed in her grief. She focused on now, on the simple tasks of buttons and laces. Soon there would be hot water and maybe alcohol. Just one drink, perhaps, but the idea of a world slightly softened appealed immensely. She couldn't afford the to be overly blurred, but just a little couldn't hurt. She needed to think and plan, and she wouldn't be able to keep any rein on her emotions if she got drunk. Not that drunk didn't sound nice. It sounded blissful as a feather-bed. Just not wise.

Rosanna pulled her boots back on and wrapped herself in the blanket. June opened the door, and Rosanna shivered at the cold breeze that slipped into the relative warmth of the hut.

"C'mon," June said. "Haul city ass, if you don't want it froze off."

Rosanna laughed, and they scuffled and slid down the last few feet to the steaming water. The snow ended a few feet away from the pool, and they left boots and blankets there. Rosanna had never gone skinny-dipping before, and it felt pleasantly naughty to stand out in nature as nature (and a sedentary lifestyle) had made her. June's body was brown and lithe, sleek and feline with muscle. She belonged out here, under the wild sky. A pair of parallel scars crossed her ribs on her right side, and they only made June look more feral and dangerous. Rosanna felt dumpy and out of place, here where paths were forged through snow, not shoveled and salted by underpaid city workers. She looked down at the pale softness of her tummy and sighed.

"Yes, you still have tits," June said. "Did you think they'd left? C'mon, I'm freezing!"

Rosanna laughed, and took June's hand. The pool was lined with smooth stones from the river, and it was a little slippery  getting in. It sloped down gently from the shore to a deep well in the center that looked more than big enough for two. Water flowed down to the river out a narrow channel on one side. They supported each other, leaning and swaying to help each other stay upright. The air was cold, and a little winter draft kept coming around, just in case they were getting too warm. The water, though, was deliciously hot; not enough to scald, but enough that each step into it felt like a step into summer. At the deepest part, the pool was hip-deep on Rosanna, and a little wider than she could reach with outspread arms. June sunk into it with a sigh, then paddled easily to the pebbled slope, stretching out with the water up around her neck. Rosanna sank down to her knees, then let the mineral-rich water float her up to the surface. Her scrapes and stitches stung briefly, but the heat felt good on her bruises. She floated with her ears under the water, listening only to the mindless murmur and laugh of the water around her. She Heard, too, Words of warming and healing in that conversation, but for the moment she was content to merely listen.

She pulled her head up out of the water when June began to splash about. Rosanna looked for her, feeling she ought to be alarmed, but too tired and warm to manage it. June had already slipped back into the pool by the time Rosanna realized she'd been out.

"Forgot my drink," June said. "You still want those apples?"

Rosanna crouched down in the water, and walked slowly to June's side, careful to keep as much of herself submerged as she could. June laughed.

"You walk like a lobster," she said. "And you're almost red enough to be one." Rosanna reached out and pinched June's toe.

"Watch it, you," she said. "We lobsters are proud and fierce."

"Mmhm," June said. "Right up to the melted butter. Here, eat something and leave my toes alone."

Rosanna took the plastic bag from June and started to eat, feeling the sweetness as another source of warmth, almost. June stole a few pieces, then opened up the bottle she'd brought and took a swig. Rosanna took a sip when June offered the bottle, but nothing more. The hot water and the stillness were relaxing her enough that she was afraid a drink would put her right to sleep. June had one more hearty drink then leaned back in the pool and contemplated her toes. Rosanna finished about half the apples, then tossed the bag back towards their boots. She crept down the slope a bit until she was a little better covered, then leaned back into the water again, resting her head on one of the smooth river-stones. The murmur of healing was stronger where she lay, and she felt some of her aches fade even more than mere hot water could account for. Even the bruise on June's cheek looked fainter, as if it were a day old, rather than hours. She rolled over onto her stomach, and traced the stones with her fingers till she found the one that whispered, and dug it gently out from the bed of the pool.

Out of the water, it was a knobbly, ugly little thing, not as smooth as the other stones, but it fit easily in the palm of her hand. June, who had been gazing off into the tree-line turned to look.

"What's that?" she said.

"Dunno," Rosanna replied. "But it's got magic in it."

June held out her hands and Rosanna passed the stone to her.

"Could be a geode," June said. "You'd have to split it open to be sure."

Rosanna shook her head.

"I wouldn't want to do that. Like I said, there's magic in it. Something healing."

"Not Trapper's doing, then?"

"No, not likely. It feels...old. And it feels like it belongs here."

"Indians used to come here, maybe they knew your magic."

"Maybe. I wonder how they put it in the rock?" She thought of her little frost word, and wondered about putting it into a stone. Would that keep it safe? Like a little Library for one? "Granny would know," she said. Tears rose up in her eyes. Granny might, but she wasn't there to ask. The web under her skin hummed quietly, like a quiet song of comfort. She let the tears fall for a little while, then washed them away with a handful of hot water.

June handed the stone back.

"Do you want to take it?" she asked.

"I don't know," Rosanna said. "It's probably been here a long time. It seems...wrong just to take it."

"Feels good to hold, " June said. "Maybe we could borrow it till tomorrow."

"Maybe we could," Rosanna said. They needed whatever help they could get. Besides, Rosanna wanted a better look at it. Maybe she could figure out how to do something similar with the Words she had, to protect them in case…in case things didn't go well.

"Well," June said, "I'm about boiled. How bout you, lobster-girl?"

Rosanna nodded, and June ducked her head to scrub the mud out of her hair. Rosanna did the same, then the both climbed out of the pool. Rosanna's legs felt weak and rubbery after the heat. She and June supported each other up to the change house, then back to the tent. A few clouds had begun to obscure the sun, and there was already a sense of twilight, although Rosanna didn't think it was much past early afternoon. Daylight didn't last long this time of year, and the mountains stole what scraps there were. Their camp was in deep shadow by the time they arrived, and Rosanna shivered with cold and exhaustion both. The stone in her pocket helped keep her upright, but she was swaying on her feet as she waited for June to open the tent. Food would have to wait on rest. June, too, was pale and shaky with fatigue.

June pulled the heater out and Rosanna crept in.

"Does it matter which one I take?" she asked.

"Suit yourself," June said. "Don't matter to me."

The tent was warm, and Rosanna shed her coat with relief. She put the healing stone on the floor of the tent between the two sleeping bags, then crawled into one. The inside was still chilly, but it warmed up soon enough with her body heat. The mat underneath was springy as a firm mattress, and she felt neither the chill nor hardness of the frozen ground beneath. She meant to have a little cry for Granny, or simply for the unfairness of it all, but warm and horizontal was all it took to send her to sleep. She was barely aware of June zipping into the other bag when the world tipped her into the dreaming dark.

# Chapter 15

Dark and cold collapsed onto Rosanna, and Trapper laughed. She fought, but couldn't move, and Granny's blood covered her hands. She wanted to howl, but she couldn't breathe.

"I died for you," Granny whispered. "I'm dead because of you." Rosanna tried to again scream, but no sound could escape the trap. "Dead," Granny said. Rosanna reached for her, but her body dissolved, poured through her fingers in terrible scarlet streams.

"NO!" Rosanna shrieked, and her eyes opened into the chilly darkness of the tent. She was tangled in her sleeping bag, and cold where she'd slithered out of it. June rustled beside her, then there was the hiss of a propane lamp, and a gentle glow lit the shelter and June's face. June hung the lamp on a hook, and scooted over to put an arm around Rosanna's shoulders.

Rosanna looked around her, comforting herself that they had escaped the diner. But not all of them.

"Granny," she said, and started to rock and weep. "Oh no, Granny, no." Rosanna could still hear her voice, and the sounds of her soul spinning away. She stroked her arm, feeling the web there, hearing the last echoes of Granny's being. How long would it last? How long would she hear Granny's final words? Tears shook her so that there was no other sound for a long while. June said nothing, just sat with Rosanna and her grief, and let the storm blow through. When Rosanna quieted a bit, June crawled out of the tent and came back with tissues and a bottle.

Rosanna snuffled and blew her nose, and took a small sip of the whiskey.

"Come on," June said. "Let's have something to eat."

It was dark out, but that meant little when Rosanna had no watch. It could have been half an hour past sunset or three in the morning. It didn't matter. It was supper-time, whatever time it was.

They bundled up in their coats, and Rosanna slipped the healing stone into her pocket. It was comfort and kindness there, a little ember that warmed and soothed her spirit as much as her body. June carried the lantern out to her cache and hung it on a handy branch while she lifted the lid. Packed inside were plastic bags of various sizes, and foil pouches. June pulled a small cook stove and a couple pots out of one corner. She handed the pots to Rosanna.

"Here," she said. "Go fill those with snow. It'll be slow but I don't feel like walking down to the river. You?"

"Not really," Rosanna said.

"Try not to get the yellow kind, city girl."

"Even city girls don't eat the yellow snow."

"Good to know," June said. "Got some kinda sense, anyhow."

"Any wild animals I should look out for?"

"Some, but they don't like the light much. Just don't go too far. And don't forget your knife."

Rosanna didn't need to be told to stay close. The shadows and the wind made her nervous. Once out of the circle of lamplight, the forest was as foreign as another country, with rustles and creaks that sounded almost like language. She filled the pots and retreated gracelessly into the comfort of light and company.

June had dropped a small pile of gear at the door to the tent, and hung the lamp on a nail in one of the trees. She set the stove on a section of log that had clearly seen that purpose before and fired it up.

"Bring those here," she said, and put the snow on to melt.

"You can pick supper," she said. "Long as it ain't the chicken stew. That stuff tastes like crap."

"Why do you have it, then?"

"Friend gave it to me. I keep hopin' she'll come camping with me so I can feed it to her." Rosanna laughed, and looked through the packets of freeze-dried food.

"Some of this looks pretty gourmet," she said. "Couscous? Curry?"

"Curry's good," June said. "Thai chicken's better."

Rosanna hunted till she found the Thai chicken, and shook her head. Camping food had come a long way from when she was a kid.

June melted snow, boiled the water, and then started the supper. She and Rosanna pulled more log segments in to sit on, then hung a tarp between some of the trees to cut the wind. Rosanna was chilly, but not unbearably cold. She was only grateful she'd gotten her boots on before everything went to hell. June sent her for more snow. It took a lot of snow to make enough water to be useful, but when the pot was full, June boiled some up for tea as  the supper cooked. Rosanna put her hands into the spacious coat pockets as she waited. The breeze had dropped, and it was very quiet. Rosanna thought she could hear the murmur of the river off in the distance, but little else. She felt herself begin to relax, if reluctantly. June handed her a cup of tea, and she cupped it gratefully, letting the warmth soak through her mittens.

"This camping thing might not be so bad," Rosanna said, sipping tea and smelling spices and chicken.

"Nope, not bad. Better in summer, though. Get a case of beer and a six-pack of bug repellant, and you're set." Rosanna laughed.

"You think I'm kidding'? Skeeters 'round here come bird-sized. Seen one fly off with a good-sized dog once."

"You sound like Trapper," Rosanna said, and sobered. Then she frowned. "Damn it, I **liked** him. He was funny and..." she shook her head.

"I liked him too," June said. "Never trusted him, but liked him well enough I mighta taken him up on all them offers."

"But you didn't?"

"Nosy," June said, but shook her head. "Almost wish I had."

"What?"

"Afore I knew all this...he was just a guy. Sorta friend. nice ass...why not? Wasn't so complicated." She looked at Rosanna and laughed, head back and teeth gleaming in the lamplight. "Why, I think I mighta shocked you. Don't you know nothing 'bout hillbilly ways? It's all sex all the time, honest. Like bunnies in the wild, wet bush." She laughed again, and Rosanna had to join her.

"So why didn't you?" Rosanna asked at last. "You had opportunity, I'm sure."

"That trust thing," June said. "Somethin' never felt quite honest about him. Not the stories, you know, but sorta deep down not real. I don't care for that. It don't make sense to waste honest on a liar."

"I don't know what I'm supposed to think about him. He's my father, but he could be anyone."

"Not quite," June said. "He's the crazy asshole that wrecked my place and killed your Granny and tried to do the same to us. That other...that's just another fact, like the colour of his eyes. Don't change nothing."

"Granny..."

"And now you're getting set to blame yourself, yeah? We don't got energy for that, okay?"

"But...I didn't save her."

"You didn't kill her neither. You only got it in you to do so much, just like anyone. You did your best. I was there, I know."

"And your place?"

"I don't blame you for that neither." June's expression went wild and feral for a moment, and Rosanna was just as glad not to be in June's bad books.

"But I brought him on you." Rosanna remembered Granny's place, and the crazy drive in the dark. Was there anything else she could have done? Anywhere else she could have gone?

"He gave me a choice, remember? I chose you, not the other way round. I coulda kicked you out if I wanted. I didn't."

"Why did you choose us? Over him, I mean? You knew him longer."

"That honest thing, I figger. You two...you was just what you said. And you needed help." June grinned. "Always been a sucker for a hard-luck case."

"What do we do now?" Rosanna said, looking into her mug of tea. There were no leaves to read. How she longed for a sign, a pointer.

"Now we eat," June said, and handed her a tin bowl full of rice and chicken.

June had been right, it was good. It was spicy enough to raise a light sweat on her forehead, but tasty and flavorful too. She ate so quickly that it hardly had time to cool, then had seconds. June put another pot of snow on to melt. There was freeze-dried ice-cream and dried cherries for dessert, and Rosanna was comfortably full as she sipped the last cup of tea.

"Okay," June said. "Now we can figure out what next. Food is always first, even for a fierce woman."

"I'll try to remember that."

"You do. Ain't no point in trying' anything hungry, even thinkin'."

"I think you just like to feed people," Rosanna accused.

"Maybe, could well be. That don't make it less true," June said. "Go on, tell me you don't feel better now."

"Yeah, a little," Rosanna said.

"There you go. Brains need energy just like bodies. No point askin' a hungry brain anything."

"Okay, okay. Yes boss. Now what?"

June shook her head, her face solemn.

"No, I'm sorry. I ain't the boss. I won't be."

Rosanna had thought she was only joking when she said it, but her heart sank a little.

"Everything I've been responsible for has gone to shit," she said, and ducked her head to hide the sudden tears.

"I ain't even gonna argue with you," June said. "You're the boss here and now, and I don't care what you done or ain't done before. We clear?"

Rosanna snuffled a little, then met June's eyes. There was no doubt there, no blame. Rosanna straightened her back, and nodded.

"Clear enough," she said. "But I'm in way over my head. Do you suppose we could try for partners?"

"I suppose we could," June said. "There's going to come decisions that need a boss, though, and you're it. If there ain't time for a vote, you get final word."

"As long as we can help each other," Rosanna said. "As long as you don't count on me to know more than I do."

"You know how to start a fire?" June asked.

"More or less," Rosanna replied. "Wasn't much of a girl scout."

"Well then, help me get a fire started, partner. I want to roast some marshmallows." Rosanna chuckled and stood.

The fire pit was a good ways from the tent, far enough that no vagrant breeze was likely to carry a spark to it. Rosanna cleared debris out of it while June got kindling and wood from her supply cache. She dumped an armful on the ground just as Rosanna finished, then laid the kindling and started the fire. The wood was dry and caught quickly. Rosanna rolled their seats closer, and by the time she was done a healthy blaze lit the clearing. June wasn't even kidding about the marshmallows. They were frozen pretty solid, but they roasted just fine on the sticks June provided. Rosanna had a couple, watching June across the fire. She looked as relaxed and casual as if this were any camping trip, just a jaunt into the woods for fun.

"We are resolved not to run, aren't we?" Rosanna said at last.

"What would be the point? If he'd kill me to get you he'd kill anyone, near as I can see. Besides, I mean to get me a little vengeance." Her eyes glinted in the firelight. "Don't you?"

"I suppose," Rosanna said. She shrugged down deeper into her coat to cover her ears.

"What do you mean, you 'suppose'? Ain't you pissed?"

"I've never been very good at angry," Rosanna said. "Right now I'm too busy with tired and grieved and scared."

"Time to turn scared into mad, girl."

Rosanna shook her head wearily. Somewhere in her, she was furious, but right now she could barely touch emotion at all. She watched the dance and play of the flames, and felt their heat instead.

"Never mind," June said at last. "You feel what you feel. But I don't mean to leave him a place to hide, not when he wrecked mine."

"I don't want this to be about revenge," Rosanna said. "That doesn't…that doesn't feel right to me."

"Well then, fine, it's about putting down another damn cougar that thinks it can hunt humans. It's about staying **alive**. That feel better to you?"

"No, it doesn't. It all feels like shit, it all feels…stupid and pointless and wrong. I can't believe this is happening." Rosanna threw her head back and shouted. "WHY IS THIS HAPPENING TO ME?" The only answer was an echo, and it died away quickly.

"Does it matter why," June said at last. "Does it really?"

"I like to know the why's of things, and all I did was come out for Solstice with my Granny."

"Well then, imagine my surprise," June said. "All I did was serve an early breakfast." She shook her head. "You can drive yourself nuts lookin' for why or what-for. In the end, it all comes back to what is, just the same. This life, these happenings, they was all gonna happen to someone, some day. Why not you? Why not me? Don't matter. All that matters is what we do with it."

"You think it's that simple?"

"Hell, no. Did I say anything about simple? But it ain't complicated. I think you're tryin' real hard to make it complicated."

"Just want to be clear," Rosanna said.

"Just love to talk is all," June said, and grinned. Rosanna stuck out her tongue.

"If the wind changes you'll freeze like that," June said. "Serve you right, too." She dug another marshmallow out of the bag.

"All right then," Rosanna said, "could we get help?"

"Ain't nobody else I know that does magic," June said wryly. "You?"

"No. I suppose there have to be more, but I don't know how to reach them, or if they could help. Police would be pulverized."

"And they wouldn't believe you in the first place."

"True. So it's you and me."

"Fierce women against the world! World better watch its ass," June said, and through the laugher, Rosanna could hear that she meant it, that she *believed* it. That was strangely comforting. Strange, because they were still only two woman against a monster, and comforting, because June was so eminently capable. It was almost contagious.

"Can we find him?" June asked. "I can track, but a starting point would be nice. Might spend all winter at it, elsewise."

"I still have my compass," Rosanna said. "I don't know if it works on people, though." She unsheathed the knife and held it loosely in her lap. It hummed gently at her touch, like a cat waking with a purr. 'Where is Trapper' she thought, picturing him in her mind. The knife tugged her hand, and she stood to brace that hand with the other. She turned toward the knife's pull until she was facing it. It was a strange sort of compass. she thought, that made her into the needle.

"That way, I guess," she said, then sheathed the knife again.

"Guess we can find him," June said. "Don't tell us how far though, or if we can go by truck."

"No compass would tell you all that," Rosanna said. "You complaining?"

"Little bit, but never mind." June paused, and speared another marshmallow. "Okay well, let's leave that part for now. What we gonna do when we find him?"

Rosanna shivered. She didn't really want to consider that. It was far more comfortable to consider where he was, to think of him off in some vague distance. A battle plan was much more immediate.

"I don't know," she said.

"Well that's no good," June replied. "We can't just walk up to him and ask him nicely to die, can we?"

"I don't...I've never killed anyone, before, you know. This isn't exactly easy."

"Girl, we're being hunted. If he could find us we'd be dead." June pulled the tooth out from under her coat. "It ain't no different than this cougar. But we got to have a plan. What do you know he can do?"

"I've seen him make monsters out of animals," Rosanna said, "but I can cure them. It's hard, but I can do it."

June nodded. "And we seen him blow up a building. Anything else?"

"He healed me," Rosanna said quietly, and ducked her head. She slipped her hand into her pocket and pulled out the stone. She could feel it working on her still, soothing hurts and easing her exhaustion more than a few hours' sleep could have done alone.

"And you? What can you do?"

"I don't know," Rosanna said, and June scowled. "Well I don't! I only just started at this, you know."

"I'm not asking what you MIGHT be able to do. What have you done?"

Rosanna thought about her little store of Words, and how she'd applied them.

"I can use ice and fire and wind, I guess," she said. "So far mostly in little ways. I can cure his monstrosities." She thought of the poisoned wolf and cringed. "Granny didn't survive my healing too well though."

"Still ain't your fault." Rosanna shook her head.

"Doesn't matter, really. She's still gone."

June looked across the fire at her, eyes gold and black in the flickering shadows.

"Everyone goes," she said softly. "Ain't nobody immune." Rosanna ducked her head.

"I…I know," she said. "But it isn't fair. We just…she only just told me all this stuff. I feel so lost! And I want her. I just…I want her."

"You're gonna have to find your own way, and that's hard," June said. "But she had faith in you. And so do I." She gave a lopsided smile. "Ain't much I got actual faith in, you know. So take it for a compliment."

Rosanna sat in stillness for a moment, listening to the snap and crackle of the fire. The tall trees around them creaked in the light breeze, and high above the stars were bright in a crystal sky. Faith seemed as far out of her reach as those stars, but perhaps she could cling to June's, just for the moment.

"Thank you," she said at last. "I appreciate that."

"Don't forget that you're smarter than he thinks," June said. "and fiercer, too."

"Ok, so we have the advantage of surprise," Rosanna said. "Even if he doesn't think we're dead, he probably doesn't expect us to come to him." She swallowed. "I kind of can't believe it myself."

"Well," June said, "I'm inclined to give him a day or two to get used to the idea of us bein' dead." She shot Rosanna a glance. "That is, if you think you can survive that long without the internet."

"Ha ha," Rosanna said. "Have I complained?"

"Not much, no. But it's early."

"I'm likelier to complain if there's no coffee in that stash of yours," Rosanna said.

"Do I look that stupid to you?"

"Well…"

"Remember," June said, "I'm the one doin' the cooking."

Rosanna shook her head. Despite the banter, the truth remained that they planned to trap and kill not just any man, (which would have been bad enough) but her father.

"June, I don't know if I can do this," she said.

"I don't know if you can either," June replied. "Hell, I don't know much of nothin', if it come to that. Don't see as we got a choice, though."

"I'm not really much of a magician," Rosanna said. She held up the healing stone. "Whoever made this probably had forgotten more than I know. Maybe more than I'll ever know."

"You can learn though, can't ya?" June said. "You done stuff at my place, I don't know what, but he didn't seem too happy 'bout it."

Rosanna thought back to the battle at the diner, at her efforts and the mingled pride and fury in Trapper's voice.

"I suppose," she said.

"Well, then, you'll do what he doesn't expect," June said.

It all felt rather unreal, out here under the stars and around a cheery campfire, unreal but for the stitches and Granny's absence. She was tired again, but more pleasantly so. The horrible sense of being completely drained had passed, and she thought the healing stone might have more than a little to do with it.

"I want to take a closer look at this stone," she said. "I have some Words that I'd like to protect, and if they're safe I can use them a little more freely."

"Why's that?" June asked. "I'd think free and wild was more powerful, like a horse."

"From how I understand it, free Words can change as they're used, get sort of corrupted from their true meanings." She shrugged. "And besides, while a free horse looks more powerful, a harnessed one can accomplish more. All the power gets directed, you know"

June shook her head.

"For someone who don't know much, you know an awful lot," she said, but Rosanna shook her head.

"It's just the basics, honestly. I don't even know how to make a little Library like this."

"Stop focusing on what you don't got and don't know," June said, and there was a note of exasperation in her voice. "Dammit, girl, you been figuring things out on your own the whole while here. Ain't you gonna pay that any mind?"

"It just seems so little," Rosanna replied.

"What we don't know is always gonna be bigger than what we do," June said. "It's stupid to focus only on what you ain't got. Makes it all the harder to use what you do."

"So I guess the plan is to rest a couple days, I'll work on making little Libraries, and then we follow my knife to the crazy person and make him...stop."

June nodded.

"In the meantime, we can do a little moving around, try to pinpoint his location a bit more."

"Are we okay on supplies?"

"For the time being," June said. "If we're goin' into the woods we might need more equipment. I got no packs in here, and we'll need those."

Rosanna's heart sunk a little at the thought of trudging through snow with a pack on her back.

"Oh cheer up, city girl," June said. "there's folks what pay good money for a mountain trek. You're getting it for practically  nothin'."

"That's not true," Rosanna said. "It's cost me my safety and freedom, and it's cost me Granny."

June put down her marshmallow-roasting stick, and came around the dying fire to rest her arm on Rosanna's shoulders.

"I know, Rosanna, I know. I was only tryin' to joke a little."

Rosanna nodded, and leaned against the comfort of the touch.

"I know you were, it's just...it's all so much, all at once."

"Come on," June said. "that's enough talkin' for now, I think." She scrubbed the bowls with snow, and tossed the dirty snow into the fire.

Rosanna was starting to feel cold again, deep to her bones, and she knew that part of that was simply being tired.

"Why don't you get some sleep?" June said. "I'll be in after a while. I want to watch the fire for a bit. It always relaxes me. Gotta put it out before I come to sleep anyhow."

Rosanna nodded.

"Do you need any help before I go?"

"Nah, I got it covered, thanks."

"Goodnight, then" Rosanna said.

"Goodnight, I won't be long."

Rosanna crawled back into the tent and then into her sleeping bag. She lay back and watched the light of the fire flicker and twist through the fabric of the tent. Once she was zipped in, only the tip of her nose felt cold, and she thought it would warm up in the tent pretty quickly. 'I'm not ready for this,' she thought. But was there any way to be ready? Granny had had her whole life, and not been ready. Sometimes, she guessed, the race started whether all the runners knew it or not. She closed her eyes, listening to the muted sounds of a fading fire, and the whisper and sough of the gentlest breeze among pine boughs. Her breathing was loud under the close tent-covered sky, but it quieted as she slipped closer to the edges of sleep. She supposed she would dream, again. The deep aches within her would not be stilled so easily. She wondered if they would ever be stilled at all.

# Chapter 16

Rosanna woke to dark again, but it wasn't quite so disorienting this time. Her weariness had lifted enough that she recognized tent and sleeping bag and June without any particular effort. Granny's absence was a deep ache in her gut, but she didn't pursue it any more than to note its presence. Just for now she gave herself permission to leave it be. It would still be there later, she knew. She had a multitude of mild aches, but nothing like the crowd of agonies she had expected. She reached out a hand to stroke the healing stone on the floor of the tent, and it murmured at her comfortingly. She would have to learn those Words before they left here. The stone belonged in the pools, and taking it away would be a sort of sacrilege, she felt; an insult to those long-gone Librarians who had left it there. But the proper use of any library was to teach, even a magical one.

It was warm in the tent, and a little damp. June had opened some kind of vent, so the air wasn't stale, but Rosanna was surprised at how comfortable she was, even outside the sleeping bag. A light breeze rattled the tent-fly and fluttered the silk.

June snuffled the last bit of a quiet snore, then turned over to face Rosanna.

"Awake?" she said quietly.

"Yeah."

June stretched and yawned; Rosanna could hear the crackles of her joints, and the hiss of her hands against the tent.

"Wonder what time it," Rosanna said, missing her watch again.

"Me too," June said. "Feels a little like morning, to me. We'll know for sure if the sun comes up."

Rosanna chuckled, but it was strange not to have her day run on hours and minutes. She unzipped her sleeping bag and sat up.

"You shine," June said. "I didn't notice last night."

It was true. Granny's web still lay golden and pale on her skin, and just under it. She thought it might be fading, but it might not. It wasn't enough light to read by, but the glow was undeniable. Rosanna brushed away a tear. Later, she would grieve later.

"I wonder what it's good for now," Rosanna said.

"Whatever it's good for, it's your inheritance, I guess," June said.

"I guess."

"Well," June said, after a pause, "I need to find a tree. You coming?"

They both crawled out of sleeping bags and bundled into coats. Rosanna stuck the healing stone back in her pocket. After the morning necessaries, June fired up the lamp and stove.

It all seemed so very normal and relaxed. Rosanna could almost pretend she was just out on a trip with her new friend. She brushed the stitches on her cheek. Almost, but not quite.

June looked up in time to catch the motion.

"How those coming along?" she asked. "I dunno if it's your pet rock or what, but I'm not near so sore today as I was yesterday."

"They itch a little, nothing much more than that."

"We'll have a better look in daylight, head down to the pools again, if you don't mind."

Rosanna laughed. "They're warm, I don't mind."

The wind stayed light, but it was cold out of the tent. She kept her hands tucked into her pockets, and her chin and nose ducked into the collar of her coat.

They had tea and a simple breakfast, and gathered up containers for hauling water. It was still deep twilight when they headed back to the pools, but the sky behind the mountains slowly brightened until Rosanna could easily make out the shapes of stones and trees around her. She expected that this close to the foot of the mountain they would remain in shadow most of the day, but it was good to see the light. Sunlight spread through a thick cover of clouds, setting a soft glow behind the sharpness of mountain peaks. Rosanna stumbled and slid a bit, still becoming accustomed to moving in the deep snow. June moved like a snow plow, and seemed to expect the world to get out of her way. Rosanna grinned to herself. If it came to that, she wouldn't blame the world if it *did* get out of June's way. There was no birdsong; just the creak and groan and sigh of pine trees in the light breeze.

Rosanna slipped once more into the hot waters, and watched the sun make its slow climb into the thick cloud cover. She was right in thinking that they would be shadowed here, but the light that fell across the valley was diffuse as well. The snow and ice on the riverbanks glistened and gleamed, but the river itself was dark, nearly black. It looked too cold to still be flowing, though she supposed the hot springs must warm it some. There was certainly more ice on the far shore than the near one.

June sploshed into the pool gracelessly, and tossed Rosanna a bar of soap.

"Is that a hint" Rosanna asked with a grin.

"Nope," June replied. "Outright fact. You stink. Plus you look like you got ten pounds of mud in your hair. Ain't attractive, girl."

Rosanna scrubbed and splashed, and it was a good thing that the pool refilled as quickly as it did, because June was nearly right. It was lovely to watch the dirt be carried away, swept out into the river. If only all her troubles were so disposable.

When they were both finally clean and dry and dressed again, both women filled buckets with water and started back up the hill to their campsite. Rosanna would have complained about the water, but it took a ridiculous amount of snow to make usable water, and she'd just as soon not be the one fetching that. June had kept several large buckets with lids in her cache for just this use, but she said there was no point in bringing more than two at a time. Just as well, Rosanna thought. They were heavy and upset her balance enough that the trek back felt more precarious than it was. It was good to feel that she was helping, though, and to find that something at least was within her skills. Her shoulders were sore by the time they got back to camp, and as she looked around, she found herself suddenly homesick. She could picture her apartment, its warm clutter and familiarity; but it was unreal, somehow out of focus. It seemed unfair that her entire life had become unnecessary and even unimportant.

"We'll have to boil the water," June said.

"Even here?"

"Oh yeah," June said. "Beaver Fever ain't just from pollution." She shrugged. "No big deal, just the way it is. But you always boil water you wanna drink, unless you got tablets, which we don't."

Rosanna picked out another lunch for them while June took care of the water, and they ate in relative quiet. There were so many things that Rosanna just didn't know. How could June be looking to her to lead this…this mission?

June had built another small fire, and Rosanna fed sticks to it, poking at the embers. All the little castles of flame collapsed into embers and ashes. It seemed appropriate.

"Whatcha thinkin'?" June asked.

"Brooding," Rosanna replied. "Feeling out of place."

"Fair enough, you *are* out of place, near as I can tell."

"I just don't know what I'm supposed to do in this, you know? I'm…gods, I'm just a glorified librarian."

"Never met any magical librarians before," June said mildly.

"I've never been one."

"Well that can't be true," June said. "Your granny didn't turn you into one, did she?"

"No, I suppose not. But...I never knew."

"And if you had a third kidney and never knew, you'd still have one, wouldn't you? Somethin' extra?"

"I guess...but...I didn't ask for this."

"Oh, so I suppose you never wished you were really special? Or that your life had some big important purpose?"

Rosanna shrugged.

"Oh bullshit. Everyone wishes that, at least from time to time. Guess what, honey. Wishes *do* come true!" She laughed. Rosanna tried to frown. June came over and poked her in the ribs.

"Look, way I see it, you can stew about what you can't change or you can claim it. This is your life. Nobody gets to choose when the shit happens. Why should you be special? Now you get to find out what you're made of. Can you ride the bull, or are you gonna get trampled? Nobody knows for sure till they have to try." There was a sparkle in her eyes that wasn't just reflected firelight. She was a primal force, there in the shadows of the wood. Rosanna tossed one more stick on the fire, and stood up.

"Fierce women don't get trampled, is that what you're saying?"

"Nah, anyone can get trampled. Fierce women don't lie down and let it happen." June grinned, her teeth a flash in the firelight.

The rest of the day passed in relative quiet. They both napped and ate as they needed to (June was quite insistent that they eat regularly) while the short hours of winter daylight slipped by. Rosanna knew that they needed to plan and to think, but she knew she needed rest, too. She spent a good deal of time listening to the healing stone, and examining its structure, but that was as close to action as she got. They had limited supplies and a murderer might be on their trail, but there only so much terror one body could hold, and right now, Rosanna's was out of room.

It snowed a centimeter or two that night, but the cloud cover meant relatively warmer temperatures, and Rosanna didn't mind it. On the second morning June checked Rosanna's stitches, and declared them ready to come out, though she shook her head over it. Rosanna was happy to have them go, and equally happy not to have a mirror. June said her cheek was healing up nicely, but what that meant in normal-person terms, she didn't know. Rosanna had never considered herself a particular beauty, but Bride-of-Frankenstein adornments weren't exactly en vogue these days. June shook her head.

"Don't worry bout it, honest," she said. "I don't think you'll hardly be able to see it, once it's all healed up. How's your arm?"

"Haven't checked, honestly. And don't ask me to take my coat off out here, either. Not gonna happen."

"Wuss," June said. "I can look before we sleep."

"It pulls a little, and it itches, but it doesn't hurt too much."

"Sounds like it's coming along, then," June said.

"How about you?" Rosanna asked. "How're you feeling?"

"Well, I don't know as I had much worse than bruises, maybe a cracked rib, but I don't hardly feel 'em anymore." She shook her head. "I'm a pretty fast healer, but not that fast. You sure you don't wanna take the pet rock with us when we go?"

Rosanna stroked the little stone. She would be sad to be parted from it, actually. It was a quiet and reliable comfort in a world that had gotten very uncomfortable of late.

"I don't think it would be right," she said at last. "Somebody left it there on purpose, you know? It's not like it just fell out of a pocket. Anyway, I'm going to try to make something like it, I think."

"How you gonna do that?"

"I don't really know how it works," Rosanna admitted, "but I'm going to learn the Words that are in this rock, and try to sort of…copy them into another, I guess."

"Will that work?"

"I dunno. But I'll try, and if I blow up or something, you'll know it was a bad idea."

"Oh. Well, if you're gonna do any blowing up could you do it away from the tent? That thing cost me near five hundred bucks."

"Oh, you're just a world of comfort, you are. Thanks a lot."

"Just sayin'," June said. "Tent's no good with a hole in it. I'd rather you didn't blow up though, if it's all the same. Don't much wanna deal with Trapper on my own."

And there was the shadow that hung over everything, no matter how bright the sun or clean the air. Rosanna didn't know if she could deal with Trapper at all. It didn't matter, though, what she knew or didn't. Time was passing and food was disappearing. June had figured they had another two days' worth of food and fuel. Already she'd been making forays out into the forest for firewood. Rosanna missed Granny's certitude, her solidity. Granny would have had a plan, she knew.

Mind you, it seemed the things she knew about Granny might be less clear than they once were. Granny had always seemed strong and sure. Perhaps surety and strength were easier to find when one had the magic to back them up. If Granny wasn't perfect, if she was only skilled, perhaps there was hope for Rosanna? Because if Granny were not innately perfect then maybe, oh just maybe, Rosanna could learn what it took to be the sort of woman Granny had been.

"You brooding?" June asked.

"No, actually," Rosanna replied. "Thinking. Having a little hope, I guess."

"Hope's good," June said. "Have more." Rosanna laughed.

"I'll try," she said. "Sometimes it's easy to forget."

"You just ain't got the habit is all," June said. "You can keep it in your pocket when you leave the pet rock."

"I like that," Rosanna said.

"That's coz you're a softy," June said. "A fierce woman with a marshmallow center."

Rosanna laughed again.

"Do we have any marshmallows left?" she asked, and June chuckled. "Help yourself," she said, and Rosanna did.

A little later, she sat beside the fire with the 'pet rock' cupped in her hands. How did it all work? She didn't want to take the Words out of their little Library. If she learned them, would she break it? That was the last thing she wanted. She remembered sitting on the keystone of her mother's Library, and *hearing* those Words, having them slip into her own private vocabulary, but that Library was damaged, and this one was intact. She thought, too, of the amount of force with which that Library had blown apart, and eyed the little stone with some trepidation. Granny had said that Libraries protected Words, and that made sense, at least it did to Rosanna. Books out in the world could get dog-eared and tattered, lose pages and meaning. Why not Words? There didn't have to be any greater metaphysical meaning than that. Like whispers around a classroom, any Word could be garbled or misunderstood. So if she were to use these Words, no matter how mangled they became by her pronunciation or memory, they would still exist in their proper form, right here in this little Library. But it was the little stone itself that interested her, as much as the Words it contained. That stone seemed to *use* the Words in some fashion. Was that just the nature of Libraries? She couldn't imagine how it would be in a normal library if all the books read themselves aloud. She'd had to focus on her mother's Library in order to hear the Words there, and the only thing they'd really done was to warm the space around them. That had seemed more like a by-product of their existence than an action on their part. So what was different about this?

She held the little stone, and *listened*, sorting through the Words, storing them all away, until she heard, only barely, the whisper of something like a voice. It was the last Word, the one that bound them all to purpose, instead of only to storage. It was the name of the stone's maker, she knew. He had bound a little of his long-ago self into the healing of strangers and even enemies, should they come to this place in need. Granny had not said anything of a Library like this, but they'd had so little time. The golden web beneath her skin glowed gently, and Rosanna thought that perhaps Granny had done something similar when she'd built that. This stone had been here for years and years. Maybe Granny would never leave her, not all the way.

Rosanna curled herself around her grief and felt it, truly felt it. She shook with tears and anger and sorrow, and hardly felt the arms that came around her. Always enough time till there's none, Granny had said. But she was wrong. There'd never been enough time, not for them.

They'd used it wrong, and just when they were figuring out how to use it right, everything else had gone wrong instead. No father, no mother, no Granny, no life, no nothing. Rosanna felt herself falling past grief to despair, and she didn't know how to halt her tumble, didn't know what to hold.

"We'll come through," June said, but Rosanna couldn't imagine it. There would never be her simple life, not ever again. She sobbed harder, finding she couldn't stop.

"Rosanna," June said, "Rosanna, please."

Rosanna wanted to run, wanted to chase the shadows into the forest until they swallowed her up. June wouldn't let her go, and she fought. She screamed, and June's arms dropped away. She filled her lungs for one more scream, the last scream, the only scream, and heard, ever so faintly, the last murmur of Granny's soul, embedded now beneath her skin.

She opened her eyes, not realizing she'd closed them, and saw June lying in a stunned heap at her feet.

"Oh my God, oh, June!" she said.

June shook her head, and drew herself shakily up onto a log.

"Temper run in your family?" she asked. She was trying to joke, Rosanna knew, but there was a flicker of fear behind those forest-shadowed eyes, a hint of distrust.

"I didn't...I was just thinking, and then all of a sudden I was thinking of Granny," she said. "I...oh gods June, oh I'm so sorry."

"You didn't hit me or nothin'," June said, "but when you shouted...it was like the air turned to an avalanche, landed solid on me."

"I don't know how...I just felt like I was drowning." Rosanna started to weep again, ashamed and frightened. "I didn't mean to do anything at all!"

June nodded her head, and the distrust faded, though she still looked at Rosanna as she might a fractious horse.

"You don't know what you can do, right?"

Rosanna nodded, and tried helplessly to stop weeping. She didn't *want* to be a walking weapon, and she wanted to be nothing like...like him.

"Well, you didn't say nothin' when you did that," June said. "not a word or a sound 'cept that scream. So even what you don't know is dangerous, girl. Problem with that, 'course, is that what you don't know is dangerous to me, too. Not too keen on that, gotta say."

Rosanna finally managed to get her tears under some control. It was too cold for crying, and she was suddenly too tired.

"Me neither," she replied. "but I don't know how to learn it all."

"Don't got to," June said. "just got to know what you *can* do, if things is right, or wrong. You get stuck, got no other choices, there's that, I guess."

"I think…oh I have a terrible feeling that doing *that*…could kill me, too."

June nodded slowly.

"Got that same feeling myself, couldn't say why, but I do."

She shook her head again, and leaned her elbows on her knees.

"You should sit," she said. "'For you fall down."

Rosanna nodded, and found another one of the fireside stumps to settle onto. June threw a few chunks of firewood onto the embers, and the flames sprung up again around them.

They sat, listening to the crack and pop of the fire, and the groan and whisper of the pine trees. Daylight was fading already, and Rosanna dreaded the night; not for what it was, but for what it meant. One more day in respite was one less day until confrontation.

"I still don't know what to do," she said. "About him, I mean."

June sighed.

"I don't know either. Can we do what's gotta be done?"

"Can I kill him?" Rosanna shook her head. "I don't know, June honestly. I've lost…I've lost everything over the last few days. I mean, not just Granny even, but…but the whole world stopped being what I thought it was."

"You a Christian?" June asked.

"Not particularly. I suppose I'm not particularly not a Christian either, I just think maybe the truth's big enough for everyone to have a piece."

June smiled. "I like that. Have to say that when the minister's wife comes to pester."

"Why do you ask? And I mean, why now?"

"I dunno, I just didn't want to upset you. I'm not particularly a Christian myself, and I kinda think…I kinda think everything and everyone comes round again. Everything goes and comes round again in different ways."

"Are you trying to make it okay to kill Trapper? I don't understand."

"Oh, I don't have to make it okay to kill him. He's rabid. But everything you lost, I think it'll all come round again. So you can't really lose it, you know? Just maybe, misplace it for a while."

"I feel like I'm the one that's misplaced. Like maybe somewhere my old life and Granny are sitting around, waiting for me to come back." Rosanna swallowed a sob. "And I found my father and lost him all in a weekend. How am I supposed to deal with that?"

"You didn't really find him though," June said. "Just some guy. Just…something misplaced come 'round again. Look, I'm sorry, I know this is hard. But you are still an orphan. Nothin' changed except this crazy man shares some DNA."

"Granny would know what to do with this," Rosanna said. "I'm the one that should have died."

"Don't ever goddamn say that again," June growled, and came around the fire to shake Rosanna fiercely. "Ever! Your Granny gave you this life and don't you EVER disrespect it. You go ahead and feel sorry for yourself some, you earned it, I guess. But if I ever hear those words outta your mouth again, so help me I'll slap it."

Rosanna just stared at her for a moment, shocked by the anger in June's eyes. There was no sympathy in her voice at all, just fury and flat statement of fact. Rosanna had absolutely no doubt that June would do exactly what she said. Suddenly, she found an answering anger of her own.

"I don't need your permission to feel whatever I feel!" she shouted. "My whole fucking life has fallen to pieces, you understand?"

"Mine too, in case you didn't notice. And I didn't ask for none of it any more than you did." June responded, her voice loud without being shouting. "Ain't nothin' left of my life either."

"It's my fault!" Rosanna said. "Everything I do is just wrong!"

"Like what? What exactly did you do wrong?"

"I didn't save Granny."

"That ain't true, and you know it. What life she had left, you gave it to her. She told me herself. She told me you saved her from a monster, she told me you drove all the way to my place and she was scared  you was gonna bleed to death. Every damn thing you done was right!"

"But it didn't work!" Rosanna screamed. "It wasn't enough! It had to be wrong!"

Finally June closed the distance between them again and took Rosanna's face between her hands. Rosanna felt the roughness of calluses and the warmth of June's palms.

"You did everything right," she said softly. "Sometimes that just ain't enough to mend the world. I'm sorry, girl. Sometimes it just ain't."

Rosanna dropped her head and let her tears fall.

"I don't want to be strong and not be able to fix things," she said at last. "What's the point of power if it just messes everything up?"

"Your power didn't mess nothin' up," June said. "You know that. All you done is try to fix the broken things that Trapper's left for you."

"What if I'm not good enough?" Rosanna whispered. "What if I'm just not good enough to fix all this, to make it right. What if I'm not strong enough to stop him?"

June laughed. The sound was startling in its brightness, like a thread of bright light woven into the darkness of the woods.

"Well then, so what?" she said. "All we can do is the best we can, girl. Don't matter if we win or lose. Must admit I'm partial to winnin', and I plan on it, but all we can give is our best."

"And if we die? Or worse, if you die? What if I fail you?"

"I don't care," June said, simply. "I don't care, so long as we stop that bastard. So long's he's out here, he's a danger to people I care about. Hell, he's a danger to the whole world, near as I can tell. He's the kind that would set it all on fire if he thought it would get him what he wants. I will give everything I got to try to stop him, and that's the best I can do."

"I don't want to be responsible..." Rosanna started, but June cut her off.

"Shut up about responsible," she said testily. "Seriously, just quit. You talk about that like it matters any who's responsible for what. It don't. What matters is what we do. What do you mean to do, Rosanna? You mean to hide in the woods till we run out of food? We could take a few more hot baths before that happens, if you want."

Rosanna shook her head slowly.

"No," she said, "no I guess I don't mean to do that." She lifted her head and smiled at June. "We're almost down to chicken stew, anyway."

June laughed again, and Rosanna felt something stir inside her, like a sleepy animal waking. She opened her mouth and was astonished to find herself laughing as well. It felt good. Granny was still gone, but she, Rosanna, remained. She didn't know what she was capable of, or whether she could succeed, but she meant to try.

"So what were you doing afore you started shouting?" June said. "Anything interestin'?"

Rosanna stroked the little rock with a finger, checking the Words in her memory.

"I think so," she said. "I think I've learned the things that are in the pet rock. I'd like to try to build one like it, but I'm not sure how, or if I need a special kind of rock, or anything, really."

"Let me see that one again," June said, and Rosanna passed it over.

"Well, this one's a little geode, I'd say," she said. "They can be tricky to find though, do you think it's gotta be one?"

"My mother's Library didn't seem to be, it was more like...I dunno, like the Words inside made it become one."

"Well then, maybe any old stone would do," June said. "Time to experiment."

Rosanna sighed. After all the energy she'd put into her outburst, experimenting with potentially volatile magic didn't really sound all that fun to her. June looked at her and cocked her head to the side.

"That don't look like rampant enthusiasm," she said.

"I'm tired," Rosanna said.

"Well then let's have some lunch and go sit in the tub for a while."

The selections for lunch were getting scant, and Rosanna wanted to leave the dreaded chicken stew till last. June had different ideas, and picked that one out of the remaining bunch.

"I want to get it over with," she said. "Plus, it'll make you appreciate my cooking more."

It did taste like crap, as June had promised. It was hot and it filled the hole in Rosanna's belly, but those were its only redeeming qualities. Rosanna was almost always hungry to some degree. The cold wasn't easy on her city-soft body, and simply staying warm took a good deal of energy. The meals they had were sufficient, but never quite enough for her to feel really full. They snacked on dried fruit and trail mix, but those were running low as well, as was the tea.

"Well," Rosanna said, after her meal. "On the whole, I preferred bacon and eggs."

"Oh don't you even get me started," June said, making a face at her empty bowl. "I'd do terrible things for a good cup of coffee, let alone bacon and eggs."

The path down to the springs was easy to see now, and the snow was sufficiently compacted to make walking easy. It was still a bit slippery down the final slope, but Rosanna felt confident enough to make the journey even by the gathering twilight of afternoon. Rosanna thought she might struggle a little on the way back, if it were full dark by then, but she was determined to make the effort. Her feet seemed surer of the way than the rest of her, so she trusted them to find it.

In the changing hut, Rosanna reveled in the warmth under her naked feet, and in the simple comfort of getting rid of her winter coat. Her clothes were in need of a wash, and she knew she wouldn't want to put them back on once her body was clean. It was simply unrealistic to try to get them washed and dried.

She took the shivery few steps out to the pool and sunk gratefully into the hot waters. She'd brought the healing stone with her, and found the place where she'd found it. It nestled back into that spot as if it had never left it, murmuring quiet healing into the waters. Rosanna wondered how far the effect carried downriver.

June dropped into the water beside her with a sigh and a smile. Rosanna could still make out her features in the dusk, and smiled back.

"So?" June said. "Any idea what kind of rock we're lookin' for?"

"Not really," Rosanna said. "But I figure if the healing stone was here, maybe some of these stones might have already picked up some of the magic. Kind of like an echo, maybe."

"I dunno," June said. "You're the expert, here."

"Some expert."

"Better than none," June replied, and Rosanna felt it unwise to argue with that particular tone of voice.

"Anyway," Rosanna said, "just feel around for a stone that...well...feels good to you."

"Feels good." June said, and nothing more.

"Look, haven't you ever carried a stone in your pocket, just because it felt good?"

"I suppose," June said reluctantly. "Like a worry stone, you mean?"

"Yeah. Something that feels like that."

"Ain't in the habit of feelin' stones, you know," she muttered. "Might be a hillybilly, ain't an idiot."

"Whatever, June, just look for one. I promise not to tell anyone, if that helps."

June continued muttering to herself, but she moved to the far side of the pool from Rosanna, and began to pull herself slowly back and forth over the stones. Rosanna did the same, crawling lobster-like to keep as much of herself under the warm water as possible.

Rosanna had always loved stones, and had several bowls of them collecting dust in her apartment. It wasn't necessarily a sparkly stone that caught her eye (though she did have a bit of clan magpie in her, as Granny used to say) but a shape or texture. Something about a stone would make it perfect for her collection, however ordinary it might appear to an outsider. She always thought perhaps someday she'd try her hand at mosaic, with all the little bits and bobs she'd collected. Somehow, that never happened, and the bowls continued to fill.

She moved slowly now, paying attention to the textures under her hands, and by the time the water was becoming uncomfortably warm, she'd set seven little stones of varying sizes and textures by the side of the pool. To her amusement, June had done as well, despite her grumblings about 'hippy-dippy bullshit'.

Together they took the collection up to the changing hut, and Rosanna put them in the pockets on her coat. The largest of the stones was about the size of her palm, but most were no bigger than her thumb. They filled the pockets but didn't seem enough to strain the seams.

She'd been right: her clothes were distastefully dirty against her clean skin. They didn't smell terribly bad yet, probably because of the frequent bathing, but they did smell worn. June wrinkled her nose as she dressed as well.

"Could be worse," she said. "We only been out here a few days. You should smell some of the *real* hillfolk, when they come down for supplies."

"Are there people like that?" Rosanna asked. It seemed absurd that her world of plowed streets and internet café's could exist alongside one populated by 'real' hillfolk.

"Sure," June said. "Not so many as there used to be. Young people keep leavin', you know? But there's families out there as never even owned a telephone, let alone a TV."

Full dark had fallen while they had been hunting for rocks, but June went slowly and offered Rosanna a hand when she needed it. They were nearly back at the camp when June stopped so suddenly that Rosanna bumped into her.

"What?" she asked, but June only shushed her and stood stock-still in the shadows. Rosanna stopped too, listening to the whistle of her breath. She heard the trees hush and hum as a breeze wound through them, but nothing else.

"What?" she asked again, more impatiently. Walking kept her warm, but she wanted the comfort of a campfire.

"Thought I heard somethin'," June said, very quietly. "Wait a minute, will you?" Rosanna stood quietly as her feet slowly turned to ice, and just as she was about to question June for a third time, and more impatiently, she heard it too. Very far away up the valley, a thread of wolfsong lifted up into the night. It was only a sliver of sound against the deeper silence of the evening, but it sent shivers down her back and raised up all the little hairs on her neck and arms.

"Long way off," June said conversationally, and started walking again.

"Are we...are we safe?" Rosanna asked.

"From them? Most likely. Ain't deep enough winter for them to be starvin', and wolves don't hunt humans if they can help it."

Rosanna remembered the wolf under Trapper's poison, remembered its beauty and desperation.

"Trapper makes them hunt people," she said quietly. "That's what bit Granny."

June paused in her steps for a second.

"Guess I missed that bit of information," she said. "But whatever wolf was singin' to the sky was a long way from here."

"As far as Granny's place, maybe?"

June whirled on her.

"Rosanna, you are the damndest person for makin' up troubles that I ever met. Either it is or it ain't, I got no way to know. Quit worrying at it, would you?"

"I'm just wondering if we should be posting some kind of guard, is all," Rosanna said, and June sighed.

"Been wondering that too, long before this. But we can't spare the energy, neither of us. You're lookin' better every day, but we got troubles ahead as well as troubles behind us. I don't know how we can protect ourselves and still be ready for what we got to do."

Rosanna had gotten used to the idea of feeling safe, and didn't like to put the illusion away. It was comforting to think of this place as a little bubble in time, where she could learn and heal before she stepped back into the fight. She thought of Granny's bubble of golden light, the net that had saved she and June both, and swallowed hard. Granny had bought this time for her. She wasn't going to waste it.

In the short walk the rest of the way to the camp, Rosanna found herself thinking about the golden web. It had protected them, yes, but it had also come with her. Listening with that particular intensity required for Words, she could still hear the faintest murmur of Granny's soul. It hadn't faded as she'd expected it to. It seemed tied to her, in some way, as whoever had made the healing stone was tied to it. If the web had protected her, perhaps it could be convinced to do so again.

When they arrived, June put water on for tea, and Rosanna started a fire. She was getting better at it, but it helped that June had found a gas fire-lighter at the bottom of her hoard. It meant she wasn't going through matches, and that she could be far enough away not to be likely to set herself on fire as well as the kindling. They heard wolves a couple times more, still very faint, but a breeze lifted up, and soon it made too much covering sound for the women to hear anything else.

Rosanna had pulled her mittens off to handle the lighter, and she could see the glow of Granny's web on her skin. She held her hand closer to the flame, and the web flared a little brighter. Gritting her teeth, she held it closer still, and the web filled out around her fingers, creating a little bubble of safety. Rosanna could feel warmth, and *hear* the little Words that made up the fire, but that was all.

June finished with her preparations, and turned around to see Rosanna with her hand in the fire.

"Rosanna, what the hell!" She bolted across the clearing, but Rosanna calmly pulled her hand back, and watched the web subside.

"I guess I know what this thing's good for," she said, and grinned.

# Chapter 17

"I swear," June said, "I feel more like slapping when I'm around you than I have since my last boyfriend."

"I'm sorry," Rosanna said.

"You don't sound sorry," June replied. "You sound plain happy with yourself. And if you don't stop grinnin' like that I may slap you yet."

"I had to test it, didn't I?"

"For god's sake show some sense! A test don't mean tryin' to set yourself on fire to see if it'll save you."

"Well, it lit up by the fire, so I thought..."Rosanna's elation dimmed a little in the shadow of June's fury.

"You didn't think. You just...you just DID. And that may have its place, but what if you'd been wrong? Don't you think I'm a little tired of patching you up?"

"I'm sorry," Rosanna said again, and June seemed satisfied by her sincerity.

"It's true we don't got much time to figure stuff out," June said. "But that means you got to take less risks, less stupid ones, anyway. You coulda tested that with a match instead of a whole fire."

"Look, that makes sense, and I'm as sorry as I'm likely to get. Do you suppose you could let it go now? I'm okay, and we have a new tool."

June grumbled away like a thunderstorm, and crashed around the campsite until she found some wood to chop. The axe strokes clapped through the woods, and Rosanna winced. It was true she hadn't thought it through, but the significance still delighted her. She had her knife, but so far as she could tell, it was only an offensive tool. She wasn't particularly good with it, though she knew the sharp end from the dull one. The web had real possibilities, too. If June was tired of patching Rosanna up, Rosanna was equally tired of the necessity. It was fine that they needed to take the fight to Trapper, but Rosanna didn't want to ever feel quite that vulnerable to someone else's malice again.

It was true that she didn't know how much the web could handle, but it had survived having a building dropped on it, and it had survived the weight of magic besides. A little fire probably wasn't that much of a risk. Rosanna knew that June was right, though. They couldn't afford for Rosanna to hurt herself figuring out her new tools.

She stayed away from the fire, and tried to see if she could use the web without any kind of actual danger. It would only be of so much use if it was purely reactive. She could hear the little golden voice of it, tied in with the sounds of her own soul. She smiled a little, hearing still the echo of Granny in it.

She remembered how it had felt with her hand in the fire, how it had felt like she pushed the web out from herself. If she could do it by instinct, she must be able to do it on purpose, at least she hoped so. She sat by the fire, concentrating, with little effect.

June stopped pounding on the poor logs and came to sit by the fire with her. Clearly she'd vented enough of her fury that she felt sociable again.

"What you doing?" she asked. "You look like you're terrible constipated."

"Ha, ha," Rosanna said flatly, and let the effort go. "I'm trying to use the web."

"The whole thing?" June asked.

"Yeah, I guess."

"You only used the hand before, why don't you try that?"

It was worth a shot. Rosanna pulled her mitten off and looked at the golden tracery beneath her skin. She pushed at it, but nothing happened. Maybe it only was reactive, after all.

"You look all constipated again," June said. "You didn't look that way by the fire. Maybe you're trying too hard."

"And how exactly am I supposed to not try too hard?" Rosanna was getting frustrated.

"Maybe you don't got to push. Maybe you just got to ask. Your granny didn't strike me as the kind of lady people pushed around. Maybe her gift is the same."

"Ask," Rosanna said. Right.

"Don't give me that look," June said, "it's no crazier than any of the rest of this shit."

"Okay, fine. Please web, would you expand around me to a nice little bubble about twelve feet across?"

Sarcastic as her tone had been, the web must have recognized the request for what it was. It lifted up off her skin and settled smoothly around the two women.

"Holy shit," June said softly, then laughed. "Talk about the magic word."

Rosanna could feel her connection to the web, though her skin felt strangely naked without it. She took a few steps, and the bubble moved with her. When it moved over the fire, smoke drifted up and through it as though it didn't exist, but the warmth of the fire seemed to accumulate just as if it were a solid shelter.

"This could be handy," June said, "especially if it gets any colder. We been lucky so far, but it can get nasty this time of year."

"I wonder if snow would fall through it," Rosanna said. "Maybe we could use it for a tent."

"That almost sounds like planning," June said. "Careful now, I might follow you."

"Oh stop it," Rosanna said. "I know we need a plan, and I've been trying to think of something but I don't know anything about forests or hunting or any of that stuff. You're my expert. How am I supposed to know what comes next?"

"Nobody knows, really," June said. "We just stumble on the next thing and pretend we meant to."

"Well then, what do we stumble on? Do you think you can find him?" Rosanna pulled out her knife, and asked it for Trapper again. It pointed in the same direction, as near as she could tell, but that didn't mean he wasn't coming closer. A direction was only so much information, after all.

"I could," June said, "I think. But I don't know how long it'll take, and we got limited resources."

"And I don't think I'd survive a trek through the mountains mid-winter," Rosanna said, but June shook her head.

"I think you under-estimate yourself, and I think you do that a lot."

"Maybe. But can you see dragging me all over the mountains looking for him?"

June didn't respond immediately, and Rosanna could see that she was really considering it.

"No," she said at last, "I guess not. I ain't prepared to chase this dog's tail any longer than I have to, and I don't know for sure if you'd be up for it." She looked at Rosanna and smiled. "But don't take it bad, 'cause I'm not sure I'd be up for it either."

"Well then," Rosanna said, "if we're not going to chase him, what are our options?"

The temperature inside the little bubble had risen enough that June pulled off her mittens with a happy sigh.

"Oh that's nice," she said, and Rosanna followed suit. The air was still cool, but the fire's warmth chased some of the humidity out of the air as well as the chill. June shrugged off her jacket with a happy sigh, but Rosanna wasn't quite *that* warm yet.

"You're the smart one," June said at last. "You tell me."

"Yeah, right," Rosanna said. "I'm the smart one."

"Well if you won't take that, you're the boss. What are the options?"

"If we aren't going to chase him, we have to bring him to us," Rosanna said, though the words tried to strangle her on the way out.

"That sounds fun," June said. "You know his phone number? Invite him over for coffee. Tell him to bring some, we're almost out."

"You are so…"

"Wonderful? Beautiful?"

"Maybe, but you're a pain in the ass, too."

"I aim to try," June said, and grinned. Her hazel eyes glimmered green and gold in the light of the fire and the web. She looked like nothing so much as a forest sprite; mischief incarnate.

"You know this is serious, right?" Rosanna said. "You know we could die?"

"What the hell," June said. "We were gonna die sometime anyway. Might as well have some fun with it."

Rosanna laughed, and the sound filled her up like champagne bubbles.

"Might as well," she said.

"You wanna bring him here?" June asked. "We got the springs and the river, gives us something safe at our back."

"I wouldn't count on that," Rosanna said. "I wouldn't really count on much." She shook her head, thinking.

"I know of a place that's warm like this, and I'm pretty sure I could get him there."

"Warm sounds nice," June said. "Less equipment to bring."

"No," Rosanna replied. "I think we should bring all the equipment we can carry, and anything we can scrounge along the way. I think we should be ready for a siege."

"Don't care for the sound of that," June said. "Never liked a trap, not even one I built myself."

"That's plan B," Rosanna said. "Plan A is less complicated."

"Oh my, aren't we big city. Got **two** plans."

Rosanna stuck out her tongue, and June laughed at her.

"Look," Rosanna said, "the thing he thinks he wants is what's left of my mother's Library. My other inheritance." Her head dropped for a moment, remembering the pictures lost in Granny's house. "I can get him there, at least."

"And then?" June said.

"I'm still thinking," Rosanna said, "but I have some ideas. I'll need to surprise him."

"Well you surprise the hell out of me on a regular basis," June said with a laugh, "so that shouldn't be any big deal."

"I guess I'm a little surprised myself," Rosanna said, and smiled at the web around her.

She could feel a slight drain on her energy to sustain the web as it was, but not freezing seemed a good return on the effort.

"Can you keep this thing up?" June asked.

"Yeah, at least for a while," Rosanna said. "I don't know what'll happen when I sleep, though."

"Never mind that," June said, "I'll get some buckets of snow to melt and we can skip carryin' water."

June put a hand through the web experimentally, and it passed easily enough. She pulled it back in and got her winter clothes back on. When she stepped through, Rosanna felt the whole structure shudder slightly, but it maintained its integrity.

Rosanna pulled a handful of pebbles out of her pocket, and sorted through them, finding the ones she liked best. There was no particular reason for it, no deep arcane meaning in her choices, only the fact that some of them seemed more right.

June clattered off into the trees, heading for the snow pack. Rosanna picked a small, smooth stone, and *listened* to it. She thought the Words for its existence must be in a Library somewhere, for it was so solidly a Stone that it did not even murmur of anything else. She whispered the little frost Word she'd found, so long ago in June's restaurant, and the stone became cold in her hand. That wasn't all she wanted, though, she wanted that Word to be safe until she could find a better place for it.

"Please," she whispered under her breath, hardly knowing that she spoke. "Please be safe."

The definition of the stone opened up, somehow, and accepted that little Word of cold, that shining little murmur of perfect cold. She felt the Word move from her mind into the stone. She still knew it, and could still speak it if she needed it, but it was written down now. Perhaps it wasn't quite a Library, but it at least it was a Book.

She was still admiring her handiwork when the web flared fierce golden around her.

"Ouch!" June said. "That hurt!"

Rosanna looked up, and by the firelight she saw June sprawled on the ground with several buckets of snow around her.

"Oh, I'm sorry!" Rosanna said. "I didn't know…well I didn't know that would happen."

"There's more we don't know than we do," June said.

"Are you okay?"

"I guess, stung like a bee, though. Nothin' major, just sort of a surprise."

Rosanna walked towards June, moving the bubble of light with her.

"Now hang on," June said, but nothing happened as the web moved over her.

"Hm," she said. "Thanks for askin' first."

"Well, you were in it before, so I thought maybe it was just a matter of me knowing you were there."

"So no sneakin' up," June said. "There go all my plans for seduction."

Rosanna laughed, and helped settle the buckets near the fire where the added heat would speed melting.

"I made something," Rosanna said, and held out the stone proudly.

"It's a rock. Good job," June said, but didn't take it.

"No really, I want to see if you can hold it."

"Your gold thing just bit me and you want to give me a magic rock?" June shook her head. "I ain't feelin' all that experimental."

"Aw, come on. I'm pretty sure it's safe."

"Pretty sure."

"Don't be chicken. I'll take it back if anything bad happens."

June sighed.

"And don't forget that there's the pet rock down in the pools if we need it," Rosanna said.

"That wasn't the most comfortin' thing to say, you know," June said, but took the little stone anyway.

"Feels…cold," June said. "Even though I know it ain't really, somethin' about it feels cold, like it's a rock with an ice cube in it."

"Perfect," Rosanna said, and took it back. "That's perfect. Now we know that you can carry the stones too, even if you can't use them."

"You really are plannin' something, aren't ya," June said. "Finally, you ain't just hidin' out in the woods with me."

"I think so," Rosanna said. "But I've got work to do, if it's going to happen."

"Well, we got enough to eat for tonight, and short rations tomorrow, then we're out."

"I'll be ready by tomorrow," Rosanna said. She wasn't sure how to define 'ready' really, but her preparations would be complete. She looked around at their campsite, and listened to the steady groan of pine trees in a lifting wind. The bubble cut the breeze too, so she could hear it but not feel its keen edge. June fed the fire, and Rosanna watched the shadows leap and quiver. No more hiding, she decided. Whatever the outcome, no more hiding.

# Chapter 18

The wind continued to pick up that night, snarling up and down the valley like a caged beast. Soon after sunset it started to snow; great fat flakes that accumulated quickly into a thick carpet. June shook her head worriedly.

"We're gonna get a heap of this," she said, and Rosanna believed her. It would have been beautiful from the comfort of a fire-lit room. From a campsite with dwindling resources, it was just one more damn problem, and Rosanna cursed it quietly.

"Well," June said, "at least we get to find out if this thing will keep us dry."

Rosanna looked up at the shimmering net above her. The snow slid off it as if it were solid, and heaped around them in a circle.

"Nice," June said, and Rosanna agreed. Around their small space of warmth and light, the storm prowled hungrily. June paced with the same restless energy.

"Do you have to do that?" Rosanna asked.

"Well, here's the choices. I can pace or I can holler."

"What? Why?"

"I hate small spaces. I hate storms. I hate running out of food. I hate not knowing the plan. So I stomp or I scream. What's it gonna be?"

"You could make supper. Or tea. Or whatever's left."

"Busy work. I ain't hungry."

Rosanna sighed.

"Look," she said, I've got to finish putting the Words in these rocks. I'm not really sure what I'm doing. You're not...well you're not helping much."

"That's the other thing I hate."

"Is there anything you don't hate right now?"

June thought about it.

"Not much," she said with a sigh. "Ain't like me, I know. I just...shit Rosanna, somethin' about this storm feels wrong, and I keep thinkin' I'm under my place again, with only those little gold threads keepin' me alive."

Rosanna put the stone she was holding back in her pocket.

"I'll walk with you," she said, and linked her arm with June's. June laughed, and tried to dislodge her, but Rosanna shook her head.

"Listen," she said, "I'm the boss, right? So if I say pace, we do it. We do it till you feel better."

She was tired, but Rosanna found that her city-soft body was firmer than it had been. Somewhere between the running and walking and climbing, her muscles had stepped up to what she asked of them. She kept pace with June around the fire, and soon found that the space was too small for her, too. She was hot under her jacket, but bitter experience made her reluctant to take it off. June had long ago shed her outer layers. Rosanna looked around the little space of their campsite, and its familiarity began to feel restrictive.

"Let's go for a walk," she said, and June laughed.

"In that?" said, nodding her head at the rising fury outside their little dome.

"No," Rosanna said, "in this!" She sent a little pulse of energy into the dome, and it flared to greater brightness.

June chuckled.

"You're getting' to be a showoff, you know."

"Well, I want a bath. What do you think?"

"I think we'd get lost out there, shiny umbrella or no. Ain't no way to tell what direction's what."

"I have a compass," Rosanna said, and patted her knife.

June put her jacket back on.

"Well, then," June said. "A bath sounds fine."

They doused the fire before they left. Even with all the snow, the wind was strong enough that it might have flung sparks where they could do damage. Without the firelight, the glow of the web was clearer. Snowflakes lit up like little sparks in its light, then spun around the protective globe and away.

Rosanna gave directions to her compass, and the knife warmed and bumped against her thigh like a happy cat.

Once they were out of the campsite, the snow was deeper than a carpet. The wind heaped it into heavy drifts at the base of trees, and the well-worn path to the hot springs was only barely visible as a dent in the deeper snow. Walking was more and more difficult, and Rosanna had reason to be glad for her new stamina.

"Thought it might get colder in here," June said after a while. "Ain't bad."

"Yeah, I don't know if it's the fire or just us working, but I think it's a lot colder out than in."

"Nice to know," June replied. "Kinda portable igloo."

It was strange to be in the lead, Rosanna found. She put a hand on the hilt of her knife. Strange, too, to be the provider. Granny had always been the one who knew the right thing to say or do. Rosanna had never imagined herself in that role. She listened to the quiet whisper of Granny Rosie's soul, endlessly murmuring through the tracery of the web. Granny had provided this tool, but Rosanna had found a way to use it. Perhaps that could be so of other things.

Rosanna stumbled against a stone, and June helped her up, chuckling.

"You look like a sugar-donut," she said.

"Oh, I'd do terrible things for a donut," Rosanna said. "or chocolate."

"Quit whining and lead, oh fearless pastry," June said, and they laughed, and walked through the darkness enveloped in light.

Even with their protection, it was slippery and treacherous down the last slope to the pools. Rosanna and June took turns handing each other down the most dangerous bits, but it was a relief to finally get to the outhouse and changing hut. When they stepped inside, Rosanna let the web collapse back into her skin, and it was a relief to feel it there. It emitted much less light when inactive, which was just as well. Rosanna thought she might like to go to a movie again, sometime in her life.

"I hope you can keep that up on the way back," June said. A note of worry underlaid her teasing tone, and Rosanna could understand it. The wind shook the wooden walls around them, and the snow hadn't let up at all.

"It tires me out a little," Rosanna said, "but not a lot. It's more like I have to concentrate than like actual work."

"All the same, we shouldn't stay long. This weather still don't feel quite right to me, if that makes any sense."

"Not really," Rosanna replied, "but I don't know much about the weather here anyway."

"It ain't just the weather, you know? It feels...well it feels some like the cold that Trapper set on us. Just...just wrong."

They undressed in the creaking dark, but Rosanna kept a handful of her pebbles. She cast the web out, and by its light they made the last dash to the springs. The snow had drifted deeply on the steps down to the pool, and they ran through it, gasping and shrieking like children. A shelf of snow lay thickly all around the edges of the water, and the heat was a delicious shock after the cold of the snow.

Rosanna lay back, watching the snowflakes whip past their little shelter. The wind howled and snarled but found no purchase on the web itself. It had to be content with bullying snowflakes.

"It's almost too bad snow doesn't come through this thing," June said after a bit. "I always love being here when it snows." She smiled and shrugged. "Never been here in a blizzard before, 'course. Got more sense."

Rosanna smiled back.

"So much for you wild hill-folk," she said. "And here I thought you'd had all the adventures there are to have."

"Nah," June replied. "not big adventures. Little adventures are soundin' better all the time."

"You were made for big adventures," Rosanna said. "Come on, miss cougar-hunter. Tell me you weren't."

"That ain't the same at all," June protested. "Sometimes you just got to do what's set for you."

"That sounds pretty much exactly like us," Rosanna said, and June was silent.

"Maybe," she said at last. "But this hurts more."

Rosanna didn't know what to say. She counted on June's irrepressible hope, and to hear it waver was frightening.

"I guess," Rosanna said at last, "it hurts more because the stakes are higher but the risk is the same. We risk us, and if we lose…we don't just lose us. People we don't know lose, too."

"That's a ray of sunshine, ain't it."

"Yes and no. We're all made up of the Words, you know. We're all part of the magic."

"I'm magic." June laughed. "I'm as magic as mud."

"It's all made of those Words, even the mud. Even Trapper. What we do…that keeps the best of the Words, the best of the magic, clean. So it hurts more because it means more, too. Because we have to try harder, and be more."

"I thought bein' mad would make this all easy," June said. "I thought that would be enough. But it ain't. I just…gods Rosanna I just ache for a normal day. For a complainer over his coffee. Feels like forever."

"I don't really know what will make it enough, I'm sorry." Rosanna said. "I promise you, though, that if we make it through this, I will do whatever it takes to give you back normal."

June chuckled, and reached out to pat Rosanna's cheek.

"Aw, stop babying me, girl. Tell me to get over it. I ain't no good at people being nice at me."

"All right. June, you're the queen of the fierce women. Get over it or I'll kick you out of the pool."

Nothing was better or fixed, Rosanna knew. But somewhere between them, the admission that the world was broken made the break bearable.

"I'm going to try to make some more of these rocks useful," Rosanna said after a pause filled only with the keening of the wind. "Any ideas?"

"Well, if you could make somethin' like that pet rock, that'd be good. And a cold rock is very special and all, but we kinda got enough cold. Maybe a portable fireplace would be nice. Running pretty low on fuel. And a light?"

"Sure, you want a coffee-maker too?"

"If you got one, I'm in favour," June said, and splashed Rosanna. "Smartass. Asks for suggestions and gets cranky when I got some."

Rosanna sifted through the Words she knew, and whispered one into each stone. In the end, it felt like she held and handful of miracles, and she looked up into the dark with a smile.

"No coffee," she said, "but try this." She handed June one of the pebbles to no apparent effect.

"Nice rock," June said.

"It's not just a nice rock, it's a *very* nice rock," Rosanna said. "If you ask it politely, it'll show you."

"Seriously?"

"Seriously."

June looked at the stone in her hand. It was an exceptionally ordinary sort of stone; just a flattish, grayish river rock smaller than the palm of her hand. She looked at Rosanna once more, then shrugged.

"Please nice rock," she said, "be *very* nice."

The stone flared up into a dazzle of light and warmth that outshone Rosanna's web. June dropped it in her surprise, and the stone glimmered under the surface of the water so brightly that they could make out the details of the trees beyond the pool. By that light it was clear that snow was falling more thickly even than before, and that the wind had not eased up even a little. June reached into the pool and gingerly picked it up.

"Wow," she said at last, examining it. "That's a really, really nice rock."

Rosanna laughed, delighted at both her success and June's wonder.

"Do I got to ask it really nice every time?" June said. "Might not always have the chance."

"Just say 'please'," Rosanna said. "I figured if it was going to shine it ought to have a trigger, you know?"

"Makes sense," June said. "Don't always feel like advertisin' where I am."

Rosanna nodded. "I did a couple up just with the warmth. I figured we could keep them in our pockets. I think I got the healing ones right. They sound right to me, but...well, I honestly can't be sure how well they'll work."

"What else you gonna do?" June asked. "much as I'd like to set here all night, that snow ain't goin' nowhere."

"I can't really think of anything else," Rosanna said. "and I'm getting kind of tired."

"Well then, let's head us back to bed, magic girl. I want somethin' to eat. We don't got much in the way of choices, but somethin's better than nothin'. Usually."

"Unless it's chicken stew, right?" Rosanna asked, and June nodded solemnly.

"'Cept for then, yeah."

As Rosanna's exhilaration ebbed, she found that she wasn't just a little tired, after all. She could clearly feel the exertion the web required of her now, minute though it was. It hadn't felt like too much effort to put the Words in the stones as she wanted them, but when she tried to stand her legs were rubbery from more than just the water's heat.

"Whoa there," June said, and seized Rosanna by the arm before she could tumble back into the pool. "That don't look so good."

"I guess I'm a little more tired than I thought," Rosanna admitted and June made a face.

"No, really? Never woulda guessed."

"Could we stop for a nap?" Rosanna asked, as they stumbled back through the snow to the changing hut.

"If we stop for any longer, I think we're gonna be right snowed in," June said. "And we got nothin' down here but us and your rocks. Don't matter how very nice a rock is, it ain't gonna feed us."

Rosanna nodded, and dropped the web while they changed. June laid the light-stone on the floor of the hut, which gave them both the opportunity to enjoy some creative graffiti.

"Damn," June muttered, "wouldn't have thought them Adams boys could spell that one." Rosanna chuckled, and stepped once more into her too-dirty clothes.

"Now I need a bath again," she said, and June nodded.

"Maybe before life 'n death and all that shit we could arrange some clean clothes," she said.

"No promises," Rosanna said, but she hoped so. June looked down at the light-stone.

"That ain't gonna burn me, is it?"

"I don't think so," Rosanna said. "I just put warm in it, and light. But maybe just check it to be sure? I'm new at this, remember?"

"Well, if it explodes, I'll haunt your ass for sure," June said, and poked at the rock experimentally. "Warm," she said. "not hot." She picked it up, then crossed to Rosanna.

"You don't look great," she said. "Seen you look worse, but you don't look great at all."

"I might have overdone it a bit," Rosanna replied. "I don't know what any of this costs yet, you know?"

"Can you get that web up? That wind don't sound a bit friendly."

Rosanna pushed at the web, and it expanded, but she couldn't hold it as she had before.

"It's too much," she said. "God I feel stupid."

June poked her in the ribs.

"Nah," she said, "not stupid. Just underfed. Try smaller."

Rosanna did, and finally found that she could maintain a bubble just big enough for the two women, but only if they were shoulder to shoulder.

"That's all I can manage," she said. "Sorry."

"Don't be sorry, that's fine," June said. "We'll just be real close pals, okay?" Rosanna nodded. When they left, each woman carried a stone for healing and another for warmth in her pocket. Whatever they had cost, at least there were tangible results of Rosanna's efforts. The quiet whisper of those stones lifted her spirits, and she could feel the healing stone's efforts to aid her. Those Words lived in the stone now, and followed their natures without her intervention. They had each cost her a little of herself, it was true, but that part of herself wasn't lost, either. Some part of her would exist for as long as the stones did.

That thought was enough to steel her for the trek back to camp. She and June hooked their arms around each other and stepped out into the howling storm. Rosanna's knife gave them their direction, and the light-stone illuminated the path like an imperishable star.

# Chapter 19

Rosanna hadn't thought the storm could become any wilder, but it did. She could feel now, some of the wrongness that June had spoken of. This wasn't just winter doing what winter does. There was a malice clinging to the winds, like a drop of poison on a sharp blade. Rosanna wore Granny's web like a shawl now, draped as it was around her and June's shoulders. The worst of the wind still slipped up and around the protection, but that hatred pulled at the strands and made greater demands on Rosanna's dwindling energy. At least with so small a space, the light-stone was enough to grant them a measure of comfort and warmth. Rosanna's feet and legs were made heavier by the weight of the snow, and the moisture dripped inexorably down into her boots. Soon she felt like every step sloshed ice-water over her toes. They took turns falling into drifts and pulling each other out, until the whole thing seemed like an endless dream.

"Should we go back?" she shouted, after another tumble into a snowdrift.

"No point," June said. "almost there."

It was a lie, of course. They had both long ago lost track of how far they'd come, and Rosanna's compass could only tell direction and not distance. But Rosanna knew they had as much chance of making camp as of getting back to the springs. They might as well try.

"Not such a nice walk anymore," she panted.

"Your idea, city-girl," June said, and even managed a smile. They stumbled on.

Rosanna was grateful for the warmth in her pocket, and for the busy whispers of her healing stone. Even so, each step became a struggle, and she found herself longing to lie down, just for a minute. She threw her shoulder against the storm as if it were a stone she meant to move, and pushed through it with her head down and fists clenched. June fell, and dropped the light, so Rosanna picked it up instead. She put an arm around June and helped her up. They were both soaked where they weren't freezing, and Rosanna's little web wasn't enough to be much more than a shield against the wind. Rosanna held her stones, her little handful of miracles, and smiled anyway. Walking through this storm was a difficult thing, but she could do miracles. What was difficult to her?

June was the first to see the camp, and she cried out. Her voice was hoarse with effort, but the joy was unmistakable. Rosanna lifted her head, and nearly fell again in sheer relief. She and June helped each other to the tent and she dropped the web with a gasp of relief. It was like dropping a heavy burden. The wind felt like it could cut her in half, and she ducked out of it to give a smaller target. The malice was clearer without the web, and Rosanna was certain that Trapper was looking for them. She tried to push the web out again, and simply couldn't.

"Go lie down," June shouted. "I'll get food."

"You could get lost just from there and back!" Rosanna shouted back. Even under the relative shelter of the trees, the blizzard confused her senses. She grabbed onto June's arm, and wouldn't be dislodged. She desperately wanted to lie down, but she'd done all the losing she was going to. June growled, then finally decided it wasn't worth the fight. They staggered together to the cache, and June handed the light-stone to Rosanna. Even with the light it was hard to make out details, so June simply grabbed whatever came nearest to hand. It wasn't like they had much in the way of options, anyway.

Together they took the last staggering steps back to the tent and tumbled in. It was cold inside, and the wind ripped at the tent silk, whipping the supple frame back and forth. Rosanna laid the light-stone on the floor and she and June huddled around it.

"Don't suppose you have anything hotter?" June asked. Rosanna shook her head.

"Might help if we touch it," she said, and took a mitten off to try. The effect was stronger, but not the immediate rush of relief she'd hoped for. She shook her head.

"It's a little better, but not much," June nodded.

"We got a little fuel left for the heater," she said, "but if I use it we don't got hot food tomorrow." Even in the warm glow of the light-stone, June's lips had a bluish cast, and both women were shivering violently.

June turned to the fly of the tent and rummaged around in the vestibule.

"Shit," she said after a moment. "last tank is out on the stove." She sighed. "I'll go get it."

Rosanna grabbed her wrist before she could match action to word.

"I don't think so," she said. "I don't think you'd make it out there, and I don't think I would either."

"We gotta warm up, Rosanna," June said. "I can't hardly feel my fingers."

"Here," she said. "hold the light for a minute."

June peeled off her soaking mitts and obliged, though she was shivering so hard that she nearly dropped it. Rosanna took her warm stone out of her pocket and tucked it into June's sleeping bag. June curled around the warmth, soaking it in. Rosanna whispered encouragement, and the stone heated up a little more. It took energy she hadn't thought she had, but it was worth it to watch the blue recede from June's fingers and lips.

"Where's your warm stone?" she asked after a few moments.

"Coat pocket," June said, and Rosanna dug it out, and put it in the bottom of her own sleeping bag.

"Come on," Rosanna said, "you best get out of those wet things and into your sleeping bag." The temperature inside the tent had already risen. It wasn't quite comfortable yet, but it no longer felt like they crouched in someone's deep-freeze.

"No, no, no," June said muzzily. "You got this all wrong. I'm supposed to take care of you. It don't go the other way 'round."

"Shut up and get naked," Rosanna said, and grinned.

"Damn, how come nobody tells me that when I ain't freezin' to death?"

Rosanna helped June out of her clothes. The ice on them was already melting as the temperature continued to rise inside the tent. June crawled into her sleeping bag, eyes already half-closed. She looked up at Rosanna once, just before she fell asleep. Golden light glimmered in her hazel eyes like a remembrance of summer.

"You gonna be okay?" she asked, and Rosanna smiled, weary though she was.

"Yeah," she said. "Head to sleep, I'm right behind you." June nodded, and rolled over. Rosanna peeled off her own layers of wet clothing. She smiled wryly to herself. It was almost like they'd gotten washed after all. Her coat and sweaters were still dry, thanks to the web, but from the waist down, she was soaked. Around her, the wind prowled and snarled with arrogant certainty, knowing its power. The light-stone made a silk cocoon of the tent, and Rosanna was content to cling to the earth and rest. She dug June's healing stone out, and tucked it in with June's sleeping form. June hardly stirred, except to vaguely protest the cooler air. She snuggled back down into the thick fabric, and snored gently.

Rosanna held her own healing stone cupped in wondering hands, just for a moment.

She heard its little voice, the pure song she'd placed within it. She felt it working to restore her depleted reserves. June had called the web Rosanna's legacy, but that was only part. This work here, the ability to make wonders, that was Granny's legacy to Rosanna, too. Tears sprang up, and she let them fall. Granny would have been proud, she thought, and that thought was as nourishing as it was painful. Rosanna herself was proud, and she wasn't sure she'd ever felt that way before.

Finally, she wiped her face, and piled all the wet clothes on top of the light-stone. She wasn't sure if it'd be enough, but she hoped the warmth would at least dry them out to some extent. She unzipped her own sleeping bag, and crawled in. There was a lovely pocket of heat down by her toes, and she sighed and stretched happily. Even under all the wet clothes, the light-stone still let out a soft glimmer, and Rosanna was comforted by it. No matter how the wind howled, her light still shone. It did not flicker, and it did not go out.

When Rosanna woke, the wind still rippled the fabric of the tent, but it no longer tore at it. This was more of a casual caress, and there was no sense of anger to it. Rosanna stretched, luxuriating in the warmth of their little space. June still hadn't moved, but Rosanna could hear the soft hush and hum of her breathing. It was lovely to be warm and dry at once. The hot springs had much to recommend them, but even there she had to pay attention, or some bit would end up chilly. Not even the tip of her nose was cold today, and she couldn't remember when that had last been so.

Well, yes, she could remember. Back in June's restaurant, when Granny was still alive. She swallowed, waiting for the grief to knock her flat. It didn't. Granny would have loved Rosanna's miracles, would have been proud of Rosanna's resourcefulness. Today it was okay not to be drowning in grief. At least for the moment, it was, and Rosanna knew now that moments were precious.

She lay back and pushed the golden web out from her. It was nearly effortless again, and she smiled. June grumbled and rolled over to peer at her peevishly.

"How's a girl supposed to sleep with that crap goin' on?" she grumbled.

"It's daylight, lazybones. Time to get up."

"Daylight don't prove nothin'. You don't got a watch. Could be any time at all. Could be time to go back to sleep for all you know."

"I'm hungry."

"Oh well now, that's just mean. Appeal to my nature like that? Ain't you got no consideration?"

"I could bleed, if you prefer. That seems to get you out of bed, too."

June made a face, and slowly emerged from her blue and orange nest. Her braids had come out in the night, and her brown hair stood out in a shaggy nimbus. She yawned hugely and scratched a shoulder.

"Don't feel too bad this mornin'," she said. "You make up some more of them pet rocks?"

"Yeah, I did one for each of us."

"Nice," June said and grinned. "You don't look near so close to death's door as I figgered you would."

"Me? I practically had to carry you last night, you lump!"

"That was all just so you could get me back to the tent and rip my clothes off," June said. "Take a woman into the woods and that's what happens."

Rosanna laughed.

"Oh yeah," she said. "I always secretly wanted to date scruffy the wonder-pooch."

"You ain't no picture of beauty yourself, smartass."

Rosanna didn't doubt it. She'd combed through her curls with her fingers as much as she could, but they were unruly at the best of times. She shrugged.

"All this isn't making me less hungry."

"I grabbed what we had," June said. "Ain't much, though." Rosanna took a quick look, and the heap of packages was pathetically small.

"Well," Rosanna said, "we knew we were going to leave today."

"We *said* we was leavin' today," June said. "Wasn't sure we meant it."

"We did."

Their clothes were nearly completely dry, even the boots, and June was impressed.

"You're pretty damn good at this for a beginner," she said. "You sure you ain't been sneakin' lessons?"

"I guess I was just meant for it," Rosanna replied. "Funny, all my life I didn't think I was meant for anything much."

"Nothin' funny about that at all," June said. "Don't you forget that, when things get hairy. You are meant for more than you ever thought."

It wasn't really a comforting thought, but it wasn't uncomfortable, either. It was like a new coat, this new definition of her. It fit, but it would take a while to get used to living in it.

They dressed, and Rosanna turned the light out with a whispered 'please'.

"That thing ain't gonna light up every time I'm polite to you, is it? A flashing pocket might get noticed."

"I don't think so," Rosanna said. "I meant for intention to count, that you have to be talking to the rock. Try it and see."

"Rosanna, please make the coffee."

Nothing happened, and Rosanna slipped the stone into her coat pocket, along with the others.

"Well then, that's nice," June said. "But where's the damn coffee?"

"I didn't quite manage that one, sorry," Rosanna said with a grin, and June sighed theatrically.

"My turn again, I suppose," she said, and unzipped the flap. A huge chunk of snow spilled in onto the floor of the tent.

"Holy shit," June said, and they both sat in silence for a second. The snow had piled up against their tent right to the top of the zipper. Rosanna could make out trees, but the snow was waist-deep.

# Chapter 20

"Well, shit!" June said again. "And we just got dry and everything."

"I think we're staying dry, at least for a bit," Rosanna said. "I feel fit and fabulous today. How about some magic?"

"Is that smart?" June asked. "Can he tell when you do stuff?"

"I'm not sure," Rosanna said. "I think, though, that if I use tools I've got, there won't be very much new magic to hear."

"Does that mean you think he heard you last night?"

"Well, there was something ugly on that storm, and it didn't come up until after I started fiddling with Granny's web. But I think that if he'd known where we were, it wouldn't just be snow at our door this morning."

"Cheerful thought," June said.

Rosanna did find it cheerful, if only because it reduced Trapper's stature in her world. He couldn't hear everything and he didn't know everything, and she, Rosanna, might be able to surprise him. She wasn't quite sure how to explain all that, so she shrugged.

"I could try melting it with the light-stone," she said, but June shook her head doubtfully.

"That's an awful lot of snow. I want to stow the tent and our other gear before we go. Maybe it sounds stupid, but I don't like just leavin' stuff lying around."

"No, I can understand that," Rosanna said. "I'm just not sure how to do it."

"We could use the rocks, but we might just as well wait for spring," June said. "I don't suppose you got a magic shovel?"

"Sure, in my pocket with the magic coffee maker."

June shook her head.

"It don't have to be complicated, we can just shovel our way out and be wet. Again."

"No, really," Rosanna said. "I'm sure there must be a way to use what we've got to do what we want. I'm tired of being cold and wet, and besides, we don't really have enough food to power any serious tunneling."

"Fine, magical genius, you figger it, but could you hurry? I gotta pee."

Rosanna pushed the web, when it reached the snow, it pushed the flakes back and compressed them, but Rosanna could feel the extra effort. Simply moving the snow this way wasn't going to work for long. She pushed enough out of the way that both women could take care of the morning necessities, but it was hard work. She was almost ready to give up and get cold and wet again. She stroked the light-stone in her pocket, and when she did the web flared brighter and the snow hissed against it. Rosanna listened, and she could hear an echo of the stone's Words whispering along the tracery of the web. That wasn't an answer, either, though. June was right, it would take forever to melt this much snow. But if the web could be connected with one kind of stone, perhaps it could be connected to another.

She pulled out her healing stone, and the web's light subsided to its more usual intensity. Now she could hear the faint sounds of earth and air Words moving within the confine of Granny's construct. She smiled. Trapper wasn't the only one who could use wind as a tool, she decided.

"June," she said, "I think I have an idea."

"Ideas are nice," June said. "Anything I'll like?"

"I think so. Come walk with me, would you?"

"I went walkin' with you last night and nearly got froze for it. You sure?"

Rosanna made a face at her. "I'm never sure. But it still sounds like a good idea to me."

June shrugged, and stepped in close to Rosanna under the golden net. She looked at it curiously.

"Looks different," she said, and Rosanna nodded. "I think I just turned it into a magic shovel, she replied," and stepped forward.

The snow still resisted, but the web itself built up a little current of air, so as she walked, the snow simply lifted up and parted. There was no shoveling, and no great exchange of energy, just a gentle shift of position. June laughed.

"Looks more like a magic snow-blower," she said. "You could make a fortune doing driveways around here."

Rosanna smiled.

"How is it? You gonna tire out?" June asked.

"Nope. It's only a little more work than just holding the web, because the stone already has the Words that I need."

"That's more detail than I really gotta have," June said, "but I'm glad it works for you."

"What's the point in being outrageously clever if I can't brag?"

"Well, miss Magic Snow-plow, do you think we can clean up camp?"

Rosanna cleared a path to the cook stove and the cache. It really wasn't so much a plow as a broom, she thought, and it moved lightly without even disturbing the trees overmuch. Rosanna shrunk the web down to just fit around them, and they tunneled over to the cook stove. They dug the equipment out by hand, and so ended up a little wet anyway, but it was nothing as bad as it would have been working through the heavy drifts under just their own power. June used the last of their cooking fuel to make tea, and Rosanna cleared a path to the axe. That was the last missing piece of equipment, and June smiled happily to see it.

"We can take that with us," she said. "If we gotta hold over some place else, we should be ready for it."

They ate trail mix and the last of the marshmallows for breakfast. Granny Rosie would have been appalled, Rosanna thought, then grinned. Appalling Granny Rosie was always good fun.

"What you smilin' at?" June said. "If you think you're havin' that last marshmallow you are mistaken."

Rosanna passed it over.

"Nah, just thinking about Granny. She always believed in a good breakfast. We used to fight about it till it kind of got to be a family joke."

"Good to see you smile, girl," June said softly. Rosanna swallowed the lump that was suddenly in her throat.

"I'm going to miss her so much," she said. "She drove me nuts, but I loved her more than anyone."

"Go ahead and miss her," June replied, "but don't forget to smile for her, when you can."

"It still feels like we were just really finding out who each other was, you know?" Rosanna said. "All this magic stuff...I never even guessed that about her."

June thought for a moment, taking bites out of the last marshmallow, then licking her fingers contemplatively.

"I didn't know your Granny too well," June said. "She was friendly enough, hung out at the restaurant some, but she never got too involved."

"That's really strange," Rosanna said. "She used to always be in the middle of everything. Every time we moved it was like she moved in and took over. Every town turned into 'Grannyville'."

June nodded. "That was kinda the sense I got of her, that she wanted to do more, that she even knew how. but that she was just...waiting. Or tired maybe, I dunno."

"What do you think it means?" Rosanna asked.

"I think she really was tired," June said. "And maybe all this magic stuff explains it. Maybe she didn't know who she was except all that, didn't know who to be."

Rosanna shook her head. "That doesn't make sense to me," Rosanna said. "She was so sure, and she knew so much."

"Don't you see?" June said. "Rosie didn't know herself any better than you, all that time. Maybe even you knew her better than she did." June chuckled softly. "Each of you learned only one side of your selfs. How could you know each other any more than you did?"

"That doesn't make it any better, really," Rosanna said. "Because she didn't get the chance."

"Nobody gets all the chances, girl. We each only get some. You two got a few extra before the end, and that's more than most people get at all."

Rosanna nodded.

"I wish..." she said, after a long pause, "I wish I had more chances with Trapper, too."

June nodded.

"I can understand that," she said. "I wish he didn't turn out the way he did."

"I don't really understand why he did."

"Does it matter?"

"Well, yeah, at least some. I mean, I know he's responsible for my mother's death, and Granny's too, but...I'd like to know why."

"Sometimes why don't matter. Sometimes ain't even a real 'why'. If you got the choice between askin' him why and puttin' him down, don't you hesitate. Whatever 'why' he's got ain't gonna change what he is." She pulled her pendant out.

"If I asked that damn cougar, I guarantee he'd still have this tooth in his crazy head."

Rosanna nodded. It was hard to put Trapper on a level with an animal. It was equally hard to align the two sides of him she'd seen. On one side, he was a man, even if he was rather a mess of a man. She'd talked to him, felt warmth and a human connection. On the other, he was a killer. She'd felt poison in him, and felt his joy in injecting that poison into other lives. Nothing was going to be easy about this. She sighed.

"We ain't there, yet," June said. "My gramma always said there's no point in worryin' bout the ditch till you're in it. She was a terrible driver." June smiled, more tentatively than usual. Rosanna reached out and took her hand.

"We can do this," Rosanna said. "And then you'll get a nice insurance settlement and we'll rebuild and go on."

June nodded, and Rosanna was sorry to have even alluded to the restaurant.

"Damn," she said, "how come it's always you that knows the right things to say?"

June laughed. "Ain't that I know, it's only that I talk so much that somethin's bound to be the right thing."

Together they dismantled the tent, and it packed neatly into several light bundles. Rosanna looked at the space it left, feeling strangely bereft. It hadn't been home, really, but it had been safe, and she thought that safe might be hard to come by for the next little while. She would have liked to say farewell to the hot springs, somehow, but it was a long walk in deep snow just to wave to the scenery. She told herself sternly that she wasn't really going to miss the place, but that she was just trying to put off the next bit.

"We should prolly bring as much of our gear as we can," June said, and Rosanna nodded.

"I have an idea of what I want to do, but if it doesn't work out just right, we'll be doing more camping."

"You go ahead and be the idea girl," June said. "I don't mind that, long as you don't mind being pack-mule, too."

In the end, they built a travois to carry the gear. It wasn't that any piece of it was particularly heavy, just that the combined weight and bulk was too unwieldy for them to carry in their arms.

Rosanna hoped June knew where they could resupply without putting anyone in danger, but they were going to have to do it somehow.

Rosanna cleared a path back to the truck, keeping the net as small as possible around them. She could still feel the slight drain on her energy, but it seemed as though those stores were growing as she asked more of them. A thick blanket of cloud lay heavy on the valley, which meant that the temperatures were kinder, and Rosanna found herself enjoying the walk. She let her body respond to the terrain, and moved with a grace and ease she never would have expected of herself. June turned to her with a smile.

"You don't look much like a city girl today," she said. "You almost look like you belong out here."

"I almost feel like I do," Rosanna said. "Although I could seriously do with about fifteen degrees warmer."

"Wuss," June said, and grinned. "You're getting' real good at moving quiet, too."

Rosanna remembered Trapper's meditation on movement, and stopped for a second.

"What?" June said. "What'd I say?"

"It's just…Trapper taught me that. Nothing about this is easy! Nothing is going to **get** any easier."

"Nope," June said. "It ain't. But we ain't in the ditch yet, so quit worryin' till we are."

Rosanna sighed, and repeated it. "We're not in the ditch, so I won't worry till we are."

"Ain't quite what I said," June replied with a grin, "but some day I'll teach you how to talk proper."

The walk back to the truck wasn't overly long, certainly not near as long as it had seemed when they arrived. The truck itself stood in the shelter of some enormous pine trees, and they had kept it from being buried quite as much as their tent had. June opened it up and took out a window-sweeper. Rosanna cleared a path around the truck, but didn't feel sure enough of her control to try to clean off the windshield. She did put the warming stones inside the cab, though, and June laughed.

"Heated seats, yet! This old bucket's movin' up in the world." Despite her laughter, June's face was lined with some private worry as she scraped ice and snow off the glass. She had a broom in the back of the truck, and took it out to sweep the box clean. Rosanna handed her up the gear, and June stowed it tidily away. She climbed down and stood beside Rosanna, admiring her handiwork.

"Well now," she said. "Don't that look nice."

"I suppose," Rosanna said. It looked like a rusted out heap to her, but she'd been fond of a few clunkers in her day, and wasn't about to make an issue of it.

"Won't run, though," June said flatly.

Rosanna's brain sputtered and stalled.

"What?"

"I forgot." June turned around and kicked at the snow fiercely. "I just…I was so damn tired I forgot."

"Forgot what? The keys? They're still in it, aren't they?"

"Not that, I forgot the damn engine jumper."

"The what?"

"To jump the battery. Got no plug-ins out here, battery is gonna be flat after this long and this cold." She kicked at the snow again. "Shit hell and damn!"

Rosanna had forgotten about the necessity of plugging vehicles in when the temperatures dropped. Her own bit of the country didn't get quite so cold, and that was really how she liked it.

"What's the jumper thingy?" she asked.

June sighed. "I bought a portable jump-starter, but I loaned it out, and I never got it back. Truck never gives me no grief, and I figgered I'd get it back sometime." She cursed some more. "I am gonna kick that man's ass when I see him next."

"Are we in the ditch now?" Rosanna asked. June scowled at her.

"That just ain't funny, unless you got some way to call in the tow-truck."

"Would it help if we warmed it up? We've got stones."

"Warm ain't the problem. Battery cells freeze and it loses current."

"Shouldn't we try, anyway?"

June heaved a sigh, and visibly tried to rein in her raging temper.

"Well, if we're gonna, we might as well warm the engine up first, give ourselves the best chance we can."

June popped the hood, and they set the stones on the block. They waited in the cab until they could see the patterns of warmth on the hood. June took a deep breath.

"Cross your fingers," she said.

"I'll cross fingers toes and eyes," Rosanna replied, "just to be sure."

June tried to smile, but it was more of a grimace. She turned the key, and the engine whined and whirred. For a second, Rosanna thought it was going to catch, but the sound just ground down to nothing. June punched the truck door in frustration, and Rosanna cringed at the resounding thump.

"How far to help?" she asked at last.

"Long way," June said. "Shit. Rosanna, I'm sorry, I got us all the way out here, and now...and now we're just plain screwed."

"Don't you dare apologize. You got us safe. There just has to be another way."

June didn't say anything, and the silence leeched the warmth out of the cab as surely as the winter air.

# Chapter 21

They sat in the cooling silence for a few more moments, then June tried the engine again. This time the engine didn't even whirr, just clicked like a broken lock.

"Shit!" June screamed, and pounded on the steering wheel. Rosanna watched in silence. It was a set-back, yes, but she couldn't believe that a dead battery could stop them when nothing else had. She waited until June exhausted some of her fury, though she worried about broken hands on top of everything. June was too hungry to carry a full tempest for long, and finally she sat, panting with her forehead leaning against the steering wheel.

"Better?" Rosanna asked.

"What do you think? We're still goddamn stuck, ain't we?"

"When you're in the ditch, it doesn't make much sense to spend your energy crying about it," Rosanna said, stung by June's tone. "We need a solution, not a funeral."

"Well there ain't gonna be much of a funeral when we freeze to death all the way out here, is there?"

"Wow, I didn't think you ever gave up."

"I ain't! It's just facts! We don't got the resources to walk out, nor even to survive here." She shook her head furiously. "It's just facts!" she repeated.

"Facts change all the time," Rosanna said. She didn't understand her own calm. Surely this was catastrophic, but some part of her didn't really believe in catastrophe any more. She listened to the murmur of her heating stones under the hood. Granny Rosie had said that cars weren't inherently magical anymore, because of use, but Rosanna could still hear echoes of the Words that made them up, and even more, she could still hear the quietest of mumbles from the old truck battery. There was only the barest of whispers of electricity, and Rosanna had never really listened for that particular Word. There'd hardly been a chance, really. But she could hear it, and added it to her own vocabulary. It sounded like another of the Words that was already safe somewhere, and she was relieved. Saving the pure nature of electricity felt like too much more responsibility on top of what she already had ahead of her.

June was swearing again by the time Rosanna shifted her attention back to the cab of the truck.

"June," she said with a smile, "Shut up. I love you dearly, but honestly, just chill. I think I have a solution."

June's mouth opened, and just for a second Rosanna expected to have her skin peeled off. Then it shut, and June nodded.

"Do you have any stones left? The ones we picked out but I didn't do anything to yet?"

"Sure," June said, hope blossoming in her eyes. "We still got three or four." She shrugged. "I didn't know if you'd need 'em, and I liked the feel of 'em. Like worry stones." June dug them out of her coat pocket, and Rosanna looked down at them. What she wanted was to encourage the murmur in the battery, but she wasn't a mechanic or an engineer. Cars did what she asked until they broke, and then someone else did the fixing. But she knew that a battery could be recharged, so perhaps if she created something that just made electricity, the battery would fill up again. She spoke the Word into the stone, and tied it there with a little of her own energies. She could hear it tumbling around inside the structure of the stone, could practically taste lightning on the air.

"I don't know if this will do it," she said, "but I'm hoping it'll charge the battery for us."

"How long?" June asked.

"Hell if I know," Rosanna said, "but if it doesn't work at least I have the Word to work with."

Some of the tension left June's shoulders and she looked at Rosanna curiously.

"You ain't the same person, you know," she said. "You ain't the same at all."

"I don't feel all that different," Rosanna said. "Dirtier, maybe." It wasn't quite true though. All her life she'd felt like a shadow not just of others, but of herself. Nothing in her life had ever seemed to quite come into focus. She was herself, still, but in focus now.

She climbed out of the truck, and gathered the warm stones up to put back in the cab of the truck. Then she set her little stone spark on the battery, where it sizzled and jumped excitedly. She whispered encouragement to it, and felt it feeding power into the battery. She grinned, and June grinned, and they both wished mightily for a hot breakfast.

"Will it take long?" June asked again.

"I don't know how much electricity," Rosanna said, "but if this is like a jump-start you could probably just try the engine."

"Let's wait a minute," June said. "For luck."

Rosanna could hear the current flowing into the battery. It wasn't much, more of a trickle than a torrent, but the battery seemed to be making more noise all on its own. They waited, not speaking, but almost holding their breath in anticipation and worry.

"Try it," Rosanna said, at last. "if it doesn't work now, we should probably set up camp for another night."

Neither of them really had any interest in another night's camp. June took a deep breath, and turned the key. The engine whirred and ground for a second, but didn't catch.

"That's better than last time," she said. "One more time." This time, the engine chugged twice, then caught with a triumphant roar. June whooped with joy, and hugged Rosanna tight. Rosanna could hear the bright chorus of electricity running through the battery, and wondered how she could ever have not noticed. She smiled to herself. Maybe it was like one of those optical illusions. Once you see the picture inside the picture, it's there forever.

She got her little charger off the battery, and tucked it in her coat with the others. It tingled her fingertips, and she considered the wisdom of carrying lightning in a pocket. Still, unless encouraged, the current would mostly just zip around inside its little stone Book. Mostly would have to do. For now, a battery charger was a pretty valuable commodity.

June grinned like a monkey as she ground the truck into reverse. Rosanna had been worried about getting through the snow, but clearly this great blue monster had seen and conquered more than a few winters in these mountains. Even in reverse it plowed through and over drifts as if they were little more than anthills. The suspension creaked and groaned, and the cab bucked like a cranky bull, but soon they were turned around and headed toward the road.

The slope was just as steep as Rosanna had remembered it, but in daylight she had a chance to admire the passing view. The trees stood solemnly in heavy robes of white, and everything glimmered in the cloud-softened light. It had been a good place to hide, and even with her magical work, Rosanna felt rested. The truck growled and muttered about the steepness of the grade, but they moved steadily away from that small pocket of safety. She didn't think Trapper was waiting for them at the road, though she supposed it was a possibility. The violence of the storm probably meant he knew they were alive, or at least that Rosanna was. Beyond that, she thought they still had the element of surprise. She had the beginnings of a plan, but they would need to get resupplied. What she had in mind might work, or it might not, but Rosanna had no intention of going into anything ill-prepared. They were meeting on Trapper's ground, and she needed to be as ready as she possibly could.

June focused fiercely on the driving, though she seemed to take delight in breaking through the deeper drifts.

"You must be killer in a bumper car," Rosanna said.

"All cars are bumper cars," June replied, and grinned.

"Any idea where we're going?" Rosanna asked.

"That kinda depends what we need," June said. "You got ideas?"

"Well, I wouldn't mind some hot food that wasn't freeze-dried, no offense to your cooking."

"Same here, no offense taken. What else?"

Rosanna sighed. She wasn't sure how they'd accomplish any of this. Her purse was back in her car, or maybe June's restaurant.

"I'd like us to have packs or something, so we can carry this gear. We're probably going to have to camp again, and I'm not sure for how long."

"So we need more food, too," June said. "Okay."

"I don't think I've got any money," Rosanna said, and June shrugged.

"Me neither, but I got friends that won't ask for none."

"I don't want your friends to get on the bad side of Trapper," Rosanna said, and June chuckled grimly.

"Trapper don't want to be on the bad side of my friends, neither. But I won't tell them, and they won't ask. They wouldn't believe the whole story, and Trapper might get one or two before they got him."

Rosanna felt her eyebrows climbing into her hairline. These were friends? June must have caught the expression out of the corner of her eye, because she laughed.

"People don't just come here 'cause it's pretty, ya know. Some people hide out here, but the ones that belong, they don't belong nowhere else. We got wildlife that ain't ever had its picture took."

"But they're your friends?"

"Dangerous friends is better than dangerous enemies. Besides, I'm more than half wild myself. I get along with everyone, till they do me wrong."

June's expression darkened, and Rosanna knew she was thinking of Trapper.

"City people like it all to be simple. You got the right people and the wrong people, and they don't hang out together. Out here we know you just got people, and the ones that are really, really wrong end up broken at the bottom of cliffs. Some springtimes the bears eat real good."

Rosanna shuddered. June could seem so civilized and then so savage, in almost the next second. She never wanted to be the cause of that shift. June was not domesticated, Rosanna decided, and that was the difference. June was whoever she was, without consultation of anyone else's code of ethics or expectations. Rosanna tumbled that thought around in her head, and wondered how it would feel to simply do what she believed was best. She shook her head a little. Right and wrong were important to her. It wouldn't ever be quite as simple as necessary or not. But that was all right, really, because between the two of them, they had all the ways to judge a situation. June knew Trapper had to die because he just had to. Rosanna knew that it was wrong to leave him loose and dangerous in an unsuspecting world. Beyond that, she would decide and judge as it became necessary. In other words, she'd worry about that ditch when she was in it. She intended to be prepared for the ditch though. She would not be caught unawares again.

It was almost a surprise when the old truck bounced over one last snow drift and onto smooth asphalt. Rosanna had seen glimpses of the road ahead, but after these few days out in nowhere, it was strange to see the work of human hands again. June nodded in satisfaction.

"Figgered they'd have it plowed by now," she said. "Probably worked all night at it." She snorted. "None of the back roads, 'course, but the government likes the highway clean. Bad for loggers, otherwise."

"Well?" Rosanna asked. "Which way?"

"That depends some on your plan, I guess," June replied. "Don't want to add more distance than we got to."

"I expect things to wind up around Granny's place," Rosanna said, but I don't want us too close to Trapper until we've got supplies.

"That's fine, then," June said. "We'll go see Bear. He practically hibernates this time of year, and if he ain't home, he won't mind if we help ourselves." She grinned. "He's got a soft spot for me."

"Is there anyone who doesn't?" Rosanna asked, then got a closer look at June's grin. "And are you sure it's just a soft spot he's got?" She was delighted to see a blush rise all the way up to the tips of Junes ears, and chortled.

"Just you close your trap, city girl," June said. "Ain't like that. Bear...he's a good guy. Real good guy. So don't...aw never mind." She focused fiercely on the road.

"I won't tease if you don't want me to," Rosanna said with a smile, and June sighed.

"Go ahead and tease, I guess. Wouldn't be you if you didn't. But...I like this one, Rosanna. Don't...I dunno, just..."

"Don't screw it up?" Rosanna asked, and June nodded.

"If it ain't too much bother," she said.

"It's not," Rosanna said.

They sped up the highway at stomach churning speeds, but June took the curves with confidence, and finally Rosanna decided that she wasn't going to worry about the real ditch any more than the metaphorical one. What was the point? She relaxed, and watched the rise and fall of the tree line beside her. They were closer to the valley floor here, and when there was a break in the trees she saw wide meadowlands, all painted in the same blue-white perfection. It looked still and beautiful from here, but it was lovely to be warm and uncomplicated, if only for this little while. Rosanna's sense of place wasn't perfect here, but she thought they were getting near June's restaurant when they turned off the road. Rosanna had expected another foray into snow drifts, but this road was neatly plowed, and June nodded her satisfaction.

"Good," she said. "He's either home or been home lately. Either way there'll be food."

The little road was longer than Rosanna had expected. It wound in towards the foot of the mountain, then up in a long slow climb that made her ears pop. June took this stretch of road with little more caution than she had the highway. The truck bumped and bucked over dips in the road. Rosanna imagined June driving in the city and shuddered.

"How far?" she shouted, over the creaks and groans of the truck's abused suspension.

"Dunno, little ways more, I think. Don't usually come out here in winter, it's harder to tell how far we are without my landmarks."

They swept around one more curve, and a fenced yard came into view.

"Damn, I'm good," June said, and Rosanna laughed.

"Good or lucky," she said, "either way is fine with me."

The fence was a huge construct; about six feet tall and made of rough-cut logs, it stretched out across the open yard and to the tree-line, where it turned and marched solidly back towards the house. Snow had drifted up to it, but didn't come close to reaching its top. June looked out at it and shook her head.

"I swear, that thing gets higher every year," she said.

"Isn't it a lot of work?" Rosanna asked, and June rolled her eyes.

"You have no idea. But he just don't quit. Does it all himself, too."

June rolled slowly up to the gate. That was made of the same graying logs as the fence, but it was chained and locked.

"He probably ain't home," June said. "Don't know whether to be happy about that or not."

Rosanna understood. It would have been good to have more help, or even just to talk to it out with someone besides the two of them. Besides which, anyone named 'Bear' sounded like a useful ally. But explaining it all would be next to impossible, and Rosanna didn't want to put anyone else in danger. It was bad enough that June was with her.

"If he's not home why is his road plowed?" Rosanna asked. "And how are we going to get in?"

"Plowin' roads means steady money around here, least in the winter it does. We work by trade a lot. Bear cuts wood for his stupid fence, sells and hauls what he don't use in the summer. Been thinkin' bout getting a plow myself." She opened her door, and Rosanna flinched back from the cold air.

"As for how we get in, that's easy." There was a small wooden box attached to one of the gate posts. June opened it up and pulled out the key. Rosanna laughed and shook her head. She jumped out to help June open the heavy gate.

"What the hell?" she said, still chuckling.

"Lock's just a 'go away' sign," June said. "Sorta local sign language for someone with an unreliable temper." Rosanna waited as June drove the blue beast through the gate, then helped close it. June didn't lock it, but hung the chain on the gate post.

"That way he knows he's got visitors, if he comes home. Ain't a good person to surprise, is Bear."

"Shoot first and ask questions later sort of guy?"

"Bear don't ask questions," June said, and smiled wryly. "But we're friends, and if we don't surprise him, he'll get a chance to see that. Only a friend would unlock the gate. Any other idiot tryin' to break in here is just askin' for trouble." She smiled again. "Bear kinda likes trouble, if you know what I mean."

"Will he mind?"

"What, us bein' here? No. Bear's been in enough trouble to know the signs. I'll leave a note. We'll keep track of everything we take, leave a list. Everyone probably thinks I'm dead." June shook her head. "I hate that. But I ain't gonna risk anyone else."

They drove up to the house. Rosanna had expected some kind of log cabin, but it was an ordinary little rancher with seventies-blue siding. June parked the truck next to a power outlet and plugged the block heater in. A wide area of snow had been cleared next to the house, but the sidewalk and steps were still drifted over.

"Yup," June said, "he ain't home. Bear always shovels his walks. Unlike some."

All the same, June first knocked on the door, then opened it and yelled in.

"Hm," she said, "dog's gone too. And it ain't all that warm in here. Wonder where he went this time?"

They took their boots off at the mat, but left their coats on. The front door opened into a living room with polished pine floors and darker wood paneling. That room led directly into the kitchen; the only real transition was from wood floor to tile. June walked down the hall until she found the thermostat and cranked it up. Rosanna heard the furnace kick in and smelled the dust rising up into the air. The place was tidy, but a thin layer of dust lay on all the furniture, and June shook her head.

"Musta been gone a while," she said. "I ain't talked to him in a couple months, but that's no different than usual. Hope he's okay." She frowned and sighed.

"Don't matter really, we got our own troubles. First thing, I want somethin' to eat. So you can have a shower, and I'll figger out what there is."

"Are you sure?" Rosanna asked. "I mean, about us being here?"

"Ain't like the city. We all need each other some time, and we know it. Besides, I told you. Bear's a friend. He'd help if he was here." She pointed. "Bathroom's at the end of the hall. Towels are under the sink."

It still felt odd to walk in a stranger's house and root through his cupboards. In the kitchen she could hear June rattling around without any hesitation, so she turned on the shower. It took a few moments for the water to heat up, and the room was still chilly, but Rosanna shed her dirty clothes with satisfaction. The towels were huge and fluffy, if a little stiff with cold, and Rosanna hung hers on the shower door in hopes that it might warm up a little. She stepped in, under the pounding water and sighed. This, she decided, was the true mark of civilization. Anything else could be fudged, but a hot shower was irreplaceable. She lathered and rinsed and then just stood for a little while, letting the water run over her.

The bathroom was warmer when she finally got out and dried off. She looked at the pile of clothes and sighed. She really didn't want to put them back on, not when she was nice and clean. She settled for wrapping the towel around herself. She borrowed Bear's comb, working out the tangles of the last few days with relief. All she really needed now was a toothbrush, but she wasn't borrowing that.

June thumped on the door, and Rosanna jumped.

"You ever gonna come out?" June shouted. "There's food out here that ain't been freeze-dried."

"Do I have to dress for dinner?" Rosanna asked, "or can you survive me in a towel?"

"Come as you are, girl. I'm too hungry for manners."

As soon as Rosanna opened the bathroom door, rich savory smells filled the air. June stood at the door with a bundle of cloth in her hands. She was blushing.

"There's um…"she paused. "I got some clean clothes you can wear if you want." She held out a pair of jeans and a flannel shirt.

"Won't these be too big?"

"Don't flatter yourself," June said, and Rosanna understood.

"So you just happened to leave a few of your things here? With your good friend?"

"Quit flappin' your mouth and get dressed or you can eat out in the snow," June said, and shut the bathroom door with a thump. Rosanna laughed, and got dressed. The clothes should actually have been a little small, but what with the exercise and scant meals, they fit pretty well. She walked out into the kitchen, where June had a couple of places set.

"I'm gonna shower after we eat," June said. "Then we can wash what we got on, and see about supplies."

Breakfast was sausages fried up with onions and potatoes. June wrinkled her nose at it a little.

"Man has no spice cupboard at all," she said. "And the potatoes are those frozen hash brown things, but it's food."

"It smells amazing," Rosanna said.

"Well, that's hopeful, and there's coffee, too."

They both ate in ravenous silence. It probably could have been anything and been delicious, providing it didn't come out of a packet. Regardless, Rosanna thought it might be the best meal she'd ever had. She took seconds when June offered, then settled back with a contented sigh.

"You're my favourite cook," she said.

"That's great, because you're my favourite dish washer," June replied, and grinned. "Though if you don't mind, I'll get my shower in first."

Rosanna sat back with another cup of coffee while June bathed. If she listened, she could hear the little Words of warmth that stirred her coffee, and faint murmurs of other syllables in the things around her. Granny had said that use diluted the Words, but they were still there, all around her in a faint susurration of endless conversation. Granny might have been in it to protect the extraordinary, bur Rosanna found herself more inclined to defend the ordinary and simple. Nobody should be allowed to make the world less than it was, just to appease his personal hungers.

It was good to be warm and dry, but Rosanna put her boots back on, and left her coat in easy reach. Some lessons were too dearly bought to forget. When the sound of the shower stopped, she ran water and washed the dishes.

She was looking out the window as she dried them, and so she saw a big man stumble out of the woods, followed by a black dog. Then, rising on the cold air and cutting it like a rusty razor, she *heard* poison, the black sound of Trapper's wolf-thing. Man and dog both ran for the house. Rosanna put her dish down and her coat on. She had her knife in her hand when they reached the door.

"June!" she shouted, and that was all the time she had.

# Chapter 22

June was still running from the bath room when the man crashed through the door. Rosanna crouched, waiting for the dog to attack, but it hung behind. The man opened his mouth to shout, and Rosanna realized that the sound of poison came from him. It was hard to tell what he might have looked like, except that he was big. His features had shifted into something other than human. He panted loudly in the silence of the kitchen.

"Bear!" June shouted, and he turned his head toward the sound. His eyes were deep pools of fury, discoloured by the poison running through his body and spirit. The dog at his heels whined, and Rosanna could hear its confusion and concern.

"Bear?" June said again, and took a step forward, hand outstretched.

"Don't touch him!" Rosanna shouted, but it was too late. Bear seized the hand, and dragged June close. He bared teeth that had become pointed and venomous. June struggled to pull away, and he lashed out with a huge booted foot. Rosanna heard a snap, a horrible sound like dry wood breaking, and June screamed and crumpled. Bear dragged her closer. Rosanna couldn't use her knife, not on June's friend, but there was no time for subtlety. She spoke lightning, hoping it would be enough to knock him out and not enough to kill. He turned his black eyes on her, and dropped June's arm. June dragged her leg but crawled out of his reach. As soon as June was clear, Rosanna pushed out Granny's web. She didn't know how well it would work against the poison, but at least it should give them a moment to run, should they need to.

"Don't kill him," June whispered, "Please, please don't kill him."

Rosanna smiled wryly. Bear was well over six feet tall, and so broad that his shoulders filled the narrow hall off the door. She didn't feel like much of a hazard, especially when her lightning had merely slowed him down.

Still, she remembered the wolf. Bear must have been bitten by something similar. As ugly as the sound of the poison was, the rough and lovely music of his essential self still rumbled below it. She had failed with Granny. She squared her shoulders. She was done with failing.

"I don't like that sound," she said. "That's quite enough of that, I think." Rather than try to counter the poison, she echoed the Words of Bear's own soul, sang them like the aria they were. Bear stopped completely, the poison warring with his true self. Beside him the dog took a tentative step forward and licked his fingers.

"This is who you are," she said. "BE this." She tied the Words into the web so that it echoed them, strengthening his essential self. Then she Spoke the clean Words of air and earth and healing. Bear's eyes began to clear, and the rasp and whine of contagion started to unravel from around his soul. The dog beside him whimpered excitedly, and licked with greater enthusiasm. Rosanna pulled the web back in, ready to extend it should that be necessary, but Bear simply stood as she disentangled the corruption from his mind and soul. He lifted his eyes to hers, and they were pale blue under his heavy brow. As she unwound the last bit of venom from around him, he staggered, then fell heavily against the wall. He shook his head, as if to clear it, then looked at Rosanna again.

"I..."he said, then stopped. "Where is she? I thought June...where is she?"

Rosanna listened, and heard no more traces of Trapper's magic on him.

"In here, asshole," June shouted from the living room. "If you try to bite me again I'll break *your* leg."

Her voice was heavy with relief and gratitude, but also with pain. The dog barked joyfully, and ran in to lick her face. Bear still looked dazed, but he followed.

"I thought you were dead," he said, and folded down to his knees beside her. "I thought…" His head dropped, and his shoulders shook. "I thought you were dead," he said again.

"Breakin' my leg ain't a polite way to say hi," June said, but her voice was thick with unshed tears.

"I did that? I didn't…June I didn't mean…" He wrapped his arms around her and wept. "I was so lost, June. I never get lost."

"I know, honey," June said, her voice gentler. "It's a good thing I brought a finder." She lifted her face to Rosanna and smiled. "We're all even for the restaurant now. We're all even and then I owe you some." Rosanna opened her mouth to protest and June frowned. "Now do we think I could get off the damn floor? This hurts. And someone better close the door. We ain't gonna heat the whole valley."

Rosanna settled for shaking her head. "Yes boss," she said, "but we shouldn't move you until I get a look at that leg.

"You a doctor?" Bear asked.

"Not exactly," Rosanna said, then paused. "But I have some skills." She was tired, but using the web had helped cut down on the amount of energy she'd had to expend herself. June's leg wasn't at an odd angle, but Rosanna had heard that snap far too clearly. She knew enough first aid to know that moving June around wasn't a good idea.

The dog wormed in between Bear and June and he resumed licking June's face. He was tall and sleek, with a dappled brown coat and whip of a tail that wagged furiously. Rosanna might otherwise have been nervous of so big a dog, but he radiated such joy and friendliness that it was impossible to be afraid of him.

"Attila, lay off!" June spluttered.

"Attila?" Rosanna asked, and June grinned.

"Attila the Honey, worst guard dog in the valley," she said.

"He's not that bad," Bear protested. "He got me home, anyway," he said in lower tones.

"We'll talk about that in a bit," Rosanna said. "I need to look at June's leg."

Her lower right leg was swollen tight against her pants, and Rosanna shook her head.

"I'm going to have to cut your jeans off, I think," she said.

"Better the jeans than the leg," June replied.

"It's probably going to hurt a lot," Rosanna said.

"Already does."

Rosanna dug through her pockets and came out with a couple healing rocks.

"I don't know how much help these will be," she said, "but every little bit, right?"

June nodded. Bear looked at them curiously, but said nothing. He stroked June's brown hair back from her forehead, then ran a thumb gently down her cheek.

Rosanna carefully slit open the seam on June's jeans, and hissed at the bruising there. The leg wasn't obviously at a bad angle, and the skin hadn't broken, but this was much more than a bump.

"We should splint this," she said, "then get some ice on it."

"Damn," June said. "I thought I was done with ice for a bit." She shivered. "Am a bit cold, though."

"Bear, we need some blankets, and something for splints. Can you do that, or tell me where?"

Bear dragged his attention away from June's face, and up to Rosanna's. He avoided looking at June's leg.

"No, I can do that," he said. He kissed June's forehead, then went off to rummage in one of the bedrooms. Rosanna could hear his heavy steps even through the walls. She took his place supporting June's head and upper body.

June looked up at her, fine features drawn and pale.

"Can't you just…I dunno, fix it?" she asked. Rosanna sighed.

"Maybe," she said. "But I could fix it wrong, and then we'd be equally screwed."

"You fixed Bear."

"That was different. That was magic. This isn't."

"It's just a sprain anyway," June said. "Nothin' those pet rocks can't handle."

Rosanna said nothing, but listened to the sounds of June's body. There was a hitch in the music there, a space in the conversation.

"No," she said. "It's broken."

June shook her head. "I don't think so," she said. "Be all better by tomorrow." Rosanna didn't reply. There was no point in upsetting June just now, and she expected they both knew the truth of it anyway.

Bear came back with a couple walking sticks and an old sheet. Rosanna cut strips off the sheet with her knife, then laid June flat to help hold the sticks while he bound them to the broken leg. June paled further as they jostled the injured limb, but they worked quickly.

"That feels better already," June said with a smile. "Told ya." Rosanna smiled.

"You did," she said. "Now let's get you to a softer surface."

"That sounds nice," June replied, and Bear smiled. He leaned down and picked her up as if she were no more than a child. In his arms she looked no bigger than one. Rosanna helped support the splinted leg, and they moved June over to the couch. Bear tucked pillows under her head, and covered her with a thick blanket.

"We can move you to a bed in a bit, but we should probably keep an eye on you for shock," Rosanna said. June sighed.

"Don't care," she said. "I'm warm, I'm dry, and I ain't sleeping on the ground."

"We should get some ice on that leg though," Rosanna said.

"Crap. I knew it was too good to be true." June looked up at Bear. "Don't suppose you got anything like a painkiller in this house?"

"Only legal ones," he said. "Sorry."

"That's okay, I know you," June said. "anything you got would be nice." Attila gave June's face one last and thorough licking, then lay down with a happy sigh. Stretched out, he was nearly as long as the sofa June lay on. Rosanna reached out to pat his sleek head, and he thumped his tail against the floor.

"Got a friend for life, now," June said with a smile. She groaned as she shifted position a little.

"All better, hm?" Rosanna said. June scowled.

"It will be. It has to be. Don't got time for lyin' around. Not if he's out there doin' shit like this to people I care about."

"I know, I know," Rosanna said. "But all you can do right this minute is take care of yourself. So stop moving around so much."

"It…hurts some is all," June said. "Just can't quite get comfortable."

Bear came back with a bottle of painkillers and a glass of water, and June gulped down a handful. Bear sat on the floor next to her. He didn't say anything, but seemed content just to assure himself of June's continuing existence.

"Oh hey," Rosanna said, pulling her first little Book out of her pocket. "I just remembered."

She folded one of the remaining pieces of sheet over June's injury, then set the little stone on top. It was cool to the touch, but she whispered to it, and it began to radiate cold with greater enthusiasm.

"And you said we wouldn't need a cold stone," she said with a grin. June tried to grin back, but it was an effort, and Rosanna ached to see it. For all her fears, she'd come to think of June as unsinkable, somehow. Invulnerable. Strange how all the pillars holding up her world kept crumbling, and yet she remained. She stroked the golden web absently, listening to the last murmurs of Granny Rosie.

"Feels good," June said. "I'm real tired, though." Rosanna nodded.

"Sleep for a bit, then," she said. "I'll wake you up in a bit to check on you."

June reached out and grabbed Rosanna's hand.

"You wouldn't…you wouldn't go without me?" she asked. Her eyes were deepest brown, with only faint glimmers of green or gold. Rosanna tried to smile, but her eyes filled with tears and she could only manage a grimace.

"Don't lie to me," June said fiercely. "I can stand anything but a damn lie."

"I might, June. I'm sorry, but I might." June nodded and released Rosanna's hand.

"Figgered," she said, and that was all. She closed her eyes and drifted off into sleep. Rosanna could hear the small magics in her stones working to support June, helping her body mend itself. But a broken leg was beyond their power to heal, and beyond Rosanna's certainty. If she were willing to take chances with June's ability to walk, she might try harder, but she wasn't. Nor could she take the chance with her own energy level or magical ability. A rebounded spell could kill. Besides, clearly Trapper was on the move and busy. She shook her head, and Bear turned to look at her. She managed a half-smile, then stood up. Attila looked at her and thumped his tail a couple of times before settling his nose back on his paws.

She swayed a little and Bear stood quickly beside her.

"You okay?" he asked, his voice a low rumble.

"Tired," Rosanna said, but she was beyond tired. As the pillars of her world crumbled, she found herself carrying the weight alone. It was bearable, perhaps, but heavy. She tried to smile at him again, with little more success than previously. "Just…tired."

"Bedroom's this way," he said, and put an arm around her waist. Just for a second she let herself marvel at the purity of the Words that made him up. Then she put a hand up to his strong shoulder, and let him help her to bed. She didn't protest when he helped her off with boots and coat, but wouldn't let him leave the room with them. He just nodded, and put them next to the bed.

"No more than an hour," she said, and he nodded again. "I mean it."

"I can tell," he said. He was just leaving when Attila bounded up onto the bed with her and curled up at her feet. Bear laughed.

"Sorry," he said. "Dog never had any manners. You want me to move him out?" Attila raised mournful eyes, and Rosanna chuckled.

"No," she said, "he's fine. I don't mind a bed-warmer."

"That's about all he's good for," Bear said, and ruffled the dog's ears. He closed the door behind him and Rosanna sighed. At least there was simplicity in being tired, she thought. Nothing to do but permit it. Attila repositioned himself to give her face one more furtive lick, and the last thing she remembered was his warm bulk stretched out next to her.

# Chapter 23

Rosanna woke in a strange darkness with an enormous figure bending over her. Without thinking, she pushed the web out, hard. There was a canine yelp, and a more masculine voice shouted in protest. She woke up enough to remember where she was.

"Bear?" she said, without dropping the web. "That you?"

"It was," he said. "I'm not so sure now."

Rosanna fumbled for the bedside light, and saw him compressed against the wall of the bedroom. She dropped the web, and just caught sight of Attila slinking out the door.

"Think you scared the crap out of my dog," Bear said evenly, as he took a deep breath.

"Not literally, I hope," Rosanna said.

"Probably not. But you're cleaning it up if you did." He chuckled, and followed Attila.

Rosanna smiled to herself. No wonder June liked this one. She put her coat and boots back on, then straightened out the covers. The room was simple and tidy, in a guest-room sort of way. It could almost have been a hotel room, it was so impersonal. Still, it was her first bed in ages, and she was grateful for it. She stepped out into the hallway, and Attila bounded up to her, tail wagging frantically.

"I guess I'm forgiven," she said, and leaned down to pat his broad chest. He licked her face with an equally broad tongue until she spluttered and pushed him away. From the kitchen, she heard the low rumble of Bear's laugh.

"Be careful," he said. "Attila's been known to kill with kindness." He whistled sharply, and Attila turned to run down the hall, nails skittering on the polished floor.

"Oh yeah," Rosanna said. "Scary, scary dog."

"There's coffee," Bear said, "if you hurry. Otherwise June will have it all."

"Lies!" June shouted from the living room. "The man lies! I seen him drink the whole pot. Didn't even offer a poor crippled girl any."

Any half-formed hopes that June would be recovered withered and disappeared. June's voice was tremulous with pain, though she made a valiant effort to cover it. Rosanna rounded the corner, and found June propped up a little higher on the sofa so she could sip coffee. Attila ran around the kitchen once, then to the door.

"Hey," June said. "Slave-boy! The dog wants out!"

Bear shook his head and smiled, then opened the door for Attila, who disappeared into the snow in great leaping bounds.

"Does that dog ever do anything at less than a full run?" Rosanna asked. Bear grinned slyly.

"Only a couple," he said, and June laughed. It was strained, and shaded with pain, but it was still a laugh.

"You can fix your coffee how you like it," Bear said. "There's an open tin of milk in the fridge if you don't mind that."

Rosanna didn't mind it a bit. After their days in the wood, it was lovely just to have coffee the way she wanted it. She sat down at the kitchen table with a happy sigh. Something about coffee meant comfort to her, meant home. Bear looked at her coat curiously.

"You not planning on staying for supper?" he asked. She smiled, though it hurt her face.

"My plans don't seem to mean much lately," she said. "I'm getting in the habit of being ready for that."

He smiled back, gently and sadly.

"Some times are just like that," he said. He looked over at June. "I assume that's why we haven't taken her to a hospital yet?"

Rosanna sighed.

"You probably could," she said. "You probably should, if she'll go."

June glared at her from the sofa.

"And who'll take care of you, city-girl? You don't know shit about the woods except that there's monsters in it. Ain't much to go by."

"Monsters…" Bear said. "monsters like me, I guess." He looked at June's splinted leg then glanced away, but Rosanna saw tears in his eyes. He was a huge man, with shaggy dark hair and a scruffy beard to match. But he had more than just a soft spot for June, that was clear.

"That wasn't your fault," Rosanna said.

"I did it, didn't I? That makes it my fault."

"Do you remember it?"

"No, I don't even remember getting here. Attila must have got me home, I guess."

"What *do* you remember, then?" Rosanna asked.

"Well," he said slowly, as if it were a long way down to those memories. "I remember being sick of the house. I remember packing up for a couple days. I thought I'd snow-shoe up to the waterfall, maybe do some ice-climbing if it was good."

"Without me? Bastard." June said with a grin, but Bear's face still held a shadow of terrible grief.

"I thought you were dead, June. We all thought…" He shook his head, and peered silently into his coffee for a moment.

"I'm sorry honey," June said softly. "We had to run, and we had no way to get hold of anyone." Bear lifted his head to meet her eyes.

"But you were just going to leave, weren't you? Go do whatever it is that's more important than a broken leg and not tell anyone?"

June sighed and dropped his gaze.

"Yeah," she said. "I didn't want you…didn't want anyone else in the trouble we're in."

"Seems I found it anyway," he said, and took a gulp of his coffee. "I don't know how, though. I just remember there was this strange sound, and Attila just going nuts to get away from it. Sometimes that dog's smarter than me, I guess. After that it's kind of a fog, except…"

"Except what?"

"There was a voice in my head with the noise. It kept telling and telling me to go home. But that noise…that sound…it was everywhere in me. it was like carrying an avalanche in my head. I was frozen and buried and lost."

"He seems to like doin' that to people," June muttered.

"Who? Why won't you tell me who?" Bear said, but June shook her head.

"I tried to explain it to him," she told Rosanna, "but I don't think he more than half buys it." She turned to Bear. "And I won't tell you who because I **know** you, and you'd be out to chase him down in less time than it takes to say his name. So quit askin'. I ain't gonna lose you to him, and you don't know enough to survive him."

Attila scratched at the door, and Bear let him in. The dog bounded into the living room to lick June's face again, then lay down on the floor beside her.

"What did the restaurant look like when you saw it? June's place, I mean?" Rosanna asked.

"It looked…"Bear took a deep breath. "it looked pulverized. It looked like there'd been a gas explosion with ice instead of fire." His hands started to shake and he put his coffee down on the table. "We looked for…for survivors, but it was all just….there weren't any pieces bigger than my hand."

"Our enemy did that," Rosanna said. "To get to me." She pointed to June. "Our enemy made you do that to June. To get to me. Worse, he wanted that avalanche in her head, too, or mine, or anyone's." She shrugged. "What's not to believe?" She pushed Granny's web out a couple inches from her skin, just enough that it was clearly visible. Bear nodded once.

"So you don't think I can handle him?" he asked.

"You've proven he can handle you," Rosanna replied. "And no offense meant, but he can. Easily."

"I might surprise him." Bear said, a low rumble entering his voice. Attila's ears flattened against his skull, and he pressed himself close to the couch.

"You might," Rosanna said, before June could respond. "Or you might die. Don't you think June's lost enough this winter?"

It was a low blow, and Rosanna would have been ashamed of it, except that she herself thought June had lost far too much this winter. Dealing with Trapper was Rosanna's duty, however it happened.

"Look, if I fail, I'll need backup. June at least knows the hazards."

"Rosanna you can't go alone," June said, and swallowed hard. "Bear could go with you."

"No," Rosanna replied, "he can't. You need a doctor, and I need to know that you're safe."

"But you don't know how to take care of yourself out here! You'll just die and…and…"She curled her hands into fists and turned her head to the wall. Bear moved the dog out of the way and knelt beside the sofa.

"June," he said, his voice a low murmur, like the sound of a heartbeat. "June."

She turned to him, her face streaked with tears and furious.

"You did this!" she shouted. "I was supposed to be there! You did this to us!"

"I know I did," he murmured, "I know. I'm sorry." She pounded on his shoulders, weeping and shouting until he got his arms around her, and then she just collapsed against him and cried.

Rosanna didn't know what to do. What had happened wasn't Bear's fault, and June knew that. Bear might not be totally sure, but the women knew what magic could do. Attila crossed the room and laid his heavy head on her lap. She scratched behind his ears, and his tail thumped against the floor. That was simple, at least, she thought wryly. She heard the murmur of Attila's being with gratitude for its simplicity and beauty. Here was a dog that lived to love. She drank some more coffee and petted the dog, taking comfort from each.

Slowly, June's storm subsided, and Bear pulled away. He kissed her gently, and June clung to him.

"It's not your fault," Rosanna said, "not either of your fault."

"I shoulda listened," June said. "You told me to wait."

"And I'm the one that…that hit her," Bear said.

"And my father is the one that set you up," Rosanna replied. She sighed. "All the blame goes to him."

"Your father?" Bear asked.

"Yeah. We only met a few days ago."

"Bummer, eh?" June said, in a perfect caricature of a Canadian drawl.

"Dude," agreed Rosanna, and laughed. Bear shook his head.

"You're both crazy, you know that, right?"

"You'd know, mister twenty-foot-fence," June replied, but he just shrugged.

"Didn't say I wasn't, just want to be sure you know that *you* are too."

"I can go with you," Bear said. "I can help. I can't cook like June, but I know a lot about the woods."

Rosanna shook her head.

"June needs to get to a hospital, and sooner is probably better."

"We could get someone else to help, then."

"And if he's set other traps? If your friends or June's friends are just like you were? Or worse? How many of those do we handle?"

The other two were silent.

"Oh come on, it's obvious, isn't it? Bear, you were sent home to wait, just on the off-chance that we might come to you. If he can do it to you, he could pick anyone."

"But then...you've got to help them," June said, horror blooming in her voice. "We can't leave them like that."

"I can best help them by stopping him," Rosanna said.

"Winter can kill you just as dead as him," Bear said. "You need a guide."

"No," Rosanna said, "I just need a trap. I just need a place to bring him. Then I need enough gear to wait for him to arrive. That's all."

"That's all? That's ALL?" June's voice rose in pitch and volume. "Are you fucking crazy?"

"Yes," Rosanna said calmly. "Probably. But the thing he wants from me...I know where it is and how to get to it. All I have to do is get there, and make sure he knows I've arrived."

"Was this...was this your *plan*?" June asked incredulously. "To...what, to sit still and just wait for him to pick you off?"

"I just need to be there a little while before him." Rosanna said, smiling. She felt a little of June's feral nature reflected in that smile, and she liked it. "Long enough to set a few surprises."

Some of the fury left June's face, and she lay back on the sofa, looking closely at Rosanna's face.

"Well now," she said slowly, "Surprises...that's another thing altogether."

"And Bear," she said, "no offense, but what you don't know about what I can do could kill us more surely than even winter could."

Bear nodded slowly.

"I guess I've seen enough to give that thought some credit. No offense taken, either."

"I'm sorry, June," Rosanna said. "I know...I know you wanted to be there. You've saved my life over and over, right since the beginning."

"You're not all that sorry," June said, and held up a hand to stop Rosanna's protests. "Oh, you're sorry I'm hurt and all that, you just ain't sorry to be doin' it on your own." She shrugged. "Maybe that's good, I dunno. You sure did look fierce when you talked about them surprises."

"If I fail…"Rosanna said, then stopped. "I don't know what you should do," she said at last. "He'll probably still be out there, but if I'm…gone, then he won't have access to as much power. I hope."

"We'll build that fence when we need it," Bear said, and June smiled at him.

"Idiot," she said, and kissed him.

"Where will you go?" June asked.

"Up past Granny's house," Rosanna said. "Well, where Granny's house used to be."

"Granny Rosie?" Bear said, and his blue eyes darkened. "Is she…"

"We lost her under June's place," Rosanna said quietly, and stroked the golden threads under and on her skin. "She saved us."

"So did you," June said. "Don't forget."

"And you saved me," Bear said. "I won't forget that, either. Whatever you need, you can have. I'm sorry about Granny, though. She was…remarkable."

Rosanna nodded, feeling the ache and emptiness where Granny Rosie belonged. Would she ever have enough time to grieve, she wondered? Was there enough time, ever?

"Remarkable, yes."

Attila nudged her hand until she started petting him again, and she smiled into his adoring brown eyes.

"I think you have a friend," Bear chuckled. "Come on, boy. Supper?"

Attila's ears perked up and he gave Rosanna's fingers one last slobbery kiss before running across the kitchen and skidding to a halt just in front of the door. He turned and pranced in a canine ballet as Bear got food and dish from the hall closet. There was a blast of cold air as they both stepped outside.

June rearranged herself under her blanket, then hissed with pain.

"Hang on," Rosanna said, "let me help."

"I don't want help," June said. "I want to be better." She scowled fiercely as Rosanna covered her up.

"You're a crappy patient," Rosanna said. "I pity the doctors already." June grabbed Rosanna's hand as she stood.

"Rosanna…"she said, "you ain't just leavin' me here on purpose are ya? Couldn't you just…fix it?"

Rosanna sighed, and met June's eyes.

"I think it's possible I could fix it," she said. "but I think it's just as possible I could fix it wrong. I won't take the chance."

"I will."

"Well, I won't."

"It's my leg," June replied. "My chance."

"It's a stupid risk. And I can't afford to lose anyone else, I couldn't…" Rosanna stopped and took a shuddering breath. "I'm not happy to do this alone," she said at last. "But I'm happier with that than with crippling or killing you."

"Killing? Ain't that a little over the top?"

"I don't know. So I won't risk it." She pushed June's brown hair back from her forehead. "We were supposed to be sisters, I think." she said. "I just won't risk you."

June nodded slowly.

"Sisters, then," she said. "You come back to me or I will kick your ass, sister mine. Got it?"

"At least we know I can find you," Rosanna said, and patted her knife. "I'll come back."

June nodded once, and wiped at her eyes.

"How's the leg doing?" Rosanna asked.

"Hurts like hell," June said. "Soon as I'm better I'm gonna kick that boy in the shin so hard he'll limp for a week."

"Just his shin?"

"Yeah," June said with a grin. "I think I'll have a use for the rest of him."

Rosanna was still chuckling when Bear came back in.

"Getting cold," he said. "And what's so funny?"

"You, as usual," said June.

"Ah. I don't want to know, right?"

Rosanna grinned at him.

"Not right now." He sighed.

"Women. Anyway, like I said, it's getting cold."

Rosanna looked out the window. It was getting dark too. She sighed. She hated the short hours of daylight this time of year. If she'd been home, this would have been a good time to curl up with a book and a drink.

"The problem is," she said, "that I don't know if he knows what I did here."

"That's a problem, yes," said Bear.

"Be right back," Rosanna said, and stepped out onto the porch. She wrapped her coat around her, and *listened*, testing the night sounds for any sign of Trapper or his magic. All she heard were the quiet sounds of an ordinary twilight, and the rasp and hush of her own breath. Attila bounded around the corner of the house and jumped up to lick her face. His breath smelled like dog-food and she pushed him down. Unrepentant, he jumped up once more, then ran off into the snow.

Back inside, Bear was busy preparing a meal of some kind, and June dozed on the couch.

"There's no sign," she said, "but..."

"But that could just mean he's really good," Bear said. "Right?"

"Right."

"Tell me who it is, Rosanna. I promise not to run out. You make sense, and June needs me."

"Thompson Trapper," she said.

"Shit," Bear said. "He's good. He's really, really good."

"Tell me about it," Rosanna said.

"No, I mean in the woods. He's…" he paused to stir a pot. "June's skilled, right? I'd take June over most paid guides. But Trapper…he's a genius."

"Are you trying to convince me to take you?" Rosanna asked. "Because you're doing pretty good."

Bear laughed, if bitterly.

"No, I'm just…I'm convincing myself that I'm no good to you. I couldn't beat him on those terms."

"So scaring me is just a side-effect?"

"Pretty much."

"Thanks."

"Hey, no problem. Glad to help. Scared is more likely to stay alive."

He turned and looked at her.

"So how good are you at that other stuff?"

"I don't know."

"You're still alive, that has to mean something."

"I guess. Good enough, maybe?"

"Good enough," he said, and smiled. "Good enough gets the job done. Any more is showing off."

She chuckled.

"Do you need to leave tonight?" he asked.

"I should," she said. "If he caught you he'll know where you live."

"Most folks do." He bared his teeth. "Most of them have the good sense not to come up here."

"Attila is pretty darn scary," Rosanna agreed, and smiled at the puddle of brown dog curled up beside June.

"I need to get June to Nelson, probably," he said. "There's no real hospital any closer."

Rosanna nodded. June looked paler, and that was worrisome. If she were bleeding inside, Rosanna didn't really know how to tell.

"Tonight would be best," she said.

"Do you know where you want to stay?"

Rosanna thought of another night in the tent and sighed with regret.

"Oh, I *want* to stay right here on your nice warm bed. But I *need* to stay somewhere closer to Granny's, someplace uninhabited, for preference." she sighed again. "I can camp, if that makes the most sense."

"I can do you a little better than that," Bear said with a laugh. "I have a little camper you can borrow. It's not big, but it has a bed and heat. You can drive to wherever you want, spend the night, and be ready for…whatever."

Rosanna had never even considered the possibility of a camper, but it was perfect.

"Are you sure?" she asked. "I'm not sure when…or if you'd get it back. Trapper has a bad habit of blowing things up because I'm in them."

"Well then, don't be in it when he finds you," Bear said, and glanced over at June.

"You gave her back to me," he said quietly. "I owe you everything."

"But she wouldn't be in it except for me," Rosanna protested.

"Your debts to her don't matter. I owe you everything." He shrugged. "Besides," he said, "It's a little beat up. A few more dings won't even show."

"Supper's ready," he said, and went to wake June. He kissed her brow, but she didn't respond.

"June?" he said, and her eyes fluttered open.

"Hurts, Bear," she mumbled and her eyes closed again. Rosanna scrambled over, and lifted up the blanket to look at June's leg. Her entire lower leg was covered with a terrible bruise, and the swelling pressed against their makeshift splint.

"Oh my god," she breathed. She could hear the whispers of her stones, but they weren't quite keeping up with the injury. She looked down at the bottle beside the couch. It was aspirin.

"Oh my god Bear, you have to get her to the hospital **now**!" She picked up the bottle and showed it to him.

"Aspirin! You gave her aspirin! If she's bleeding inside…"

Bear paled.

"I didn't even think," he said. "I didn't…"

"Never mind guilt," Rosanna said. "We don't have time for guilt. Action. Now."

She checked June's pulse and it still felt strong to her, but she didn't remember enough about shock to know how long that would last.

"We have to keep her warm," Rosanna said.

"If she's bleeding inside she could die," Bear said. "I might have killed her."

"Just quit babbling! We have to get her to the hospital!"

"I can't drive her like this, what if we make it worse?"

"Well then, what?" Rosanna shouted. June's eyes fluttered open again.

"I'm thirsty," she said plaintively. "Can I have a drink?" Her eyes drifted closed before they could respond.

"An ambulance," Rosanna said, "Can't you get an ambulance?" Bear shook his head.

"No hospital, remember?"

"Well what do you do when something bad happens? There has to be something?"

"Stop shouting at me!" Bear roared. "I can't think with you shouting at me!"

Rosanna gulped down a deep breath. She hadn't realized she was shouting, but the echoes of her voice bounced around the room for a second after she stopped.

"Can't you fix her?" Bear asked.

"I don't dare," Rosanna said. "I could kill her trying."

He nodded.

"Ambulance. Air ambulance."

"Call," she said.

The phone was in one of the bedrooms, but Rosanna heard Bear shouting his distress through the walls. She smoothed back June's hair, and murmured Words of earth and healing. She couldn't do anything specifically about the wound, but it felt right to strengthen June's body and being as best she could.

June's eyes opened again, and she smiled a little.

"You're a good nurse," she said. "But it hurts."

"I know," Rosanna said. "Bear's calling for an ambulance."

"Ah, hell," June said. "That means helicopter. I hate flying."

"Tough beans," Rosanna replied. "Bear will be there, anyway."

"Gettting rid of both of us at once, hey? Nice job, girl."

"I don't think I should be here when the ambulance is," Rosanna said. "I can't afford not to deal with Trapper now."

June nodded.

"Better get goin' then," she said. "People tend to run when Bear hollers."

Rosanna nodded. She kissed June's forehead, and June reached up an arm to hug her. Her eyelids fluttered and she passed out again.

Bear thundered out of the bedroom.

"Half hour," he said flatly, and looked at June. "She'll...she'll be okay for a half hour?"

"Keep her warm and keep her still," Rosanna said. She took her cooling stone off the broken leg. "Did they tell you whether to ice it?"

"Yeah, I'll pack it with snow." He thumped his forehead with the heel of his hand. "Aspirin! Stupid idiot!"

"I shouldn't be here when they arrive, Bear," Rosanna said, as gently as she could. She smelled something burning and turned off the stove. Canned ravioli bubbled in the pot, and the smell of it scorched was revolting.

Bear met her eyes from across the room.

"What if she gets worse," he said. "I can't save her."

"I've done everything I dare," Rosanna said. "Those stones she's holding, they'll help as long as she's in contact with them."

"You could stay," he said. "You could take some time and get away from this for a few days."

"And give him more time to do this? No thanks. And it wouldn't be a few days. There's going to be questions about how this happened." She swallowed. "Police questions. And about June's restaurant. And maybe Granny's house. I can't afford to be locked up when Trapper finds me."

"You can't just leave us!" he said. June's eyes opened.

"Shut up," she said, quite clearly. "Help her." She licked her lips. "I'm so thirsty!"

"Sorry, they said nothing by mouth," Bear said miserably.

"Gimme a kiss then, and go help her."

Bear kissed her tenderly, then stumbled away, eyes full of tears. He went first to a long line of keys hanging on the wall, and picked off a two sets.

"Come on," he said roughly, and led her outside.

Attila, sensing the mood, slunk quietly at Rosanna's heels as they left the house. Bear cleared a path through the snow just with his own bulk, around the house and to a garage. He unlocked the door, and it slid up to reveal a rusted-out red truck with a white camper settled into the box. Rosanna worried that she might need her charger, but it turned out that Bear had one of his own, already plugged in.

"I like things to be usable," was all he said. He handed her the second set of keys. "Turn 'er over, make sure it's running okay."

The truck started on the first try, sounding smoother than its advanced age suggested it should.

"Drive it up to the house," he said, "I'll go check June."

The truck handled well in the snow, though it creaked and bounced just as much as June's blue monster had. Rosanna pulled it up near the porch and parked it there. She climbed down, taking the keys with her. She transferred all the camping gear from the blue truck to the red, not bothering to open the camper, just piling it all onto the seat. The camper would do for a night or perhaps two, but Rosanna's trap needed more open ground.

Bear met her at the door.

"She okay?" Rosanna asked.

"Same, says she's thirsty," Bear said. "All I got for food is mostly frozen or canned." He shrugged. "I never know when I'll be home." He handed her a cardboard box. "Should be enough for a few days, I didn't know what you'd need."

"That should be fine, I mostly need propane now." Bear nodded. "Camper stove and heater run on propane, got a little tank on the back. Should do you fine."

"Bear..."she said, but he shook his head. "You don't have time. If you can't fix her, you don't have time to be here talking to me."

Attila edged between them, looking up with worried brown eyes.

"Bear please, I don't have any choice!"

"Don't talk to me about choices," he said. "I know all about choices."

"I can't save her from this, don't you see? But I might be able to save her from him. That's what's in me to do."

The stiffness of his shoulders dropped a little, and he nodded.

"Go do it, then," he said, more gently. "Do it well, and do it till it's done."

"I will," she said. "I promise."

"Take this idiot with you," he said, giving Attila a rough pat. The dog food and dish were still out on the porch, and before she could protest, he opened the camper door and threw them in. Attila barked once, joyfully. Clearly this had a meaning that he recognized.

"No time to argue," Bear said, "and I don't expect I'll be here to take care of him."

It was true, so she opened the driver's door. Attila leaped up onto the seat and sat behind the wheel until Rosanna shoved him over. It was crowded with all the gear, but she found herself glad for the crowding. Bear was back in the house by the time she restarted the engine. She thought...she hoped...she heard the sound of a helicopter as she made her careful way down to the main highway, but all she saw was the black road ahead.

# Chapter 24

The weight of the truck and camper were unfamiliar, and skidded and bounced strangely when she least expected it. Grateful though she was that the road was plowed, it was still slippery in places, and full dark had narrowed her world to the span of her headlights. Rosanna wanted to creep down the slope and around the curves. She could easily imagine herself as a rusted-out snail on a snowy track. But she didn't know what the response would be to Bear's call. This area might not have its own ambulance, but Mounties were everywhere. Would they respond? Once the questions started she didn't imagine they'd end, except perhaps with a padded room and a little medication. She skidded on a turn and clutched tightly to the wheel. Some nice medication didn't sound too bad, actually. Attila woofed happily, and scrambled over the camping gear to look out the window.

"I'm glad you like it," she said, and continued their descent.

Her hands hurt by the time she reached the highway, and she was only too happy to turn onto proper asphalt. It was still going to be slippery, she knew, but at least its curves were designed for logging trucks. One idiot with a camper shouldn't be overtaxed by them. Without thinking, she had turned left, headed to June's and to Granny's. In the rush from

Bear's place, she hadn't had time to truly consider her destination. How close to Trapper did she want to be?

There were occasional rest-stops and scenic views along the side of the road, and she pulled out at the first one she found. It had only been plowed in a half-hearted sort of way, but the truck handled the lines of snow like a ship breasting waves. Rosanna pulled to a stop and dropped down out of the cab of the truck. Attila jumped down after her, and disappeared among the snow drifts.

Rosanna was weary, and worried about June. It was strange to be so alone, out in the dark of winter again. She *listened* to the wind, and thought she might hear just a whisper of something further up the valley, but there was no poison on the air. What she heard might just as well be her mother's broken Library as anything else. She unsheathed her knife and asked it where the Library was, and it swung her without hesitation. She smiled again at the compass that made her the needle, and the knife bumped in her hand. Strange, what a person can get used to, she thought.

"Am I used to this?" she wondered out loud. Attila bounded through the waves of snow, sleek as a porpoise. He jumped up, and put his paws on her shoulders, the better to give her face a good lick.

"Get down!" Rosanna spluttered. "Bad dog, down!"

At the terrible words, Attila dropped to the ground at her feet. His tail pressed to the ground and he whined mournfully. Rosanna sighed. She didn't really know the right thing to say to anyone, it seemed.

"Never mind, boy. Want some supper?"

That turned out to be the perfect thing to say, and Attila was up and dancing as she opened the camper. Bear had put her box of supplies inside the door, and his idea of a 'few days' was generous. There was frozen sausage along with assorted tins of meat and fruit and vegetables. There was even a bag of pancake mix. She tried to take the box to the cab of the truck, but it was too heavy for her, so she moved part of its contents, then shoved the rest further into the camper. She felt ridiculously short, trying to climb up, then found the steps that folded out. That was an improvement, but she had to push Attila out of the way three times before he'd let her make the climb.

The interior was cold and cave-like, but she found a light switch near the door. She flicked it, not knowing whether to expect anything, and a small but enthusiastic light warmed up over her head. Attila whined at her heels, so she scooped a bowl full of his food out, pushed him out of the way, and set it on the ground outside. She hoped the light wasn't pulling off the truck batteries, but at least she had some recourse if it were. She put a hand in her pocket and felt the quiet tingle of stored electricity.

Lit, the space was small and efficient, but no longer cave-like. She folded out the small kitchen table and set her supplies on it. She might as well unpack them as trip over them, she decided, and stowed the cans and packages away. There wasn't a lot of cupboard space, and it took her a moment to figure out the latches that would hold them closed during travel. It was comforting to have a full larder, however small the larder was, and it was practically decadent not to be crouched in the tent or beside a campfire.

Attila scratched at the door and barked, but she decided it might be easier to manage without him for a little longer. Bear had said something about a heater, and she found it. Luckily it was not only easy to start, but had pictures explaining its operation. The air was soon warming nicely. The sleeping space was a nook above the truck cab, and while the mattress was soft enough, it had no bedding. She went out into the cold to get a sleeping bag from the front. She glanced at the supplies she'd tossed onto the front seat, but she figured everything there would survive the cold just fine. She smiled wryly. Built-in freezer, yup. Attila wove circles around her ankles as if he were no bigger than a cat, and nearly pitched her into the snow more than once.

"Would you just calm down?" she asked, but he wouldn't, and she didn't mind overly. She thought she could cope with lonely, but alone might have been too much. The sky above was velvet-black, with glittering diamond stars. They looked cold too, glinting above the valley. She wondered what Words might make up a star, and shivered at the thought of knowing. There was so much she could learn, and yet...she never wanted to be that cold, or that distant. All she wanted was her own place, and a chance to explore it. It seemed ridiculous, after everything she'd come through, not to have greater aspirations. She had an idea now of what she could do, but she still didn't really know what she was *for.*

She shook her head at herself. There'd be time for that after, or not. But until she got to 'after' there just wasn't. She thought of Granny's 'lots of time till there's none' and sighed.

The camper was warmer when she climbed back in, and she looked up at the light with a growl.

"I'm an idiot," she said. Attila had come in behind her, and was happily taking up nearly the entire floor. She dug her stones out of her various pockets, thinking sadly of the pet rocks. She hoped they'd help June. She hoped she wouldn't need them too badly herself. She unrolled her sleeping bag and popped a couple warming rocks into the bottom of it. Then she set the light stone on a counter and whispered 'please'.

It glowed with a warmer, kinder light than the little fluorescent bulb, and she was happy enough to stop using electricity. Attila grunted in protest when she nudged him aside to get to the switch, but otherwise seemed disinterested in Rosanna's miracles.

Rosanna still didn't know what time it was, but she was becoming accustomed to that. It was dark, and she was hungry, so she ate. There was a little stove in the camper, but she found she didn't care for any more fiddling. Besides, she didn't mind beans straight out of the can, although Granny had always been appalled by it. For dessert, there was canned pineapple. She considered canned peaches as well, but decided to save them. There might be a day after tomorrow, who knew?

She turned off the furnace before she went to bed. She still didn't know where it was drawing from, and she wouldn't need it while she was sleeping. The warming stones should keep that little cubby just fine, even if she turned out the light.

Attila snuffled in his sleep, and kicked out with his hind legs a couple times.

"Bed-time, boy?" she said softly, and he opened his eyes. He stood and stretched, yawning hugely. She patted his sleek brown head, and he licked her fingers a couple times, then casually climbed up into the sleeping nook and lay on her sleeping bag. He turned and gave her a doggy grin, and she shook her head and laughed.

"Move over, you," she said, and shoved him to the side so that she could get the stones out of the bag. There turned out to be some bedding up top after all, once she'd crawled up there, and she laid a blanket over Attila. He was already slipping back into doggy dreams, and the rabbits were everywhere. She chuckled at him again.

"Get 'em, boy," she whispered, and he whuffled and kicked out. There was a curtain she could pull between the sleeping space and the main area, so she did, and left the light stone active. It would be nice not to wake up cold, after all. She missed June. She even missed Bear, though she'd barely gotten to know him. She missed Granny, too, but she missed normality most of all. She had a feeling that normality was gone for good, and it had left fewer traces of itself than any of the people she missed. She left her coat and boots in easy reach.

She woke because she couldn't breathe. Something heavy was compressing her ribs and stomach, and she gasped and kicked out. Her foot struck the side of the camper, and Attila made a sleepy noise but didn't move. Just that sound was enough to anchor her to here and now, and she realized that it was Attila's head that was squashing her. Not only that, but he'd maneuvered her to the edge of the bed so that she didn't even have room to roll to get him off her. She groaned and pushed at him, and he grunted in protest.

"Why do men always hog the bed?" she asked, and Attila lifted his head to lick her face.

"Ew," she said. "No good morning kisses till you brush your teeth, my friend." She pushed aside the curtain, and the unfaltering light of her stone streamed in on her. It wasn't exactly warm in the main room of the camper, but it wasn't uncomfortably cold, either. It was still dark out, but that didn't mean much. She felt rested, so she hoped that meant it was morning.

There was no coffee or tea in Rosanna's supplies, but Bear had included a couple bottles of water. She was grateful not to be melting snow, but something hot might have been nice. Attila didn't stir until she opened the door, then he poured down from the nook like a waterfall of dog. He wagged sleepily and yawned enormously. She waited for him, and he wandered off among the snowdrifts to take care of his morning business. She did the same, then got the sausages out of the cab.

She left Attila outside while she figured out the stove. He scratched and whined until she put out a bowl of food for him. She found a plastic bowl and set out some water for him as well. The stove was pretty straight-forward, and soon the smell of cooking meat filled the camper. The instructions for pancakes were simple, too, but she didn't much feel like adding to the dirty dishes. Instead she had more beans from the can. She opened up the peaches and had them for dessert. It wasn't a June-class meal, perhaps but she was pleased and fed. She finally let Attila in when she was done, and he went straight to the empty frying pan. He looked at her accusingly, and she laughed.

"It's all right," she said. "I saved you one" He took the sausage from her fingers, and swallowed it nearly at a gulp. The frying pan would survive with just a wiping, she thought, especially if she needed to use it again. There was a good bit of frozen sausage still, and she wasn't tired of it yet. Toast would have been nice, maybe, but at least nothing had come out of little packets. Rosanna rolled up her sleeping bag and put her light-stone in her pocket. She squared everything else away for travel, and stepped back out into the chill. The sun still hadn't made an appearance, but the sky seemed paler behind the mountains. Time to go, whatever the hour really was.

Attila sniffed the cold air happily, and hit the ground without even touching the stairs. He leapt up just as happily when Rosanna opened the truck door for him, and she had to push him aside again to get in herself.

"You don't drive, you know that right?" she said, but Attila only grinned, and took the opportunity to lick her face as she climbed up on the seat. The truck grumbled when she asked it to start, and she wished she'd thought to put a warming stone on it. It didn't matter, though, because the truck only grumbled the once, then started up with a confident purr. Attila barked once, joyously, as Rosanna put the truck into gear. She wished she felt the same way. She felt deeply tempted just to drive on past, to let it all go for another day. Maybe for a warmer day, or a city day, or no other day at all. Attila had his nose pressed to the window, watching the trees flash by. Ahead, the sky brightened, and the clouds started to thin and drift, like paper boats upon a great cold river. The weight of the truck was comfortable on this larger road, she found. She felt more secure on the packed snow, and had good traction up hills and around curves. She'd always liked to drive, but never really understood the appeal of trucks in general. Maybe there was a point, after all. She swept up a hill and found herself next to the ruin of June's place. She gulped, and slowed, but only a little.

Bear had not exaggerated. The building looked like it had been demolished with explosives. She didn't pause to have a better look. The mundane sounds of the truck drowned out any sense she might have gotten of the magical whisperings of the place. It was enough to recall that this was Granny's grave. Any desire to flee left with that remembrance. Attila turned from his window and whined once, low in his throat. Rosanna reached out a hand to pat the solid bulk of his shoulder.

"I'll be okay, boy," she said, hoping it was true. "Don't worry, I'll be okay." He licked her hand once, just a solemn declaration of solidarity, and she laughed through the tears that threatened.

"What did I ever do to deserve such fine friends?" she asked, and put her hand back on the wheel to handle the next curve. The sun was truly up now, and parts of the road were becoming slipperier where daylight struck. She saw little traffic, though one big logging truck overtook her in a swirl of snow and recklessness that stole her breath away. Her world narrowed down to this moment on this road, and she was glad of that focus. There was no knowing what waited for her at Granny Rosie's house, and that alone was going to be difficult to bear. Right now, she drove in sunlight under an irrepressible blue sky, and that was good.

She thought she recognized the turns of the road now, and slowed a little. Granny's driveway was marked only by her mailbox, but Rosanna recognized that from a distance. She sighed, and drove up to the turning. It didn't look like anyone had been up the driveway; certainly it hadn't been plowed, and there were no fresh tire-tracks in the snow. Rosanna hoped the truck was up to the climb. June's blue monstrosity could probably have handled it without a second thought, but Rosanna wasn't sure how the extra weight would affect the truck. She crept forward and the truck bounced noisily over the drift at the side of the road. She looked up, surprised that the driveway was not near so steep as she remembered it. Compared to Bear's, this was just a bump in the road. The truck made it up easily, and she pulled to a stop at the edge of a snow-covered heap.

She took a deep breath, then another, before she opened the door. It was warmer out that it had been in days, and there was a dampness in the air that made her hands ache. Still, it was nice not to feel that her lungs were being frozen a gasp at a time. Attila jumped out behind her, but took a sniff of the air and pressed close to her legs. Rosanna bent to pat him.

"I know, boy," she said. "It's not a good place." She stood to look around. "It was, once."

A fair bit of snow had fallen here, but not as much as farther up the valley. Rosanna could clearly make out Granny's porch, and the general shape of the little house under the drifts. Trapper hadn't been quite so thorough in pulverizing this building. Maybe this was his first try, and he'd perfected the art at June's. Rosanna stood frozen by the destruction, all the same. This had been hers, once. This was a place of memory and safety, and he had broken it. She *listened*, but heard no clear sign of Trapper. That didn't necessarily mean much, but she thought she'd know the sound of him if he was within shouting distance. There was a very faint murmur though, like a slowing heartbeat, from the middle of the rubble. Rosanna reluctantly stepped out onto the drifts. It felt sacrilegious, like stepping on a grave. Boards creaked and shifted underfoot, and Attila wouldn't follow her. She didn't blame him. It was probably stupid, and it was definitely dangerous, but she couldn't help herself. Part of the chimney still stood up among the other detritus, and it was from there that the sound originated. She made her careful way over to it, and laid a hand against the stone to steady herself. The sound was a little clearer, but it was still barely more than a whisper. Rosanna repeated the Word she heard, and the little fire pixie floated up from the ashes in the fireplace. It shivered, and its glow was dimmed, but it still possessed a perfection and purity that Rosanna could never have imagined. It hovered in close, and she got a sense of its gladness to see her.

"I'm sorry," she said, "I had to run." It was starving, she thought. Granny had said something about giving it the fuel it needed. She looked around. The house was made almost entirely of wood, but the little sprite had not touched it.

"You could have the house," she said, but it shook its head, and Rosanna could feel its sorrow as deeply as her own. This had been home to more than she and Granny, after all.

"Let me get you something," she said, and the pixie drifted down to the ashes again. It lay there like the smallest of embers, as if Granny's fire had only just gone out.

Rosanna stumbled  and skidded off the ruins as quickly as she could, and found Granny's woodpile largely intact. She picked up an armful, and made her way back with greater care. She stacked it carefully around the pixie, then went back for another armful. When she returned, a thin thread of smoke lifted up from among the ashes, and she was heartened to hear the growing strength of the creature's being. She laid the other logs around the tiny fire, enjoying the warmth.

This was where all magic had begun for her, she realized. All the magic in her world had started exactly where she stood. Suddenly, too, she understood Granny's sense of stewardship. This little being was too perfect and lovely to be allowed to perish. There were too many flaws and too much ugliness in Rosanna's life for her to permit it. It wasn't about what the pixie had done or might do. It was only that she couldn't bear the thought of its absence.

"I'll try to come back," Rosanna said, and a waft of cinnamon scent swirled up around her like hope. "I have to stop this, though."

She moved several more armloads of wood, but she knew she couldn't stay. Her life and the pixie's were both tied now to her success. She looked up at the smoke and sighed. She couldn't count on surprise anymore. It didn't matter, really. A large part of her plan had evaporated when Bear broke June's leg. The tools she had would have to suffice.

"Be well," she whispered, and felt a pulse of warmth in response. The snow around the chimney was already melting, and Rosanna could make out the shapes of familiar furnishings, like ghosts among the ruins. She would be back if she could, to see if anything could be salvaged. For now there was both comfort and sorrow in standing among her memories of Granny Rosie.

She shook her head at last, and walked back to the truck. Attila met her with subdued happiness. This place made him very unhappy, but he made no move to desert her. She looked at the pile of camping gear and sighed. How was she supposed to move all that? She didn't know how long it would take for Trapper to find her. Probably not long, if she didn't hide. She didn't want to be out in the cold and unprepared, but it was just as likely that he was on his way here.

She found a canvas duffel bag under the truck seat, and decided to carry only what would fit in that. In the end, that meant the tent and both sleeping bags, and enough food for no more than two very frugal days for both her and Attila. She set down a bowl for him before they left, and he ate enthusiastically. Rosanna was getting the idea that Attila could always eat, whether or not he was hungry. She hoped the cold wouldn't be too hard on him, but he didn't show any signs of suffering from it. She took a good drink of water, then hitched the bag up onto her shoulder. She sighed again. That was going to be very uncomfortable in a very short time. It was a good thing, she thought, that she'd had a chance to get used to uncomfortable. It was all a matter of perspective. Compared to having a building dropped on her, this would be quite pleasant.

She laughed out loud, and Attila perked up at the sound.

"Go for a walk, boy?" she said, and he wagged. Rosanna laughed, thinking that not all magic words were Words of power.

The snow was not as deep as she expected. Perhaps the only true malice of the storm had been vented on her and June. It helped that she was stronger, and well-rested. She remembered Granny's relentless march up the mountain and grinned. Granny would have been proud, she thought, and stopped to readjust the bag on her shoulder. Would Trapper? She shook her head. That line of thought was not useful. Trapper had to be stopped, no matter who or what he was. She tried not to think of what that might mean. Clearly there wasn't going to be a reasonable conversation ending in tea and treaties.

Attila roved around her, freely but not too far. Rosanna was surprised when they reached the eaves of the pine wood; she'd remembered it as much further away. There was hardly any snow under the trees at all, though there were a few clear places where drifts had formed. The wind ruffled through the needled boughs with delicate fingers, barely making more than a whisper of sound. Rosanna stood still for a moment, *listening.* Beyond the endless murmurs of the trees themselves, she heard a faint but clear burr of Unbeing. It ground against her nerves and lifted the hairs on the back of her neck. He wasn't far, then. She would have to choose her ground.

That was simple enough, really. There was only one place of safety that she knew of, though she'd hoped to choose a place of power, instead. Without access to the rest of her mother's Library, she didn't know what hope she had of defeating him. Some hope was better than none, she supposed. Maybe.

She asked her knife for directions, and it bumped against her leg, leading her deeper into the pine-scented shadows. Her body seemed to know the way in any case, so she let it take the lead. She was tired of worrying about things she couldn't change, and there was a deep peace in deciding to stop. Things would happen as they would, and worry cost energy she couldn't afford. Attila stayed closer to her heels now, moving like a breath of wind himself among the thick needles of the forest floor.

She came to the edge of the green glade and stood just outside it. Trapper was closer, she thought, but not waiting at the grave. She took one step, and stood for a moment, poised between winter and spring. She stopped again, savoring it, but Attila ran headlong into the clearing with a joyful bark. She laughed and followed him in. He leaped among the grasses, wagging and barking until she called him back. He trotted up to her with a great doggy grin, and sat on her left foot, tail thumping the ground. She leaned down to pat him, and he got a few good licks on her chin before she managed to push him away.

It should have seemed disrespectful, but Attila's happiness was the perfect response to this place. It was another miracle, and Rosanna felt tears of mingled joy and sorrow rising up in her eyes. It was like coming home. She walked to the little spring, and took a drink of the warm water. It smelled and tasted of minerals, but not unpleasantly so. She dipped her water bottle in the basin, and filled it, as well.

Granny had said she meant to release the Word holding this place, but Rosanna doubted it. This was like Granny's web, and such remnants were precious. Rosanna listened, and *heard* that last murmur of her mother's being. It filled her up, poured into her like light and water. With it came memories, small polished bits of recollection that shone in her mind and heart with their purity. She remembered the blue blanket, and how Momma would wrap it round them both and sing in her wobbly voice till Rosanna laughed. She remembered the pink teacup, and the smell of lilies. With those memories came a bare handful of others. She remembered a man's laughing voice, and being lifted up into the air so high that she thought she was a bird. She remembered a rough chin and wide hands that always, always caught her.

Rosanna gasped, as winded as if she had been struck. This man she hunted...he wasn't just Thompson Trapper, he wasn't just the villain who had to be stopped. He was hers. He was part of her. He was all that remained of her long ago and far away. What was she supposed to do now?

Attila whined and licked her fingers, and she reached out to him and rested her hand on his shoulder.

"I'll be okay," she said thickly, trying to convince herself more than him. He licked her fingers again, and leaned against her, offering what simple canine support he could. She smiled down at him.

"You're a very good dog, Attila," she murmured. "Good boy." He bounced up, and ran a wide circle, just for happiness' sake, and she laughed at him.

The foul sounds on the wind were getting louder, so Rosanna made what preparations she could. Attila sniffed at the basin, but wouldn't drink out of it, which was probably just as well for her. She made sure he got water and food, then ate as well, though she wasn't very hungry. She stashed her supplies off in the grass, just in case she survived. It seemed absurdly optimistic, but she wasn't in the ditch yet. She set the light-stone in the center of the glade, in case she got to use it as a distraction or even a weapon, and made sure that her other little wonders were within easy reach. June might have known more about traps of the mundane sort, but Rosanna didn't, and June was far away. Perhaps that was for the best,

Rosanna thought. She pulled out her knife, and admired its keen edge. Attila sniffed at it, then backed away with a surprised little growl. Rosanna chuckled.

"Sorry boy," she said, "this thing has a mind of its own."

Up the mountain, the Library pulsed out its low chant of power and Being, and the scent of lilies rose on the air  around her. Rosanna smiled. If any place belonged to her, this one did, and she to it. Whatever came next, she had been precisely who and where she was supposed to be, at least once in her life. Some people never managed that much, but she had.

# Chapter 25

Attila snarled, and something howled poison and hatred from outside the circle of green. Rosanna stood.

"Doesn't that trick get old?" she shouted, but there was no response. Attila stood stiff-legged, with all his teeth bared and his ears flat to his skull.

"Attila, stay," she said firmly, and he looked up at her in protest. "Stay," she repeated, and though he quivered with the effort, he held himself still at her side. The poisoned beast, whatever it was, circled the glade, but she turned to follow the sound. It seemed reluctant to enter the ring of green, and she wasn't surprised. There was a deep strength in the purity of this place. Nevertheless, she expected that Trapper's will and the madness of his poison would overcome that reluctance in time. She stepped to the line between seasons, and caught a flash of silvery black slipping back behind a tree.

"I see you," she said softly. "And I hear you just fine."

She stepped out into winter, though Attila pressed against her legs. The animal stepped out, and stood silent in the tossing shadows of the wood. Then it lifted its eyeless head and keened venom onto the breeze.

"I know you," Rosanna said. "You've forgotten, but I know you."

The thing closed in on the sound of her voice with hideous speed. Its mouth was full of dark teeth that glistened with echoes of destruction. Attila lunged forward to meet it.

"Attila! Stay!" she shouted, and pushed the web out with enough force that the monster rebounded off of it and lay still for a stunned moment. Attila pulled back at the edge of the golden net, and stood growling through it at the monster.

Underneath the pulse of Trapper's magic, she could still hear the barest sense of this creature's true being. She spoke that Word into the web, as she had with Bear.

"Be this," she said, and strengthened that whisper until it was loud as a shout. "Be what you really are!" It lifted its eyeless head and screamed to the sky, fighting with the fury of the magic that rode it. It pushed at her again, but the web held strong, though its claws scythed sparks off the threads of gold. Rosanna shuddered with pain, but stood her ground. She could feel her connection to the web, not only in the strength it took to hold against her foe, but as if it were just a larger expression of her spirit. Those claws sheared against her very self, and though they found no purchase, Rosanna was scarred by their passing. She could feel the corruption trying to push back towards her, but Granny's web held strong. The darkness began to unwind, with greater and greater speed until a wolf began to emerge. Rosanna smiled. It was easier each time, and if Trapper had no better tricks than this…

Then a shot rang out through the clearing, and Rosanna staggered under a terrible concussion. She hadn't thought of guns. Why hadn't she thought of guns? She stumbled another step and felt something soft underfoot. Attila yelped and scrambled to get out of her way. She didn't think the bullet actually hit her, but her body rang as if she had been flung against a wall. Rosanna had been rear-ended by a speeding truck once, and it was like that, except for the sound of breaking glass. Instead she heard a snarl of triumph, and the beast  leapt against the weakened web. She pushed out, but her thoughts were tangled and uncertain, still ringing around that appalling pain. The web collapsed into her skin, and the beast crashed into her and knocked her to the ground. Its claws raked through her coat effortlessly, and she sucked in her belly and tried to scoot backwards, but its weight pinned her down. The sound of it so close was deafening and repulsive, but she could still hear the animal's essential self, somewhere under the layers of compulsion and disease. She kicked out with a booted foot, and connected solidly with one of its hind limbs. The animal grunted, and shifted a little, then lowered its head to within a finger's breadth of her face. Those teeth glittered, and she could see Trapper's victory reflected in them.

She heard Attila whine beside her, and suddenly she was angry. She was beyond angry. She glowed incandescent with fury at him and at all the pointless destruction. Anger anchored her, and solidified her. She spoke a Word of ice, and another of wind, and held the beast in place. She looked into the daggers of its teeth, and she remembered that she was a fierce woman. She might get trampled, but she wasn't going to just lie there and watch it happen.

She pushed the web out, and though she could only manage a hands breadth from her body, she felt it push the monster up and off her. She tied the words of its true being back into the web, and felt their strength and purity. This was another wolf, or the same one re-enslaved. Faster and faster the corruption unwound from around that spark of pure Being. The face of a wolf emerged from under the darkness, then the fur and feet and tail. It stood, transfixed still by her spell, but quivering with the desire to run. Rosanna smiled, and released the words that held the animal in place. Then a shot rang out again. Rosanna pushed hard at the web, but this was not aimed at her.. The wolf yelped, then fell heavily on its side. She heard its being spin away, heard the last beat of its heart. She cried out in surprise and horror and rage, and drew herself up to her feet. Attila stood beside her, though he trembled and swayed. He lifted his head to nudge her fingers, and she laid her hand on his head.

Trapper's voice rumbled through the clearing.

"That could be you, city-Rose," he said. "I have a nice clean shot. Or maybe your doggy friend, hm?"

There was a horrible cheerful friendliness in his voice.

"It'd be worse to bleed to death, I expect," he said. "Listening to your own life drip away. A clean death is best, don't you think?"

"You coward!" she shouted. "You chicken-hearted son of a bitch!"

"Now, now," he said, "that's your grandma you're maligning. Your *other* grandma. I bet you don't know anything about her."

"I suppose you're here to tell me about the family tree?"

"No dear, I'm here to tend that tree. Prune it if necessary."

"With a bullet in the back?"

"I'm not proud, my girl."

"Liar. Proud is all you are."

"Don't make me shoot you," he said. "We could still talk this out. It's not so much I'm asking, really."

"What is it, exactly, that you're asking?" she said.

"Don't play stupid, little Rose, it doesn't suit you. I want the Library. I want it all, and I don't want to have to fight you for it."

"What good could it possibly do you? What do you need more than you already have?"

A shot rang out again, and she staggered under the impact to her web. It collapsed into her skin, and she knew it would be at least a few moments before she could make use of it again. Granny's soul was tied into it, but so was Rosanna's. It was not an endless resource, and not proof against such violence for long.

"I'm not here to debate," he said. "and I've done all the asking I'm likely to. There's no shame in losing, city-Rose. The only shame is in foolish waste. Don't waste your life on another's principles."

"You weren't always like this, you know," Rosanna said, and her head dropped. "You always used to catch me. What happened to that?"

He was silent, and in that moment of respite she could hear the low keen and cry of poison. She might not be a genius in the woods, but her sense of hearing seemed to be improving every day. He was moving, very slowly circling around to her right.

"Things change," he said at last. "I found...other things to catch."

"Trapper, yes," she said. "But there's some of that other person left, I think. You keep telling him no and shutting him away, but he's there."

"Lord, you're a philosophical sort, aren't you?" he said with a chuckle, but it seemed forced. "You must have gotten it from your Granny, I suppose. Your mother was always more of a doer."

"Do you miss her?"

There was a long silence, touched only by the low murmur of a passing breeze and the distant sound of sparrows calling. She stopped trying to spot him, and simply listened to the sounds between his words. She couldn't make out any sound from the gun, but there was a mutter of incipient fire somewhere near him. She thought perhaps it was a bullet, or several.

"I did," he said at last. "For a long time, I did. But time came I couldn't afford to miss her anymore. It cost me too much, made me too weak." He paused. "Like you, standing there with a third-class guard dog and a handful of tricks. All that thinking hasn't brought you any good, has it?"

"Not much, I suppose," Rosanna said. "But you still need me."

He laughed, and the sound scraped her nerves like a glass file.

"There's no guarantee I do," he said, "and if you're going to be too difficult, it's easier to shoot you and figure it out on my own."

"You've spent a lot of years trying to do it without me," she said. "Are you sure you want to spend more?"

"Have you come to your senses, then?" he asked, suspicion warring with triumph in his voice.

"I don't know," she said. "I'm just tired of being out of my depth."

"Good way to drown," Trapper agreed genially. "but I'm not sure I believe you."

"If we're going to talk can I at least step back into the grass? It's cold out here."

He paused for a long moment.

"I suppose I can afford small kindnesses," he said at last. "Two steps only. Take any more and I shoot your dog." He chuckled, and she realized how close he must be, because she heard it clearly. "I might shoot him anyways. Bloody useless animal. I'd be doing Bear a favor."

Two steps might not be enough, but she had to hope.

"What's the shield thing you had up?" he asked with casual interest. "Never seen anything like that."

"Granny made it," she said, and he laughed. She wanted to kill him then. She hadn't ever wanted to kill anyone, and she didn't like how it felt. It felt like the shadow of his corruption laid on her spirit.

"Crazy old bitch," he said. "Always finding new ways to do the ridiculous."

"If you want to talk, I'd rather you didn't talk about her."

"Why not?"

"She's dead."

"No, really?"

Rosanna didn't respond, listening instead for the exact position of her light-stone.

"You dropped a house on her," Rosanna said. "That was the point, wasn't it?"

"Seemed appropriate," he said, and laughed again. "A house always falls on the wicked witch."

"You're just baiting me now," Rosanna replied. "What do you really want to say?"

There was a long silence, and then Rosanna heard his voice from a slightly different position in the shadows. Attila growled, and she put a hand on his shoulder to keep him still.

"I still want the Library," he said, sounding closer as well as further to the right. "Don't you want your life back?"

She laughed, and was as surprised as he when the sound burst out of her.

"Granny was the only life I had," she said. "My parents died, remember?"

"We could be strong together," he said, "we could find each other again."

Rosanna shook her head.

"I can hear the poison running through you. Is that your idea of strong?"

"Yes!" he shouted. "Haven't you seen what I can do? With more power...with greater Words...just imagine it!"

For just the briefest of moments, Rosanna remembered that she was alone in the world. This man represented all that remained of a life she'd never known, one that she'd dreamed of and mourned for nearly as long as she could remember. She was born into promise and family, and had been left with none of it. What did she owe anyone? But she spotted him, then, still circling stealthily, even as they talked. Whoever it was that looked at her down the long cold barrel of a hunting rifle, that person wasn't anyone she knew, or ever had. She belonged to the tribe of fierce women, now. That would suffice.

"No," she said.

"I *will* shoot you," he said, and she heard the rustle and click of his gun, watched him work the bolt. He was clever, all his motions rippling as silk, and nearly invisible in the shadows. She hoped she was clever, too. She put her hand over Attila's eyes.

"I'm getting mighty tired of asking you for what's rightfully mine."

"You could stop," she said, and then shouted, "Please!", sending all her fierceness to the light-stone. She managed to push the web out just far enough to touch the stone, and connected stone and web. She poured her energy into those small Words of light and heat, and fed through Granny's web like electricity through a wire. Even through her closed eyelids, the flash was nearly blinding, and she heard Trapper cry out. She heard heavy footsteps stumbling away from her, and focused on the sound. She still couldn't get any impression of the gun itself, so she focused on the small but focused mutter of trapped fire. She gave each one a nudge, and the bullets exploded with cracks and pops like fireworks. The gun fired, but no bullet even seemed to pass near her. She released the roar of light and heat, and let the web sink back into her skin. When she opened her eyes, a faint corona of light haunted the edges of her vision, but she could make out Trapper's form as he retreated gracelessly into the woods.

He turned and spoke a Word of cold, but she countered it easily. Her time in the woods had taught her all about cold, and she had no reason to fear it anymore. She spoke lightning, and he turned that aside. A small fire started in the dense needles of the forest floor.

"I can always find you, you know," she said, and caught a glimpse of his face in the weak winter sunlight. "I didn't come here to hide." He no longer held the gun, and he had a series of little cuts all over the left side of his face and neck. One on his cheek bled freely into his close-cut beard.

He shouted fire at her, and the grass in the circle ignited all at once. The lilies shriveled into ash, and Attila cringed at her feet. She spoke wind and ice, and caged the fire. It swirled around her like a magician's cape, then went out. He gasped and stumbled as his spell rebounded. He stood panting, and leaned down to rest one hand on his thigh. He looked up at her, and she could see the planes and shadows of her own face there, buried under years and obsession.

He smiled at her ruefully.

"I've underestimated you every time, haven't I," he said.

"No," she said. "I did it for you."

He shook his head, and she realized that she was weary, too. Her knife was still in her hand, but only out of habit. She wasn't fierce, she was just hollow.

"We could let each other go," he said. "A truce maybe?" His eyes were earnest and open, but she knew the falsity they concealed.

"And you'd just leave me be, I suppose," she said.

"If you left me be, yes."

"And the Library?"

His eyes darkened, and the curling whine of poison threaded up on the air.

"It's yours, of course."

"Of course," she said, and forced the web up just in time to deflect his thrown knife. He'd backed it with a whisper of wind, and it shook her nearly as badly as the bullet had. She fell to the ground with a curse. Her head struck the ground hard, and her vision dissolved into gray sparkles for a breath or two.

When she managed to clear her sight, she saw Attila coursing over the scorched grass towards Trapper. She scrambled for her knife and to stand.

"Attila, no!" she screamed, but he threw himself at Trapper with silent determination. Trapper laughed and opened his arms, then whispered that one terrible Word. Attila yelped and Rosanna screamed again, wordless fear and hurt.

"Truce," he said. "We could have a truce. I keep the Library, you get the dog." He paused. "Better trade for me, I'll admit, but there's nothing here you want."

Attila kicked out, but the venom of that Word crouched around him, caged and tormented his true self.

"You said it yourself," she managed. "He's not much of a guard dog."

"But you love him," Trapper said, and his smile was a scar across his face. "You don't love those old stones, do you?" He shook Attila again, and the dog whimpered.

"All right," she said. "All right. Just give him back, please let me fix him."

"Do you promise?"

"I promise," she said, weeping. "Anything, oh please, just don't...I can't stand anymore."

"Very well then," Trapper said. "We are agreed. I will go my way, and you will go yours. We may have this conversation another day, but we are done for today. Right?"

"I promise!" Rosanna said, head down. "Whatever you say."

"Might as well start fixing now, before it's set. Only gets harder," he said amiably, and let Attila go.

Rosanna called up her web, as strongly as she could manage.

"Father," she said, and he turned. He was beautiful in victory. It shone on his scarred face like the light of a summer sun. It shaped the lines of his shoulders into the lines of a hero.

"Be this," she said, and spoke the Words of his true Being. She could still hear them, nearly lost among the black discourse of venom and hatred. That self still existed, somewhere. She tapped into the Word that held her mother's grave, and into the heat and light of all her pocket miracles.

"Be this," she repeated, and wove a net of her father's own self in which to trap the trapper.

"No," he said, and staggered back.

"Be this," she repeated, calling and calling, seeking out those neglected remnants of a truer soul. She could hear strands of poison lifting into silence.

"You promised!" he shouted, but she could spare no breath for simpler conversation. Maybe she could write a better ending to this tale. Maybe there was still enough time.

He looked into her eyes, and shook his head.

"I won't," he said. "I won't go back."

"Be this," she said, and he laughed. It was a sound like a scorpion sting, and it wounded her. She staggered back, but did not drop the web or her Word.

He took a step towards her, and another, though it looked like he was walking upstream in a mighty flood.

"I won't," he said again, even as she heard more of the poison unfolding from around him. There was so much, so many layers of ruination and evil. She could hear his truer self more clearly, but it was too slow, much too slow. Then the process began to take on a momentum of its own. More and more the darkness unwound, but he was closer, and she was out of energy. She fell to one knee, holding her knife before her. It was no defense anymore, she knew. But she had saved him, she could see that. It would take time, but she would have her father back, and he would catch her. Then he stood before her, panting.

"You…promised," he said, and she smiled.

"I lied."

"Like father, I guess," he said, and smiled a strange bitter smile, half poison and half…something else.

"But I made who I am," he said. "And you may not unmake me."

She couldn't resist as he took her hand, and pressed the knife to his chest. She tried to fight him, but simply staying conscious took all the breath and blood and will that she possessed. He was there! She could see him, the man of the laughing eyes and warm hands, he of long ago and far away. He was right there!

"I'm mine," he said. He put his cold, roughened hands around her wrist, and pressed forward one more step.

# Chapter 26

Rosanna stepped out of the camper and into the bright spring sunshine. Months had passed since the glade, but somehow every day was still that day, and she could not take much pleasure in any of them. The air bubbled and sparkled with birdsong, and she took a deep breath. She tried to smile, but the expression wouldn't come. There was something broken in her, she supposed, something lost. Attila sploshed through the mud and leaped up on her, grinning rapturously. She smiled then, though it was a crooked sort of half-formed thing that did not linger.

"You are unbelievable," she said, and pushed him down firmly. "Down, Attila." It worked for a moment, but only until the energy in him overcame his desire to please. Then he danced around her in circles of endless, transparent joy.

She could hear the workings of his spirit, clean and lovely without any trace of lingering poison. She wished her own spirit felt so unsoiled. She looked down at her hands, and at the knife strapped to her thigh. She'd wanted to throw it away or destroy it, but couldn't. She'd invested some part of herself into it, made it almost a living thing. She'd done all the killing she ever wanted to. The wide sky above was blue as hope and forgiveness, and yet she could find neither.

She sighed and looked at the house. It was coming along well, though it wouldn't ever be Granny Rosie's house again. They'd salvaged the stove, and the chimney was almost completely intact. Some few of the furnishings had been fixable, and Rosanna had recovered quite a few books and pictures from under the snow. Most were damaged, but that seemed appropriate. Damaged but usable suited her perfectly. Bear had helped Rosanna build a shed to house the things until winter passed.

She heard the roar of June's truck behind her, and the squeaking protests of its shocks as it came over the last bump. She turned to see Bear getting out of the driver's seat, and waved. It wouldn't be long before June would be driving, whether or not she was supposed to. That woman was impossibly resilient, and Rosanna had supported that healing as best she could. June had moved in with Bear until things got sorted out with the restaurant, but neither seemed overly concerned with how long the arrangement lasted. Rosanna could hear the connection between them, and she thought that they were moving beyond 'friends with benefits' into something else entirely. Attila bounded over to greet June and Bear, but then came to stand beside Rosanna. She rested her hand on his head, comforted by the sleek fur and the tumble of sound that was him.

Bear shook his head, and smiled.

"No mistaking where I stand in his affections, is there," he said.

"I'm sorry," Rosanna said. "He's your dog, I didn't mean…"

"Don't be ridiculous. He's your dog now, you know that."

She did know. Her car had survived the destruction of the restaurant, and Bear had towed her back to the city. She'd gone back to her apartment there, and hated it. Hated every dusty, dull, empty, purposeless inch of it. Nobody had known she was gone. She couldn't read or eat or even watch television, so she'd simply been in that space reliving moments best left to dwindle into silence. Bear had called to tell her June was coming out of the hospital, but that Attila wasn't well. She had gotten her windshield replaced, and driven the curving snow-path back to the mountains. Attila had been thin as a whisper when she'd seen him, and she'd been afraid that somehow she'd been wrong, that somehow Trapper had left poison on that pure spirit. As soon as she'd spoken, though, his head had come up, and his love had been a symphony. He'd run to her, put his paws on her shoulders, and licked her face. She had wept down in the snow with him, heedless of June or Bear, or the whole damn world. He'd put his solid brown head under her chin, and pressed into her, and that was that.

Her apartment wouldn't have been a good place for a dog, so she'd gotten rid of it. She'd taken a leave of absence from work, citing Granny's death. By then, the searchers around her house had declared her missing, but unlikely to have survived the explosion. Nobody knew what had caused it, or the one at June's place. Rosanna had expected many more police questions than there were, but this wasn't the city, and the police were spread thin. Since there was no sign of fire, and since Bear and June had vouched for the city girl, the questions had stopped and the world had moved on. Rosanna put her things in storage, and moved into the camper in Bear's yard for the rest of the winter.

By the time spring came, she'd figured she'd stay, and she and Bear had started to clear the site of Granny's house. It turned out that Granny's will had some provisory clauses in the case of her prolonged absence, and Rosanna could live on the place as long as she pleased. After a year, she would own it. She didn't know how to feel about that, nor about the trust fund that had kicked in. It wasn't a fortune, but it was enough to live on, providing she didn't expect to live like royalty. It was enough to rebuild. So she and Bear had worked at it, while June had growled and fretted at them for not letting her do more. She had learned about hammer and saw, and was surprised to enjoy it.

She looked at her hands in the brilliance of the new day, and found them roughened by the work. It pleased her to be that much further from her empty, dusty life. She reached down to pat Attila's chest, and he looked up at her with adoration gleaming in his deep brown eyes.

"Yup," June echoed, "that's your dog for sure. You poor thing." She grinned, and thumped along with her walking stick. She reached down and patted Attila too, and he wagged his tail happily. More attention was always better, in his world. June stood and took a look at Rosanna.

"Are you eating?" she asked.

"Of course," Rosanna replied. "Have you ever known me to stop?"

"Let's get specific, how *much* are you eating?"

Rosanna shrugged.

"Enough," she said. "I move, I breathe. I'm just not as good a cook as you."

"You come by for dinner, then," June said. "You're getting too thin. You're gonna steal all my men."

Rosanna tried to smile, she did, but the effort slid off her face like poorly applied makeup.

"You aren't eating, are you," June said, and put her arms out.

Rosanna stepped into the hug, and rested her head on June's shoulder. She didn't mean to weep, not anymore, but the tears came anyway. After a moment June pulled back and put her hand under Rosanna's chin.

"Are you ever going to tell me what happened? I thought maybe I could just give you time, but you ain't...you ain't healing, Rosanna. I mean, this leg of mine is doing better than you."

"I can't," Rosanna replied. "I try and try, but...I can't."

June sighed.

"Well that's just bullshit," she said softly, and with a smile. "You can. You done miracles, and I seen them myself. This is just talking, and lord knows you're good at that."

Rosanna shook her head. How could she? How could she even speak the words? She'd replayed the images a million, million times in her head, but how could she possibly give them voice? It was too awful. She'd told them it was finished, and that was all she'd ever been able to say about it before the storm of sorrow and guilt and regret stole her voice.

"I think it's time you showed me, then," June said.

"What about your leg?"

"Doctor says exercise is good for me," June replied. "Is it far?"

"Not so far, no," Rosanna said. Without the snow it was hardly an effort at all. She'd been several times to the edge of the woods, but no further in than that. She stalled for time scratching Attila behind the ears, but June's eyes were mostly gold today, and that usually meant 'stubborn'. Rosanna sighed.

"We'll go as far as you can manage," she said at last. June nodded.

"Bear, we're going for a walk."

"Good," he shouted from across the yard. "Take that dog, would you? He gets into everything."

Rosanna took the slope at an easy walk, but June didn't seem troubled by it. Rosanna could hear the wholeness in June again, and thought that meant the bone was healing well. Still she whispered a little encouragement, just a quiet echo of June's own being. June stopped on the trail and Rosanna turned to look at her.

"You did something," June said. "Didn't you."

"A little," Rosanna admitted.

"Thought you couldn't heal me."

"I can't, I just kind of…lend a hand. I help your body remember to be whole."

"Sounds like healing to me,"

"Well it's not, really. I'm not doing it, I'm just reminding your leg that it isn't going to be broken forever, that it wasn't made that way."

"And you?" June said. "Who reminds you that you aren't going to be broken always? Who reminds you that you weren't made that way?"

Rosanna shrugged.

"Maybe I *was* made broken," she said at last. "Maybe I just didn't know."

"Some days I don't know whether to hug you or slap you," June said. "Honestly, girl!" She shook her head and waved Rosanna on. "No, don't stop to argue, just get a move on."

What had been a snowy slope was now a stone-speckled meadow. Bright yellow lilies stood among anemones and clumps of vibrant purple flowers that Rosanna didn't recognize. She saw the tender leaves of wild strawberries, and thought she might be visiting this spot more often in the summer. Birds swooped and danced like acrobats in the air, everyone working without a net. Rosanna heard the sharp cries of some small animals off in the distance. Attila ran off with a bark to chase the small and the furry. He never caught anything, but Rosanna didn't think he ever really meant to. It was quieter under the pine trees, and the bright sunlight was filtered and dimmed, although it still pooled to brilliance where the trees stood further apart. Attila ran back to them, tongue lolling and chest heaving with exertion and delight.

"How's the leg?" Rosanna asked, and June scowled at her.

"You're worse than Bear," she said.

'That doesn't exactly answer the question."

"Wasn't supposed to. Just walk. I could run circles around you, and if you don't pick up the pace, I might."

For all her bravado, June's limp was more pronounced, and Rosanna could hear the hitch and mutter of pain.

"June…" she said, and June glared.

"More walking less talking."

Rosanna did. She slowed as they approached the glade, though. She could see sunlight glowing there, but it was too bright. She would see too clearly, and she knew what to look for. There would be scorched grass, and the dark stain. Everything was tainted, everything. She stopped. Attila pressed against her legs, and she rested her hand on his warm, satiny fur.

"I can't."

"Maybe not," June said. "We can. I remember you were whole. You ain't supposed to be broken like this, Rosanna. You got more to you than the broken place." Attila licked her fingers.

"Is it there, then?" June asked, and Rosanna nodded. "Don't look so bad," June said, and linked her arm with Rosanna's. She leaned more than a little as they stepped forward, and Rosanna was ashamed. June would do anything for her, anything at all. If her leg were in a dozen pieces, she would still be making this journey, because she thought Rosanna needed it. Rosanna was only alive because of June's generous spirit. She owed June the courage to walk those last steps. So, what she had tried and failed to find for herself, she found for June instead, and stepped out from under the cool shadows of the pine trees and into the shimmer of spring sunlight on new grass.

It wasn't charred, as she had expected. New grass lay in a thick carpet all around the basin and spring. The stone basin itself showed some dark markings, but the water in it was pure and clean. New lilies, yellow and white, nodded in profusion around the stone, and their scent filled the clearing like a blessing. Rosanna stepped further in, waiting for the sting of poison or death, waiting for some castoff remnant of violence to rise up and strike her.

"This don't look so bad," June said again cautiously. "Is it?"

Rosanna could hear the life around her, not just the grasses and flowers, but myriad birds and insects. She could hear the faint echoes of her mother and grandmother here. She could hear the rumble and recitation of the Library further up the mountain. Everything she was existed here, everything except the hands that would always catch her, and the soul that would not be saved.

She started to weep, and June turned to her and wrapped her arms around her. Rosanna felt the comfort, but only from a great distance, it seemed. Attila whined and nosed at her fingers. She shook in the storm of tears, and it seemed she had never wept before. These tears burned and seared, and she didn't know how to stop. She heard her grief sweeping up into that terrible sound, the death-song, and if she had been alone, she would have allowed that shriek to pull her away and spin her off into the darkness. But June held her, and Attila licked her hand. She wasn't alone.

"I could have saved him," she said at last, still crying so hard that the words were only barely intelligible. "It was working. I was bringing him back, you understand? I was bringing my *father* back!" She collapsed to the ground, and felt the edge of a stone. She pulled it up out of the grass, and held her light-stone, her pocket miracle. She clutched it tightly, and wailed and rocked, and June said nothing, but rocked with her.

"But...but he wouldn't let me," she said at last. "he wouldn't...he would rather die than be with me." She pulled her knife out of the sheath, and looked at it. She could feel the piece of herself that existed in the metal, that would always exist there. Every piece of her that existed had his blood on it.

She looked at June.

"When it was working...he said I couldn't have him. He...he walked onto my knife." She dropped the knife on the ground. "I killed him. I could have had him back, and I killed him."

"No honey," June said quietly. "He did it. He chose it. You ain't broken, you didn't do wrong. "

"But it was working! If I'd done it some other time, or surprised him, or..."

"Stop it. You could tell him how it was to be whole. You couldn't make him be it."

"He didn't have to die!"

"You didn't get to decide that, Rosanna. We all got to decide whether we live with what we got. He decided."

"But it's my fault."

"No, it ain't. Me, I woulda just killed him. You're different. You're more. You gave him a chance to make everything better, and he decided not to take it. You can't make people decide. You can't make them be. You know that."

"I hoped..." Rosanna whispered.

"I know," June replied, and put her hand on Rosanna's shoulder. "Ain't nothing wrong with hope. But he broke it, not you." She looked around at the glade.

"Did he die here," she asked.

"Yes," Rosanna said. "It's my mother's grave."

"Did you bury him?"

"No," Rosanna said, remembering only with reluctance. "I...let the Words go that made him up."

"It's time to let the rest of him go, then too," June said firmly.

"But I remember a better man," Rosanna said. "How do I reconcile that?"

"You don't," June said. "You just have both. You have the best and the worst, and neither one cancels the other out. They just are."

"I killed him," Rosanna whispered again.

"He killed himself, and you know it. You just don't want to."

That was true. Rosanna remembered his rough hands wrapped around hers as he stepped into death. Her knife, his will.

"This doesn't feel any better," Rosanna said, and started to sob again. Tears turned the glade into a blur of green and gold.

"Of course not," June whispered. "It ain't going to feel better until you're healed. But you know the hurt now, right? You can see it?"

That was true, at least. She could feel within herself the hitch and stumble of injury, and recognize it for what it was. Perhaps she wasn't ruined, only damaged.

"I've lost so much," she said at last, and June nodded.

"Yes," she said. "But you have me, and you still have you, and that's more than he had at all." Attila laid his heavy head on Rosanna's thigh with a sigh, and she laughed ruefully.

"And I have you, too, don't I," she said, and he grinned his most loving grin and reached up to lick her chin.

"Been a while since I seen a smile on you that I believed," June said. Rosanna nodded.

"I don't expect you're done here," June said, as Rosanna stood. "But at least you've started. Can't finish what you don't start."

Rosanna helped June up, and listened again to the lazy intonations of her mother's Library.

"No," she said. "But I have time."

Made in the USA
Middletown, DE
07 December 2020